SON OF MERCIA

MJ PORTER

Boldwood

First published in Great Britain in 2022 by Boldwood Books Ltd.

Copyright © MJ Porter, 2022

Cover Design by Head Design Ltd

Cover Photography: Shutterstock

A CIP catalogue record for this book is available from the British Library.

Paperback ISBN 978-1-80280-754-7

Large Print ISBN 978-1-80280-750-9

Hardback ISBN 978-1-80280-749-3

Ebook ISBN 978-1-80280-747-9

Kindle ISBN 978-1-80280-748-6

Audio CD ISBN 978-1-80280-755-4

MP3 CD ISBN 978-1-80280-752-3

Digital audio download ISBN 978-1-80280-746-2

Boldwood Books Ltd
23 Bowerdean Street
London SW6 3TN
www.boldwoodbooks.com

For Jake and Janet.
Both Mercians. And both gone before their time.

Designed by Flintlock Covers

CAST OF CHARACTERS

Main Characters:

Icel, orphaned youth living in Tamworth, his mother was Ceolburh
Edwin, Icel's friend
Cenfrith, Icel's uncle, brother of Ceolburh and one of the Mercian
king's warriors.
Wine, Cenfrith's horse
Wynflæd, an old herbwoman at the Mercian king's court

The Kings of Mercia:

Penda, King of Mercia r.c633–655
Coenwalh, brother of Penda, it was through his line that later
Mercian kings descended.
Æthelbald, King of Mercia r.716–757
Offa, King of Mercia r.757–796

Ecgfrith, Offa's son, King of Mercia, 796 only

Coenwulf, King of Mercia r.796–821

Coelwulf, King of Mercia r.821–825 (deposed), brother of King Coenwulf

Coenwulf, Coelwulf's son, Lord of Kingsholm

Ælflæd, Coelwulf's daughter

Beornwulf, King of Mercia r.825–826 (killed)

Lady Cynehild, the wife of King Beornwulf, retires to Winchcombe nunnery

Ludica, King of Mercia r.826–827 (killed)

Lady Eadburga, the wife of King Ludica, and daughter of Ealdorman Oswine

Wiglaf, King of Mercia r.827–

Lady Cynethryth, the wife of King Wiglaf

Wigmund, Wiglaf's son

The Ealdormen of Mercia

Under King Beornwulf:

Alhheard, Beornoth, Eadberht, Muca, Mucel, Sigered, Wynfrith (fictional)

Under King Ludica:

Bofa, Eadric (fictional), Eatferth, Muca, Mucel, Oswine (fictional), Wilfwald, Wiglaf (later king)

Under King Wiglaf:

Ælfstan, Athelhard, Æthelwald, Beornoth, Eadwulf, Muca, Mucel, Sigered, Tidwulf

Before Mercia was Mercia, there were many smaller sub-kingdoms, the Mægonsæte, and the Wreocensæten were two of these smaller kingdoms, just as the Hwicce and Lindsey were.

Æthelweald: Bishop of Lichfield
Bealdred: Lord of Kent
Beorhtwulf: Bealdred's son

Kings of other kingdoms

Athelstan: King of East Anglia
Cyngen ap Cadell: King of Powys
Eanred: King of Northumbria
Ecgberht: King of Wessex
Merfyn ap Gwriad: King of Gwynedd

Misc. (fictional)

Æthelryth: inhabitant of Tamworth
Acha: inhabitant of farm steading
Ansfith: horse at Kingsholm
Beornwyn: inhabitant of Tamworth
Brother Fassel: inhabitant of Kingsholm
Brute: a horse at Bardney
Cuthred: inhabitant of Tamworth
Eadburh: Edwin's mother
Eahric: commander of the king's household warriors
Hatel: at Kingsholm
Leonath: inhabitant of Tamworth
Ordlaf: Mercian warrior
Osbert: inhabitant of farm steading
Osmod: Mercian warrior
Oswald: at Kingsholm

Oswy: one of Wiglaf's warriors
Pega: at Kingsholm
Sigberht: inhabitant of farm steading
Sigegar: inhabitant of farm steading
Siric: inhabitant of Tamworth
Sewenna: horse at Kingsholm
Waldhere: Mercian warrior
Wulfheard: Mercian warrior

Places mentioned

Bardney: in modern-day Lincolnshire. An important monastic site.
Hereford: on the River Wye, sixteen miles east of the modern-day border with Wales.
Kingsholm: associated with the ruling family of King Coelwulf, close to Gloucester.
Lichfield: an important bishopric. King Offa had attempted to make it an archbishopric to rival Canterbury but had been ultimately unsuccessful.
Lundenwic: modern-day London
Peterborough: an important monastery site, founded by the Mercians in the seventh century.
Repton: a royal mausoleum for the Mercian dead. At this point, King Æthelbald was buried there. Repton has a stunning Saxon crypt built in the eighth century.
Tamworth: the capital of the Mercian kingdom.
Wroxeter, a Mercian settlement
The Kingdom of the East Angles: had been part of Mercia at the end of King Offa's reign but reclaimed its freedom under the reign of King Beornwulf of Mercia.

The Kingdom of Gwynedd: part of modern-day Wales (north Wales), shared a border with Mercia.

The Kingdom of Powys: part of modern-day Wales, shared a border with Mercia.

The Kingdom of Wessex: roughly speaking, this covered the area south of the Thames, not including Kent, or Dumnonia (Cornwall and Devon).

THE MERCIAN REGISTER
AD826

'Much uncertainty and discord exists between the Mercian kings and their nobility.

'King Coelwulf of Mercia, the first of his name, has been deposed and King Beornwulf now rules in his place, swept to power by the ealdormen of Mercia, and in doing so, breaking the powerful line of succession that has run from the mighty pagan warrior, Penda, for nearly two hundred years.

'But all is not well; King Beornwulf has suffered a huge defeat at the hands of the resurgent King Ecgberht of Wessex, losing control over Mercia's prized possession of the Kingdom of Kent.

'With unease at his failing kingship growing, King Beornwulf has ridden to the kingdom of the East Angles to face their self-proclaimed King Athelstan, in an attempt to quell his failings and replace the loss of the Kingdom of Kent with the acquisition of another, that of the East Angles.'

PART I

1

AD826

I move through the hall, wishing there were more people to hide behind. But with Beornwulf, king of Mercia, away with the war band battling the upstart, Athelstan, king of the East Angles, there are too few. I don't wish to feel the gaze of the king's wife, Lady Cynehild, cutting me, even from such a distance. She sits on the raised dais, arrayed as though she rules without the aid of her husband. A cold woman, I've yet to discover why she detests me so much, but hate me she does. I know that. As does everyone else within that great hall, its blackened rafters reaching far above my head. Not that any of them will tell me why she despises me. I doubt they know the cause of her animosity. When I've asked Wynflæd in the past, she's dismissed my query quickly enough.

'Icel, why would Lady Cynehild, the queen of Mercia, hate the nephew of one of her husband's warriors? An orphan boy with no one but his uncle to care for him?' Her words cut me. I don't like to be reminded that my mother died birthing me, that I have no father. I'm entirely reliant on my uncle's goodwill. And before that, on the care of a woman who was not my mother who ensured I lived.

Still, for all Wynflæd's dismissive words, I know Lady Cynehild watches me.

I nip here and there, bending low, thinking to do all I can to stay out of Lady Cynehild's sight.

She's a terrifying woman. I can't deny it. I've known her cold gaze to freeze me, a flick of her fingers to find me running far away from my food, even when my belly growls with fury. On those occasions, I've taken shelter elsewhere, been fed by the sympathy of others, by Wynflæd, or Edwin's mother, by those who don't sit within the king's hall for their meals.

'Where have you been?' Edwin, my foster brother, hisses the words to me as I rear up beside him. He's saved me a place on the bench reserved for the children of the ealdormen and the king's warriors. Edwin always does. I notice his flushed cheeks, his lips set in a thin line of anger, his dark hair as unruly as ever. I also see the stain on the arm of his tunic, no doubt snot from his nose or fat from the piece of meat he thrusts into his mouth even as he speaks.

'I was with Wynflæd.'

His tutted reply tells me what he thinks of that. 'You should spend less time with that useless old crone and more time with the horses or the warriors, or with your uncle. They'll teach you what you need to know.' His words are mangled round the food he chews, but I understand them all the same. It's not as though they're anything new for me to hear.

I shake my head, clearing the long, dark hair from my eyes, reaching across him for a piece of warm bread just out of reach. Taking pity on me, he hands me the bread, while other hungry eyes glower at me from further along the table. I meet those eyes evenly, only turning aside when I fear the scrutiny from the dais. The other youths know that I can't withstand that gaze. A few smirks remind me they know the Lady detests me.

Some might say it's an honour that the Lady even knows who I am. I would sooner merge into the tables and stools as the other children do. Why Edwin and I are allowed to claim space here, in the king's hall, I don't know. But I know we don't belong, all the same. I've asked my uncle about it, but like Wynflæd, he dismisses my concerns.

'You are my nephew. The king and queen honour me by feeding you, and Edwin, your foster-brother.'

Again, I begin my familiar retort to Edwin concerning Wynflæd and why I spend so much time with her.

'She knows a great deal, about the old kings, about Mercia, about healing. You should come and listen to her. It's all well and good knowing how to kill, but healing is magical.' We've had this argument many times before and will continue to do so. He would rather learn to maim and kill; I would sooner know how to heal.

'You only spend time with her in the hope she'll speak about your mother, that you might find out who your father was?' Edwin's words are angry. He doesn't approve of my desire to know who my father was. Edwin thinks I should be content knowing that his mother fed me when I was a babe, that my uncle ensured I lived, that Wynflæd nursed the pair of us through the colds and fevers that we endured when we were small boys. 'Don't.' His single word brings me up short, just as I'm about to resume the argument.

I duck again, using his broader body to shield me from whoever eyes me. Only Edwin looks elsewhere, I realise, seeing his neck turn outwards, and not towards the dais. It's a warm day. I've not noticed the arrival of the warrior because the door stands wide open, the stifled breeze from outside doing little to lift the fug from the interior of the hall, the hum of conversation drowning out all noise from beyond. It smells of cooked meat and rancid fat, and unwashed bodies. I wrinkle my nose, even as I feel my eyes drawn to the figure. I'm standing, even as Edwin pulls me back down, his large hand on my clean tunic. I turn to remonstrate with him, but his other hand, greasy from the meat, covers my lips, head dipping towards the dais, eyes wide with meaning, and slowly, slowly, my mind begins to make sense of all that's happening.

Cenfrith, my uncle, has returned from the kingdom of the East Angles, but his eyes are hooded, a dirty bandage wrapped round his head, stained black with his blood. More importantly, his face is bleached of all colour, his eyes seeking out the figure on the dais, not me, and my blood runs cold.

My uncle is one of the king's fiercest warriors, a man I admire and could never hope to emulate.

'Where is King Beornwulf?' I mutter through my clenched teeth, but Edwin shakes his head again, hair sticking out with the movement, his greasy hand still over my mouth.

My heart thuds too loudly as silence envelops the hall, all eyes settling on the trembling figure of my uncle.

'My Lord?' Lady Cynehild stands, her fine blue dress, despite the terrible heat of a summer's day in the heart of Mercia, pooling round her, the soft shush of the expensive fabric audible even from where I sit. The colour suits her; I admit that. It brings out the flush of her rosy cheeks and the lightness of her long, tightly braided blonde hair. She's not a tall woman, but there's something about her posture that makes her imposing. And terrifying.

'My Lady,' my uncle huffs, and I've escaped Edwin's clawing hand and skipped over the bench I perch on, taking my wooden beaker of water to my uncle's side. He notices the water, not me, swilling it into his parched mouth with a filth-encrusted hand. Dust stains his face, his clothes, and his weapons glisten with what I suspect to be the gore of the battlefield. And he stinks. Of sweat and horses. And perhaps piss as well. I'm staggered by the state of him.

My uncle has fought in many battles for Mercia. I've never seen him like this.

'A rout, My Lady,' Cenfrith manages to gasp.

I eye the darkened stain of his tunic with worry, considering how Wynflæd would tell me to heal such a wound; with hot water, a little vinegar and then moss and honey to cover it while the skin works to knit together. She would offer a draught to ease the pain.

But my uncle hasn't finished speaking. Far from it.

'I regret to inform you that Beornwulf, the first of his name, king of Mercia, is dead. Beornoth, Eadberht, Alhheard and Wynfrith, four ealdormen of Mercia, died with him on the slaughter-field battling the upstart king of the East Angles. Only a few of the king's household warriors have survived. I've ridden hard to bring you the news in fear that King Athelstan of the East Angles will invade Mercia now that he's slain the king.'

A shriek of horror fills the hall, but it doesn't come from Lady Cynehild's mouth, but from another, no doubt one of the recently widowed women. I don't track the sounds of the sobbing woman as her cries are quickly stifled by others, evidently keen to hear the news. Stunned by it as well. This is King Beornwulf's second failure in only a year. And this time, it's a fatal one.

If there was silence in the hall at my uncle's arrival, it now feels as though no one dare breathe, let alone speak.

I move even closer to my uncle, desperate for him to acknowledge me, Icel, his nephew. I should be the only one who matters to him, even amongst the king's widowed wife and those who now scent the time has come for them to claim their birthrights.

I'm relieved Cenfrith lives when all others of the king's warriors are dead. Yet, I fear for his life with the terrible injuries he carries. He needs to get to Wynflæd. She will heal him.

'Not now,' my uncle offers, his pained eyes meeting mine for the first time, as he pushes me behind him, out of sight, the strength remaining in his hand assuring me he'll live.

But, of course, I've forgotten about Lady Cynehild and her hatred of me. I think to slip away, but I'm exposed on all sides, and the horrified eyes of Edwin, as he shakes his head from the bench, remind me to stay where I am. Despite the news Cenfrith brings, Edwin thinks only of me, his foster-brother. I'm grateful for his concern.

'Who—' the word is cut off, and I swallow once more, fear almost turning my innards to fluid. Lord Ludica has risen from his honoured seat close to Lady Cynehild. While King Beornwulf has been riding to battle, Ludica, Bealdred and Lady Cynehild have ensured Mercia was ruled well. I can determine his intentions now, and yet my concern is for Cenfrith, not Mercia.

Ludica is a youthful man, too young to rule Mercia as he has no battle glory to his name, and yet, with the death of King Beornwulf, he's the obvious choice to become king. He's Beornwulf's closest relative, a cousin, I believe. Not that I pay much attention to the men and women in their rich clothes, with their near-constant arguments and complaints that one or other holds more wealth and honour than them.

The only other choice for Mercia's next king would be Bealdred, who sits to the other side of Lady Cynehild. Lord Bealdred is an older man, with some battle glory to his name, and much loved by the dead Beornwulf. But Lord Bealdred has already failed to hold Kent against the incursions of the Wessex king. Bealdred is tainted with that failure and doesn't even think to counter Lord Ludica's claim from his place beside Lady Cynehild.

Lord Ludica is older than me by only six years and yet thinks to be king. More, he can be deemed a man with seventeen years to his name, whereas I'm still no more than a boy, and scrawny with it.

The girls my age tower over me, already becoming women, as Wynflæd tells me, a caution in her eyes that I don't need.

But I'm still a boy, with messy black hair, stick-thin legs and a nose I hope to grow into one day. I often feel that my features are too large for my slight face. I might overtop Wynflæd but not by a great deal. I wish I were taller, if only so I didn't spend so much time on tiptoes reaching for objects just out of reach on the shelves in her workshop. I would never think to call myself a man for I am certainly still only a boy and treated as such by those within Tamworth. Ludica is a man in the eyes of everyone here and he's welcome to it.

Lord Ludica certainly dresses as though he has a royal treasury to support him. I've never seen a man wear so much gold and silver in his clothes or round his neck and along his arms. If I wore as many rings as him, I'd never be able to cut the herbs Wynflæd instructs me to slice so small. My arms would shake too much from the weight.

'When did this happen?' Lord Ludica's words crack with surprising force, and a sigh of unease ripples round the room as everyone realises what his words actually mean.

I note the look on Ealdorman Sigered's face. He's old and lined with his years, as though a split tree trunk. He should have been with King Beornwulf but arrived at Tamworth, some would say, purposefully, two days too late for the muster.

'Five days ago,' my uncle admits, his words softer.

'Five days is too long. Where have you been?'

But my uncle doesn't respond. I don't know where he looks as I still shelter behind him, but I can imagine.

'The boy,' Lady Cynehild states, her words flat and unfeeling. I can't believe she wishes to berate my uncle, here and now, when her husband is dead and Mercia under threat. Yet, the words are unmistakable, ringing through the air, and I feel everyone in that room stare at me. I wish I'd stayed beside Edwin then. Equally, I wish I could dart through the servants and slaves who carry platters of meat, jugs of ale and wine, all held in place as they absorb the news my uncle carries.

But I'm saved from further scrutiny by Mercia's king-in-waiting. There is no choice. Mercia has few enough æthelings, men deemed worthy of the throne. Of late, Mercia's kings have spectacularly failed in their duties to provide heirs, preferring to bicker over who should be king, now rather than in the future. And those who did have heirs, have seen them die too soon, or even before they could become king after their fathers.

'I'll call my warriors together, prepare a counter strike.' Lord Ludica strides from his place on the dais, words flung over his shoulder, even as he dismisses my uncle with a contemptuous air.

Ealdorman Sigered doesn't move with the snapped commands, but Lord Bofa does, Lord Wilfwald as well. Both men must sense a new possibility now that King Beornwulf is dead.

Only then Lord Ludica arrests his forward momentum, seeing me where I cower behind my uncle, and he draws up short, dark eyebrows knit together.

He's not a tall man. I think he might still have some growing to do. Wynflæd has told me many times that boys will continue to grow taller long after girls have become women. Lord Ludica wears his hair tightly cropped, a black beard and moustache working to cover the youthfulness of his face. I can see the resemblance to King Beornwulf in the sharpness of his nose. But there all similarities end. King Beornwulf was a warrior. Lord Ludica is softened by his time spent sitting close to the king in his royal hall, rather than riding at his side.

It's almost as though this is the first time Lord Ludica has truly seen me. He stares, his black eyes pits of nothingness, and then shakes his head, remembering he commands here now, and this is not the time to notice a warrior's nephew, an orphan with no mother or father to speak for him.

'After we've convened the Witan, and I've been confirmed as Mercia's king, we'll ride to the kingdom of the East Angles,' he announces, and I expect Lady Cynehild to argue.

I risk peeking out from behind my uncle's protective back, but she stays silent. Instead, her lips form a tight line. I quickly appreciate why. Lord Ludica might be a young man, but he has a wife already, and even now, Lady Eadburga makes to stand at the urging of her father, Ealdorman Oswine, to replace Lady Cynehild as Mercia's queen. Lady Cynehild's marriage to Mercia's king wasn't quite the safeguard she thought it was.

For a moment, I think there'll be a battle as fierce as that which killed King Beornwulf and the four ealdormen of Mercia, but suddenly Lady Cynehild deflates, stumbling for her chair. Her weakness surprises me. Yet, she has no child to rule after King Beornwulf, and with no child, she's nothing now. She'll be forced to retire to a nunnery, live a life of quiet contemplation far from the royal court. Never again will she rule Mercia. Never again will she preside over feasts or wear rings that flash with rich gems and jewels. I would feel sorry for her. But I can't. She's made my life a misery.

Bishop Æthelweald stands on the dais, summoned from the church inside Tamworth by one of the servants who thinks to earn a reward from him. I've not noticed him passing, but evidently my uncle has as he doesn't startle as I do. The bishop's hands are clasped before him, eyes lowered in sorrow for all his chest heaves with the speed of his arrival. As he puffs and pants, his rich cloak shimmers in the light from the open doorway. I've never liked the older man, just another who knows me and always seems to be there to witness my transgressions, which are few enough, but always seen.

'We'll call the Witan for tomorrow morning. It seems that we require a new king and new ealdormen, both.' Bishop Æthelweald's words echo through the still subdued hall, the soft weeping of women the only sound to be heard above the thudding of my heart.

I eye Bishop Æthelweald. I detect the hint of eagerness in his clipped words. A king's death should be a time for mourning, but as with Lady Eadburga, Ludica's wife, the bishop senses that everything is different. Now he'll help Mercia's new king to rule. It will make him even more powerful. I don't doubt that.

Mercia is to have a new king, Ludica, the first of his name. Perhaps my life will become easier without Lady Cynehild's keen gaze watching my every movement. It seems the bishop, the lords and Ludica's wife aren't the only ones to realise everything has changed with the news my uncle carries.

'Uncle.' He staggers before me, almost down on one knee, and I rush to his aid, grateful when Edwin is beside me as well. Then, with the departure of Lord Ludica through the open doorway, and the submission of Lady Cynehild, Edwin and I are released from the hesitancy that has always marked our actions within the king's hall. 'We need to get him to Wynflæd.'

This time there's no argument from Edwin or my uncle. That worries me more than it should. My uncle's eyes flutter open and closed, even as he rests his full weight against me, head lolling to one side so that I can hear his laboured breathing. He's almost too heavy for my slight arms and legs to carry, and yet I refuse to buckle. I will support him.

As we make our way outside, the bright light almost blinds me; the world I knew changed in just a few words by the death of the king. I notice my uncle's solitary horse, Wine. Head down, slick with sweat, mouth foamed from her exertions. One of the stable-hands moves to curry the animal, his words soft, while another rushes with a bucket of water for her to drink from. I would go to her, thank her for bringing my uncle back to me, but I hardly know her. She's my uncle's horse, not mine.

I'm grateful, even as I realise how few horses there are now. She stands alone outside the stables. Within those stables are the horses of the ealdormen who didn't escort the king, including the horse used by Lady Cynehild. If I ventured inside the stables, I would find it less than half full. King Beornwulf took his men and his wealth of animals to claim back the kingdom of the East Angles from King Athelstan. None of them has returned, other than my uncle and his faithful mount.

King Athelstan of the East Angles will be wealthy now, and not just in terms of horses. He'll carry the knowledge that he killed the Mercian king.

I can hardly believe I'll never see Beornwulf again. His scrutiny was almost as unwanted as Lady Cynehild's, and yet he was Mercia's king. Why he'd notice me, I never knew, but he did, and that protected me, even as Lady Cynehild's disdain ensured I was bossed about by the servants as well as my peers.

I realise I will miss King Beornwulf. That thought surprises me.

2

TAMWORTH

Wynflæd stands outside her workshop, almost opposite where we erupt into the daylight from the king's hall, the low-hanging thatch roof threatening to sag, and yet staying up all the same. She might be bent nearly double, but her eyes are intense as she frantically beckons us onwards. News of my uncle's injuries has reached her already.

'You should have come here first,' she berates Cenfrith, her words like a knife over stone. They jolt my uncle to wakefulness from where he's fallen into a daze, his head coming up and swaying as though his neck can't hold the weight.

'The king...' my uncle begins, his voice too light, only an exhalation. His weakness fills me with dread.

'Isn't going to get any more dead,' the caustic response, as Wynflæd leads us inside her home.

The too-familiar smells assault my nostrils; the heavy aroma of garlic, the lighter fragrance of herbs and other plants I've yet to learn to name. There's a brisk fire in the central hearth, the flames lighting the space, the heat unneeded other than for cooking and concocting her medications. Already, I'm sweating.

It's too hot on such a summer's day when there's no wind to drive the heat away.

Wynflæd is so old, I've never thought to determine her age. Not only is she stooped, but she's also diminutive. It was a game amongst the small children of Tamworth to see who would grow the quickest to tower over her as a small child. Edwin won the competition between us, laughing once he could look down on Wynflæd's scrawny neck and see where her hair had worn away to nothingness.

It took me longer, and I found no joy in being able to effortlessly grab for the objects as she tasked me time and time again with such small jobs. Only now does she let me do more than tie the bunches of herbs in just the right way and hang them at the correct angle from her blackened rafters. Only now does she trust me to collect the most common herbs, to prepare them for use in her medicines, all under her vigilant gaze, of course. But outside of her workshop, I watch all that she does when she harvests the rarer herbs and plants used to cure the ills of the men and women of Tamworth. I'm learning the secrets of being a healer, even if she doesn't openly share them with me.

'Put him here,' Wynflæd instructs me with a point of her finger, indicating the bed where her patients lie when they need to stay the night with her. She shuffles off to her blazing hearth and flings more items into a cauldron that already stinks and boils with whatever she's been brewing.

Edwin coughs, the acrid stink making his eyes water. I'd laugh at him, but my concern for my uncle overlays everything, and even I'm struggling to breathe.

Cenfrith must live or I will truly have no one other than Edwin and his mother to name as my family.

'Strip him.'

My uncle startles from his daze at Wynflæd's command, but my hands are reaching for a sharp knife on Wynflæd's work surface to cut through the padding of his filthy byrnie.

Edwin rushes to remove Cenfrith's boots to expose starkly white feet. Everything above Cenfrith's ankle is either bloody or dirty as Edwin moves to cut his trews away.

Cenfrith flails at my eager hands.

'I can do it,' Cenfrith mutters, but he can't. Instead, his hands merely slow my progress, his nails caked with blood and grime.

'Leave the boy,' Wynflæd's words snap with authority.

My uncle sags back against the bed. He takes instructions from few men or women, but Wynflæd has the same effect on everyone, I've noticed. Far better to do as she says or her potions will taste vile. She'll spare the honey to make a point.

I gasp as my uncle's chest wound is fully exposed as I gently pull away the tunic he's stuffed in place to absorb the blood. A particularly stubborn part of the fabric refuses to move without tugging at the skin. My uncle gasps at the pain, and I turn to Wynflæd, unsure how to proceed, but she's already there, hovering with a clean cloth in her hand. She smells of her herbs. They override everything else, not even the reek of the cauldron scenting the immediate air.

'Hold it steady, and slowly pull it when I say.'

I bow my head, showing I'll do as she asks. I can feel the heat from the cloth she carries, but as she presses it against my uncle's flesh, he lets out a single sigh and stays silent, eyes closed against the pain. Edwin stands close by, unsure what to do. Wynflæd must note him from the corner of her eye.

'Get me more water, boy,' she instructs him stridently. 'Two buckets full, and make sure it's clean. Don't scrape the bucket on the side of the well.' I would chuckle at her oft-quoted phrase, but the tunic is finally released, and now I can see the deep gash on my uncle's chest.

Wynflæd makes no comment, although her hands are busy.

Instead, she snaps out commands to me as she works. I collect the sheep's gut from her neatly arranged shelves, I place the needle into a bowl of boiled water, burning my finger in the process, and all the time, I worry about my uncle.

His eyes remain closed, his body relaxing as he finally sleeps. But his chest only rises and falls a little way. Is it too late? Not that I voice the question. Wynflæd would banish me from her workshop for such thoughts. She would send me to pray in the church, telling me that I must petition our Lord God if I can't trust her. I know what she thinks of Him, so I keep my lips tightly closed, doing all that she asks.

I would sooner believe in Wynflæd's craft than the honeyed words of the bishop with his rich tunic, copious amount of food and pious reprimands when the people of Tamworth indulge as he does and earn the wrath of our Lord God. His God is not my god.

Edwin staggers in and out of the open doorway, carrying bucket after bucket of water, far more than just the two. I decant the first into a fresh cauldron, leaving the water to boil, as Wynflæd commands, and using another to soak my uncle's tunic, although I'm sure it would be better to discard it altogether. The water quickly turns a dirty red colour, more like rust than blood.

Wynflæd works to stitch Cenfrith's wound, having Edwin hold a light, close, so she can see what she's doing, only to chastise him for using the 'good' candles made from beeswax and not the stinking ones of pig fat.

She moves to my uncle's forehead, tutting at the blood there, but it comes away easily enough, and all that remains behind is a cut running above his left eye that has long begun to heal. Still, she prises it open and dribbles salted water into it.

At this, Cenfrith startles awake with a shriek, and I rush to hold him down before he hits Wynflæd with his jolting body.

I notice when the blood is cleared away the tight muscles on my uncle's chest and exposed arms; the way his neck bulges in a way that mine never will, and the strength in his hand when I grip it, and he reciprocates with a squeeze that almost brings tears to my eyes even though he's wounded and weak.

Cenfrith is a warrior. He has the body of a warrior, honed through years of training, through the many battles he's fought. But he's also sliced with long-healed cuts. Red streaks, some long-faded and others still angrily pink, and above where his heart lies, an object rests, attached round his neck by a long cord, a depiction of some winged-creature in silver, that might or might not be hollow. I think to touch it, to see what it is, only for Wynflæd to slap my hand aside from my meddling.

'Leave it,' she cautions, brokering no argument.

I've long wanted to touch the object, but it's been hidden from me. On one occasion, I asked my uncle about it, and he refused to tell me anything. It's one of the few times I've felt his anger directed at me. I've not made the same mistake since.

I nod, chastised once more and hurry to begin cooking the pottage Wynflæd instructs me to produce. Into it, alongside the oats, go a handful of many of her herbs, garlic, nettles amongst them, the aroma pleasant, for once, making me consider that I might still be hungry. She keeps me stirring it while she continues to tend to my uncle. I can do little but sit and glower, ensuring I stir the mixture constantly, singeing my hand in the process. Usually, she would allow her concoctions to cook with only slight interference. I know I'm being kept busy on purpose.

Into another cauldron of water she orders me to add yarrow and wild carrot, woodruff and the leaves of a dandelion, wrinkled at the edges, but good all the same. I've seen her make this salve before and know that she'll apply it over the wound when she's finished with it.

When my uncle next opens his eyes, he turns his head, offers me a tired smile, but then Wynflæd moves in front of him, and I can hear them murmuring one to another, although I'm not to hear what they say.

Edwin has long slumped to sleep on one of the stools, arms folded on the table, and his head resting there. He snores softly, and I stifle a yawn with my other hand. Behind him, every bucket within Tamworth is filled with water, as outside the darkness of night has coated the land. While I've stirred the pottage, he's done as Wynflæd commands, and then more. I'm grateful that he's not left me to return to his mother for the night.

'Keep stirring,' Wynflæd snaps, sensing my preoccupation, although her back is still to me. She really does seem to have eyes in the back of her head, as I've heard some of the other children comment when they're trying to steal items from her store as some rite of passage amongst them all.

I've never taken the risk, grateful to be allowed the easy access that I have to her workshop and all the items she keeps inside it, ready for when they might be needed.

'He'll sleep now,' Wynflæd eventually announces, stretching her back as she does so. I look from her to the cauldron, incredulous, and she cackles softly. 'He'll eat it when he next wakes. Now, you and Edwin should go and rest. Well, you should,' she announces dryly. 'It seems Edwin already is. That boy,' and she shakes her head fondly. She likes Edwin.

'Will Cenfrith heal?' I'm forced to ask because she hasn't offered the reassurance and I need her to say it to me.

'Of course he will. Don't doubt me or my skills. I've told you that before. Now, shoo, and take Edwin with you back to his mother's. I need to sleep as well. Leave the cauldron on the side of the hearth, away from the direct flames. It would be a shame if it burned now, after all your hard work. Before you return here, you must bring me more wood. No, not now,' she barks as I reach for the sack on the floor that she uses to bring wood for her fire. 'Later, when you've slept.'

Far from gently, she slaps Edwin on the back, and he jolts awake, mouth open, a line of drool reaching from his forearm to his mouth.

'Go to your beds,' she instructs him, and I stumble to my feet via my uncle, checking that he breathes easily and that she has tended to all of his wounds. I hear a huff of annoyance from Wynflæd, but I have no remorse. After all, Cenfrith is my only true family. Edwin and his mother had made me one of their own, but Cenfrith is my uncle. He belongs to me, as I belong to him. We have no one else.

Outside, it's fully dark but with the hint of grey showing dawn isn't far off, the birds in the nearby trees, trilling loudly to one another in a hum.

Inside the king's hall opposite, lights are blazing from lit candles, an orange and yellow glow spilling onto the ground outside. I can hear heated conversations taking place, but I direct Edwin to the stables. I'd sooner curl up beside Wine. And I don't want to risk waking Edwin's mother from her sleep.

I find Wine quickly enough, dozing in one of the stalls. Her saddle has been removed, her reins as well, and she's been washed so that the dirt of the road doesn't stain her grey coat. My uncle will reward the lad who tended to her so well.

Wine opens half an eye as I unlock the door but promptly settles once more. She knows who I am even if we don't spend much time together.

Edwin tumbles to the hay-strewn floor and is asleep before he's even horizontal. It takes me longer to find sleep.

Beornwulf, first of his name, king of Mercia is dead, and for some reason, I feel a tear trickling over my cheek to land in the hay on the floor of the stables.

3

I find myself outside as the men and women of the Witan appear the following morning. I've slept deeply but not for too long.

I don't know all those entitled to attend the Witan. Well, I know of them, I suppose.

Eager to have something else to worry about other than my uncle, I perch to watch on one of the upturned buckets that Edwin filled during the night and which has since been put to good use. Any more water in Wynflæd's workshop and she'll need to swim.

The ground beneath my feet is scuffed from the passage of too many feet and hooves. My thoughts turn to the dead Beornwulf. When he was king, such wouldn't have been allowed. I shake my head, surprised I've become used to thinking of him as dead already. At how quickly Tamworth has ceased to be run under his strict instructions. He liked his capital to be clean and tidy, for everything, and everyone, to know their place. It's only been a day since we all knew he wouldn't be returning.

As though summoning them just by thought, the new king-in-waiting, Lord Ludica, and his wife appear next, heads bowed and speaking closely together. I eye them with mild interest, just waiting for Ludica to turn his gaze my way and acknowledge the child sitting on the bucket. But he doesn't, instead hurrying to gain entrance into Beornwulf's great hall.

I startle. I need to start thinking of it differently. It's no longer Beornwulf's. I sigh, the sound long and filled with emotions I don't understand.

Next to appear is Lady Cynehild, her passage laboured as she willingly takes the support of one of her women to either side. She wears the same dress from yesterday, and I consider that she's not slept. Perhaps she's spent the night praying for her husband's soul in the church that the bishop presides over – the only person to have done so because no doubt everyone else has been busy plotting how they can benefit from the king's death.

I watch Lady Cynehild, too tired to be fearful of her gaze and criticism, but then she, of all people, does look my way.

Her eyes seem to offer sympathy. In the bright daylight, I can see the warmth of the hazel in them. My forehead furrows, and then it does even more as I find myself standing and trying to straighten my sleep-tossed tunic. It's seen much better days, and in all honesty, I've grown a good few inches since it was made for me.

'Icel,' she speaks softly, having left her two women behind to come closer to me. Her steps are slow and strained, and yet sure, all at the same time. 'Tell me, how is Lord Cenfrith?' Of all the things she could have said to me, this is not what I expect.

'He's well. Wynflæd believes he'll be fine, but for now, he sleeps. There's no fever. Even I know that's good.' No one else has asked me about Cenfrith as they've gone about their duties this morning. Not the stablehands, not the women preparing food, and not the ealdormen who yet live or their wives. I find the words rushing from me, showing my relief that my uncle will live through his injuries.

'Good.' The tension in her tight lips ease as she speaks. Is she as pleased to hear that news as I am to tell it? The thought comes unbidden, and I dismiss it. Lady Cynehild and my uncle aren't friends, even though my uncle was one of King Beornwulf's closest allies. I imagine she merely asks because she wants to hear more about how her husband died on that far-away battlefield. About why my uncle has returned when her husband hasn't.

Her following words perplex me.

'Be wary, young Icel. A new king and his lady rule here now. Unfortunately, I can't say what that will mean for you.'

I nod because I'm unsure what else to do.

Surprisingly, her hand reaches out as though she'll caress my face, only she pulls up short, stopping the action. I accept that more easily than that she might have touched me. I notice the paleness of her flesh and the bulky rings which cover three of her fingers, priceless gems flashing brightly in the daylight. This time, her smile is tight, given through pursed lips.

'Remember me to your uncle when he wakes.'

'My Lady.' I bow deeply, as I've seen the men and women of the court do. I can't think that we've ever spoken in such a way before. And she's gone, to be swallowed up by the flow of men and women into the great hall. I'm not sure how so many have managed to congregate so quickly. But I suppose an entire night has passed, and men and women will push horses if they think there's a prize to be gained at the end of it.

It makes sense to me that a new king must be confirmed for Mercia. I know Lord Ludica has already made it clear that he's 'throne-worthy' and will be the next man to rule. But Wynflæd whispered to me earlier when I went to check on my uncle that another has a claim as well. But she cautioned me that they'd not dare step foot in Tamworth, which confuses me. If there's someone who could be considered for the kingship, then they should be here, and they should be considered. But what do I know? I'm merely the nephew of one of the king's warriors, and that king is now dead.

'What you doing?' Edwin's words come from behind one of the wooden buildings.

He beckons me to his side, and I give up my position and go to him. He's far from clean, and I wrinkle my nose at the ripe smell. I imagine he's rolled in Wine's green shit but hasn't realised. I left him to sleep when I slipped away from the stables.

'How's your uncle?'

'Wynflæd promises me he'll live.'

'That's good,' Edwin huffs.

'What have you been doing?'

'With the king's warriors. They'll let me train with them now.' He beams with pleasure as he speaks, but the news fills me with unease. Will they expect me to train as well now that so many of the king's warriors have fallen beneath the seaxes and war axes of the king of East Angles? I hope not. I don't want to be a warrior. I always thought my wishes would be allowed. Certainly, my uncle had long ceased trying to teach me how to protect myself. There was no anger with the action, just calm acceptance. But, of course, there's a new king now. Maybe everything will change. 'Are they the men and women of the Witan?' Edwin asks, jutting his head towards the few still hurrying inside Beornwulf's hall.

Silently, I correct my thought to the king's hall.

'Yes, but I don't know many of them. It seems strange to think we'll never see Ealdorman Eadberht again or any of the others.'

'Maybe these lot will be better than King Beornwulf and his dead ealdormen. I mean.' He chuckles to himself. 'All they need do is not take on the might of Wessex and fail, lose the kingdom of Kent, oh, and die in battle on the edge of King Athelstan's blades.'

I wince at Edwin's neat summary of what's happened since Beornwulf became king. Maybe Beornwulf was no great king after all. He stole the throne from the rightful king, Coelwulf, who succeeded his brother, Coenwulf, to the kingdom. Until now, no one has questioned that. I only know because Wynflæd does like to speak about the past.

'What of King Coelwulf, first of his name?' I suddenly ask, not wanting Edwin to continue naming Beornwulf's failures because I find they upset me.

'What of him? I thought he was bloody dead.'

'Is he?' I ask, the news surprising me. 'I thought he'd been allowed to live by King Beornwulf on condition that he relinquish all rights to rule Mercia under oath and while touching the holy relics of Saint Oswald.'

'If he lives, where is he? I've not seen him at Tamworth attending upon Beornwulf.'

'Would you walk into the wolf's den?' I ask Edwin.

He shrugs his shoulders, releasing a foul smell of sweat at the same time. If King Coelwulf does live, I'd expect to find him somewhere close to Gloucester, from where his family originates.

'Don't you ever bathe?' I ask Edwin, my thoughts distracted by his stench.

'I smell like a man,' he juts out his chest as he speaks. I would laugh at him, but Edwin doesn't take kindly to having his manly aspirations dismissed so quickly.

'You smell like a stinky man, yes,' I mutter under my breath.

The men and women inside the king's hall have fallen silent, and although I'm not inside, and the door has been shut, I can still hear Bishop Æthelweald when he begins to speak, his words slow and measured.

'Today, we mourn our king, Beornwulf, the first of his name. But now, we must ensure a new king is duly elected to rule Mercia.' His words are met with a rumble of conversation.

'Not even a prayer for the old man, poor sod,' Edwin offers.

I'd been expecting more prayers, I admit. But, in fact, I'd also anticipated some of the king's men to be sent to recover the bodies of the dead as soon as it was light enough for them to ride out. After all, Lord Ludica said he would ride out to gain revenge against the East Angles. Neither of those two things has happened.

But Edwin stands before anything else is said. Something is happening at the main gate, and he wanders away, intrigued by it all. He's such a nosy git. But it means he knows a great deal of what happens here, even things that Wynflæd doesn't hear as she administers to the inhabitants of Tamworth.

But before I can refocus on the bishop's voice, Edwin is back, his face pale.

'It's the rest of the Mercians. You better get Wynflæd.'

I'd forgotten my uncle said there were more survivors.

'How many?' But I'm already running to fetch Wynflæd from inside her workshop.

'Four, maybe three. I think one of them might be dead,' Edwin calls to my back.

'What is it?' Wynflæd demands unhappily when I dash inside her workshop.

'More survivors. Edwin says four, but maybe three.'

Her lips thin at the knowledge, and she jerks her chin towards her basket, filled with a collection of supplies she uses the most.

I catch sight of my uncle as I rush to do as she asks. He sleeps, but his naked chest and face are slick with sweat. She told me he didn't have a fever. It must have just started.

'He'll be fine. It's always the way with a wound left untended for so many days. He should have stopped and at least cleaned both of them rather than allowing the head wound to fill with dust from the road. Now hurry. These men will be in just as bad condition as your uncle.'

Outside, I match my steps to her far smaller ones. More and

more people not included in the Witan are hurrying to see who the survivors are. There are still women and children hoping their husbands or fathers might have lived through the attack. Cenfrith didn't stop to give names of the survivors before collapsing. No one has dared risk Wynflæd's wrath by demanding the answer.

I watch them all, hope on their faces, and realise how lucky I am that my uncle has returned.

Edwin walks ahead of Wynflæd and me, using his broad back to clear a path to the exhausted horses. There are five of them, and they all foam at the mouth so that some of the other youngsters have already rushed to gather buckets of water from which they can drink. One of the horses has no rider.

The men who remained in Mercia are trying to help the wounded dismount, giving the horses some ease, but it's far from simple. And at the rear, the man on a black horse, who paws at the ground, is definitely dead, slumped in the saddle, with a crust of dark blood down his beard and spilling onto his chest.

A woman shrieks at the sight, while Wynflæd shakes her head.

'It would have been better to leave him behind.' But already she's examining the first man who lies on the ground.

I recognise him because of the scar on his forehead, a jagged wound that was caused last year when he fell while drunk and hit a piece of stone on the ground. His nose is a bloody mass, flies buzzing about it, and both of his eyes are so swollen that they don't open. He also has an oozing wound on his left leg, which Wynflæd quickly examines.

'Clean it,' she urges me, and I bend to do as she asks, using a piece of clean cloth to move aside the filth of the road. Beneath it, I can see that it's not a deep cut, and if the wound-rot has stayed away from it for this long, it won't take now. 'Waldhere,' Wynflæd speaks to the man while I work.

I turn to Edwin, and he rushes away, back to her workshop. I need cooled, boiled water.

'Waldhere,' Wynflæd calls again. Her tone is insistent. Even as he is now, Waldhere would be a fool not to respond to her.

He coughs, body shaking, as his eyes flutter open. They startle at seeing Wynflæd so close to him.

'Urgh,' he cries.

'Tell me where it hurts,' she demands to know, not at all concerned by his surprised shriek. Wynflæd hasn't ordered his clothing removed, but if he doesn't answer her, he'll be naked in no time at all.

'My face, my leg, nowhere else.' He gabbles the words quickly as she presses on his nose and a loud squelching noise can be heard.

'You'll never be pretty again, but then, I don't think you ever were,' she informs him and only then turns to look at me.

Edwin has staggered back with his burden, and now I use the water to clear away all of the filth on his leg wound. It's long, running from his knee almost to his ankle, but it's no deeper than the nail on my small finger.

'Is it well?' she asks me.

'It will be,' and she nods.

'Take him to his bed,' she orders the men who are mingling around. There's no sign of a wife for Waldhere because he's never had one, and that actually makes it easier.

The other two men have sobbing wives and children clustered all round them. It falls to Wynflæd to shout in order to clear them all away, the force of her words surprising me. Even then, I can't get close enough to see what ails them. So instead, I listen to Wynflæd as she speaks to the men and then calls for me to collect items for her. I run to her workshop, only to return and find her gone, along with everyone apart from Edwin and two other lads a similar age to us, who lead the five exhausted horses back to the stables.

'She went in there,' Edwin calls to me when my running footsteps abruptly stop right in front of him, pointing towards the hall where the king's household warriors sleep.

'Thanks,' and I run from him.

As I aid Wynflæd throughout the afternoon, I hear indistinct arguments coming from the king's hall and eventually cheering and acclamation.

At the sound, Wynflæd looks up from stitching an open wound on one of the men's backs. 'Well, at least that's bloody resolved. Perhaps we can all get on with what needs doing now.' Her tone is barbed, and I entirely agree with her. It's all been a farce, because Lord Ludica was always going to be the new king, no matter the rumour of another with a similar claim. Now we need to see how capable our new king of Mercia is. Ludica, first of his name, king of Mercia is now responsible for every man, woman, child and beast within Tamworth and within Mercia itself. And more, for ensuring the advances made by the kingdoms of the East Angles and Wessex are halted.

I can't see how a youth who's barely a man can take on the might of two kingdoms when Beornwulf, a man with the reputation of a warrior, has so spectacularly failed. The thought unnerves me.

4

I nurse my uncle that night. Wynflæd makes no comment as I mop his brow and dribble water into his partly closed mouth. She's content he's well, but I remain to be convinced while he's slick with sweat.

She sleeps in her small bed, little more than a lump of furs, the snores she makes loud enough to keep me awake every time my chin nods onto my chest as I blink grit from my eyes. And all night my uncle mumbles in his sleep.

'The king,' his words are just loud enough to hear, the fear in his voice, evident. 'The banner.'

He speaks of Mercia's banner, held aloft before the king when he rides out to make war. I've always been thrilled to see the eagle there, sharp beak, even sharper eyes on a blood-red background held high by the king's banner bearer. I don't know where the banner is now. I imagine it's lost on the battlefield. Perhaps even hung in the hall of the king of the East Angles, a sign of his victory.

'It's too hot,' the next words pour from Cenfrith as he lies without moving anything other than his tongue. Sweat drips from his forehead, the smell ripe. I wrinkle my nose, and use another cloth to wipe it clear. I don't know if he's too hot now, or if it was too hot on the battlefield.

In my mind, I can see the summer-baked ground where the two sides joined battle, hear the sound of ravens high overhead, and know his fear. The scops tell their tales well enough that although I've never seen a battlefield, I can imagine one.

I nod in sleep once more, startle awake thinking I'm on that slaughter-field, but I'm not. Wynflæd's loud snores assure me of that. The dead are far more silent.

Cenfrith's right arm rears into the air. It wavers. He must think he still fights the bastard East Angles. He stabs outwards, bringing his elbow back, before hitting me in the chest with all of his strength as I bend over him, thinking to tend him. I struggle for breath. My uncle is a strong man.

'The king,' Cenfrith cries, as though summoning the men he fights beside even now.

I bow my head low. There are many men I'll never see again. The king is just one of those.

And then my uncle begins to sob. The sound startles me. I've never seen my uncle cry, even when mourning my mother, his sister, on the joint anniversary of her death and my birth. So often a sombre day, and one made difficult with false cheer.

'Cenfrith, you're well,' I call to him, but he doesn't hear me above the sound of his tears, the thrusting of his seax arm.

Now he thrashes on the bed, and I fear he'll wake Wynflæd, and that it will be my fault.

Again, Cenfrith raises his right hand high, stabbing and slashing for all there is no seax there. His legs move and I know he battles in his dream.

'Beornwulf, my brother,' he calls eventually, the cry hoarse, and I bow my head again, cuffing tears from my eyes. My uncle relives

the moment Mercia's king lost his life against King Athelstan of the
East Angles.

I know why King Beornwulf thought to make war against Athelstan. Everyone inside Tamworth knows.

For over fifty years, the kingdom of the East Angles has sworn
its fealty to the Mercian king. First King Offa, and then his short-
lived son, Ecgberht, and then King Coenwulf. Then King Coelwulf,
the first of his name, the mighty war-axe against the Welsh kingdoms of Powys and Gwynedd. And then some madness saw King
Coelwulf deposed, his place taken by King Beornwulf. But King
Beornwulf hasn't earned himself the name of the war axe, sword or
seax of anything.

He rode to battle King Ecgberht of Wessex within Wessex itself.
Beornwulf thought to make himself king over all the kingdoms of
the Saxons – the East Angles, the Mercians, the West Saxons, the
men and women of Kent. Perhaps even the kingdom of the
Northumbrians far to the north. But the battle of Ellendun left
Mercia weak, not strong, her men dead or injured. The kingdom of
Wessex wasn't contained; if anything, it was resurgent, claiming
back the long-held kingdom of Kent from Mercia. And Athelstan of
the East Angles scented the chance for a victory as well, for the East
Angles to claim back the right to rule their own kingdom.

King Beornwulf, determined to save his tattered reputation,
spoke of taking back the kingdom of the East Angles from beneath
King Athelstan. Of killing the man who thought to stand against
him. Of restoring wealth and positions to the nobles of Mercia left
with nothing after the East Angles declared their freedom.

The East Angles, beneath their snake banner, must have been
far stronger than King Beornwulf believed. There can be no other
explanation for the king's failure.

I would know why my uncle has survived, but I will not ask. I
offer soft prayers of thanks that Cenfrith has returned to me.

Eventually I sleep, but in my dreams, I hear the roar of men fighting to their death. I smell their fear. I taste their blood, and in the morning, my uncle's fever has passed, and he sleeps more naturally.

* * *

My uncle eschews Wynflæd's aid three days later, bursting from her workshop as though he's been kept captive, which he hasn't. She watches him go with an indecipherable expression on her lined face. I hear her barbed comment all the same.

'A man can only take so many wounds,' she grumbles, as she moves to clear away the mess left by his lying on one of her straw beds for three days.

I think to follow him.

'You have work to do,' she barks at me, no sympathy in her words. 'Your uncle has his own concerns,' she tries to explain.

I turn from watching Cenfrith's back to her and know that there's no choice.

Only later do I find my uncle, sitting in King Ludica's hall, unchanged from when Beornwulf ruled here, other than the layer of dust that coats everything, a furious expression on Cenfrith's pale face beneath his healing wound. His left eye slightly swollen. It gives him a lopsided appearance.

Cenfrith nurses a wooden cup before him, but I know there won't be wine or ale within it. My uncle isn't one to indulge in either. He's a warrior. He likes to keep his head clear from the fogginess of ale.

Edwin is already sitting as a silent guard next to my uncle. I raise my chin to him, thanking him even though I didn't ask him to help. Edwin nods with all the solemnity of my uncle. I might laugh if the two didn't look so enraged.

I take a seat beside them. Wynflæd has had me running round
after her, and the wounded men, and horses as well. We've also
tended to the wife of the dead warrior, offering her herbs to help
her sleep, her two children, wide-eyed and terrified at their mother's grief. My feet throb, and I'm thirsty too, but all that is driven
from my mind on seeing my uncle and friend.

Cenfrith looks far from hale. I would sooner send him back to
bed than allow him to sit within the king's hall. But I'm not going to
order him. Wynflæd is the only person I know, other than King
Beornwulf, from whom my uncle will take orders. As she's allowed
him to leave her workshop without further argument, I have no one
else to rely on.

'What?' I ask, but my eyes are drawn to King Ludica as laughter
floods the king's hall.

King Ludica and his special allies sit on the dais together,
drinking and gaming. His wife looks on with a proprietorial gaze as
though daring anyone to question him and his right to rule. How
quickly things have changed. I've even heard that Lady Cynehild
has left Tamworth for the royal nunnery at Winchcombe. Not that I
feel any freer within Tamworth. In fact, if anything, I feel as though
more eyes watch me now, and even Wynflæd, for all she still bays at
me when I do something wrong, is less caustic than usual. Does she
sense the change as well?

The fact she's released me from other duties is a mark of that. In
the past, she would have me working until I slept and then prod me
to wakefulness once more as soon as there was light enough with
which to see.

Above my head, I eye the long line of shields ranging from one
side of the king's hall, all the way round to the other. Some of them
are barely held together by the spiderwebs and dust, too dark to
determine what's actually depicted on them. Others are brightly
painted, showing the winged eagle of Mercia's kings, or just the

head, or two heads. Several kings have used different variations on the same theme of the Mercian eagle emblem. All of them menace, the eyes of those birds seeming to watch everyone within the king's hall as though they're there to judge what happens in the kingdom.

Rumour has it that one of the shields once belonged to King Penda, over two hundred years ago. It's said that he used it in battle when he overcame the might of Northumbria's kings. I don't see how it can be the same shield. Surely by now it would have crumbled to little more than dust.

'They should be riding to recover the bodies of their king and the ealdormen who perished.' Cenfrith's voice is too loud, as though he wants to start a fight with the new king and his group of allies. Luckily, given my uncle's current state and hoarse voice, no one seems to hear him.

Edwin nods as though the wisest of men, his cheeks flushed with mirrored fury. 'They don't deserve to be left for the ravens and wolves, the foxes and the birds of prey.'

I shake my head, eyes wide at Edwin's statement. But Cenfrith doesn't grow angrier, merely nodding in agreement, downing yet more water and reaching for the jug to fill his beaker with more. He still glowers at the king. My uncle is making it clear he thinks little of King Ludica.

King Beornwulf was my uncle's friend. Not for the first time, I consider why my uncle didn't die beside Beornwulf. I can't see it being by choice.

'We could go?' I suggest it because I don't know how else to solve the problem, how to drive the wrath from my uncle's face. King Ludica said he would avenge the king's death, but since he muttered those words, they've not been spoken of again. Mercia's new king seems to prefer drinking to spending his time on the training field. Tonight there will be a feast. Tomorrow, there will probably be another.

Slowly, Cenfrith turns to meet my gaze. I expect to see fury on his face at my presumption, but instead, a smile lifts his pale cheeks, his bruised face making it look far from friendly. But he means it to be friendly. His following words assure me of that.

'Really, Icel? The youth who wishes to heal, not fight, would truly venture into disputed territory with the kingdom of the East Angles and reclaim the bodies of King Beornwulf, Ealdormen Eadberht, Beornoth, Alhheard and Wynfrith?' He arches a dark eyebrow at me, even though it pains him as his eyebrow pushes up his wound. Cenfrith quickly straightens his face.

My uncle might once have been an attractive man, but it's difficult to find it amongst the ruin of his face. The wound he took above his eye is going to leave another jagged scar along his forehead.

'Well, um, yes, actually, I would. It's only right that they're buried with all honours due to them.' I try to sound as confident as possible.

And now Cenfrith's expression turns murderous, and he stands, knocking the table so violently, Edwin, on the far side of him, almost tumbles from his place on the stool.

'Do you hear that, My Lord King,' Cenfrith's words ripple with disdain, suddenly far louder than I thought him capable of when he answered just me. 'Even this boy here, who's never killed in his life, knows that you're honour-bound to reclaim the dead.' Cenfrith's voice is so forceful, I almost clamp my hands to my ears.

King Ludica stands, unsteady on two feet, his elegant wine glass clutched in his hand. He has no problem with drinking deeply. It looks as though he's been doing it all day.

I eye the new king, taking in the sight of him. Somehow, King Ludica has endeavoured to dress in more finery than before he was named as Mercia's king. He's even found a small silver diadem to thread through his hair, no doubt because the king's warrior helmet is still lying on a stinking battlefield, being picked clean by the ravens and the East Angles.

'Cenfrith,' King Ludica lacks the power of my uncle's statement. His voice is weaselly, almost soft in comparison. 'You're a traitor. You left your king to die while you escaped with your life. Don't give me that crap about being sent here to warn us of an attack by the East Angles. If one were coming, they would surely be here by now.'

King Ludica's words are greeted with a rumble of acclaim from those who sit with him.

But my uncle doesn't even answer the king. Instead, he directs his ire at the ealdormen who yet live; those who didn't ride with Beornwulf.

'Tell me Ealdormen Sigered, Eatferth, even you Wilfwald. The three of you supported Beornwulf when he became king. You stood at his shoulders while he deposed King Coelwulf, the first of that name, and now you sup from this pup's leftovers. Do you call yourself Mercia's ealdormen? Do you?' The roar is noisier even than thunder this time.

I gaze at each of the ealdormen in turn. I'm having to hold my jaw tight to prevent my mouth from falling open. Edwin is in no better state than me, his eyes wider than the flat bowls Wynflæd uses for her potions.

My uncle reveals something I didn't know. I was unaware that these three were such fervent supporters of King Beornwulf. I consider then why they weren't part of the king's attacking force. Well, I know why Ealdorman Sigered wasn't. But not the other two.

'Sit down, Cenfrith,' Ealdorman Sigered, the oldest of the group, mutters, his words far from heated. 'We all mourn here. Those men we lost had been our friends and allies for years.'

'And yet you leave them to be picked over, to have their flesh torn from their skin. To have their eyeballs devoured by the ravens.

What do the holy men say of this? Aye, what did the bishop advise you?'

Ealdorman Sigered looks far from subdued by my uncle's questions. But King Ludica's face is turning ever redder as he sways from side to side. If he's not careful, he'll fall and wound himself on the edge of the wooden table. What a kingly wound that will be.

'It's not your place to question your king?' Lady Eadburga calls from her position behind her husband. Her words have more volume than King Ludica's. I can see that her father, Ealdorman Oswine, has muttered to her, forcing her to speak.

'We can't restart the war,' Ealdorman Sigered continues, as though this conversation takes place only between Cenfrith and him, as though Lady Eadburga hasn't even spoken. 'We don't have the warriors, and the season is late. The fyrd are needed for the harvest or Mercia will starve through the coming winter.'

'I haven't asked you to restart the war. I've asked you to collect the king's remains. It's only right that he's buried in Mercia, at Repton, and not left to rot.'

'What does it matter?' King Ludica demands, spilling maroon wine as he sways. 'King Beornwulf is dead, and so is his aspiration for a dynasty to rule after him. His wife was a barren bitch. Now there's nothing. Better to forget Beornwulf was ever king.' But this statement, offered with slurred words, causes a stunned silence to fall within the hall, and all eyes settle on him.

Now even I allow my mouth to drop open in shock.

'You bloody fool,' Lady Eadburga hisses too loudly so that we all hear her. Her father doesn't tell her to say those words.

'What?' King Ludica asks, slumping in his chair; all of his good cheer evaporated. Even he must know what he's done by saying such. He's called into question Beornwulf's reign; Beornwulf's kingship. He's made nothing of the men who bled their last on that far away battlefield.

'It will be arranged,' Ealdorman Sigered speaks into the silence, eyeing King Ludica with incredulity. His words have forced the matter. 'We'll send men to retrieve the dead and ensure they receive a decent burial. And let that be the end of it.'

Cenfrith bows his head, I think to Ealdorman Sigered, and not to the king at all, and then stamps from the king's hall.

I follow him, Edwin as well, into the courtyard, where the sound of the blacksmith at work rings loud in the confined space. I look that way but don't see Edwin's mother. She married the blacksmith after Edwin's father died.

There are a group of seven children playing a game between the king's hall and the row of workshops. They use sticks of wood as swords, two of them at the heart of the battle, while the rest roar on their favoured winner. I note it with a smile, as the girls far outnumber the boys.

Cenfrith doesn't stop walking, for all he limps heavily, favouring the right side of his body that hasn't been stitched by Wynflæd's steady hand.

I look to Edwin. His face is still locked in a rictus of unease, and my uncle doesn't speak. I follow him as he makes his way through the gateway of the king's compound, guarded by men who call his name, these new warriors who didn't die on the edge of a blade on the battlefield, although Cenfrith doesn't notice them.

Edwin thanks them, his voice soft as we follow Cenfrith. Edwin knows these men better than I do. These must be the ones he trains with on a daily basis.

I don't know where my uncle's going, but it's no great surprise when he stands before the church, dedicated to St Chad. It seems Cenfrith needs to pray.

Inside the small wooden door, the interior smells of fresh wood cuttings, no doubt a repair being carried out at the bishop's instructions. It overrides the cloying scent of incense. Perhaps, I consider, all churches should smell of fresh wood.

Cenfrith makes his way to the front of the church, bending his head low. I keep mine upright, as does Edwin. But we both leap forward when Cenfrith almost pitches onto his face as his knees fail him.

I grip his right arm, Edwin his left, and we lower him to the wooden floor. Then, with a hissed intake of pain, Cenfrith brings his hands together, clasping them before him. I see the tears that mar his face, that stream without ceasing, and I swallow my grief as well.

In the tussle to decide who will rule Mercia next, it's been forgotten that these were men who died. Men with wives, and sons, and daughters, with friends, allies as well as enemies. The realisation shocks me. I've determined that King Beornwulf is dead, that I'll never see him again, and yet, it saddens me, though I never even spoke to him while he lived.

I join my uncle, with tears flooding from my eyes.

For the first time in my life, many, many men have died, all at the same time. And I'll never see them again or hear their complaints, or watch them as they train against one another.

Mercia is indeed bereft without her warriors.

PART II

5

AD827

The interior is almost too dark to see by, but I don't want to look up from my task, not yet, and so I'm working more by touch than sight. Wynflæd, with a soft cackle, has left me to count the supplies of birthwort, betony and agrimony while she's gone to eat in King Ludica's hall, summoned by Lady Eadburga.

Once more, I feel the sting of not being invited, but it's a sensation I've become used to ever since Ludica became king last year. I'd never thought of myself as unique, but it seems that, for some reason, King Beornwulf had determined to treat me well, much better than now. I always had new clothes, new boots, a good cloak to call my own, but my clothes are over a year old, much repaired by Edwin's mother, and I desperately need a new pair of boots because my current ones pinch my toes, raising bloody welts along the top of them.

My uncle has failed to notice. I know better than to prompt him. He's been sullen of late and I don't like to remind him of my existence.

My uncle, of course, has been on the training ground once more, but not me. And, of all the men, only Edwin and Cenfrith don't tease me about my aversion to the place. If not for Wynflæd's insistence that I learn her crafts, I'd find myself beside Edwin, sweating and shivering on the training ground, no matter the weather, while King Ludica tries to replace the host of men lost in battle against the East Angles a year ago.

King Ludica, if he knows who I am, is more likely to spit on me as little more than one of the slaves than praise me for learning so much under Wynflæd's instruction. But it's summer, and Ludica isn't at Tamworth. No, he and his warriors are off, tempting King Athelstan of the East Angles once more. Although he'd never have been king without the death of King Beornwulf, Ludica has, belatedly, vowed to seek revenge against the men of the East Angles. It's either that or he'll lose the support of those who acclaimed him as king.

Cenfrith says such revenge has been too long in coming. But he's ridden beside his king all the same. He hungers to avenge the death of King Beornwulf. Only now do I realise that they counted one another as friends. Only now do I realise that, somehow, I was included in that friendship.

Wynflæd is dismissive of the king and his thirst for battle glory; of my fears for Cenfrith.

'Icel, your uncle is a warrior. A gifted warrior,' she's informed me, her voice lacking all sympathy for me and admiration for my uncle. 'He'll return. He always does, no matter the wounds, and no matter the losses to Mercia.'

But as the days of their absence stretch, I know there's more than just me worrying about when the king will return.

And that's why Wynflæd is now seated beside Lady Eadburga in the royal hall, in Ludica's royal hall. She's there to assist the woman should her child decide it's time to be born. Eadburga's a tall woman, with long, brown hair, which some might have called chestnut, but which I know to be only dull brown. She's not as terrifying as Lady Cynehild had been when Beornwulf was king. But I believe much of that is because, just like her husband, Eadburga doesn't take any notice of me. I could be a slave or a servant for all she knows.

It makes me miss Lady Cynehild's cruel scrutiny.

I take only some small pleasure in being invisible to Lady Eadburga, even as, for some reason, Wynflæd tuts and moans about it as she moves about her workshop, busy with the day-to-day tasks of healing blisters and broken fingers, seeing to aching ears and snotty noses, toothaches and the complaints of the women as they go through their pregnancies. I don't know why it upsets her. It's me that's ignored.

Unknown to me as I labour, Edwin has entered Wynflæd's workshop, the rafters hung with an assortment of drying herbs, as well as the odd, stranger object, such as a desiccated rat, a salted hedgehog and a snake stuffed with straw, so that a yellow strand pours from its open mouth, sharp teeth on display. I know that Wynflæd just likes to keep such items as a means of terrifying the youngsters who try to meddle with her precious medicines. I'm not about to inform Edwin of this, even as I notice him looking aghast at the objects.

'What do they go in?' he asks, not for the first time.

I hold up my hand, lips moving, trying to show that I'm counting. He lapses into silence, but I can hear him walking around, inspecting odd items as he goes. Wynflæd won't like it, but I'm not going to send Edwin away. He's my only friend, other than Wynflæd. I'm pleased he seeks me out inside her workshop.

Eventually, I finish.

'They're used in some healing potions,' I offer, as I always do. But Edwin's standing in the doorway, his attention elsewhere. Only now do I hear the rumble of horses rushing into the settlement.

My forehead furrows, fear of the previous year when so many of the king's men died forcing me to join Edwin, leaving my stool upended on the floor of the workshop.

'What's happening?' I demand, breathless.

Edwin just about fills the doorway. In the last year, we've both gained inches in height, and Edwin, with his warriors' training, also has cords of muscle on his shoulders and upper legs for all he only has twelve years to his name, as do I. There's no room for me to see if he doesn't move aside.

'I don't know. I'm going to find out.'

'Don't,' I call, but he's already gone. Anything to do with warriors and horses, and Edwin believes he has the right to know. I hang back. I don't want to hear the ridicule of those warriors who know of my decision to learn the healing craft and not the killing one.

I gaze towards the king's hall. There are figures there, moving through the late dusk, the feast held in the evening, almost during the night, to take advantage of the cooler temperatures. My breath catches as I glimpse my uncle, but he walks firmly, back erect, no sign of the limp from last year. There are also no bloody bandages round his body so I know he's well as he returns from the king's eastward march. This then is the returning party of King Ludica.

There are many more warriors than when King Beornwulf died, so it must have been triumphant. Yet, it seems to be largely devoid of the joy of success I was anticipating, and there is no sign of King Ludica. Perhaps he remains in the kingdom of the East Angles, reasserting Mercia's dominance in holding it as well. Or perhaps not.

Across the distance, my uncle senses my scrutiny, turning to meet my eyes only to shake his head quickly from side to side.

'Again?' I mouth, but he's gaining admittance to the feast, having mumbled to the door wardens, and offers nothing further.

I could run to him, but I'm not the same boy who did that last summer. I'm not often to be found in the king's hall taking my meals, and I'm certainly not invited to the feasts.

I receive all the confirmation I need when I hear a shriek from Lady Eadburga only moments later coming from inside the hall.

Edwin rushes back to me then, eyes wide with shock, desperate to share his news. He's not alone in pouring into the roadway between the houses, workshops and the king's residence.

'The bloody king is dead,' Edwin gasps. 'King Athelstan of the East Angles came against the leading force, which contained the king, and by the time the rearguard caught up, the king was dead, along with five of the ealdormen, and the East Angles were running back over the boundary line. They're naming King Athelstan the King Slayer.'

'Two kings in one year. King Athelstan must truly hate the Mercians who once ruled over his kingdom,' I mutter, trying to make it sound lighthearted even while my heart flutters.

King Athelstan of the East Angles is indeed a Mercian king slayer. A very successful one. He's certainly ensuring that his kingdom stays independent from Mercia. He's making it clear that the kingdom of the East Angles will not again be forced to pledge their oath to Mercia and be subordinate to it.

This is catastrophic; there's no other word for it. With the kingdom of Powys eager for revenge after King Coelwulf's attack there only a few years ago, before Beornwulf deposed him, and with the Wessex king determined to press any advantage from the south, Mercia simply can't be kingless once more. I suppose we should be grateful that the East Angles are merely happy to retain hold of their kingdom. The attack by Mercia was only in retaliation for the death of King Beornwulf. In the last year, the king of the East Angles has made no provocative attacks inside Mercia, not even to hunt.

'Who is there in Tamworth who can be king now?' Edwin shrugs his growing shoulders, and I can sense his confusion in the lines above his eyebrows.

Everything changed a year ago, and now, everything will change again. Both of us are still adjusting, and it seems we must start the process once more.

'There'll be someone within Mercia, and it's not for us to worry about it. It's not as though either of us is destined to be king.'

And although Edwin nods in confirmation, unease fills me. I've not enjoyed the year without King Beornwulf. Whoever steps from the shadows to replace King Ludica will be relatively unknown to me and everyone within the king's compound at Tamworth. It's been assumed that Ludica's son would rule after him. But a babe can't rule.

'Icel,' my name cracks through the night air. Wynflæd stands in the door to the king's hall, beckoning to me with her clawed hands.

I dash across the hard-packed earth, sending up clouds of dust in my wake. Perhaps a new king will see the area swept clean once more as under Beornwulf's strictures. He was a man who believed in everything being in its place.

'What is it?' I ask, noting that her eyes blaze and her lips are tight, her thin, tufted hair drifting in the wake of my speed.

'Get my supplies. The lady is about to have this child, no matter the death of its father.'

I bow my head quickly and run back to Wynflæd's workshop, hastily gathering the equipment she wants, even as there's a growing thrum of conversation from outside, and over it all, there's an increasing scream of agony.

I wince. The poor woman. Pushing forth a child is every woman's bloody battle. I hope she's more successful than her husband.

* * *

'A daughter.' I share with Edwin early the following morning, stifling a yawn for my long night. The child has been born, hale and screaming, but a girl. Not much use for a kingdom without a king. Not that a baby could be a king anyway. A babe can't lead the men from horseback against Mercia's foes, and Mercia has too many enemies.

Lady Eadburga is well, unlike when my mother birthed me and bled to death. Every birth within the compound makes me think of my mother. I should have liked to know her, speak with her, and even know who my father was. But I never will. I've long accepted that. My uncle will not speak of my mother. Wynflæd always changing the subject when I ask her. I don't quite count Edwin's mother as mine, but I hope I care for her in a similar way as I should, if she had been my birth mother. Certainly, she does what she can for me, even though I'm not her son, and her husband complains of the expense of feeding two growing boys who are not her own now that Edwin and I are no longer as welcome in the king's hall as when Beornwulf ruled.

'There are rumours,' Edwin offers, 'that the new king will be either Ealdorman Wiglaf or Lord Beorhtwulf.'

'Lord Beorhtwulf is too young, and no one will support him.' I speak with the assurance of Wynflæd's words behind me, shared during the night as we tended to the dead king's wife. These rumours aren't new to me, and I now know the identity of both men.

Lord Beorhtwulf is the son of King Bealdred, the failed sub-king of Kent, dead since midwinter. Some would say of shame. Wynflæd would disagree with them. I would as well, if anyone thought to ask me. Which they don't. We tended to him as he grew weak and unable to eat. A pitiful death.

Edwin stays silent. We both know I speak the truth. What I don't say is that Ealdorman Wiglaf has no right to become Mercia's king. Wynflæd has made that clear to me. His claim as an ætheling, as 'throne-worthy,' is no secret within Tamworth, and even Wynflæd spoke of it with derision. He only became an ealdorman last year when there was no other option after the death of the four ealdormen besides King Beornwulf. Wiglaf doesn't have the credentials to be Mercia's king. If he had, just as Beornwulf before him, he would have been welcomed at Tamworth long before then.

'Have you met Ealdorman Wiglaf?' I ask Edwin, out of curiosity. I don't believe I have.

'No. It's just a name to me, although some of the warriors seem to know who he was. He has royal blood in his veins, although none are too sure from where. One of them mentioned King Æthelbald as an ancestor.'

'What, the king murdered by his own supporters he was so hated? Hardly a great recommendation. What of the ealdormen?' Once more, I'm grateful that Wynflæd has taught me so much about Mercia's past rulers.

'Those who died will need replacing. Again.' Five of the ealdormen went with King Ludica to East Anglia. Of those, I knew who Bofa, Eatferth and Wilfwald were, Oswine as well. Eadric I'd never seen at Tamworth. It might be the honourable thing to do, to lay down their life for their king, but what of Mercia? Although, well, Ealdorman Sigered has survived once more. He always has some excuse to stay behind when the king calls his warriors together. And I add Ealdormen Mucel and Muca to that list as well. All of them have survived the East Angles cull of the last year.

To become an ealdorman involves winning the support of the man named as king. It's holding the position that's harder to do, especially when there are so many wars to fight. Staying alive seems to be half the job, or so it seems to me.

I think the ealdormen do little but shout in the Witan, demand to be heard and expect the king to provide them with the wealth they deem they deserve. This is what I believe of them. Wynflæd assures me there is much more to the task.

The men chosen for the honour must have the support not only of the king but of the men and women in the areas over which they have command. It helps, she says, if the ealdorman can claim, however indirectly, some connection to the ruling family who reigned before those truly ancient kingdoms became part of the growing Mercia over two hundred years ago.

At the moment, there are almost none of those. Any links between those who yet live and those who once ruled as kings have become so weak, even the holy men can no longer truly uphold the claims men and women make. And they have vellums to note down their observations and track the births and deaths of those families.

'Has your uncle said nothing to you of what will happen now?'

I shake my head. I've not seen my uncle other than when he slipped into the king's hall to inform yet another woman that she was a widow. I'm sure there'll be many asking how my uncle has lived through this battle. But my uncle has survived many such altercations. He's a warrior, a true warrior of Mercia. I'm proud to call him my uncle. Perhaps the ealdormen, and the king, could have done with adopting some of his training techniques. 'He's busy, elsewhere, no doubt with the churchmen and the would-be-ealdormen and those few who remain.' Ealdormen Sigered and Mucel have become the great survivors of recent years. There are few others who've retained their position without riding off to war with one of Mercia's overly ambitious kings.

'Will Cenfrith never claim an ealdordom for himself?' Edwin demands, but I shake my head again.

'He's a warrior. You know that. He has no interest in running an estate, in presiding over the courts, in dealing with matters of the law. His place is here, at the king's side, as one of his sworn men. He pays scant attention to the lands he already owns even though they're close to the border with the kingdom of Gwynedd.'

Once more, Edwin remains silent. We've discussed this on countless occasions. As we both grow to adulthood, there are many things that no longer seem to make sense, and other things equally that finally make sense. It's a world of confusion, but Wynflæd, and my uncle, anchor me. I'm pleased to have them, even if I would sooner have a mother as well.

At least Edwin has the same questions I do. I'm pleased not to be alone with such thoughts.

'Will Lady Eadburga retire to the royal nunnery at Winchcombe, as Lady Cynehild did?'

'I imagine she will. She has a daughter but not the son for which she must have hoped. Like the deposed King Coelwulf, before Beornwulf became king, she doesn't have the legacy to play more of a part in the future of Mercia.'

From behind us, I hear a soft chuckle, and we both turn. I flush at being caught talking about Mercia's kings and their wives.

'Cenfrith, you are well?' I immediately ask to cover my embarrassment. I note his eye is more than half-closed, and he now limps slightly, no doubt with exhaustion, but there's no great wound on his forehead, or across his chest, as when King Beornwulf died.

'I am, yes, although heavy-hearted. King Ludica took too great a risk. He should have waited for the remainder of his warriors, but he was always hot-headed and too eager to prove himself as Mercia's king. And now listen to you two, discussing politics as though you know what you're talking about.' Although it's a rebuke, Cenfrith speaks with a rare smile. 'It's not our place to determine the future of Mercia.'

I look down, noting my square-cut nails, clean and devoid of all muck. So unlike my uncle and Edwin. Even Edwin carries scars, and they're only from the training ground.

'Then you know who'll replace King Ludica.' I say

But Cenfrith shrugs his broad shoulders and rubs his hand through his wiry beard. 'I don't, no. That's for the holy men and remaining nobility to determine. I've listened to their arguments, and I know my preference, but that's of little consequence.' My uncle won't meet my eye when he speaks, and I consider what secrets he holds close to him now. He might refute all discussions of him becoming an ealdorman, but he's one element of continuity amongst the mess of the last few years when Mercia has lost not just two kings in battle against the king of the East Angles, but a further one as well through old age. There's not been the longevity that King Offa or Coenwulf's reign provided during the last sixty years. Far from it.

It strikes me once more that a kingdom's successes and triumphs should not ride only on the shoulders of one man. When the Witan determine who they will elect to the kingship, perhaps they should question them about their intentions. Mercia, my uncle tells me, can take no more war.

'The Lady Eadburga? She's well?' My uncle surprises me by asking.

'A daughter.'

'At least she need not worry that her child will be taken from her,' my uncle announces, something flickering in his eyes that alerts me to yet another of his secrets.

He walks away then, calling for water to bathe in, and Edwin watches him with unfeigned admiration. My uncle is the very warrior that Edwin wishes to be when he's finished his training. I wish him luck with that.

6

I eye the new king with unease. Wiglaf is an older man than Ludica, and he carries himself with confidence, not swagger. He's not as tall as my uncle, a member of the group that surrounds the new king, and neither is he as young. I detect hints of grey running through his hair and the beard and moustache that cover much of his face, but it's his eyes that absorb me.

He sees everything, even while giving his attention to the man who speaks into his ear. This is Ælfstan, one of his ealdormen. Ælfstan owes his new position to the deaths of the ealdormen who died fighting with King Ludica against the king-slayer of the East Angles.

Ealdorman Ælfstan has no relation to his predecessor in the position of ealdorman, Wilfwald, but he is a member of the nobility who've long ruled in the ancient kingdom of the *Magonsæte*, centred around Hereford, and close to the border with the Welsh kingdoms. That's important to the new king. My uncle agrees as well.

'It's always much better if the ealdormen can claim close ties with the people and places they rule over.'

I have no opinion on the matter. I decide I don't much like the look of King Wiglaf or Ealdorman Ælfstan.

My uncle has been firm with me. I'm to stay away from the new king, his wife and son. I'm to take my meals in the king's hall only when there's no excuse not to, and most of my time is to be spent with Wynflæd, hidden in her workshop, or out, collecting the herbs, plants and insects needed for her medicines. Little has changed in that regard. It was the same when Ludica was king, and Edwin and I ate with his mother and her husband. I don't ask if I'll get a new cloak and boots. My uncle has seen to that requirement already because I couldn't attend the royal funerals or coronation in the clothes I had.

Today, I've been forced into the king's hall because this is a feast celebrating his new kingship. King Ludica and the dead ealdormen have been buried in Tamworth with much weeping and wailing. Bishop Æthelweald presided over every funeral Mass. It was a dreary day, although the sun blazed fiercely overhead, making everyone sweat and itch in their new or finest clothes.

Lady Eadburga had to be escorted away from the church, unable to stand, having buried not just her husband but her father as well during the course of the same day. Her baby daughter's wails rose into the sky, where she was held tightly by one of her women attendants. I know how the baby felt to have lost her father. At least the babe will know who he was.

Only when Ludica and the dead ealdormen, Oswine, Eatferth, Eadric, Wilfwald and Bofa, had been interred beneath the rich soil of the church at Tamworth, dedicated to St Chad, did Wiglaf allow himself to be led to Lichfield, to be proclaimed as Mercia's king by Bishop Æthelweald. Bishop Æthelweald placed Mercia's warrior helm upon his head at the front of the full church. Not the same helm that Beornwulf wore for his coronation. This one had been made specifically for Ludica after the loss of the item in battle against the East Angles. A pity he was never to wear it.

Not that I was allowed inside to witness the actual ceremony. Wiglaf doesn't wear the helm now as he sits on the dais. Instead his hair is devoid of all symbolism as he feasts with his ealdormen, king's thegns and thegns – those who yet live and those newly come to the position.

The Mercian warrior helm, which rests before him, lit by four candles, is bedecked with flickering golds and silvers depicting the wings, feathers, beak and piercing eyes of Mercia's eagle, speaking of a symbolic and mighty item. The red horsehair which crowns it is almost not needed. The helm shimmers enough as it is.

Still, I'm grateful not to feel the weight of King Wiglaf's stare as I fervently spoon the hot vegetable pottage into my mouth, the meat for the feast already long devoured by men and women keen to indulge, if not to necessarily celebrate the new king. I'm hungry. I'm always hungry these days, and even Wynflæd has taken to preparing me food alongside her own. She says I need double portions if I'm to achieve my potential. I'm appreciative that she shares with me, and without the snippy comments I receive from Edwin's stepfather.

King Wiglaf is married and has a son, Wigmund, someone to rule after him. Wigmund can be no older than I am, but at least he's not a tiny baby. If his father lives only a few years longer than King Ludica managed, then Wigmund will be deemed warrior enough to inherit the kingdom.

Wigmund has worn fine clothes to his father's kingmaking cere-mony. Now I watch as he fidgets and itches in his especially deco-rated tunic, gleaming beneath the light from the candles that sit on the dais. He would be more comfortable in something less elabo-rate, but his mother smacks his hand away, time and time again, when he tries to scratch his neck and wrists. I wouldn't like to have her for a mother. Even no mother is better than having Lady Cynethryth.

Wigmund looks like his father, apart from where he fails to grow a beard and moustache to match that of the king. Wigmund is too young for such, even if he shares his father's height. Lady Cynethryth watches everything he does, bending to speak conspiratorially into his ear. Lady Cynethryth is the most richly dressed of all. I've heard Wynflæd mutter that she's surprised the woman can walk beneath the weight of so much silk, embroidery, fur and that's not to mention the jewels that run through her greying hair, round her wide neck and across her dress and cloak.

If the king's ceremonial helm shows images of the Mercian eagle, then Lady Cynethryth has ensured she wears even more. Eagles flutter on the brooches that adorn her dress, on the stitching down that dress, and they seem to take flight from her iron-grey hair. She is not, I think, a beautiful woman.

My gaze turns towards King Wiglaf. He's entirely different to those other kings I've known in my life.

Perhaps it's just that I don't know him, as he's always been a stranger to Tamworth, but I think not. He strikes me as a sly man. He watches everything, perhaps notes everything, and I imagine he remembers everything he sees.

I can't yet tell whether he'll do any better than the kings he's succeeded. It must be hoped he does, yet he's broken the rules that dictate who can rule in Mercia. By rights, and as Wynflæd has laboured to tell me, the kingdom should have been returned to the still-living but deposed King Coelwulf, first of his name, as the only descendant of King Penda, who ruled two hundred years ago, or rather Penda's brother, Coenwalh. Coenwalh was never king of Mercia, but it is right that Mercia's kings claim descent from him anyway. That the deposed King Coelwulf still lives came as a surprise to more than just Edwin.

Coelwulf's claim is more genuine than Wiglaf's, who became ealdorman of the *Wreocensaetan* only last year, and is now already Mercia's king. Another is ealdorman there now, Eadwulf.

I have only vague memories of the deposed king, Coelwulf, as I was no more than a small child then. Beornwulf took the crown from Coelwulf. I don't believe Beornwulf acted correctly, but I liked him, or thought I did, so I find it difficult to criticise his actions.

King Coelwulf, Wynflæd assures me, was a mighty warrior, eager to battle against the many Welsh kingdoms, the sort of man needed to keep Mercia safe. She's dismissive of all who've followed in his footsteps. She's furious that he's been locked away ever since at Kingsholm.

Wynflæd would welcome Coelwulf as Mercia's king, but she's not a member of the Witan, and there are none brave enough to speak up for Coelwulf. They were all, in some capacity, complacent in his deposing.

Ealdorman Sigered, with his even greyer hair, seems to be wary of King Wiglaf. Still, he's held his position for many long years, no doubt, because he avoids war with Mercia's enemies and conflict with whoever is king. Edwin is far from approving of him.

Ealdorman Mucel is the same. Both of them are veterans of the politics and war that has ravaged Mercia throughout my short lifetime. They could argue that they're too old to ride to war. But if an ealdorman can't defend the land he governs, then there's little point to him. Babies can't rule because they can't command warriors, so why should old men, who eschew leading their warriors, be treated differently?

But, for all I'm uneasy about our new king, my uncle hasn't been forced to embarrass him regarding his predecessor because he himself brought back the bodies of the dead when he returned to Tamworth.

That doesn't stop Cenfrith being troubled by Wiglaf's pretensions. I can understand why.

Wiglaf parades around Tamworth as though he's a warrior-king, with victories to his name, when he has nothing of the sort. He didn't join either of the last two king's attacks on the kingdom of the East Angles. He didn't participate in the failed attack against King Ecgberht of Wessex at Ellendun while Beornwulf was king. Wiglaf played no part in trying to force the Wessex king's son out of Mercian Kent. I doubt he's even held a blade against the throat of one of the many Welsh warriors who routinely harry the borders to the west of the kingdom.

As much as I never wish to do those things, it worries me that even our king can't do the same.

Edwin is silent beside me, brooding rather than eating, and that alerts me that all is not well, even without the purpling bruise round his eye. I know the story, but not from Edwin. I'm unsure whether he'll share with me what happened the day before on the training field. Not that he must tell me what happened. I think no less of him.

Only then Edwin turns to me, his one good eye blazing with fury from beneath glowering eyebrows. Edwin has a new tunic as well. It almost contains his growing body and has some smart iron decorations running along the cuffs and round his neck. He might not wear silver and gold, as the king and his family do, but his mother has ensured he looks the part, all the same.

'Lord Wigmund is a worm.' The words are so quiet I hardly hear them as he whispers them to me. 'He has no warrior's skills. He'd never have struck his blow had I not tripped over the byrnie he left on the ground. He doesn't know how to hold a seax, or a shield, or even how to pull his own byrnie on.'

The words are double-edged. I know that Edwin wishes I stood beside him when he trained with the king's warriors, that one day we would stand shield to shield against Mercia's foes. As such, when he complains about Wigmund, it could be about me that he speaks.

'It will heal,' I quickly offer, because it's the truth.

But Edwin turns to glare at me, his bruised eye bulging uncomfortably. 'It doesn't matter if it will heal or not. What matters is that Wigmund didn't fight with the honour of the king's son, and if the son is like that, then how can the king ever be honourable?' The words are a sharp whisper, spoken directly into my ear. He won't speak more loudly for fear of being overheard by the other noble children who share our table.

Immediately I appreciate Edwin's fears. They mirror my own too closely, and I seek out Cenfrith amongst the king's men. But he's not there any more. I know a moment of outrage that he gets to leave the feast while I must endure it. No doubt, Cenfrith's off on some secret business about which I'll never know. He'll only ever say that he works on behalf of Mercia's king.

I eat, but the food suddenly has no taste any more. This might have been a feast for Mercia's new king, but Wiglaf's the fourth king in as many years, and promises to be no better.

The following day, my uncle seeks me out in Wynflæd's workshop, his eyes fierce. He's dressed for travelling, and I swallow uneasily. I hardly see him these days.

'I'm riding out with the king's men, to the south. King Ecgberht has been sniffing around close to the River Thames once more. That man senses weakness within Mercia.'

'Then travel safely,' I order him, my voice quivering with unease.

'I always do,' he assures me, laying his hand on my shoulder before turning and leaving without speaking any further. I noticed, as he grazed my shoulder, that his arm no longer hung low. I'm growing taller, perhaps even as tall as him, and that pleases me.

Wynflæd tuts from her place behind me. When I face her, she's shaking her head, nimble fingers working through a large pile of mushrooms gathered that morning. She knows the ones she wants. I find it impossible to tell some of them apart.

'This will not end well,' she cautions me, sucking her tongue with concentration as she holds one of the mushrooms closer.

'Not for my uncle?' I demand.

She shakes her head, the thin rags of her grey hair hardly moving at all with the movement. 'Your uncle can handle himself. He always has in the past.' The words are slightly reassuring. 'Come, here, look at these,' and she points to some bright red mushrooms, the sort that looks deadly to eat. 'Don't use these for food. They can be used for other purposes.'

I nod. These are the ones I always avoid. I don't even like to touch them.

'These...' Now she points to dull brown specimens, small and hardly worth harvesting. '...will make a good pottage and can be found growing in the woodlands of Mercia. They taste delicious, hot or cold.' And she pops one into her mouth, chewing it with evident pleasure.

I'm enjoying the lesson, even if I refuse all of the mushrooms she offers me. Only then the doorway darkens, and I'm startled to look up and meet the eyes of Lady Cynethryth, accompanied by one of the king's household warriors. His name is Oswy.

She enters Wynflæd's workshop without permission. I open my mouth to rebuke her, only for Wynflæd to shuffle in front of me, a caution in her eyes as she advises silence.

'My Lady.' She dips her head, but only slightly. In contrast, I bow deeply.

Lady Cynethryth's eyes move over the objects on display, pausing on the desiccated rat with some horror on her face.

'Why is he here?' are the first words she speaks.

I wince at the harsh tone, but consider what she sees as she looks at me. I'm taller than Wynflæd. Edwin's mother says I look like my uncle, but I'm not sure I do. I do have long, black hair, tied behind my neck with leather ties, and Wynflæd says I have a stubborn chin. I'm not sure what that means. My clothes are well-worn, but at least they fit me. I'm slight, not at all like Edwin, whose physique grows almost daily. I'm tall and skinny, that much I do know. But it's easy to appear so next to Wynflæd.

'Every herbwoman needs an apprentice.' Wynflæd's words are honeyed, not at all the tone she uses when speaking with me, or, in fact, any of the men, women and children within Tamworth when she treats them.

'Should it not be a girl to help the women with their births?'

'There are enough birthing women within Tamworth and, indeed, throughout much of Mercia. It's the art of healing that the lad learns. That's entirely different and needed outside the monasteries as well as within.'

'Then he's your apprentice?'

'Of sorts, yes. He's here through choice and with the permission of his uncle, the famed warrior, Cenfrith.'

Lady Cynethryth's eyes narrow at my uncle's name. I don't know what that means, and quickly, she's once more berating Wynflæd.

'He should be learning to fight, with my son, to protect Mercia from her enemies.' As she speaks of her son, a fierceness enters her stormy eyes.

'Perhaps, My Lady. But when the wounded come home – should they make it home – my skills are needed, and he's the only one who wishes to know the secrets of how to cure ailments, knit wounds together and counter the sicknesses that sweep through our settlement each winter. Even the young girls are more interested in learning the ways of blacksmiths and silversmiths, moneyers and farming.'

I've never heard Wynflæd speak about me in such a way, and a glow of pride replaces the leaden fear that Lady Cynethryth will order me from the workshop.

'Well, if that's the case, I don't wish him to hear our conversation. Begone, boy. Far from here. Wynflæd and I have much to discuss.'

Wynflæd again bows her head, just low enough to be respectful, making 'hurry up' motions with her right hand beneath the table.

I slide between the king's wife and the old herbwoman, desperate not to knock anything over or step on Lady Cynethryth's rich dress of deepest blue linen that pools on the ground by her feet, covering her shoes entirely. Eventually, I escape beyond Oswy, the king's warrior, dressed as though we are all in danger, bristling with seax and swords, who watches me with hard eyes.

No doubt, news of what's happened here will be all round the settlement by nightfall.

I consider whether the warrior knows the identity of my uncle. He probably does. But as I've refused to take up blade and shield, it offers me no protection.

Erupting into the bright daylight, soft clouds floating in the summer sky, I turn aside, wondering what to do. It's not often I have time to myself. Wynflæd keeps me busy, as do the illnesses which befall the people to whom she ministers. I find myself drawn to the shouting coming from the training ground down by the river. I know the way for all I rarely visit the place.

The area round the king's hall and Wynflæd's workshop is almost silent, apart from the rhythmic banging coming from the blacksmith's, and I raise a hand in greeting to Edwin's mother, Eadburh, where she tries to speak with her husband. A brief smile touches her cheeks, driving back the years which sit heavily on her.

I quickly realise why no one else is about as I draw nearer to the training ground on the exposed land where the river flows in the near distance, glistening beneath the heat of the sun. In the middle of winter, the flat land can flood when the rains fall heavily, but it's an inviting place in the middle of summer. All of the inhabitants of Tamworth seem to be gathered here, all of the small children with nothing better to do, even the bishop and a handful of his monks. I strain to see over the top of everyone's head, but it's impossible.

There are just too many people to see why there's so much jeering and roaring.

Instead, I slide between them, into spaces left by others as they move forwards and backwards to gossip with friends or comment on something else entirely, and then I realise what's happening.

In the wake of the losses of more of Mercia's warriors, the king's commander has made it clear that men and boys need to join the household troop. First, it seems, King Wiglaf has determined on seeing which of the recent recruits are ready to ride at the king's side.

I spy Edwin, sweating in his old and torn byrnie, his broad face set into a line of determination as he fights with a blunt weapon against another lad, perhaps no older than him but of a slighter build. They clash time and time again, dulled blade against dulled blade, sweat dripping from their faces, their feet driving up a cloud of dust as they move round one another.

I watch Edwin's movements, noting that they're smooth, if not the fastest. He holds his seax well, his grip firm, face lined with concentration, for he wears no helm to protect him. After all, this is merely play-fighting, not the real thing.

Then I gasp because Edwin fights none other than Wigmund, the king's son, and the king is watching from the side, with his ealdormen surrounding him. Considering my uncle has just left Tamworth once more, no doubt on some urgent errand for the king, I would expect at least some of the ealdormen to be missing from the king's side, if only to supervise their estates and to ensure the borders are protected.

But, no, I note them all. There are seven ealdormen at the moment. The king has replaced those who died fighting with Ludica: Bofa, Eatferth, Wilfwald, Oswine and Eadric, and of course, some, such as Sigered, Muca and Mucel, have long held their position.

Ælfstan, Athelhard, Tidwulf and Eadwulf have taken the positions of the lost ealdormen. The men range in age, size and shape so that virtually all type of men are included amongst them, from Ælfstan, the youngest of them all, to Sigered, who served not only Beornwulf and Ludica but the deposed Coelwulf and his much longer reigned brother, Coenwulf, before that, long before I was born.

Ealdorman Sigered is a wily old fox, so my uncle assures me. He speaks with the king now, although the king is hardly listening. Still, it's good for the people of Tamworth to see that Ealdorman Sigered has the ear of yet another king.

Ealdorman Tidwulf draws my eye now. He's a tall man, well-built, and he stands furthest from the king, hardly seeming to watch the fighting at all, his attention directed elsewhere. He's a good friend to Wiglaf, though. His disinterest speaks of a man who knows his worth to the king. Rumours of some murky task undertaken for the king abound to account for Tidwulf's advancement, for Mercia doesn't often have men with black skin, and tight furled hair, amongst their numbers.

But Wynflæd assures me there's no truth to the rumours. She and Tidwulf can often be found murmuring to one another. She tells me he knows much about the art of healing, learned from a book he once read, and that intrigues her. It fascinates me as well. I should like to know how he learnt to read, for I would like to learn the skill as well. But, unfortunately, the bishops and monks hoard such knowledge to themselves as though it can't be shared.

Ealdorman Tidwulf's weapon of choice is a long curling blade. I've seen him use it. It's sharper than it looks. In the hands of a novice, it would cut the bearer. He doesn't wear a thick byrnie but instead stands proud without one. Nor does he use a shield in practice but rather turns and dances as he fights, evading his opponents with ease. I can't see that being much use in a shield wall, but what do I know?

And then I look at Muca. Muca was one of the men who supported Beornwulf's usurpation of the kingdom from Coelwulf. Muca is not a Mercian by birth, but I don't know whether he comes from the Frankish kingdom or perhaps even further away, for he too has an unusual appearance. He wears a thick black beard and moustache covering much of his face, and his black hair is longer than Lady Cynethryth's. Not that he wears it long, but rather tied up round his head, as though a crown. He has piercing green eyes, and I prefer to stay far away from his unflinching gaze.

I swallow against the worry that burns in my belly as my eyes are drawn back to Edwin. This could be Edwin's moment to make a name for himself before the king and the king's ealdormen, but to do so, he must overwhelm the king's son, who Edwin already believes has no honour. I can't imagine that will have a happy outcome.

Wigmund is taller than Edwin, not by much, but enough that his arms have the greater reach, if they lack the same muscle as Edwin's. They have no shield between them but a seax each, and they thrust and counter around one another. There are four such battles taking place simultaneously, but every eye is on Wigmund and Edwin, apart from Tidwulf's disinterested look which focuses on the river.

The king doesn't seem to blink from where he stands, wearing a short-sleeved tunic of crimson without a cloak. It's a warm day, and a servant hovers close by, refilling his wooden cup whenever he wants it. Better to have wood out here than the delicate glass goblets that can be used to impress in the king's hall.

Wiglaf speaks with his ealdormen as he watches, as though the outcome of the fight means nothing to him, but his gaze belies his disinterest. I wish I'd known of this before now. I would have had my uncle urge caution on Edwin. He's so desperate to be counted as one of the men that he'll do anything to take his place amongst the king's warriors. Edwin won't even consider that the way to do it is not to prevail against the king's son.

And, of course, Edwin does have the greater skill. He has spent the last year doing all he can, attending training with the king's warriors, running round Tamworth to increase his strength, all activities the other warriors endure day after day. Beside him, I can only run half his distance and in twice the time.

I chew my bottom lip as Edwin rushes into Wigmund, close enough that he could threaten him with a headbutt if he wanted to do so. Only at the last possible moment does Wigmund thrust Edwin aside with his dulled blade, and there's a smirk on Wiglaf's face at the movement. But even to my untrained eye, it speaks of desperation.

Wigmund doesn't wish to be humiliated before his father, but Edwin is battling for something else entirely.

They clash once more, blade against blade, Edwin forcing Wigmund backwards with the speed of his attack. Back and back, they go, and I know that Edwin will win this attack. He'll crow about it, chest puffed up as he takes his place beside the rest of the king's warriors.

Only then, the king's commander is there, Eahric, his face showing worry, as his hand strokes his auburn beard, watching this attack unfold. Behind Eahric, I spy Wiglaf, watching on, conversation forgotten about, hand raised to shush Sigered, as the crucial part of the altercation nears.

Edwin will win. I know he will. He can't lose as he rushes against Wigmund, blade moving through the air so fast I can't see it without the aid of the sun on it, glinting and almost blinding me, while Wigmund can do nothing but retreat to evade the cuts.

Again, I look at the king, trying to decide how he'll react to his son's humiliation. By the time I look back, recalled to what's happening by an unhappy murmur from the crowd, Edwin is flat on the dusty ground, Wigmund's dull blade at his throat. Wigmund has prevailed, not Edwin.

I furrow my brows, listen to the words whispered one from another and quickly realise that this isn't by chance. No, Eahric has interfered in the fight, tripping Edwin over so that he stumbled and fell backwards, opening himself up for the defeat that the king demanded.

Edwin rushes to his feet from beneath Wigmund's blade. His face is covered in sweat and purple with anger. I think he'll attack Eahric, or even lash out at Wigmund, but, instead, Wiglaf's words echo round the training ground, holding him still.

'You see, Mercia's new breed of warriors must be men as skilled as my son. Noble sons, not, as this boy is, the runt of the litter.' Wiglaf's words ripple with scorn; his hand extended towards Edwin. There's an uneasy silence at the words. I doubt there's anyone there who would call Edwin a runt. Everyone here, even Eahric, who looks far from apologetic, knows that Edwin must become a warrior and has the skills to do so or he'll have no means of supporting himself when he reaches adulthood.

Edwin looks from the king to his triumphant son with disbelief, mouth open as his chest heaves. The king's son looks as though he's just dressed. There's no hint of sweat on his face, unsurprisingly because he's done little in the mock fight other than allow another man to ensure his victory.

I try to catch Edwin's eye, willing him to silence, pleased when he bows jerkily, to Wigmund and then to his father, and shoulders his way into the crowd. There's a ragged cheer as Eahric proclaims Wigmund the victor, holding his arm high, but I rush to Edwin's side, this time a path opening up quickly for me. Walking beside Edwin, without speaking, we make our way back to the central part of the settlement, rushing up the steep embankment, both of us eager to be out of the sun and away from the king.

As we near the gateway through the defences surrounding Tamworth, a deep ditch and a tall palisade that can block the sun during the day, I see Lady Cynethryth, Oswy, and a few of her adherents coming the other way. She eyes me with undisguised loathing. At the same time, one of the servants rears up before her, having beaten us back from the training ground, and bows to her. He whispers something in her ear. A slow smile spreads across Lady Cynethryth's face at the news, and she walks into our path, making it impossible for us to avoid her and to forego bowing low to her because, at this part of the road, the ditch is below us. We'd have to tumble into the stink of the foetid water and the ruins of filth that people discard within it.

'I see the herb boy is an ally of the youth my son beat in a fair battle. Perhaps he should join you, learn to harvest the herbs that cure the minor ailments of people and beasts. It seems both of you have the skills required to pare roots and fruits, but not to kill a man.'

I tense at those words, dismayed by the taunting from the woman who is the king's wife, aware that Edwin is close to exploding with his fury.

She eyes us, hand on hip, while her women look on and the warrior, Oswy, who guards her struggles to remain impassive at such an unlooked-for rebuke.

Somehow, we both manage to bite our tongues and, when neither of us replies, Lady Cynethryth sweeps past us, no doubt to join in her son's triumph, and we escape from the king's wife. We seek sanctuary from the heat and the prying eyes in Wynflæd's workshop. Her expression is far from serene as she spies us.

'The bitch and the bastard should be ignored,' she comments sharply, without either of us having to speak. 'Neither of them knows how to be Mercia's king, and with some luck, we'll have a new king just as quickly as last time.'

I nod, tears threatening to spill from my eyes, even as Edwin bangs his fist onto the table, sending all of Wynflæd's carefully prepared herbs flying to the ground so that I wince, expecting her wrath and fury, her barked instruction that he tidy up the mess.

She doesn't even rebuke him.

* * *

When Cenfrith next returns to Tamworth, he seeks out Edwin and me. It's been over a week since Edwin's humiliation, and although he's returned to his training, it's only because I've made him. And only then because Wynflæd told me to ensure he did so. If not, I would have happily sat with him and spoken of little or nothing, just passing the time of day with him. Instead, I've walked beside him to the training ground and watched him with the other, specially chosen warriors, and every time, my rage towards Wiglaf and his despicable wife burns.

Edwin is covered in cuts and bruises, as though he's forgotten how to fight. Every warrior he faces takes advantage of such a lack of faith in his abilities.

His face is burned by the sun, and he looks thinner than I'm used to seeing.

'Walk with me,' Cenfrith instructs us both.

Only when we're far from prying ears and eyes, with the sound of the river in our ears, does Cenfrith speak again, stopping in front of us and fixing first Edwin and then me with his comforting gaze.

'Edwin, you're a fine warrior. One day you'll have your place restored to you. The king risks his already failing dynasty should he actually send Wigmund into battle. And, Icel, whatever Lady

Cynethryth implies, you know no one within Tamworth belittles you for your skills and, quite frankly, for tolerating old Wynflæd.'

The words bolster me, and I feel myself standing a little taller.

'But I would caution you both. I'm often absent from here, and Lady Cynethryth has too much of the king's ear. She's asking questions about both of you, trying to cause problems for you. Without me here, as often as I'd like, you must grow thick skins, ignore the words and look out for one another. Wynflæd is always your friend, as are others, and your mother, Edwin, even Eahric. He regrets his actions but can do little to make amends. Not at the moment.'

I gaze at the river, noting how it shimmers in the far distance as though made of ice, even though it's so hot, sweat beads on my forehead just from walking.

'Perhaps,' Edwin asks, 'I could ride with you on your duties for the king?'

'No,' Cenfrith snaps quickly and then seems to regret such haste. He places his finger beneath Edwin's chin, forcing him to meet his eyes. I note that the distance Edwin has to look up is much smaller than in the past. 'You two must look out for one another. Unfortunately, you're both too young, for now, to be called upon to do more than you already do.'

'But it's impossible,' Edwin whines with frustration.

'Nothing is impossible,' Cenfrith counters with a grim smile. 'It just takes a lot of bloody practice.'

PART III

8

AD828

The men of Mercia are once more behind the closed doors of the king's hall. Edwin walks beside me as we brood on what's happening now.

King Wiglaf has survived his first year as Mercia's king. Some are unkind enough to mention that's because he's done little but sit on his arse, eat fine food and order feasts and scops to sing his praises. That he's sent Mercia's wealth to placate the kings of Wessex, the East Angles, and even the Welsh kings. But that's all changed now.

I've seen little of Cenfrith since the snow melted. King Athelstan of the East Angles has been busy on the eastern borders, the Welsh warriors of Gwynedd and Powys harrying on the western, and there remains the menace of King Ecgberht of Wessex from the south. One thing is sure; Kent is truly lost to Mercia. For all time. Or so people mutter. And my uncle is being kept busy riding from one border to another. His face is always grim when he returns, his reports to the king never taken as seriously as they should be.

Wynflæd's dismissive attitude towards Mercia's new king means that many will share their thoughts with her when she tends to their ills. Few within Tamworth are happy with the king. It bolsters me to know that there are more than just Edwin and I who wish the king's wife and his son gone from Tamworth, the king as well. It would be a relief if they just visited the properties of some of the ealdormen; after all, Mercia is far broader and longer than just Tamworth. But Tamworth is Mercia's capital, and Wiglaf is too keen to stay within the comfort of her sheltering walls.

'What's happening in there?' Edwin asks, his chin angled towards the king's hall. Wynflæd has sent me to the well to collect fresh water for her, with her usual caution not to hit the sides of the well with the buckets. It's hot and heavy work. Edwin doesn't offer to help, and so my words are spoken between grunts of effort.

'The ealdormen and the bishops.'

He looks at me, lips downcast, and I startle to see almost a man looking at me and not my boyhood friend. We've celebrated the day of his birth already this year. I still have some months before I can celebrate mine.

'Will it be war?'

'How should I know,' I complain irritably.

'Cenfrith said that the Wessex warriors moved over the River Thames without fear of reprisal, while King Athelstan of the East Angles eyes Peterborough and its wealth.'

'And that's not to mention the kings of Powys and Gwynedd.' I shake my head, a bucket in either hand, sloshing water over my boots as I go. Mercia, Powys and Gwynedd are enemies of each other, the one always happy to take advantage of the vulnerability of the other.

It surprises me how weak Mercia is, considering it's only been six years since King Coelwulf's great victory over the men of Powys and Gwynedd. Some would say that if King Beornwulf hadn't stolen Coelwulf's crown, we wouldn't be in this position now. I might agree with them. But Wynflæd has cautioned me about the ease of remembering things as golden in the past, when they weren't so. Her words shocked me. I thought she wanted Coelwulf back as Mercia's king, but I've not yet plucked up the courage to ask her.

'He tells you more than he does me,' I mutter. My uncle has grown distant of late. It's not just that he's so busy with the king's business. I wish I knew what it was. Wynflæd cackled when I asked her. Told me it would be a woman who's won his heart, but my uncle has never sought a romantic relationship with any woman. Ever. And there was something in her eyes and forced cheer that worried me.

'Well, I'm sure he'll tell us when he emerges from the Witan,' Edwin mollifies.

'What, he's here?'

Edwin's forehead furrows. 'Yes, he arrived last night. Haven't you seen him?'

It's obvious that I haven't, and my reply is silence, as Wynflæd's workshop comes into view before me. I eye the sagging roof once more. At some point, the men and women within Tamworth will be forced to rebuild it by paying her with their labour, or all of her potions and stores will be ruined by the rain and the cold, not to mention the sun and the heat.

'There'll be no water left in those by the time you get there,' Edwin comments, stopping to turn and eye my slow progress. His words are far from helpful.

'You could take one, lighten my load.'

'I could, yes, but if the bloody king's son, Wigmund, sees me, he'll tell Eahric, and I can't be doing with the teasing. I'll never live down that day on the training ground last summer. Now all the warriors think I should be an apprentice to Wynflæd, beside you. It's all I can do to get them to forget for long enough to swing a blade and shield at them all. It doesn't seem to matter how often I break noses or inflict bruises, either.'

'Well, good to know what those arseholes think is more important than watching your friend drown his feet.'

'Ah, come on, Icel. You know what it's like?' he coaxes, eyes fierce and without remorse.

I do know, but equally, I don't feel like admitting to that. Not right now. I've stood beside him when he failed against Wigmund. The least he could do would be to return the favour. After all, he might be teased, but he has the build of a warrior. I still lack his muscles. I imagine I always will.

'If there's war, they might need more warriors, and then I can join the household troop, even if it's just because they have no one else to count amongst their number.'

'The ealdormen will bring their household warriors with them,' I retort, knowing the words are cruel and will wound.

'So, what? I'm only ever to be put to use when the king calls out the bloody fyrd?' Edwin's feet stamp at my side.

I grimace. I meant to rile him, but I'm immediately remorseful. He's my foster-brother. I should be kinder to him.

'No, Edwin, I'm sorry. Come on, you know I didn't mean it.'

'Bugger off, Icel. Maybe I should stay away from you. It would make all this,' and he raises his hands to indicate the interior of the king's enclosure, 'so much easier.'

I pause, watching him stamp away to his mother's home. I won't call him back. Not this time. He knows full well he should have helped me.

I hustle into Wynflæd's hut. She doesn't look up from examining Cuthred's leg. The boy is no taller than my waist and, because of it, gets into all sorts of places he really shouldn't.

'You two should argue where others can't hear you,' Wynflæd mutters, not meeting my eyes even though she criticises me.

I slop the buckets down, more water overflowing to sizzle into the hearth as I do so, where a fire burns even though it's warm inside and outside.

'What have you been up to now?' I ask Cuthred, my curiosity overwhelming my bad temper, moving behind Wynflæd and wincing at the large piece of wood just beneath the skin on his lower leg.

He grins at me, sun-browned face highlighting the paleness of his eyebrows. I can't help feeling that Cuthred gets away with so much because he's such a likeable young lad.

'I was climbing in the woods.' His face alights with excitement, and then it falls away. 'I fell, bashed my head,' and he touches the back of his head, only to grimace.

'But that's the least of your worries,' Wynflæd mutters. 'A bang on the head might force some sense into you. A splinter such as this can grow infected too quickly. Even something like this could see you close to death. I've told you to be more careful.'

Cuthred nods vigorously, earning himself a slap on the arm from Wynflæd's curled left hand.

'Stay still, boy.'

I grin at Cuthred to take the sting from her words and her hand.

'Can I help?'

'Yes, you can bring the good candle closer. I can't see enough.' Used to her martyred tone, I do as she asks without question. I could suggest she went outside, but I imagine Wynflæd is as keen to avoid the scrutiny of the king as the rest of us.

King Wiglaf is a harsh taskmaster, even when we do exactly as he demands of us.

'There it is,' and Wynflæd sucks her tongue with delight, holding up the large splinter so that Cuthred and I can both see it.

'Now, get me some clean water, and a cloth, and a dab of honey as well. I'll need a small cloth to wrap round it too.' The wound bleeds freely, and Wynflæd bends low and sniffs it, looking at Cuthred as she does so.

I know what she's going to say next.

'If this starts to stink, like the horses do, come and see me. Straight away. No matter the time of day or night. And keep it clean.'

Placing all the items on the table so that she can reach them, I watch her working quickly to clean and protect the wound.

Cuthred moves to leap up when she's done.

'If I hear that you've been near those trees again, I'll send the rat for you.' She leers, and with a terrified look at the remains of the rat in the rafters, Cuthred scampers from beneath Wynflæd's hands. 'That boy,' she mutters to herself, her fondness for him impossible to ignore. 'I once knew another boy like him. Look what's happened to him.' She eyes me, moving to sit beside the hearth, pulling her ragged cloak tightly round her, for all I'm sweating.

I hold my tongue. Sometimes, when the mood takes Wynflæd, she regales me with stories of my childhood, although I'm sure there's been a few occasions when she's muddled me with someone else.

'What's happening out there? There's been a lot of coming and going.'

'Witan,' I reply quickly.

'Ah, will King Wiglaf finally protect Mercia?'

'I don't know,' I huff, frustrated to be asked the same question once more.

'Well, if he doesn't, there'll be no Mercia left to rule soon enough. When the king of the East Angles has taken his share, and the Wessex king his, no doubt the Welsh buggers will decide they need some as well. It's not like it was in my day or my mother's.'

I stay as still as I can. There's nothing better than one of Wynflæd's stories about the old kings of Mercia.

'That Offa, he was a real character,' she starts. 'What a man he was. And what a fool as well. If not for him and his fervent wish that his son had no one to stand against him when he died, Mercia would have better men with a claim to rule than King Wiglaf, and before him King Ludica.' This is a familiar complaint from Wynflæd.

Fifty years ago, King Offa's tenacity in stripping away so much of Mercia's wealth in æthelings – 'throne-worthy' men – has led to this crisis. Offa's son and heir, Ecgfrith, died mere months after his father, leaving Mercia with no one but King Coenwulf to rule her. The short-reigned King Ecgfrith left no son of his own.

King Coenwulf, the first of his name, ruled well and for over two decades but once more, his only son and heir died before he did.

Mercia then fell to his brother on his death. King Coelwulf didn't rule for long before Beornwulf usurped him, despite King Coelwulf's successes against the kingdoms of Powys and Gwynedd.

And now, with Beornwulf and Ludica dead, the available list of men to rule has grown so small that Wiglaf, a man with no true connection to either of the previous ruling families, can claim Mercia as his own, and without any great argument from anyone within Mercia.

But Wynflæd is speaking once more. 'King Offa killed so many æthelings; I'm surprised his hands weren't permanently stained with blood. Although he has ensured that his name will never be forgotten. I can't see King Wiglaf being anywhere near as lethal or single-minded. If there were alternatives to his kingship, I don't believe that he'd silence them. Strange to think of that as a criticism.' She cackles at the end of her tirade, and I laugh along with her. Sometimes, I don't fully understand everything she says, and it's better to pretend to it. 'Now, boy, your uncle came to see me late last night, full of worry about you. I assured him you were well and happy with your endeavours at my side. I hope I spoke true?'

'You did, yes, thank you. It would have been nice if my uncle had thought to ask me himself.'

'Ah, he's a busy man. Be kinder to him. He grows so thin; I think he could do with eating half a haunch of beef all to himself. He's run ragged by the king, his poor horse, Wine, as well.'

It seems I'm to find no one who will criticise my uncle, other than myself. I sigh softly. 'If there's war, he'll ride out with the king's household warriors once more.'

'He will, yes, but your uncle has the greatest luck of all apart from ealdormen Sigered, Muca and Mucel, and most of theirs is because they don't join the warbands.'

We both turn towards the door simultaneously, the sound of angry conversation coming from close by drawing our attention. I purposefully slow my steps so that Wynflæd reaches the doorway first. Over the scuffle of her feet, it's easy to decipher the words being shouted. All the same, I only catch some of them.

'Athelstan, at Peterborough,' and my heart sinks.

'What proof do you have of this?' It's Eahric, the king's commander, who counters the assertion.

'Proof,' the messenger bellows.

I'm close enough to see now. He's someone I've not seen before, perhaps sent by the local reeve because the ealdormen are all in Tamworth at the king's instruction. The messenger is covered in dust from the road, and his horse's head sags tiredly between her front hooves.

'Yes. You carry no cuts or bruises or show any signs of being involved in a fight. How am I to believe you are who you say you are?'

The man looks affronted now, and the door of the king's hall opens with a loud groan.

'What is this?' It's Ealdorman Sigered who speaks, his lined face twisted with fury at the interruption. But I note he's too damn nosy to have sent another to look. He needs to know for himself. No doubt, I think sourly, so he can escape before the king orders him to mount up and fight for Mercia.

'My Lord,' the messenger takes to his knees immediately.

'Speak, man, speak.'

'King Athelstan of the East Angles has breached the boundary. He's surrounded the most holy site of Peterborough and means to take it as his own.'

Resignation covers Ealdorman Sigered's face as another voice is raised querulously from inside the king's hall.

'Come inside, tell the king all you know,' he states flatly.

The hubbub dies down as the door closes on the man, others who've been drawn to the commotion turning aside to return to their duties.

At the doorway, Wynflæd turns and looks me in the eye, her gaze unwavering.

'It'll be war,' she affirms. 'It has to be.'

Not that I have long to think about it. Siric, the stablemaster, stumbles inside Wynflæd's workshop as the day is drawing to an end. She looks up from her meal in surprise. I eye Siric and then rush to support him before he falls to the ground.

'You should have come sooner,' the oft-quoted phrase brings a smirk to my face, which I hide as I lower Siric to the low-lying table she uses for her patients. He's sweating profusely, the smell of him sickly sweet. 'When did this begin?' She's checking his eyes, lifting his eyelids and peering into the depths of them. Even in the glow of the candle, I'm shocked by how yellow they are, and how yellow all of his skin appears.

'Three days ago,' Siric admits, his voice a whisper.

'Did your piss turn yellow?' she demands, opening his mouth

and looking beneath his tongue. Its blackness shocks me.

'Yes, it did?' There's wonder in his voice that she knows this.

'So what, you thought, I'll give it three days and if I'm still alive, I'll seek some aid from Wynflæd?'

'I...' Siric begins, and then snaps his mouth shut. Her words are tight with fury.

'You thought it better to just curl up in a corner and die, did you?' There's no sympathy, as she peers at his skin, ordering me silently, and with just her hands, to move the candle closer, to bring water, to add a cauldron to the flames to boil water.

'I...' he tries again.

I fix him with a gaze, trying to convey some sympathy. He swallows heavily, eyes not leaving Wynflæd as she moves round him, and then turns to her jars and selections of dry herbs and leaves. Her movements are sharp and assured as she opens lids, sniffs contents and then pours her requirements into her hands. Some she adds to the water, others she places to the side, no doubt for use later on. I know what she means for me to do.

'Bramble bark,' I comment, noting the first item left to the side.

'Next,' she barks.

'Birthwort?' I ask, unsure if that's right. 'Next,' I sigh, feeling much like Siric now.

Wynflæd never tells me if I'm right or wrong, not until I reach to use it next time, and she offers something along the lines of, 'choose more wisely this time.'

'Radish.' I'm on firmer ground with the thin, bright slices. 'Elecampane,' I press on, 'and sweet flag and nettle.' The last two I know are correct.

'Is all that to drink?' Siric asks, his words horrified.

'Do you want to be treated?' Wynflæd demands, hands on her thin hips.

'I...' Siric stutters, and I turn aside, hide my amusement. It feels so good when grown men are as cowed by her as I am.

'Good, now, lie here, and do as your told. I'll have this ready for you shortly, and then you're to do as I say when I say it.'

Siric nods, and I see his throat bob as he swallows.

* * *

I stand beside Edwin as a host of thirty warriors pours from inside Tamworth. The king leads them, but I doubt he'll do any actual fighting.

Edwin is devastated to be once more excluded even as Wigmund watches on with a smirk on his broad face, while his mother stands proud beside him. Wigmund isn't riding with his father. No, he's to rule with his mother in the absence of King Wiglaf. A pity, really.

My uncle is also a member of the host, but before he mounted up this morning, he sought me out.

'This won't amount to much.' He tried to reassure me. 'It might seem as though Mercia has no warriors left thanks to King Athelstan of the East Angles, but that's not the case. And the East Angles lost just as many, if not their actual king. This is all posturing and strutting to see who'll withdraw first. No, the real problem is with the men of Powys and Gwynedd. Not that the king sees that. But he will.' Cenfrith gripped me on my shoulders and held my eyes with his brown ones. 'Stay safe, and do what Wynflæd asks of you. And keep Edwin occupied as well. One day soon, he'll earn his place in the king's household warriors.'

I nodded to him, reassured him that I'd do all he asked.

Now I watch him ride away, Wine pliant beneath him, cantering as he commands, and take solace in the fact that he's always returned to me before. Always. It would be nice if he looked back, though.

Edwin, disgruntled, takes himself to the stables once the men have gone. I watch his slumped shoulders and open and shut my mouth but find no words for him. A bit of sweating amongst the empty stalls, in place of Siric who still ails, cleaning them out ready for the return of the horses, and hopefully, he'll find a smile for his face.

I return to Wynflæd, who has me making another restorative for Siric. He's not as yellow-skinned this morning, but Wynflæd is still unhappy. She's determined he'll bathe in some new concoction she's devising and it will aid him. I wish I knew all that she does.

She keeps me busy until we're both drawn to some fresh ruckus outside.

Ealdormen Sigered, once more declining to ride beside his king, has been summoned from inside the king's hall.

Another messenger, this one a man I recognise, is calling to all and sundry, not waiting for Sigered to deliver his message.

I listen to the man's words.

'The Powys Welshmen are massing on the border. They mean to attack Wroxeter. The king must send out his warriors. There are hundreds of them. The bishop sent me here. Where's the king?' His voice rumbles to a stop as Ealdorman Sigered appraises him with a look of disbelief on his face, white hair tumbling in the gathering breeze.

'The king left, this morning, to ride to Peterborough.'

'Then he must be caught, told of events with the Welsh.'

Lady Cynethryth, with her son beside her, has joined the ealdorman. Her lips are pursed with fury; cheeks flushed at the intelligence. Or, at least, I take it to be for that reason.

'The bishop will have to call out his warriors,' she announces as though that solves the problem. 'And the men of the settlement who owe the king their dues for keeping out the warriors of Powys.'

'My Lady?' the man is stunned at the pronouncement and

unsure what else to say. His head moves from Ealdorman Sigered to the king's wife, as though waiting for Sigered to speak more sense.

Sigered sighs, his entire body quivering, and then he straightens his stance, almost as though he's being pulled tight.

'Form up twenty warriors who've not ridden with the king. I'll lead them to Wroxeter and deal with this minor inconvenience.'

Beside me, Wynflæd gasps at the words, and I turn to her, aware my eyes are wide with shock.

'This will end badly,' she announces, shaking her head, the wisps of her hair rising and falling with the wind before turning aside.

Edwin, summoned by the commotion, glances at me, a flicker of hope in his eyes, but I already know Edwin won't be a part of this force either. No. It'll be the older men, those who by rights, should no longer be fighting for the king, having spent a lifetime doing so. But there's really little choice. The king has taken his best warriors with him.

* * *

Three days pass with dull routine, Siric coming and going from Wynflæd's workshop, other injuries needing tending as well; a limping sheep amongst them, an edge of fear making people sharp with one another. Only Lady Cynethryth seems unaffected, but Wynflæd, summoned to her side on the second night, shakes her head and mutters that it's all an act. Lady Cynethryth demands something to help her sleep and Wynflæd provides it quickly, because many of the women are suffering the same. I find it far from reassuring.

Time and again, my thoughts tumble towards my uncle. What is he doing? Where is he? Will there be war?

On the fourth day, the sound of a horse approaching at speed entices everyone away from their duties so that we're all waiting impatiently for the man to be admitted inside the compound.

I recognise Osmod, one of the king's warriors, more by his striking grey horse than anything else, and my heart sinks. Osmod was not with the king or with Ealdorman Sigered. This then is something else.

Osmod dismounts quickly and strides into the king's hall, as silent as the rest of us, waiting for news of what has befallen Mercia now.

I swallow, tasting nothing but my tongue, fear making my heart thud too loudly.

It takes only moments for one of the servants to hurry outside, whisper to the first person he sees, Ordlaf, before rushing back into the hall.

Ordlaf, his eyes wide with shock, faces us all as he scrunches the extra length of his tunic between tight-fisted hands. 'King Ecgberht of Wessex has called his warriors together. They mean to attack Lundenwic.'

Outrage burbles from all those waiting for news. This isn't what we wanted to hear.

Wynflæd tuts loudly, and I follow her back inside her workshop, only to hear her whispered words.

'Mercia is surrounded and will fall for she can't fight three enemies at the same time.'

I hardly needed Wynflæd to tell me as much, and yet hearing the words spoken aloud by Wynflæd sends a stab of fear into my belly.

King Wiglaf has brought Mercia to her knees. But I can't help blaming King Beornwulf, and Ludica as well. If only King Coelwulf were still Mercia's king, with his descent from the great warrior kings of the seventh century who ruled over the many kingdoms on this island. Perhaps then Mercia wouldn't fail as she does now.

The king doesn't return to Tamworth any time soon, neither does Cenfrith.

Instead, nothing happens. After Ealdorman Sigered rides out to Wroxeter, and the king travels to Peterborough, no news is heard at Tamworth for days. No one is sent to aid Lundenwic.

Wynflæd keeps me busy, and even Edwin is forced to assist me in the end. It's impossible to keep up with Wynflæd's demands for herbs and spices, for tree barks and dead bees, when she has me rushing to and from the well every other breath. Edwin takes over that duty, his unhappiness at being left behind by the king and his warriors meaning he makes no complaints. After one such journey into the hinterlands round Tamworth, I return to Wynflæd's workshop to find Edwin being instructed in how to correctly cut the celery and the radish that I harvested the day before.

A wry smirk touches my cheeks, quickly banished as he gazes at me from beneath his thick eyebrows, begging me to aid him. Wynflæd slaps his hand and berates him for cutting pieces as wide as his finger, and not as thin as his nail.

'I can do that,' I offer cheerfully. What I really want to do is

smear Wynflæd's pot of sunburn lotion over my long arms and
pulsing neck. I've been out for much of the day, stepping through
the thick woodlands to the west and the dense bed of river plants
on the way back to Tamworth itself. I took a hat with me, but, of
course, in the heat and with the flies and bees buzzing round me, I
cast it aside. So now, my nose aches with the burn, while on my
thumb, a bee's sting throbs uncomfortably. I immersed myself in
the river when I came close to Tamworth, but while that removed
the dust and sweat from my body, the cold water simply made
everything else ache and throb.

Wynflæd turns to glare at me.

'Edwin is hardly needed elsewhere,' she mutters, and I wince at
the implied criticism that Edwin isn't riding with the Mercian
warriors. 'You're only going to talk to one another. You may as well
do something helpful at the same time.' It's almost an apology. I
grin at Edwin.

'Where have you been?' he demands to know as Wynflæd waits
for me to unload my collection of finds. There's a long line of
wooden bowls on Wynflæd's preparation table and three or four
wooden boards that all show where she's been busy chopping and
grinding different seeds and plants. I'll have to scrub them clean
later.

It's a busy time of year anyway, not helped by the fact that in
light of everyone's fears for Mercia, they all seem to have discovered warts and boils they didn't know they had before. And, in
the heat of the summer, some of the pregnant women are struggling as well. More than one has appeared, shaky and pale-faced
in Wynflæd's doorway. She's sent them away with a simple
remedy and a directive to rest as much as they can, even though
it's impossible for them to do so. The thick pottage Wynflæd's
made for the women smells delicious, and she's made it clear that
of all the many ingredients contained within it, the most impor-

tant is the generous liver given her by the slaughterer of the king's animals.

Such delight from the dark red piece of meat almost made me turn aside with disgust.

'Deep in the woodlands to the west. There's...' But Wynflæd slaps me on the arm, and I snap my mouth shut with a growl. 'There's something that Wynflæd needs that grows there.' The sack that I've thrown to the floor is heavy and dirty. It's filled with everything I was asked to find and some other things besides, worth collecting before she thinks to send me away once more; I've discovered more dandelions and dock leaves. I've risked a rash in cutting back the nettles she prefers to use, even though they're more potent than others that don't sting as much. I've found wild mushrooms, and garlic, blue-headed flowers, purple-headed plants and even something bright yellow that I don't know the name of, but I'm sure must be useful.

'I hope you kept the body of that bee that stung you,' Wynflæd announces, even as she smears my thumb with something that smells of garlic but instantly soothes. 'Leonath is desperate for more of the ointment to treat his lack of hair.'

Poor Leonath. He's a young man, and yet his hair is falling out. Wynflæd says there's no reason for it other than that it is. After much persuading, she's attempting to help him, but the concoction requires bees, and they're not the easier things to hunt down and kill. Well, not when you actually want one.

I open the leather sack at my belt and pour its contents onto the table. The dead bee tumbles onto the surface, alongside a spider that I'd not realised was there. Edwin grimaces away from it, but Wynflæd pounces on it with delight.

'Come, I have a use for you as well.'

'How do you do this?' Edwin almost whines as I take the knife from him, the wooden board as well, and begin to carefully slice the radish into small pieces which will be dried and kept in one of Wynflæd's many clay jars.

'It's interesting. I mean, look, you'd think this was just a radish. You wouldn't know it can aid those who lose the use of a leg or an arm, or even of both legs, or those who fall into a deep sleep and don't wake.'

'How do you even know that?' Edwin continues, surprising me by asking a sensible question rather than whining.

'You do know the bishop has books filled with the knowledge that Wynflæd carries in her head, don't you? These aren't just random objects and items she asks for on the off chance. They work... or at least sometimes work.' I rally quickly. From time to time, it's impossible to help those who are ill. My thoughts have turned to poor Æthelryth, whose child was born blue no matter the precautions she took only two days ago. Sometimes Wynflæd can't save the frailest members of the community, yet the child was born too soon. I saw the tiny shape of the body before it was taken away. At least the grieving woman lives to try again. Or so I think, but the thought is little comfort to her, or to myself.

'And what does the dead bee do?' Edwin demands to know.

I shrug my aching shoulders. 'It's needed for the poultice to cure baldness.'

'How does it do that?'

I shrug again, aware my shoulders are much narrower than Edwin's warrior-trained ones. 'Wynflæd hasn't taught me why things do what they do, only that they do. Go and ask the bishop if you want more information.'

I think he might just do that, but then Edwin stands, stretching his arms over his head and yawns widely.

'I'm going to find something to eat,' he bends to whisper to me. 'I'll come back and bring you something,' is his quick response to my outraged cry. I'm hungry as well, and I've done far more than be bossed about by Wynflæd that day.

Quickly, I collect another radish, chopping it into the small slices Wynflæd demands, and I'm just about to do the same to the three pieces of celery when Edwin rushes back into the workshop.

'King Wiglaf has returned,' he cries, face lit with a smile.

'Is that a good thing?' I ask.

Wynflæd looks up from her mutterings over one of the cauldrons that slowly bubbles, just out of the direct heat of the flames.

'A wise question to ask.' She cautions Edwin, moving her hands to shoo us from her space. Certainly, she doesn't share Edwin's evident belief that it means there's been a victory. 'Find out what's happening. All of it.' She fixes me with a firm gaze, one eyebrow high. She means for me to report back to her.

I follow Edwin outside. There's still enough light from the sun to see by, even though the moon is a faint glow in the sky. It's continued to be hot, with no breeze to trouble my hair or the dust lying thickly on the hard-baked ground. I have never had my wish about the interior of Tamworth being kept as smartly as during the reign of King Beornwulf.

From the king's hall, Wigmund appears, his mother not far behind, and an expectant hush falls. In it, I can hear the sound of horses coming closer and closer, the odd jingle of iron on iron assuring me that at least some of the Mercian warriors are returning.

Edwin steps through the crowd of people, sliding through the small spaces they leave between one another, using his shoulders to force a path when they don't move quickly enough for him, but I remain where I am. It's not as though being closer will give Edwin the news he wishes to hear any sooner. If the king remains mounted, we'll all know soon enough.

The creak of the enormous gate opening, the rhythmic sound of hooves over the short wooden bridge that covers the deep ditch, and I glance upwards. King Wiglaf is there, hand raised, asking for silence. He comes dressed as a warrior king, even his shimmering helm in place. But, still in the half-light, I note that no dust fouls it or the byrnie he wears. His horse stands as proud as the king. The animal is white and has been groomed recently. The beast doesn't even foam at the mouth.

Wynflæd will relish in these details. I know exactly what she'll say about our king.

'King Athelstan has been defeated, sent back to the kingdom of the East Angles, his tail between his legs.'

A muted cheer greets the words, and for a moment, I sense some unease in the king's gaze. Perhaps he expects us to accord him more respect for such a task. But his words don't speak of a great triumph and, certainly, nothing to counter the losses the Mercians have endured in recent years.

His eyes narrow, and I think he'll demand more. Only a man behind him suddenly roars with triumph, the sound ricocheting between the tightly knit wattle-and-daub-covered buildings of the stables, the blacksmith's and the king's hall. In the wake of such a call, more and more of the crowd begin to cheer, the sound coming louder and louder, but I turn aside.

I need to inform Wynflæd of this. I want to hear what she has to say about the king and his victory, and I can't see that anyone is about to tell the king about the problems with the kingdom of Powys. I also know that it's to Wynflæd that my uncle will come.

I've noted him, and Wine, to the rear of the king's force. It's enough for me to know that he's survived the king's defence against the king slayer, King Athelstan. A quick tally assures me that every man who rode from Tamworth has returned to it. No one will mourn that night.

When I duck back into Wynflæd's workshop, she's murmuring

beneath her breath, passing a pouch from one hand to another, and occasionally waving it in the small amount of smoke burbling from the fire, tinged with the purple of some herb, the smell pleasant. I step more quietly. She doesn't appreciate being disturbed when working on one of her charms. I know she doesn't like the charms, but sometimes, when there's little or no hope of recovering from an ailment, she confers a charm on her patient. On the odd occasion, they even seem to have worked. I'm unsure who this charm is for, but then, Wynflæd has just as many secrets as Cenfrith.

Silently, I return to my task. From beyond the thick walls of her workshop, I can hear the conversations of men reunited with wives, children and friends, but there's none of the joy I expect to hear. I'm curious about what my uncle will say about the whole thing, but I'm content to wait.

Edwin doesn't join me. That doesn't surprise me. He'll have been put to good use in the stables or been tasked with cleaning and sanding seaxes and byrnies. Not, I think, that a great deal of use has been made of the sharpened blades.

Only as I'm yawning and considering my bed does the doorway darken and Cenfrith appears. Wynflæd's finished the charm work, the item hanging next to the dead rat now, just waiting to be claimed. I eye him, ensuring he's well, while he bows his head respectfully to Wynflæd before settling before her hearth. We've shared a few words about the king, but nothing more.

Wynflæd offers Cenfrith a beaker of water, and he takes it willingly, swigging it back and then rubbing his hands over his eyes.

'The king should have ridden to the kingdom of Powys,' Cenfrith begins. 'King Athelstan is the king slayer no more; he merely stole a fortune in priceless artefacts from the monastery and then scarpered back to his kingdom. We've done little but eat dust. There was a small altercation; four of the East Angles were killed as we ran them across the border.'

'Yet the king means to say it was a great victory?' Wynflæd's words drip with scorn.

I stay quiet, try to make myself as small as possible. I want to hear Cenfrith and Wynflæd speak, and they're likely to send me away if they realise I'm listening.

'He needs to do something. Support for his kingship is poor, even amongst the ealdormen. I can't imagine that Ealdorman Sigered is pleased with him either.'

'And will the king send men after Sigered to Wroxeter?'

Cenfrith's response is silence.

I risk turning to watch the pair of them. Cenfrith is pensive. His eyes fixed on the hearth, where blue flames leap from one side to another. It seems that Wynflæd has been burning some of her precious driftwood, perhaps to imbue the charm with the requisite magical properties.

Eventually, Cenfrith speaks. 'I'll lead a force of twenty men in the morning. It's to be hoped we're not too late.'

'And what of the border with the East Angles?'

'Ealdorman Tidwulf has remained behind. He'll do whatever needs to be done. Icel?'

I'm startled that Cenfrith acknowledges my presence. 'Uncle?'

He meets my eyes. I see the frustration in the way he twists his mouth. Not that my uncle is a man to smile readily, but I don't think I've seen him smile in recent months. Not once.

'Tell me of the king's son.' The request surprises me.

'I have little to do with him. He's most often to be found in the company of his mother.'

'So, he wins his victory against Edwin and puts it to good use.' It's evident that Cenfrith expects no answer to his assertion.

'It seems to me that Mercia finally has a king with a son, but that son will never make a suitable replacement to his father,'

Wynflæd speaks softly, no doubt hoping that her words won't be heard beyond the confines of her walls.

'He's young. He may yet learn,' Cenfrith announces, standing abruptly. His head almost brushes the hanging snake in the rafters. Sometimes I forget how tall he is.

'Youth can't be used as an excuse forever,' Wynflæd offers, her lips downcast. And then their impromptu meeting is at an end.

I stifle a yawn.

'Get some sleep.' Cenfrith notices my action, and his words are devoid of malice. 'It'll be tomorrow soon enough.'

* * *

From the doorway to Wynflæd's hut, I watch the ealdorman and warriors as they prepare the following day. Of the twenty men who'll ride with my uncle, it seems that Ealdorman Athelhard is to have the command.

I only know him by name and reputation. He is, of course, one of Wiglaf's special allies. He's an older man, and I remember Wynflæd's words that he's a man who should have long ago made a name for himself but has failed to consistently. Only the deaths of so many of Mercia's ealdormen has allowed him to claim his current position. He's not unlike King Wiglaf in that respect.

Ealdorman Athelhard rides a tall brown stallion, white socks on the animal's feet, making him distinctive. Beside me, Edwin sighs.

'You'd like a horse like that?'

'I'd like any bloody horse.' Edwin complains. He's heard enough stories from the returning warriors to know that he didn't miss a chance to claim battle glory for himself, and, if anything, that's made him even more disgruntled. 'I see Cenfrith is included in the riding party.'

'Yes.' I offer nothing else. I don't need to.

'If I didn't know better, I'd think he couldn't stand the sight of you.' Edwin cackles at the statement, but I swallow my unease. Sometimes, I think the same; I can't deny it.

'Has there been no news from Ealdorman Sigered, or from Lundenwic?' I ask, keen to change the subject away from my uncle.

'Nothing.'

'That can't be good.' I muse.

'Probably not,' Edwin agrees, striding away from me, following the men as they ride from Tamworth.

I stay behind. My uncle waved to me before he left, and I held my arm aloft in reply. I'm sure that Edwin is wrong about my uncle. But, well, sometimes I'm not sure he is.

* * *

It's ten days before I see Cenfrith once more. The men who return from the west haven't taken the time to polish their dented helms or groom their mounts. Neither do they come with feigned triumph but rather a sullen victory.

And half of their number is missing.

The two ealdormen ride at the front of the group, Sigered with a purpling eye, his cheek so puffed up he can't wear his helm, whereas Athelhard sits slumped in his saddle. I can't tell what his injury is, not from where I stand, but on seeing my uncle, his face strained, but apparently uninjured, I rush back to Wynflæd.

'The ealdorman,' I advise her quickly.

She nods, not to be disturbed from her task of tending to Beornwyn and her gnarled fingers. I believe Beornwyn to be not much older than Wynflæd, and yet she's twisted and misshapen. Nevertheless, she and Wynflæd spend a great deal of time together. I often hear them laughing softly, speaking of men and women long dead, sometimes with the softness that speaks of lost loves, and other times, of contempt for fools. I prefer the thought of fools than of them sharing their beds with another.

Now, Wynflæd massages ointment into Beornwyn's hand, made from pigeon dung and goats' dung, dried and then ground down. My arm still aches from grinding it to Wynflæd's requirements. Mixing it with the honey and butter was her task. Beornwyn's other hand rests in a bowl of hot water, a stone from the hearth ensuring the pungent mixture stays warm. I know Wynflæd is worried that if Beornwyn's hands are this bad with the warmth of summer all around her, they'll be beyond painful when the winter chill comes.

'Will you go?' I ask.

But Beornwyn shakes her head and only then does Wynflæd speak.

'Ealdorman Athelhard has no use for me. He'll seek aid from the bishop and his monks and will be the worse off for that, perhaps. So he'll not consult me.'

I feel my mouth open in shock and then snap it shut with an audible pop, but she's not finished.

'Ealdorman Sigered admits to no frailty, so I won't be needed by him either. Your uncle is well?'

'Yes, yes he is.'

'That's good. He'll tell us what we need to know in good time.'

From beyond the walls, a gentle wailing has begun, and the two women, with resignation in the slump of their shoulders, eye one another. There's to be more mourning for the women and children of the settlement.

Once more, I can't help but blame King Wiglaf. He might have taken a small victory against the East Angles, but it's not enough to re-establish Mercia's feared reputation, and he was hardly keen to send warriors to Wroxeter.

* * *

When my uncle enters Wynflæd's workshop, Beornwyn has gone. Even with the tales the two women share, they've long since run out of things to say to one another. With some movement back in her hand, Beornwyn was keen to be away and doing something helpful, such as tending to the youngsters.

'Wynflæd.' Cenfrith bows his head low. I believe he shows her more deference than he does King Wiglaf.

'You look tired,' is Wynflæd's less than gentle response.

I watch my uncle's shoulders tense, and it takes him effort not to snap at her criticism.

'We returned in less than a day, pushing the horses onwards, ourselves as well. The ealdormen were eager to announce their triumph to King Wiglaf.'

'And was it a victory?'

'No more than against King Athelstan of the East Angles. We lost more men but retained the treasures the Powys Welshmen thought to steal.' Cenfrith runs his large hand through his hair as he speaks.

He's weary, I can tell from the way he's slumped onto one of Wynflæd's stools. I see his wounds starkly in the half-light, especially the most healed gash on his forehead from when Beornwulf lost his life fighting the East Angles.

'It won't dissuade them from attacking again,' Cenfrith admits. There's resignation in the set of his hard jaw, and it dismays me to see him so lifeless.

'You need to sleep,' Wynflæd mutters, for once her words less acerbic. I think she senses his frustrated impotence as well.

'Yes, I do, but when I wake, there'll be some new disaster for Mercia.' Cenfrith's eyes bore into me as though he sees me for the first time. I catch a glimpse of the emblem he wears round his neck, for once openly on display. I notice the flashing eyes of the winged creature, the silver seeming to live with the dull flames from the hearth. He eyes me, lips pursed, and then sighs heavily and stands. He reaches over, rubs his hand through my thick hair, a rare show of affection, and then leaves without speaking further.

Wynflæd watches his departure as keenly as I do. That neither of us speaks again assures me that she shares my worries about Cenfrith. He takes too much upon himself. Much more than King Wiglaf does.

PART IV

10

AD829

A hand on my shoulder, and I startle awake. I've fallen asleep over the table in Wynflæd's workshop once more. It happens too often these days. But better to avoid the malicious gaze of the beleaguered King Wiglaf and his acerbic wife than risk leaving the safety of the workshop. Inside, I'm safe and protected. Outside, anything could happen.

'What?' I gasp, meeting my uncle's firm brown eyes, thanks to the glow from the banked hearth, surprised to see him. It's been many weeks since we last so much as said hello to one another. He's been busy, as last year, rushing all over Mercia, trying to keep track of what her enemies are planning next.

'Get up, pack your things. We're leaving.'

'What?' I demand once more, reaching for a beaker of water and swallowing it quickly.

'Get up and pack your things. We need to leave here.'

'Why?'

'Icel, ask fewer questions and follow my orders,' Cenfrith snaps his command to me, his words a harsh whisper as he doesn't wish to wake Wynflæd, that much is clear from the way he glances towards her sleeping shape.

My body moves to obey even as more and more questions form in my mind. What should I take with me? Will I return here? What of Wynflæd, who snores on her bed in the far corner of the room?

But my uncle is gone, slipping through the door and moving around outside. I would follow him, but there was just something about the look in his eyes that makes me do as he asks rather than continue to question him.

I turn to grab the sack I use when foraging, moving through Wynflæd's supplies to take the things I know will be useful: some linen strips to be used as bandages, some honey and even some mint to chew to make my breath sweeter. I snag a handful of her mushrooms for eating, stuffing them into a hemp bag, a packet of some elm bark that makes a good healing tea and some dried woody nightshade, which can be used to cure every ailment. I even have clothes here, brought to me by Edwin on the instructions of his mother, because she knows I so often sleep here. These follow the other items into my sack.

I test the weight, thinking of what else I might need. My good knife is already on my belt as I eye the small wooden bowls and containers lying waiting for Wynflæd's next concoction. It would be helpful to have at least two of them, just in case.

These I place in my sack as well, hoping she won't object to me borrowing her things, as her snores continue to fill the air.

And then Cenfrith is back, moving so quietly I startle when I realise I'm no longer alone in the darkened room, lit only by the glow of the embers in the hearth.

'Are you ready?' he demands to know.

I nod mutely, unsure what to say or even how to feel.

'Follow me, do what I do and go where I go. If I stay still and don't move, then you must do the same. Your life will depend on it.'

I swallow, my knees trembling to hear such words. What has happened? But, of course, I've resolved not to ask him, not yet.

'Stay close, stay silent and try to move quietly.' His orders end with an entreaty. I almost smirk. My body is difficult to control these days. My arms are too long, my feet too big, and my legs... Well, it's best not to think about them. Wynflæd has assured me that I'll grow into my new body, but I can't see it. I would sooner be much smaller and not just because it would be easier to avoid the critical eye of Lady Cynethryth. That I'm even taller than Edwin now has not gone down well. The herb boy who towers over almost everyone but some of the king's warriors. I can hardly hide myself these days.

Outside, there's little light from the moon overhead, clouds scudding quickly across the sky. I shiver. It's the summer, but it's a cold night after a day of near-constant rain. I expect to see my uncle's horse outside, but Wine is missing. A flame flickers from the main gateway, but the only sound to be heard is that of the soft exhalations of people sleeping, coupled with some snoring, some grunting, which I don't think about for too long, and the gentle croon of a mother speaking to a fretful baby.

My uncle springs forward, gesturing for me to follow him, as we slip from the shadows of one building to another, from Wynflæd's home to the blacksmith's forge where Edwin and his mother sleeps, on to where the closed gate offers no chance of escape.

Cenfrith's pace doesn't ease, and then we're walking in the shadow of the enclosure, the built-up defences, not as well-maintained as they should be, speaking of a time when Mercia itself was far from peaceful and her kings eager to have somewhere in which to shelter. It always surprises me that the gates are monitored as they are, but the ditch is an effective deterrent, even if only because of the smell of rotting food and shit that rises from it when it's hot.

Only now do we pause.

'When I move forward, follow me, not too quickly, but quickly enough,' Cenfrith whispers urgently into my ear, and I notice that he only has to bend a little to do so. Perhaps my recent growth is welcome after all. My uncle has always seemed half-giant to me.

I swallow my fear and nod, eyes peering all round me, drinking in the sight of the only place I've ever called home. It seems it's not to be for much longer.

A scuff of feet alerts me that my uncle is on the move. I scurry to follow him, mirroring his movements, sliding through the small crack in the huge, joined gates, somehow come open, while the guard isn't looking. And then we sprint, over the built-up beaten track, towards the curling river in the distance, over the training ground and to a covering of dark trees.

My breath is harsh in my throat, and more than once, I fear I'll tumble amongst the long grasses where the herd animals should have been grazing had they been allowed outside the king's enclosure. The damp grasses coat my trews up to my knees, the fabric tightening with every step I take.

Once inside the trees, my uncle hurries onwards, standing taller now, his shoulders less hunched. Unease gnaws at me, and I'm convinced I can hear something following on behind. Not a man, but a beast, something that's caught our scent and wishes to hunt us down. There have been reports of wolves in Mercia after the harsh winter, but not so close to Tamworth as this. Perhaps this is the first one to be forced to venture so far from its usual home.

I open my mouth to speak, but Cenfrith holds up his hand. I snap my mouth shut, standing as still as he does. He must hear the same as I, but rather than showing fear; his shoulders slump beneath the light of the moon.

What is this?

'What are you doing?' Edwin's whisper reaches me even before I can see him.

Cenfrith groans.

'What are you doing here?' Cenfrith demands, fury making the words clipped.

'What am I doing here?' Edwin all but shrieks. I notice then that he carries a bulging sack, just as I filled one with my possessions. How he knew to bring such with him, I don't know but he must suspect Cenfrith's intentions. He makes carrying it look easy. For the time being, we both have fourteen years to our names. Yet, I'm still slight and narrow, Edwin broad and powerful.

'You'll have to stay with us now,' Cenfrith cracks at him. 'You should have stayed behind. Now, hurry up, and stay silent. We must be far from here when the sunrise comes.'

Edwin's standing, mouth open, gazing at my uncle in shock beneath the light of the moon. I'm not far from doing the same.

'Tell me what's happened?' I demand.

'I will, when we're safely away from here, not that anywhere will be safe now, but I hope to save you – and Edwin, now as well, I suppose. Follow me, keep up and stay silent.' Cenfrith appears far from easy at the doubling of his charges.

Ahead, the sound of the river is growing stronger. I consider whether we'll have to cross it or not. It runs deep and will be even deeper after the heavy summer storm of yesterday. If we use the ancient bridge to cross it, we'll be exposed and might be seen by the guards on duty outside Tamworth.

I receive my answer when I hear the welcome nicker of Wine as we emerge from the trees. Wine stands patiently, her white eyes easy to see in the gloom, the hint of grey in the sky auguring the advent of another day.

'Quickly, over the bridge. Stand to the far side of the horse. You won't be seen then. I'll ride.'

My uncle mounts up, having first secured my crammed sack to the saddle.

'Stay close, Edwin,' Cenfrith urges him, not unkindly, although there's a hint of frustration in the words.

I've walked this bridge many times in the past. Now it feels similar yet different because my movements are furtive. Will I ever return this way? Beneath my feet, the wooden struts groan with our passage, the horse's hooves echoing in the silence of the dawn. There's not much room for me to walk beside the horse, not with Edwin there as well. But no one calls to my uncle, no one demands to know what we're doing, and then we're once more passing into a heavy band of trees. My uncle dismounts, leading Wine, but still offers Edwin and me no explanation.

'Are we going to Watling Street?' Edwin, braver than I am, eventually asks the question from his place behind me.

Once more, there's no reply.

We walk single file, my uncle leading his horse, then me, and Edwin at the rear. I notice that Edwin's hand rarely strays from his seax on his weapons belt. I wish I had something other than the small, sharp blade I use to prepare the herbs and roots for Wynflæd. I hope she won't miss me. I also wonder why my uncle didn't wake her. It seems she doesn't need saving, as I do, from whatever is happening.

Every so often, I look back over my shoulder, fearful that we're being hunted, but no one ever appears, beast or warrior. As the sunlight grows, my uncle emerges from the trees and onto the clearly defined, if ancient, road that cuts through much of Mercia, from Lundenwic in the south to Chester in the north-west. Weeds and grasses cover much of the track, but the stones and gravel have stayed in place for many long years. They fight to stop themselves from being overwhelmed by the summer growths.

I finally see Cenfrith clearly then, note the many rips in his byrnie, the bruising round his right eye, the tear in his left cheek that glistens as though blood still seeps from it, and know that something is very, very wrong. My uncle must sense my scrutiny. He licks his lips, and begins to speak.

'King Wiglaf has abandoned Mercia.' There's disgust in Cenfrith's voice. 'Even now, King Ecgberht of Wessex rushes to Tamworth to claim it as his own.' Contempt enters my uncle's voice. 'Everyone in Tamworth will become subject to the new king. But I won't swear my oath to yet another false king, and neither will you, Icel. Or you,' and he directs this to Edwin. Edwin, who'd wanted to ride with King Wiglaf but who'd been refused permission to do so by the king's commander, the sting of that defeat by Wigmund, still enough to keep Edwin from taking his rightful place as a member of the king's household troop. 'There are many dead, again, and King Ecgberht has numbers that swamp those of Mercia's. We'll escape into the border regions with Powys or Gwynedd and see what happens next. If King Ecgberht of Wessex remains Mercia's king, we must think of leaving Mercia altogether, perhaps travelling to Northumbria. I don't know. I can't see any of the Welsh kingdoms welcoming us. Not at the moment.' He pauses, the words seem to exhaust him, and my body has grown even colder with fear.

It was bad enough when Mercia's kings kept dying but now Mercia's king is a coward and all will know of it.

'I just know we need to be far from King Ecgberht of Wessex. He'll claim Tamworth first, Mercia's capital, and then probably Lichfield, secure the royal enclosure and Mercia's premier bishopric. He already has Kent and the archbishopric of Canterbury.' The words are heavy with unease.

'What about everyone else in Tamworth?' Edwin surprises me with the unhappiness in his voice.

'They're not my concern,' Cenfrith's reply is short, his words laboured, as he moves to mount Wine. The animal's head hangs low, and I can detect the exhaustion there, just as I'm feeling it.

'So, you've just abandoned them?' Edwin has stopped, hand wavering above his seax.

I'm shaking my head. Now isn't the time for a war of words.

'I'm not the bloody king,' Cenfrith roars, his brown eyes wild and crazed.

In the harsh light, I can see all the wounds he's taken for Mercia, starting at the one that cuts above his right eye, the other that took much of his cheek, making his face appear lopsided now, the stitches too tight. There's one that snakes beneath his byrnie, down his neck, and more on his exposed forearms; the tip of his left middle finger missing for all the years I've known him. He's fought an entire lifetime for Mercia, and now the third king in a row has left her in jeopardy.

'King Beornwulf, for all I loved him as a brother, had no right to claim Mercia, none at all. Just think, without his actions, King Ecgberht of Wessex wouldn't have had the means to take Mercia. It's his fault, and King Ludica's and now King Wiglaf's. I'm done risking my life for such arseholes, and I won't risk my nephew's life either. Icel is all the family I have left. And, Edwin, you've been almost a family to me as well, for many years now.'

I gasp. I've never heard my uncle talk in such a way about Beornwulf. He's always supported Mercia's kings. He's always told me that Mercia must be protected no matter what, and no matter the lives lost. I've never heard him speak of me with such affection.

'I don't care about that. I care about my fellow warriors, about the women and children left there. I even care about Wynflæd.' Edwin's words are edged with resolve.

'Wynflæd and the women and children will come to no harm. It's the men and the boys who will be the victims here.' Cenfrith's words are tired now, slowing. 'King Ecgberht of Wessex will only care about injuring those who might one day be warriors.' Silence falls between us. And then my uncle is recalled to the here and now. 'We need to press on. If we can make it beyond the abandoned settlement of Wall today, we'll be able to rest before continuing along the ancient road to the borderlands with the Welsh kingdoms.'

'I'm going back,' Edwin announces, his words filled with determination.

'Edwin.' Cenfrith meets his eyes, his words filled with remorse. 'If you go back now, you're as good as dead. Stay with us. I should have come for you. I apologise for that. But you can't go back. There's no time for you to help them.'

I think Edwin will argue, but instead, he runs his hand over his seax once more, a threat there, I'm sure of it, and starts to walk away from Tamworth, towards Wall and whatever the future holds for us.

Eventually, we stumble to a stop having just made it beyond the broken-down ruin of Wall. It's Wine that leads us away from the road, close to a small brook from which she drinks thirstily, before making it clear she's too exhausted to go on, by trying to lie on the ground, saddle and all. I eye her. I'm feeling exactly the same.

We're surrounded by trees and other plants, many of which I name to myself as a means of trying to find some clarity in what's happening. There are nettles, and apple trees, and an ash tree and even a beech one. They mask us from other road users, just as the burgeoning hedgerow does, the promise of berries in the future evident in the fragile whiteness that covers the green. Not that we've seen many other people.

I tumble to the grass, unheeding of the dampness that still clings to it despite no rain having fallen that day. Edwin isn't far behind me, but Cenfrith stays upright, speaking softly to his horse as he removes the saddle and brushes the sweat from her long legs before she finally settles to the ground.

'Do you believe him?' Edwin's words are thankfully only just loud enough for me to hear.

'Why would he lie?' I retort, dismayed by my friend's lack of trust in my uncle.

'Who knows.' He shrugs his vast shoulders. 'He doesn't seem like his usual self.'

'He's just witnessed his king running away from a greater threat than Mercia has faced for decades; what do you expect him to be like?'

'A fair point.' Edwin yawns, covering his mouth with his hand and blinking in an attempt to stay awake.

'Get some sleep,' Cenfrith instructs us both, having handed me a water bottle and watched me drink much of it before passing it to Edwin.

'Tomorrow, we'll find food, and I'll tell you where we're going.'

'What of a watch?'

'Sleep with your weapon close to hand.' My uncle's words aren't reassuring. 'I can't see the Wessex warriors reaching here so soon. We should be all right, just for tonight.' His face is drained, fatigue evident in his laboured movements.

I move so that I'm lying down, able to see the sky overhead through the branches that partially protect me. I think I won't sleep, and for some time I listen to the steady breathing of Edwin and Cenfrith, the nicker of Wine, and only then do my eyes close, but my dreams are far from peaceful.

* * *

I wake again to a hand on my shoulder.

'Come on. We need to get going.' Cenfrith speaks normally, with no attempt to mute his words.

I startle awake, trying to work out why I have branches for a roof and why the sun is burning so fiercely into my eyes.

Edwin is no better beside me. He struggles to open his eyes and then gasps in outrage.

'I thought it was all a dream,' he explodes, remembering his anger from the day before.

'This is no dream,' Cenfrith mutters. 'Mercia's king has left her weak and without protection, despite the best attempts of her warriors to drive back the pretensions of the kingdom of the East Angles, Powys and Gwynedd as well. The Wessex king will claim all of Mercia's wealth. I don't think he'll stop there, either.'

'Tell me what happened?' I ask, realising that Cenfrith has hardly given many details.

'What would you know? That we faced the Wessex warriors at Lundenwic because King Ecgberht had crossed the River Thames and claimed it? That we were entirely overwhelmed? That the Wessex king had more warriors to his name than Mercia has ever numbered? That King Wiglaf abandoned his warriors and fled from the battle, thereby rescinding the oaths given king to warrior?' Cenfrith stabs his finger into his open hand with every point he makes.

'What of the Mercians?' I ask.

'King Wiglaf left them to fight to the death or be claimed as prisoners by King Ecgberht of Wessex. No doubt those who survived will be sent to the Carolingian slave markets, or used poorly in the mines so that King Ecgberht can repay those who helped him claim Wessex as his own. It won't be far for them to travel to the ships that will take them away from Lundenwic and Mercia. No, it isn't something I wish to discuss.'

'Then how did you escape?' Edwin retorts, his face furious once more.

'The king ordered me to return to Tamworth before the battle even started. To demand more warriors from Lady Cynethryth, although from where I don't know, but it was too late. Even as I rode away, I could see what was happening behind me, and I confess, I turned to watch. I witnessed King Wiglaf fleeing when he realised victory was impossible. Alone.' Cenfrith's words ripple with barely suppressed rage, but I'm impressed that he answers Edwin's questions. So far, he's told me nothing. 'I saw King Ecgberht beginning to send his men into Mercia, running with their dreaded wyvern banner before them. They would have caught me, but I know the secret paths to Tamworth and I beat them to it.'

'And did you tell Lady Cynethryth of the king's request?' Again, Edwin's words echo with outrage.

'Of course I did. I told her to escape Tamworth if she could after I told Icel we were leaving. She wouldn't have left anyway. She didn't believe me. Called me a liar and a coward in the same breath. The look she gave her son, I knew exactly what she was thinking. If her husband is dead, she'll merely be the mother of the next king.'

Edwin's mouth opens and then closes as though he's run out of questions to ask. But I haven't.

'And what will we do? With no king and running from the man who claims Mercia as well as Wessex.'

Somehow, I expect Cenfrith to know the answers to this, but his silence speaks of a man who has no idea of what the future holds.

'I haven't thought that far ahead yet. All that mattered was ensuring our freedom from the Wessex king.'

I glare at my uncle, astounded by his admission.

'Now, hurry up. We're not yet far enough away from Tamworth to linger.'

I gather my few possessions, thinking time and time again of the people left behind in Tamworth. I've known those people all of my life. I think of Edwin's mother – the woman who kept me alive when my mother died. I hope they survive whatever's coming. I hope Wynflæd doesn't hate me as much as I hate myself for abandoning her.

11

'Can we not just go to your estates?' Edwin asks the question of
Cenfrith. I admire him for persisting with such a line as I wipe
sweat from my face again.

'No, that's the first place whoever is tasked with finding us will
look.' There's logic in the answer, but still, I'm disappointed. I've
never been to Cenfrith's home. I should like to see it even if he's
dismissive of it.

'We can't loiter in the borderlands forever. We need food and
oats for the horse and perhaps news of what's actually happening
in Mercia.'

I expect Cenfrith to react angrily, but he doesn't.

'You're right, Edwin. I'll go to Hereford, find out what I can.'

Immediately, Edwin's downcast face clears, but I pause.

'Just you, or all of us?'

'Just me,' Cenfrith states. 'A solitary man will arouse less suspicion than if I take you with me. I'm sorry.'

I note the mutiny on Edwin's face. I'm not far behind him.

'It's been seven days since we left Tamworth, and we've done
little but trek around in the woodlands and forests, up hills and

down hills, skirting rivers and brooks, all trying to stay hidden from anyone. And now you get to go into Hereford? I should like to go. To actually see a new part of Mercia? To eat bread, or see people.'

'Icel, those are petty requests where your safety is concerned. I can't risk you and Edwin being seen.'

My forehead furrows. 'Surely, you as one of the king's sworn warriors are more likely to arouse suspicion than Edwin and I? We're just youths on a journey.'

But my uncle already shakes his head from side to side.

'It's out of the question. I'll go to Hereford, alone, or we'll stay here, hidden from sight and eating whatever you manage to find for us.'

My belly rumbles at the words. I've done my best, but mushrooms and the roots I've found aren't enough to fill me. We've not been able to catch any of the small woodlands creatures to provide meat. We don't have the skills or the weapons to hand that a hunter might have. Or the patience to wait.

'Fine' I know I sound petulant. 'We'll stay here, and you can go to Hereford, but you must bring back bread and oats and other items to make this... well, whatever this is, more pleasant.'

Cenfrith agrees, nodding eagerly, his brown eyes keen. I've not seen him looking so alert since he woke me in Tamworth in the middle of the night and took me from the only place I've ever called home.

'You'll need to take the horse to transport everything required.'

'I am aware of that.' Cenfrith's words are hard-edged when he speaks to Edwin. There have been occasions over the last few days when I thought Edwin might take aim at my uncle with his seax. Certainly, I know he regrets his haste in following us on that fateful night. But I'm grateful he's at my side. My uncle isn't the most talkative of men. Cenfrith's brooding silences would make our exile intolerable.

As he rides away, Cenfrith turns back one final time, his eyes on Edwin.

'Don't follow me,' he reaffirms. 'If he follows me, Icel, you're to leave here and go elsewhere. I'll find you in good time.'

I turn to Edwin, ready to argue with him, but he sags to the floor, all defiance gone from him.

'If I follow him, I'll have to return to Tamworth or have nothing, and that's not what I had in mind. I want to be a warrior. I don't want to die on the blade of a Wessex warrior without the ability to defend myself.'

'Good,' I offer. 'I don't want to be here on my own.'

Silence falls between us. We're sitting beside a small stream, water burbling through a collection of rocks, a gentle counterpart to the turbulence in my heart. If we're lucky, a fish might happen into our hands.

'What do you think's happening in Tamworth?' Edwin eventually asks. He's not alone in having his thoughts turn to Tamworth, to Wynflæd, to his mother.

'I have no idea.'

'It won't be like when Ludica and then Wiglaf became king. They merely allowed the Witan to proclaim them as king, and then everything stayed just about the same.'

'No, it won't be like that,' I confirm. I have no idea what will happen, but it's not likely to be pleasant with the Wessex king. He's a man who has no problem killing to achieve what he desires, so Cenfrith has told us both.

'What do you think King Wiglaf will do?'

'If he ran from the battlefield, I can't see him amassing a force to counter the Wessex king.' I'm not skilled in politics or battle tactics, but I can understand his desire to stay alive.

Edwin is silent, and then he begins to speak, hesitantly at first and then gaining in confidence.

'I think King Ecgberht will move against the men of the East Angles as well, perhaps even the Northumbrians. He wants to rule all of this island, apart from the Welsh kingdoms and the kingdoms of the Picts and Strathclyde. Or maybe he'll take them as well, although they're not Saxons.'

I gasp at Edwin's vision of the future.

'You've thought about this?' My words are almost a shriek.

'It's what the king's warriors believe. I've heard them speak of their fears often enough. They believe Kings Beornwulf and Ludica should have turned towards the Wessex kingdom. Already, they've claimed Kent from the Mercians. What will be next? Although, I can't see that they ever imagined Mercia falling so completely under his control.'

I consider Edwin's suggestion, allowing my fingers to touch the water, the coolness of it refreshing. It's the height of summer. Even here, beneath the trees overhead, it's still too hot. 'Would King Ecgberht be able to do all that? Surely the Wessex king can't have so many more warriors than the Mercian king?'

Edwin shakes his head, dismissing my words. 'The number of trained warriors in Mercia has fallen hugely in the last few years, with the battle against Ecgberht in Wessex, and then the two offensives into the kingdom of the East Angles, as well as the altercations last year at Peterborough. Not to mention the problems on the borders with Gwynedd and Powys. Without all those losses, Mercia would have twice the number it has now.'

It's hardly a comforting thought.

'You should let me train you,' Edwin leaps to his feet with excitement.

I shake my head quickly, holding my hand out at the same time. 'I'm a healer.'

'Not if you can't continue your training.' His words are hot. This argument has been brewing for some days.

'If you fight in the name of Mercia, do you not want someone who can heal your wounds?' My words are as angry as his.

'It doesn't have to be you?' Edwin thinks he's won, knowing that we're so far from Tamworth and Wynflæd.

'Then who will it be? Tell me? Wynflæd hardly has a host of interested young men and women to train. Do you even know of anyone else who wants to learn her craft?'

'It still doesn't have to be you,' Edwin argues, and I bite back my caustic response. Edwin has never understood my desire to heal rather than maim. I doubt he ever will.

* * *

The day passes slowly. Edwin grows bored quickly and takes to fashioning pieces of wood into strange creatures with his seax. I think he'll cut himself.

'It's a bloody horse,' he explodes when he asks me to guess what it is, and I suggest a chicken.

'A horse? Where's its tail?'

Edwin surges to his feet, disappearing amongst the tightly packed trees, and I shiver at suddenly being alone. The animals of the woodlands are scampering hither and thither, occasionally a raucous cry from a bird bringing me to my feet, heart pounding, knife in my hand. But I'm entirely alone.

Eventually, I grow tired of the stream and go to lean against a tree. The bark of the old tree, an oak, is remarkably smooth behind me. I allow my eyes to close. It's one way of countering the hunger in my belly.

I only wake when Edwin slumps down in front of me as though made from planks of wood and not flesh at all.

'I hate this,' he begins as my eyes flicker open in surprise. 'I hate this so much.'

'It won't make it right, though, hating it.'

'What if your uncle is wrong?'

'Have you ever known him to be wrong?' I ask this softly.

'No, but...'

'There aren't any "but" s. This is how it's going to be. I don't like it any more than you, but blaming Cenfrith when it's not his fault is a waste of time.'

'Then who should I blame for this shit?'

'King Ecgberht of Wessex and King Wiglaf of Mercia. Wiglaf more than Ecgberht.' I know who I'm holding accountable for this. I was wary when he became king. When King Ludica inherited the crown from Beornwulf, I didn't know enough to think it wrong. But now I do.

'And King Ecgberht is far from done.' My uncle appears, the sound of his approach with Wine masked by our argument. We would not survive in the wilderness without him.

'What do you mean?'

'King Ecgberht has summoned the Mercian Witan. He means to be proclaimed king of Mercia by right of conquest. Even the soap maker in the market at Hereford was aflame with the news. In Hereford, they fear being overrun as Tamworth has been. They speak of burning fields and slaughtered Mercians. I don't know if they speak the truth or not.'

'And who might these ealdormen be?' Edwin demands to know, no doubt deciding to focus on that rather than whether his mother still lives.

My uncle looks tired once more, his eyes hollow in a gaunt face as he hands me a loaf of bread, a wry smirk on his face. 'Whoever is shameless enough to serve the wrong king. And there will be enough of them to ensure Mercia stays firmly under King Ecgberht's command. There'll be those who've been slighted by King Wiglaf and those unhappy with Beornwulf's usurpation of Coelwulf. I imagine Ecgberht might even seek out the deposed King Coelwulf and have him swear an oath to him. That would further legitimise his claim.'

I break apart the bread, hand half to Edwin as my uncle falls silent. The bread, which should have tasted amazing, is suddenly sodden in my mouth, almost tasteless. I had hoped for better news.

'Certainly, no one knows where King Wiglaf has gone. He's not been seen since he ran from the battlefield, but his body wasn't found.'

'So Mercia is truly at an end?' Edwin forces the words through tight lips.

My uncle's face is filled with sorrow. 'For now, yes. For now. We'll see what the future brings, but I don't hold out much hope for Mercia driving King Ecgberht all the way back across the Thames and into Wessex. Not without a king, anyway.'

Once more, I feel my uncle appraising me, and I'm unsure why.

* * *

We're not far from yet another of the ancient roads when my uncle hisses between his teeth, and we know enough to step into the darkness caused by the shadows of the tree.

The weather is on the turn, but each day dawns bright enough, only later, and later, and in the evenings, darkness draws in ever earlier. There's a chill in the air every day, and it's not just the silence that so often rings between us all. Sometimes, I find it hard to stay warm, and the fires we light each night never seem to hold the heat of a hearth in a dwelling.

'Warriors,' my uncle informs us both, doing his best to join us, encouraging Wine beneath the low-hanging branches.

'From where?' Edwin queries, hand on his seax. I would chuckle at the way he mirrors my uncle's posture, but I'm terrified. There have been rumours heard in Hereford and the other settlements, my uncle has risked visiting in recent weeks, that King Ecgberht sends his warriors into the forests and woodlands seeking out those who shelter there, but this is the first time we've encountered them.

Above my thudding heart, I can detect the sound of hooves on the stone road and the cries of men laughing with one another. Certainly, the Wessex warriors aren't terrified, even so close to the kingdom of Powys. They should tread with more care. The Powys warriors, as I know from my uncle's stories, are a vicious lot. They fight with whatever they have to hand, not necessarily sharpened edges and cruel blades. They can kill with anything they can find.

Wine obediently follows his commands, only my uncle slips from her back, handing me the reins. I can't clearly see his face in the shadows of the tree, but his hand is on his seax.

'Don't,' I whisper to Cenfrith, but he's gone, slipping once more to the side of the road. I tremble with terror, itching to reach out and hold onto Edwin because I fear he'll follow my uncle. Instead, I grip Wine tightly, taking comfort from her now familiar scent. She watches me, eyes bright in the darkness. I'm growing to know my uncle's horse.

From amongst the trees, I can hear the sound of men, of horses, but nothing else. I caution Wine to silence, fearing she might nicker a greeting to the animals.

I breathe out slowly, not realising I've been holding my breath, but still, my uncle doesn't return. What does he think he can do? A man alone against King Ecgberht's Wessex warriors.

Edwin bites his lip so that it flashes whitely, and I shake my head at him. His hand remains on his seax, his body poised to dash after Cenfrith. I hope it won't come to that. If Cenfrith can't contend with the enemy, then how can Edwin? He has no experience of fighting a battle, of knowing his life is entirely in his hands. I shudder at the thought, tasting bile in my mouth.

Time stretches, too much of it, and still, we're alone, even though the sounds of men and horses does finally die away. Eventually, Edwin turns to me, eyebrow high, but I shake my head, almost too terrified to move. Wine has begun to crop the grasses at her feet. Certainly, she's calmer now; she must think the danger is gone.

I close my eyes, try to blot out my fear, focusing on the sound of the woodland creatures, and when that doesn't work, working through one of Wynflæd's favoured recipes: take plantain and feverfew and pepper and beat them and then strain onto the boil. I wish I knew more complex ones.

And still, Cenfrith is absent. Eventually, Wine becomes fractious, moving slowly forwards and backwards, as though wanting to leave my side but unsure whether she should. I speak softly to her, running my hand down her long nose, noting the white star on it, stark in the shadowed light, trying not to consider what will happen if my uncle is lost to us.

'There's more of them than I'd like,' Cenfrith announces, his words too loud after the prolonged silence.

My head turns to gaze at him. He wears a grim expression, shaking his head from side to side.

'King Ecgberht of Wessex is far from content with what he's accomplished so far. It seems he means to enforce his rule on every part of Mercia.'

'Can we still cross the road?' Again, it's Edwin who asks.

'If we're careful. The problem will be on the far side. There's not the tree cover to keep us from prying eyes, not immediately. We'll have to move when it's dark and go far more quickly than I'd like to. It'll be tricky with you and Icel on foot.'

My uncle had intended to head northwards, not to the lands that owe him their rents but somewhere he's convinced we can shelter within during the coming winter months. I'm eager to reach it. I'm weary of constantly travelling, of sleeping somewhere I don't know and rising the next day just to journey to somewhere else I don't know. And the cold is becoming insidious, the threat of the first frost never far.

'It would be better if we travelled separately, but as neither of you knows the way, that risk can't be taken.'

'Shall we go now, then?' Edwin is eager. I've noticed with each morning that his hands are paler and paler, any warmth from the sun long since drained from his skin. His eyes have also become furtive, his sleep more disturbed.

Silence greets those words, my uncle tilting his head from side to side as he considers. I think he'll say no, preferring to plan what's going to happen next, but he surprises me.

'Yes, better to do it now, as I know where the bloody Wessex warriors have gone.'

I open my mouth, but Edwin dares me to argue with a fierce stare, so I hold my tongue. After all, what do I know about such things?

All the same, we wait until darkness coats the land before we emerge onto the old road. The feel of stone is oddly reassuring after so many weeks of grass or spongy pine beneath my feet. But it's over far too soon. Cenfrith leads Wine; Edwin and I following so closely behind, I fear that if Wine shits, it'll land on my hard-worn boots.

I glance in both directions along the road, but there's not enough light to see far. I take some reassurance from the lack of flames or lights in the night sky. There's no one making camp close by either.

On the other side of the road, we drop down into lower-lying land, and my uncle is right; there are no trees here, not like the dense covering we've been hiding within. Although it's dark, the feeling of so much space round me is as terrifying as when I first slept in the woods. Here, there's nowhere to run and hide, no handy tree that will shelter me beneath its boughs.

I feel exposed, and I don't like it, not at all. That surprises me. I thought I hated the woodlands and the denizens who live there. But it seems I've become used to what little protection they can offer me, in this strange landscape, the border between Mercia and the Welsh kingdoms, which feels entirely different to the life I've known in Tamworth.

Breathing hard, almost running to keep up, I keep my eyes forward. The ground is far from flat, for all there are no trees. I think we must rush through cultivated land, and then I hear sheep nearby and immediately worry that an older man, or a young boy, will be close at hand, keeping a watchful eye over the animals at the end of their summer grazing.

But my uncle doesn't stop. Instead, he presses onwards, Wine seeming to have an uncanny ability to avoid every stone and dip in the land while I trip and stumble with regularity. Overhead, the sky is thick with clouds, and although it hampers me, it also masks our progress.

'We need to stop,' Edwin eventually huffs. I've been thinking the same for some time, and I'm pleased he dares to say as much.

'Just a little further,' my uncle informs us, and I don't know if that means to our destination or to where we can stop. The sacks of supplies that Cenfrith has collected to carry us through the coming winter, are heavy, the ropes digging into my shoulders, and although I should be cold, I'm too hot. Cenfrith has been planning how we'll survive the winter undisturbed ever since his first trip into Hereford.

I hobble on, the fact I don't fall more to do with the weight at my back pulling me backwards rather than onto the ground. Every breath is harsh, and then my uncle stops and I do collide with the rear end of Wine. Luckily, she doesn't shit on my boots.

'Steady,' Cenfrith urges me, dismounting quickly.

I drop the sacks, two loud thuds to either side of me, and fall to the ground. Edwin doesn't even manage to lower the bags, instead rebounding off one of them and settling against the other as he joins me on the cold ground. Only then do I notice my surroundings. We're not amongst the trees. Instead, from relatively close by, I can hear the sound of water.

'Where are we?' I eventually huff.

'Just somewhere we can rest for a while.'

'So we're not staying here?' Edwin asks, his words tinged with exhaustion.

'Just for a while.' There's sympathy in Cenfrith's words. He has a horse to ride and no heavy sacks to carry, unlike us.

I'm just pleased to be still, and although I drink deeply of the water bottle Cenfrith passes to me, thankfully carried by the horse and not by Edwin or me, I quickly fall asleep.

The next day is dark and overcast, with the threat of rain imminent, and Cenfrith, after we've eaten and rested for as long as he'll allow us, forces us onwards. In the distance, almost as black as the clouds overhead, another line of trees quickly comes into view. As soon as I pass beneath them, I feel much safer and stop looking behind us as though we're being chased.

'We should arrive today,' my uncle assures us both when our steps flag almost immediately. It seems as though there's nothing round us to walk to, but my uncle knows best. Of that, I'm sure.

'And then what?'

'If we can, we'll stay there for the winter.'

In my mind, I ask, 'and then?' but Edwin holds his tongue and enquires instead, 'Do we have enough food to last through the winter?'

My uncle has been gathering supplies for some time now on his trips in and out of the larger settlements of Hereford, and the outlying farms, and that's why Edwin and I are so weighted down.

'If not, we'll get more,' my uncle assures Edwin.

I've never considered where my uncle gets his wealth from, and it concerns me now. I know he's spent a great deal on the supplies we currently have. But, while they weigh me down, I have no idea if there's enough to last all winter long. And, if Cenfrith can't return to his lands, how will he get the coin his lands produce to keep us fed?

Edwin and I have new cloaks and new boots, although I'm carrying mine, not wearing them. I don't want to add the pain of blisters to the uncomfortableness of our journey. There are also thick furs and a collection of needles and thread to make more if required. My uncle also has a new heavy cloak, while Wine has a blanket to keep her warm. Cenfrith seems determined that we survive without needing to ask others for assistance.

The ground begins to climb, the trees round us slowly fading away as we march ever higher, as though older men whose hair has started to leave their pate clear. I think of the bee that stung me all that time ago, the one I kept and gave to Wynflæd for her cure.

It's hard-going, more challenging than ever before. I try not to look upwards, but it's impossible. The slope is so steep, Cenfrith dismounts, urging Wine upwards, not prepared to take the chance that she'll slip and injure herself. I'm forced to pause, breath harsh in my throat, to cough away the dryness. I turn, take the opportunity to look behind us.

We're high enough to see much of Mercia stretching out before us, and it all seems surprisingly calm from here. In the fields in the far distance, tiny shapes can be seen busy about the harvest, the animals who yet live taking the last of the goodness from the grass before a winter indoors, should they escape the slaughter.

It all seems very normal. Too normal. And I'm entirely outside it all. I'm not helping Wynflæd harvest the roots she needs, slicing them, boiling them, or suspending them in vinegar or salt to prevent them from corrupting. I swallow, aware tears are forming in my eyes.

'Come on, Icel,' Edwin calls, and his words are jaunty.

'What?' I demand, and then I see. Ahead, the hillside continues ever upwards, but the hill seems to almost buckle in on itself, a small, reasonably flat piece of land that's invisible until you're facing it. And there is a dilapidated dwelling, made from stacked pieces of stones and wattle and daub and planks of wood, with a small shelter to the side. It's to that my uncle has brought us.

My pace increases, onwards, the bags no longer as heavy as before, and I step down, two steps, then three, and I abandon the sacks on the ground. The wind has abruptly stopped, the air has warmed. Edwin grins at me, amazed by where we are. I can feel the same on my face.

'Edwin, Icel, get your arses over here,' Cenfrith calls, and we both dip, grab our bags and rush to find him. He's opened the door and while it smells old and little-used, there's warmth inside the dwelling, a hearth easy to see on the floor, and there are alcoves for four people to sleep within. 'Will this do, for now?' Cenfrith asks, the hint of a smile on his lips. I've not seen him smile for long weeks.

'Yes,' I gasp, Edwin doing the same.

'Good, then let's get sorted. We should be quite safe here, even the smoke from our fire will be masked by the colour of the heather behind us, and there's a small stream to the back. The only problem will be wood. But we've got time to collect it yet.'

And neither Edwin nor I ask how long we're to stay there. Suddenly, it doesn't seem to matter.

12

I open my eyes, gazing into the grey haze of a new day, aware I'm alone. No one sleeps in my workshop now, just me.

I don't like to admit it and certainly never would to that catty witch, Beornwyn, but I miss my young apprentice. And not just because without him, there's no one to set to the tedious tasks that mark every day. In order to tend to the sick and wounded, I must have stores of all the ingredients I need. Aside from the butter I use when making Beornwyn's salve, which comes from the royal dairy, everything within my workshop has been carefully harvested and preserved by my hands or those of Icel's. Or those of his mother's, Ceolburh, long before he was born.

I think of her often, of her long fair hair, so different to Icel's. Of her fierce intelligence and even quicker temper. Icel didn't get that from her. The years have been long and hard without her at my side, and now they'll become even more so.

On legs grown frail and weak, on feet grown unwieldy, difficult to bend, and always cold, I make my way to the hearth, stirring up the embers and adding more wood to the dull glowing red of a fire in retreat. I know how it feels as it refuses to yield to my attempts to conjure up new flames. I would rather fade away as well.

From beyond the walls of my workshop, I hear the cries of men and women as they begin their day. Despite knowing otherwise, I listen for Icel, for Edwin, and even, after all these years, for Ceolburh's light footstep. I've not heard it for many years now.

I think back to the day I lost her. I could not help her, even with all my years of knowledge. Icel was a big baby, but more than that, she was a small woman, delicate, narrow-hipped. I should have warned her sooner of my suspicions, but as she watched me that day, I believe she knew what would happen. Perhaps she always had.

Over the years, I've lost many a babe, born blue or barely breathing, too frail to survive separate from its mother, but never another mother. Only ever Ceolburh. I'd never seen such blood or felt so useless. Even now, sometimes I wake, sweating and feeling drenched to my elbows in the blood of another. The horror never leaves me, and neither has the sorrow.

Lord Beornwulf forgave me, although he mourned long and hard, never acknowledging Icel as his son before the Witan. Leaving the boy unclaimed because of it. Cenfrith forgave me as well, grateful when Edwin's mother offered to suckle his nephew besides her own babe. She never allowed the fact that few knew of his parentage to stop her from loving him.

But I've never forgiven myself and never will.

And now Icel is lost to me. I don't blame Cenfrith for that, but rather King Ecgberht of Wessex. A man I despise. Worse, a man I fear.

I hear him now, heavy boots outside, ordering his men to arms. I would take myself to determine where he goes now, but I don't wish to witness his iron-grey hair, his tight jaw, his hollow cheeks in the bright daylight. He's filled with nothing but ambition. I wish it were misplaced, but I see what he's achieved and know he's a genuinely great commander, even if I loathe him.

The day he arrived in Tamworth, come as a conqueror of Mercia, riding in on a wave of smoke from the burning fields, sparing the women and children of Tamworth, although he left the king's hall standing, I knew King Ecgberht would succeed and that, one day, he would be my death. He came on a high-stepping stallion, the animal a uniform brown, hardly the sleek black of a true warrior's mount, and yet that animal knew its worth and continues to do so.

King Ecgberht is a man who knows how to dress for his position. He wears riches and wealth on his arms and fingers upon which men could live a lifetime, if not seven lifetimes. His hair is cut short, his beard and moustache neatly trimmed, his nose just the right size for an average face. But his eyes, as grey as his hair, are sharper than any knife I've ever wielded. He saw me that day, and he knew me for what I am.

Not that he stopped my work or even acknowledged me, but it's enough that he sees me. It fills me with fear, and I'm too old to know such terror.

'We're ready, My Lord King.'

I wait, hardly breathing, to hear that voice, to know that he's gone. King Ecgberht, not content with claiming Mercia for himself, means to have the submission of the men and women of the north as well, of Northumbria beyond the massive River Humber. I pity them, but at least their king has capitulated rather than run with his tail between his legs.

No one has seen King Wiglaf since his cowardly flight from the battlefield. His wife and son have since disappeared, but again, no one knows where, or even how. Rumour has it that Cenfrith informed Lady Cynethryth of her husband's failure, urged her to leave Tamworth before it was too late, but she didn't believe him.

Not until reports of mounted warriors leaving a trail of smoke behind them were brought to her. Then she left under cover of dark, taking her son with her.

She must have decided her son didn't have the support to stand against King Ecgberht. In that, she showed more wisdom than I would have expected from her.

'One moment,' King Ecgberht responds, and now I hear booted feet coming my way.

I rise, legs awkward, back complaining, ready to face him. I've been waiting for this moment. I knew it would come. King Ecgberht shouts of his faith, and yet...

'Good woman.' For all I hate him, his voice is pleasant, filled with warmth and command as he enters my workshop, blocking out all light from the brightening summer's day.

'My Lord King.' I attempt a curtsey, even as my knees twinge and my back protests.

'Is it ready?'

'Of course, My Lord King.' Carefully, I hook the charm from above my head, noting how heavy it weighs in my hand.

King Ecgberht, licking his lips as he eyes my prize, reaches out to take it from me.

'You have done it correctly?' he asks, hesitating.

'Of course, My Lord King, exactly as you requested. The herbs, the smoke, the collection of items as specified.'

'And it will work?'

'Of that, there is no guarantee,' I caution, as I always do with such requests.

King Ecgberht pauses in the act of assessing the tightly packed charm inside the small sack of finest silk, tied securely to conceal everything that lies within, jumbled together. For a moment, I think he won't take the charm I've laboured over for three days, allowing no one entry inside my workshop. Cuthred has been forced to leave buckets of water at my door. And I've been forced to scoop out the contents, only taking what I could carry.

'Then you have my thanks.' And into my hand, he presses a small sack of great weight, the clunk of the coins forcing my eyes wide with shock.

'There is no need for payment,' I urge him. To pay will be to undo all that I've done on his behalf. Does he not know that?

A smirk, his lips tight and downcast as he snatches the money back, the charm as well with his other hand. I note the wyvern emblem covering all that he wears: from the enormous golden ring on his left hand to the depiction embroidered onto his tunic; to the symbol he wears more openly around his neck, so similar to the one Cenfrith owns, and yet so different. His wyvern is a sullen beast etched in silver, tail turning, tongue as well, eyes picked out with cold sapphire.

'Then you've done as I've asked. I'll ensure you never go without anything you need. A woman of your age requires some assistance. There are rumours a youth once aided you, a boy?'

I curse whoever has been speaking of Icel, but my face remains blank. I hope they've not spoken of their suspicions. It's been so long, most people within Tamworth have forgotten that Beornwulf and Ceolburh were ever married.

'I have had many such apprentices. Alas, they think it more exciting to become mothers or warriors, or warriors and mothers than aid an old woman and her meagre collections of herbs.' I've heard the bishop belittling my endeavours. And yet, it's to me that the king has come. That amuses me, even though I wish King Ecgberht had been content with his religious paraphernalia to justify the trail of destruction and dead men he's left in his wake.

'Perhaps,' he muses.

I think King Ecgberht knows more than he lets on. Is this some sort of test?

'I'll require another when I return from the North. Ensure it's exactly done as I specified. Do not veer from the instructions.'

'My Lord King.' I bow just my head this time. I shouldn't be forced to such subservience by a mere king, and yet, it's what he expects and easier done than raising an argument.

'When I return, I'll hear more about this boy. Perhaps I can find someone else to assist you. Or maybe I can have him hunted down and punished for deserting you.' King Ecgberht smirks as he speaks, and my feet turn ever colder.

He knows. Someone has told King Ecgberht of Icel's birthright. The thought is more terrifying than anything else I've ever endured.

'My Lord King,' I attempt, but my voice is older than the ancient stones I've heard stand a silent watch far to the south.

He turns, leaving me to my worries and my thoughts, and they are innumerable. I listen to the sound of the retreating horses, and only then do I reach for my sack, prepared with all I can carry.

I can't stay here. I won't stay here. I will allow the King of Wessex to drive me from my home, and there is only one man I blame for all this. And his name is King Wiglaf.

Outside, I blink in the brightness, pleased to see Cuthred waiting for me with a slight horse, the animal small enough for me to ride.

Cuthred's expression is cheerful as he helps me mount. I've not told him of my intention, only that I must leave Tamworth and collect supplies from the summer meadows. He's been happy to oblige me. I wonder if he'll feel the same when I tell him we won't be returning while King Ecgberht has command of Tamworth.

I only hope King Ecgberht of Wessex will fail, and soon, but in my heart, I know he won't. Not when King Wiglaf, the craven fool, is the only alternative.

PART V

13

AD830

The snows have rattled the wooden door, blocking it for a day or two at a time, so that poor Wine has had to fend for herself in the makeshift stable, but now, at last, each day dawns clear from low-hanging, pink-tinged clouds, and Cenfrith has announced that the snows are done for the year.

I've made my way partly down the hillside that faces towards the west, towards Gwynedd, seeking long grasses and roots for Wine to eat. It's not that we've run out of food after our time hidden away, but rather that we've all grown so tired of it, there's no taste or enjoyment in each meal. Not any more.

Once more, I long for warm bread and pottage that tastes of something other than onion and garlic. Even Wine has become sniffy about her food.

As so often the case of late, my stomach grumbles at the thought of decent food. There's been no meat all winter long, not after we'd eaten the last of the dried strips of beef and pork Cenfrith had purchased in Hereford. We've not been able to hunt small creatures, because they're all in hiding, just as we are.

I'd even happily eat the liver that Wynflæd used to flavour her pottage for the pregnant women back in Tamworth.

Not for the first time, my thoughts turn to what's happening in there. I can't see that King Ecgberht of Wessex will have harmed Wynflæd, but perhaps he has a particular hatred for women who know more about healing than the holy men. I wish I knew. I wish that my uncle had thought to bring Wynflæd with us. At least, with her extensive knowledge of what is and isn't edible, we might not be quite so tired of our food.

I stand, pulling my cloak tightly round my face. It's cold outside, not the bite of impending snow, but rather from the wind that blows along the hill. It's fierce, and I can feel that my cheeks are already pink and raw from it. Further down the slope, Edwin is foraging for twigs and wood from a sparse coppice; no doubt planted long ago by whoever built the structure that's been our home for the last however many months. We've been careful not to take too much from any of the trees, but we need to keep warm, and Cenfrith won't allow Edwin or I to travel far away from the steading, either into Gwynedd or into Mercia.

'Bloody bollocks, it's cold,' Edwin calls to me. He has a dark covering of beard and moustache on his face. Cenfrith has offered to teach him to shave it away, but Edwin has so far refused. At least he doesn't have to contend with pink cheeks from the cold. He looks almost unrecognisable. He's taller now, broader as well. His mother won't know him, should he ever return to Tamworth.

'It is, yes,' I agree.

The silences between the three of us have begun to grow in recent days. We've exhausted the topic of King Ecgberht, Mercia, King Wiglaf and what the future holds. We don't know. That's the simple answer. There's only so many times we can say the same thing.

We've seen no one since we first came here. No one. For the first time in my life, I've come to appreciate the constant visitors that Wynflæd once had in her workshop. It was rare for there to be a morning or afternoon when she was left undisturbed. There were always stories to be heard and intrigue to gossip about, even if I hoarded much of the wealth of conversation to myself.

'Have you found anything?' Edwin huffs, standing in front of me, arms bent against his chest as he cups what wood he's found. He should have brought a sack with him, but it seems he's forgotten once more.

'Not much, no. It's the wrong time of year.' I have half a sack full of straggling grasses for Wine. I doubt she'll appreciate them even though it's taken me all morning to collect them.

'Do you think Cenfrith will return to one of the settlements for food?' Edwin is as hungry as I am. Sometimes, he lists all the food he's going to eat when he visits Hereford or Wroxeter. It always ends with the wish that he could taste bread infused with summer fruits. He's always had a sweet tooth and we have no honey for eating. I have only a small supply left and I must keep it in case of injury.

'I don't know.' We've discussed this before, but no matter how hard we try, it's impossible to get Cenfrith to share his plans with us. He's secretive and silent for much of the time. Only when we play *tafl* or games of chance, the pieces made from anything we can find, does he become alive. I think he misses being busy, but more, I see him fingering the half-hidden emblem he wears round his neck, a pensive expression on his lined face.

'Well, can't you bloody ask him?' Edwin's words are flecked with frustration.

'I have asked him. You know that.' My reply is too hot. I don't appreciate the criticism.

'You'll have to get him to tell you, for once,' Edwin huffs, walking away from me, the wind stirring his cloak so that it rises up his back. He's miserable, but I can't remind him that it was his choice to follow Cenfrith and me from Tamworth. That argument has resulted in too many fights between us, Cenfrith forced to tear us apart in the confined space of our hut. Edwin always wins when fists are flying because I lack his skills.

There's just the three of us, and we need to rely on one another. If not, I have no idea what will happen to us.

I pause my work, turn to stare down the hill, towards the kingdom of Gwynedd, and a gasp escapes my mouth, even as I drop to the ground. I inhale the smell of cold and dampness, barely able to breathe. I try to turn to see if Edwin has disappeared over the crest of the hill, but I don't want to make too big a move.

There are four horses at the bottom of the slope, no bigger than sheep at such a distance, cropping at the winter grasses, while four men gesticulate towards the top of the hill. I swallow heavily, fear almost making me piss myself. I try to recall then if the smoke from the hearth fire was visible while I was gathering the grasses. But I can't remember.

I daren't draw my eyes away from the men as they point and talk, their movements extravagant enough that I almost think I can hear and see everything they do. The wind doesn't bring their actual words to me. The horses are well rugged beneath their saddles, and they don't look as though they've endured much hardship during the winter months. They're certainly not as thin as Wine has become.

I stuff my hand into my mouth, desperate to stifle the moans of fear that threaten to erupt. I wish Edwin were with me. He'd know what to do. My other hand reaches for my knife. I have no other weapon to hand. I consider how long it might take the men to reach me. It's a steep hill, so I would have enough time to return to Cenfrith. But what then?

If we have to fight the men, it'd be four against one. I would be no help, and Edwin has yet to face a warrior one to one in a real battle. I don't know how he'd react. Edwin might just run away, fear making him weak when he should be strong.

I risk lifting my head slightly to better view the men, and my heart sinks. They've abandoned their horses, and now the four of them have begun to climb higher, two in front, two behind.

The only thing that brings me comfort is that they don't carry shields, although weapons are evident on their belts when the clouds part enough to let thin slivers of light through.

I lower myself to the ground again, looking all round for some means to hide. I can't make it up the slope. I can't risk the men glancing upwards and seeing me crab towards the summit. Here, the slope is sparsely covered with the remnants of the foliage that grew the previous summer. There's not even the hope of a stone to hide behind. There's nothing.

Almost too afraid to look, I fight my desire to simply stand and run. I wish my uncle were here. He'd know what to do. But he's not. Cenfrith stayed behind to protect our few possessions and to watch the despised pottage didn't boil dry. There's only me.

And then, I can hear the men calling one to another, laughing as they do so, the sound burbling towards me along with the wind. It feels strange to listen to voices that aren't Cenfrith's dull rumble or Edwin's slightly higher-pitched tone. Even though I don't understand their rolling language, it reminds me of how long it's been since I spoke to someone other than my uncle or Edwin. I know then that the men are indeed from the kingdom of Gwynedd.

I don't know whether to be cheered by that or not. At least they're not Wessex warriors or Raiders from the far north, but the

Mercians and the Welsh kingdoms are just as much enemies. The fact they won't know who I am, should they capture me, brings some solace, but it's short-lived. Now, I can hear them, as though they stand close to me, and I still haven't moved.

I consider what they'll do to me, should they find me. Will they take me as a slave? Or will they simply kill me, here and now? Perhaps, these men own the steading we've claimed as our own. Maybe they'll want to bring me to justice for stealing their property.

My chest aches with the effort of breathing slowly. I'm still fighting the urge to run, the desire to be away from them, and then, I can't hear them any more. I only realise slowly, eyes closed as though not being able to see them means they can't see me. My breathing calms enough that I can focus on more than just my fear and the need to piss. I open one eye and then another, looking down the hillside, unable to see the men from where my head is pressed so tightly to the cold ground. My trews are wet and cold, my cloak little better, and I'm sure I'm lying on last year's sheep dung, the rounds digging into my cheek.

I risk lifting my head and see the men, backs to me, leading their mounts away along a twisting and narrow trail that's long intrigued me. I want to know where it goes, what lies beyond the tightly packed mass of trees, but Cenfrith has forbidden Edwin or me to go that far. He believes that, provided we have the advantage of higher ground, we'll remain hidden.

I wait until the last white tail of the rear horse disappears along the track, and then I wait a little longer, just to be sure. Only then do I rear up and run up the hill, breath rasping a white cloud before me. I remember Wine's grasses and clutch the sack tightly in my hand.

When I'm over the rise of the summit, I finally slow my steps, sucking in much-needed air, aware that my tunic and trews are stuck to my body because of the wetness of the grass. Immediately,

Cenfrith appears before me, from where he must have been tending to Wine, concern on his face, which only grows as he sees my agitation.

'What is it?' he demands to know, his voice instantly familiar, immediately calming.

I suck in air and let it all out with the words, 'Four horsemen. They came so far up the hill on foot, but then turned aside and have gone.'

Cenfrith's eyes cloud, and he stamps forwards to retrace the steps I've just taken.

Edwin peers at me from beside the steading and then comes running as well as he realises something isn't right. I take no comfort in knowing that I look so terrible, even Edwin is concerned for me. That must be the first time that's ever happened.

'What?' he demands of me, following Cenfrith and not waiting for a response.

'Horsemen,' I call after him weakly, my legs shaking so much beneath me that I tumble to the ground, drinking in the familiar view from this side of the hill. Mercia lies spread before me, and Mercia is my home, even if I'm distanced from it, for now.

I focus on the thin trail of smoke coming from the roof of the steading while my heart thuds loudly in my ears. I can hear Edwin demanding answers from Cenfrith and Cenfrith's furious response, followed by a querulous counterargument from Edwin. And still, I shake, hand clenched on the sack that contains the grasses for Wine.

I feel sick with fright, terrified of what this all means, and then Cenfrith returns, his footsteps quick and heavy.

'We'll have to be more careful from now on,' he mutters, offering me his hand and pulling me upright. He pats me down as though seeking injuries, although I have none. 'They might return. There's no way of knowing.'

'And if they return?' I ask, my voice breaking on the final word.

'We'll have to leave here, return to the woodlands, stay out of sight.'

My heart sinks at the thought of running away from our comfortable existence. I might have resented the lack of bread, the repetitious nature of our meals, but I have felt safe here, safer than I did throughout the previous summer.

'And what then?'

I don't turn to Edwin. I can hear the frustration.

'Then, we'll decide what to do next,' Cenfrith assures him, the heat gone from his words.

Once more, I feel Cenfrith eyeing me, as though assessing me for something, but then we're inside the stable that Wine sleeps within, and I'm handing her the grasses, watching how she sniffs at them with as much enthusiasm as I feel for the pottage we eat.

'We just need to be more vigilant now the snow's cleared. We came here late in the season. It's possible the shepherd's sleep in it, or someone comes here for the summer months. If that's the case, then we'll leave. It's been good while it lasted.' If the words are meant to reassure, they don't.

Edwin looks at me, his expression bleak, his complaints about food all gone as well. Sometimes, it's easier to forget that we're hiding away from the Wessex king who's taken Mercia for himself. Just as King Wiglaf of Mercia, we've run away to keep our lives.

* * *

For all Cenfrith's reassuring words, he grows increasingly morose over the following days. I hear him moving round at night when he believes I'm asleep, and more than once, I eye him fingering the amulet round his neck. He also sleeps more during the day, and I can't but conclude that he keeps watch all night, although he never says as much.

And then, seven days later, just as dawn is breaking, the dull glow of a new day rousing me from a deep sleep, I hear a sound I've been anticipating and dreading in equal measure.

There are voices from outside our steading.

Cenfrith, already alert, stands by the door, finger pressed to his lips on noticing that I'm awake. I reach over and shake Edwin as well. He could sleep through the thunder of a hundred horses on the march.

'What?' he garbles, but then hears the scuff of boots and the shouting of men to one another. The sounds ring too loudly. There's no wind to cover the noise.

'Bugger,' Edwin explodes, moving quickly to stand beside Cenfrith while I struggle to follow, legs tangled in the fur that covers my lower body. My uncle shakes his head at me, making motions with his hands to show that I should stay where I am. I'm relieved that he doesn't expect me to fight.

I watch as Cenfrith bends his head close to Edwin's ear, but I don't hear the words. Only when Cenfrith wrenches the door open, emitting the grey haze of dawn, do I realise what he's about to do.

Cenfrith darts outside, moving so quickly I almost don't realise that he's gone. In his wake, Edwin closes the door firmly but quietly and beckons for me to join him.

I do, trying not to trip or fall over Edwin's discarded boots.

'What's he doing?' I demand to know, my words laced with concern.

'Be quiet,' Edwin urges me. His eyes are hard, daring me to argue with him, as he holds his head close to the door, trying to hear everything that happens beyond the comfort of the warped wood. All winter, the door has allowed as much cold in as it's kept warmth in, but it's the best we had. I doubt it'll provide much protection from blades, but it reassures me, all the same.

I hear shouts of outrage and the softer sound of someone sobbing from beyond the walls, and the thud of something heavy hitting the icy ground. Edwin's terrified eyes meet mine, even as he runs his finger over the edge of his seax.

Cenfrith gifted it to him after Edwin begged him to continue his warrior's training. The two have spent some time each day fighting against one another, running round the summit and even working on building Edwin's physique so that he has arms almost as wide as Cenfrith's. To begin with, Edwin was desperate for me to join in, but I busied myself in trying to collect a supply of medicines to aid us through the winter colds and ailments I knew we'd have to counter.

For ten days, we shook and shivered, Wine being tended to only every other day, but the pottage and potion I made eased some of our aching throats and hacking coughs. Even now, with the threat of an enemy beyond the doors, I think I spent my time wisely. At least Cenfrith and Edwin are hale enough to defend us.

A cry that I know to be from Cenfrith has me fumbling with the door latch, but Edwin shakes his head, long hair cascading down his shoulders as he does so, and I know he won't yield to my entreaties.

'He said to stay inside, no matter what we heard,' Edwin states firmly, the tremble in his voice showing me he's just as terrified as I am.

Frantically, I listen to the crash of iron on iron, the huffs of men fighting for their lives, and then there's ringing silence, broken only by an outraged whinny from Wine.

'You can come out,' Cenfrith calls through the door.

With groping hands, Edwin undoes the door latch and steps into the watery light of morning. I follow behind, seeking out my uncle, relief almost making me stumble when I spy him, whole before me.

He stands over the body of a man, blood leaking from a wound beneath his arm into the spiky grass fashioned when the temperature dipped low enough for ice to form. Cenfrith is breathing heavily, blood on his nose and along his byrnie, but he smiles, all the same.

'How many?' Edwin demands to know, eager now that the fighting is done.

'Four of them, as Icel said there would be.'

I swallow down my disgust at the splayed body and follow Edwin to the next dead man. He's lying on his back, throat slit, the skin stained with the burgundy of wine from the south that King Ludica liked to drink. His green eyes have darkened, his fair hair matted with the blood. The next man still gasps, air gurgling through his mouth, where my uncle's seax is embedded beneath his chin.

'Cenfrith,' I call.

'Edwin, end it for him. He won't recover,' my uncle announces exhaustedly.

Edwin nods, biting down on his lip, seax in his hand. I look from my friend to the dying man, running through all I know in my mind, aware that there's no way of healing him. Not from such a wound and yet desperate to try, all the same.

I can't believe my friend capable of killing someone so powerless, and yet, it's the kindest thing to do; I acknowledge that.

Edwin bends beside the man, and I hear him murmur something to him, and then, before I can look away, Edwin stabs down with his seax into the place where the man's heart beats. The man emits a long, wet sounding sigh, before falling still.

I bend double, vomit onto the ground, the smell sour and filled with my fear.

Edwin stands, looks at me with barely concealed disgust and then moves to the next man. This one is entirely dead, his face crushed against the well-trodden path between Wine's stable and the steading. The back of his head is devoid of all hair, and I can see the wrinkles where his head meets his neck.

But before I can say anything else, my uncle is beside me.

'We need to leave here. It's not safe any more,' and my heart sinks even further.

Where will we go now? Where is there to go that offers any safety from all those who mean us harm, be they from Wessex, one of the Welsh kingdoms, or even the Raiders. But I stifle my question. Cenfrith's face is tight with fury and exhaustion. My questions aren't going to make it any easier for either of us.

14

'Where will we go?' It's not the first time Edwin has asked the question. But, as I turn to gaze upwards, to that cleft in the hill inside which our home for so much of the winter nestles, I feel nothing but sadness.

Up there, away from the sight of everyone who meant us harm, I felt safe, coddled. It was even easy to forget that Mercia had been overrun and now the Wessex king rules her. My thoughts turn to Wynflæd, to Beornwyn, Siric, Waldhere and young Cuthred. I hope they still live inside the walls of Tamworth.

Wine steps carefully, mindful of the damp and icy grass. She's not ridden this far since before the winter storms came. I've not walked as far either. Already it feels like too much effort, fatigue threatening to force me to the ground. Miserable, I huddle deep inside my cloak, grateful only that there's less for me to carry than when we first mounted the hill. We've eaten almost all the food, and we wear all of the clothes and cloaks on our backs.

I don't want to leave here. But there's no choice, not now Cenfrith had to kill the men from the kingdom of Gwynedd. When someone realises they're lost, more warriors will come, and Cenfrith won't be able to kill the warband they'll send.

'I know where we can go.' Cenfrith announces the words reluctantly but says nothing else.

Edwin sulks at my side, his face hidden in the shadows of his hood, but every so often, he huffs with annoyance. I would do the same, but I can't help blaming myself for our current predicament. If only I'd not been seen, we wouldn't have been forced to flee the place I'd begun to think of as my new home.

All round me, the landscape is muted, the browns and greys of winter overlaying everything. The hedgerows are bare, the rivers and streams either flooded or iced over depending on their depths, and the landscape, where it sinks too low, boggy and unpleasant underfoot.

'How long will it take us to get there?' None of us has spoken for a long time. Edwin's words startle me. We're entirely alone in the landscape, only the odd curious crow or robin looking up from where it bends low to the ground or flutters to a sparsely covered hedgerow.

'When we get there,' Cenfrith replies.

Both of them are foul-tempered, and I want to do nothing but cry. This is all my fault. I know it is. Yet, Cenfrith hasn't blamed me. Far from it. He's even gone so far as to say we were lucky to survive undetected for as long as we did. It doesn't comfort me as much as it should.

It's bitter outdoors, my breath pluming before me, my hands wrapped tightly in the folds of my cloak. I don't even sweat, even though every footfall is agony. I can't believe that we managed to walk so far during the long-ago summer.

'Are we going back the same way?' I'm eventually forced to ask. We travelled this way under cover of darkness, and yet I sense some familiarity as we pass from the thick band of trees that once sheltered us.

'Yes, we'll make it back to the old road and then into the wood-lands to the far side.'

'And from there?' Edwin is still furious, the set of his wide shoulders showing his anger.

'A week, at most, perhaps more quickly.'

I expect Edwin to explode with rage, but instead, his shoulders settle as though knowing the length of time we'll be walking for drives his anger away.

'We'll freeze to death,' Edwin eventually states, the words lost and small in the vast expanse, filled with resignation.

'No, we won't. We'll find caves and trees to shelter beneath. We'll have fires each night and pile them high to keep us warm until the next day.'

'If there's any dry wood,' Edwin grumbles, Cenfrith wisely ignoring his sour comments.

Quickly, the winter day begins to draw to an end, and grate-fully, I see the road in front of us that we once travelled over to evade capture. It's much quicker going beneath the grey expanse of the gloomy day. It matches the mood and provides some comfort.

But Cenfrith presses on, and I scoop to gather dry pieces of wood and thin branches and twigs so that when he finally brings an end to our onwards march, I immediately bring forth a flame. I rub my hands over the small spot of heat, Edwin doing the same, while Cenfrith removes Wine's saddle and ensures she has no sores from wearing her saddle once more.

As she's thinner than when we first left Tamworth, he's had to clinch the saddle more tightly closed, but she doesn't seem to mind. She noses the ground, seeking out grasses, while Edwin mournfully pours a handful of oats into a simmering cauldron and stirs them. It won't be a feast.

'We've made good time,' Cenfrith thinks to cheer us. 'Perhaps it'll only take four days.'

'Where are we going?' Edwin tries once more.

'You'll find out when we get there.' Cenfrith offers nothing else.

* * *

'Nearly there,' Cenfrith announces three days later.

I don't look up. The rain has been falling without ceasing since the middle of the previous night. If I raise my head, the cold water will pool down my neck and back, making me even more miserable than I already am.

Even Edwin doesn't speak, although I hear his steps hasten to keep up. We've left the thick tree cover behind us and now walk beside a river that threatens to burst its banks at any moment. Already, water pools to either side of the vast expanse, dark and menacing. My boots are soaked, my feet so cold that I can't feel them, and my nose has done nothing but run all day long.

Despairing doesn't even begin to describe how I feel.

'Hail,' Cenfrith's voice startles me, and involuntarily, I do look up, mouth dropping open in surprise to find we're outside a sturdy-looking wall, a wooden gateway offering the chance of admission.

'What do you want?' The voice is far from friendly, although no face appears.

'My name is Cenfrith, Lord of Budworth. I beg admittance with my nephew and his friend. We are allies of your lord.'

'Where are we?' Edwin hisses to me, but I shake my head. I have no idea. I don't even know which river we followed to get here. Being beneath the trees for so long, I'm entirely turned around.

From behind the gateway, I can hear the squelch of someone walking through puddles and whispered conversation.

The sky has remained uniformly grey. I can't tell how late it is. I can only measure time in my wretchedness.

And then a large wooden gate creaks open, and we're being beckoned inside by a long arm and nothing else. Cenfrith dismounts and quickly leads Wine forwards; Edwin follows, but I stand back, looking at the wooden structure, forehead furrowed in confusion. If we're here, why couldn't we have come here before now? I shake my head, dislodging droplets of water to the ground, only for more to sting my eyes and land in my mouth. It truly is abysmal weather.

Behind the gateway, a settlement quickly comes into view before me. A sizeable wooden hall, with a sloping roof that looks as new as it can beneath the onslaught of rain, a collection of buildings to the far side of it, the sound of horses coming from inside.

The man at the gate slams it shut behind us, leaving us standing there, in the rain.

'Come inside here. Leave your horse there.' He points towards a small building close to the gate, and another one, just behind it.

Cenfrith turns to hand me Wine's rein, and I trek to the indicated place. It's dry inside, and there's enough room for Wine to stand away from the rain, although it's filled with sacks and crates of items. A storeroom, perhaps. I can't see what else it could be.

Quickly, I remove Wine's saddle and reins, hanging them over a handy-looking sack and offering her an apology that there's no food. Her head drops. But there is a bucket, just outside, and sniffing it, I appreciate it's only rainwater and offer it to her. She drinks eagerly and then settles in the small space. Like me, I imagine she's just pleased to be out of the torrent.

From inside the other room, I can hear my uncle talking to the man who's allowed us inside.

'You'll have to wait here until I'm sure you're welcome. It won't take long.' This perplexes me. He's already allowed us entry. Doesn't that mean that we're wanted?

Another voice joins the first, both of them thinking they speak quietly, one to another, but I hear the words easily enough.

'Go and ask Lord Coenwulf what he wants me to do with Cenfrith. Tell him who he is.' The words are heated, filled with trepidation.

Slowly, I run my hand along Wine's long grey nose, forcing the dark coat aside to reveal the white star, taking comfort from her, even though she stinks of damp, wet and sweat. I can't see that I'm much better. I fling my cloak over both shoulders, letting the water pool to the ground, but wait beside Wine. I don't much fancy being in the same room as Edwin right now. He's no doubt furious at finding our welcome less than warm.

I slump to one of the chests, resting my head against Wine's back. Slowly, my eyes close until I'm startled awake by the conversation taking place next door.

'Lord Cenfrith.' The greeting surprises me. Cenfrith doesn't demand the 'lord' part from anyone. I'd almost forgotten he was a lord.

'Lord Coenwulf,' my uncle speaks warily, if respectfully.

The name 'Coenwulf' startles me. It's unusual. I know of no one named it other than Mercia's now dead king.

'Why are you here, of all places?' I can't tell how old the other man is who speaks, perhaps my uncle's age, maybe a little younger.

'It was important we leave Tamworth before the arrival of the Wessex king. We've spent more than half a year living rough or on a hillside, almost in Gwynedd. But those places are no longer safe, and the weather is not our ally.'

'So what? You thought to be received here?'

Silence falls. I can tell the man who speaks is angry but not furious. And he's undoubtedly quizzical.

'It seemed the right choice to make,' Cenfrith offers slowly.

'For who?' Lord Coenwulf retorts too quickly. I can imagine the two men facing one another, perhaps not making eye contact, having to choose their words carefully so as not to offend. I can also imagine Edwin, wide-eyed, head flicking from one to another. He'll be as perplexed as I am.

'For all of us,' Cenfrith rallies.

I hear a heavy sigh.

'Thank you, Oswald. I'll allow the two of them entry.' He must speak to the gate warden.

'My Lord, there are four of them, a youth and a horse,' Oswald offers quickly.

Another aggrieved sigh. 'Then I'll allow all four of them entry. But, Lord Cenfrith, you're not welcome here. Be careful what you say and what you do, and should you say or do the wrong thing, you'll be ejected, whether it's snowing, hailing or a drought bakes the land. You're no friend of mine or of my family. I allow you to stay only because of how much my father once loved you.'

'My thanks for your hospitality,' Cenfrith replies, his words as edged with caution as Lord Coenwulf's.

There's a scrape of boots, and I stand hastily, guilty at falling asleep and eavesdropping, all at the same time.

'Bring the horse,' Oswald states, appearing in the doorway, and quickly, I go to a drowsy Wine and encourage her once more into the rain. We both stand in the doorway, sharing a look of dismay, before rushing to keep up with the fast-moving figure of Oswald, my uncle, and Edwin in his wake. I'm burning with questions but know better than to demand answers.

Instead, I glance through the sheeting rain at the place to which Cenfrith has brought us. The smell of smoke is ripe in the air, carrying with it the scent of cooking food, perhaps some pork and a heavy dose of garlic and onions, I can't quite tell. Smoke escapes the roof of all the buildings, but it lies flat, seeming to cling to thatch as the rain pushes it downwards, almost making me cough.

'In there,' Oswald instructs me, and I lead Wine into a large stable complex, the curious eyes of about twenty or thirty horses watching me as I guide her to an empty box. Here, there's plentiful hay, and she begins to chew contentedly. Only then do I realise I've left her saddle behind. My heart sinks at having to go out in the rain once more.

'Hurry up, Icel,' my uncle calls from the door, and I rush to catch up with him, eager to admit my mistake, but the words die on my lips as we're escorted to the large hall. Above the door, there's a representation of a bird. I can tell from the hooked beak that's what it is, but what startles me more is that it looks so similar to the creatures depicted on the shields in the king's hall at Tamworth.

I look to Edwin. He's seen the same as me, and his fierce eyes greet me, mouth open in shock.

'Welcome to Kingsholm,' Oswald states with a flourish, gaining us admittance into the great hall.

I gasp. Inside, away from the rain, this place is as richly decorated as the king's hall at Tamworth. There are just as many, if not more, shields hanging from the rafters, and here they're not dirty or dusty, but brightly painted as though new, for all they can't be, not with the seax and sword marks that mar them.

I sneak closer to Edwin, careful to avoid my uncle's gaze as he sweeps his head round the vast space, noticing the long tables, the stools filled with men and women, the huge cauldron suspended over the enormous hearth that burns blue at the centre of the hall.

'Why are we at the home of King Coelwulf, first of his name?' I demand to know, working out where we are, finally. The name of the lord my uncle spoke to should really have made me realise before now.

Of course, Edwin has no answers. Nor do I, and I'm not about to ask Cenfrith. He doesn't smile. He doesn't look pleased, but at least we're warm and will be dry soon enough.

'I'll be back soon,' I mutter to Edwin.

He doesn't seem to heed my words.

With a heavy heart, I rush out into the rain, retrieving the mislaid saddle from the wooden building close to the gate. It gets wet and so I'm forced to use straw from the floor to swipe the rain from it. Wine watches me between mouthfuls, and I reach across to stroke her long nose, the white star there catching my eye now that she's no longer drenched from the rain. She breathes warm air onto my face and I grin at her.

'It's better here, isn't it?' I say to her, before hastening back to the great hall, where Edwin and my uncle have made themselves comfortable before the hearth, bowls of meaty pottage empty in front of them. I look round hopefully, and a young lad rushes to bring me the same. I eat it quickly, relishing the heat.

That night, we sleep before the hearth, warmer than we've been for many months, and during the night, I hear a conversation between my uncle and a man I assume to be Lord Coenwulf. I recognise the voice from beside the gate.

'You have no right to be here, but for the love my father once showed you before you were implicated in his usurpation, I couldn't turn you away.'

'Then you have my sincere thanks, and how is King Coelwulf, first of his name?' Cenfrith sounds humble as he speaks to Lord Coenwulf.

'Dead, during the winter. He was frail, and news of King Ecgberht's success only made him weaker. Do you know the Wessex bastard has taken the submission of the Northumbrians? I never believed King Eanred would allow it.' A soft fury floods those words. I can understand why.

'It was poorly done,' Cenfrith admits, I think referring to King

Coelwulf's usurpation, the words heartfelt and met with a bitter laugh.

'Poorly done? King Coelwulf was your anointed and God-given king. He was a great victor, against the kingdom of Gwynedd, against the kingdom of Wessex. See how well King Beornwulf has done now? See how well his successor has done, oh, and then another successor, as well. My father lost no kingdom. And he lived.' The words drip with condescension.

'And yet you stay hidden here?' It seems my uncle isn't going to apologise any further.

'I don't have the support or the inclination to rule. My sister would, perhaps, but not me. My father knew that. I believe it's one of the reasons he accepted King Beornwulf could take what was rightfully his without further bloodshed.'

The conversation lulls, and I strain to hear, not wanting to miss anything.

'Was it worth it?' Lord Coenwulf eventually asks, resentment in his words.

I think Cenfrith will hold his tongue, say nothing further. But he surprises me.

'I think you know the answer to that, My Lord.' I've never heard my uncle speak with such vehemence, and I squeeze my eyes tightly shut, hoping not to be seen.

'You can stay until the weather changes, and no longer. And stay away from my sisters, including the younger one. I won't have them tainted with your treachery.'

'My thanks, old friend.' But the only response Cenfrith gets is the sound of steps walking away on the hard wooden floor.

My mind tumbles, trying to unpick the conversation I've heard. One thing is sure; we're not welcome here, and yet here we are at the home of King Coelwulf, and his son has provided my uncle, Edwin and I with shelter from the weather, for now at least. It doesn't make any sense, and yet, I'm too grateful to question it further.

* * *

The following day, I wake, unsure what to do with myself. There's no sign of my uncle, while Edwin is busy filling his belly with a steaming bowl of sweetened pottage. Already, he's made an ally of another lad, about our age, and they chat together. I catch the tail end of their words and realise Edwin is bragging about the man he killed on the hillside, while the other lad watches him, eyes wide with horrified delight.

I stagger outside. It's still dismal, but the rain has stopped. Not that it makes it easy to see. A fug of smoke continues to obscure the settlement. I turn to where the stables are, thinking to check on Wine, only to spy my uncle scurrying away from the buildings.

Ignoring my hunger, I follow him. There's more mystery here, and I don't understand it. None of it. But perhaps I can find some truths if I just follow him.

A few others rush about their tasks, but mostly, I hear voices from beneath the roofs of the buildings. There are more of them than I realised last night.

I keep my head down, focused on avoiding the worst of the puddles; some of them would reach my ankles, not just my toes.

When I do look up, I startle and stop. Before me, a church has appeared, the carved cross over the door indicating what it is. I watch as my uncle enters through the small wooden door. I don't know what to do now. If I follow Cenfrith, he'll see me. But my curiosity wars inside me. I hesitate, and as I do so, another person appears.

She looks up from beneath her cloak, a bemused expression on her delicate face.

'Who are you?' she asks, standing directly in front of me. I'm surprised she's forced to look upwards to meet my eyes momentarily forgetting how much I had grown.

'I'm Icel. I arrived last night.'

She still looks on me through slit eyes, biting her lip. And then recognition flashes.

'Ah, you came with Lord Cenfrith.'

'I did, yes.' There's no point denying it.

'I'm surprised my brother made him welcome, but then, he has a gentle heart, for all he's angry much of the time.'

'You're Lord Coenwulf's sister?'

'Yes, I am. I'm Ælflæd.'

I don't know how to respond to that. She speaks with confidence, and yet I'm standing here with soggy boots.

'Were you going into the church? I think the monks are in there at the moment. But I'm sure you can listen to their service.'

'Um,' I feel flustered, not wanting to admit that I was sneaking after my uncle.

'Or were you going somewhere else?'

My mouth opens and then closes. I have no idea what to say.

She watches me, a smile on her lips, wavering as I stay mute. My saviour comes from an unlikely source.

'Ælflæd, your brother wants you.' It's Oswald who calls across the saturated ground. The noise startles me, and Ælflæd pretends not to notice.

'Bye,' she calls, picking up her skirts to run towards the hall.

I shudder at my ineptitude, only to see my uncle exiting the church and proceeding to the rear of the building with purpose. Quickly, I move to follow him; a sliver of an idea forming in my mind, which is confirmed when he enters the enclosed graveyard, old oak trees standing as guards to the four corners of it, with a stone wall joining them together.

I don't know who my uncle came here to mourn, but I imagine I have a good idea that he goes to make his peace with the dead King Coelwulf, the first of his name, a man, it seems, he willingly betrayed. I always knew my uncle had many secrets, but now it seems he has even more than I could imagine.

I retrace my steps, not wanting to witness my uncle's weakness, pausing at the church door to listen to the words spoken by one of the monks, or perhaps the abbot, the Latin a gabbled sound I don't understand but which is familiar all the same. Then I take myself to the stables to tend to Wine.

I might find the walls of Kingsholm pleasant, offering me the security I've missed from Tamworth, but I can't see we'll be here for long. And then where will we go?

15

I'm restless. Inside these walls, where everything is provided for me, there's nothing for me to do. I'm surprised that I miss the constant foraging for food that's categorised so much of my time since leaving Tamworth. Edwin has found his way to the warriors, and he and Cenfrith spend each cold day sweating in the training ground, returning to the hall only to eat, drink and sleep.

I'm lonely and bored, restive as well. What am I to do? In Tamworth, Wynflæd kept me busy every day, sending me on expeditions to find the supplies she needed, rain or sun, snow or frost. I even had to dig out old roots from ground so frozen it made my fingers bleed just to paw through it. I would seek out the herb woman here, but I know there's no such thing.

No, inside Kingsholm, the monks hold sway. They have an infirmary where they treat the sick: a rich herb bed filled with all they might need and a beehive they can take all the honey from they want.

I'm not even allowed beyond the confines of the walls alone. Oswald won't permit it, and nor will the others. I can't even use exercising Wine as an excuse because she's comfortable inside the stables and has so far refused all attempts to get her to leave. The other horses aren't forced to exercise either.

I find myself wandering round, listening to the sounds of others inside buildings, busy about their tasks, shivering inside my cloak. I almost wish I could sit by the hearth, with the older men and women, eager for the heat to infiltrate their bones. The women busy their hands, enjoying the warmth on joints grown tight and unyielding, spinning wool, while the men work on weapons that they might never use again. The smell of grease and fat fills the air.

And then I hear a sound from inside the stables that's entirely out of place. A soft sob, quickly stifled, and my feet take me inside, half an eye to Wine, but she must sleep or lie down because her inquisitive head doesn't respond to my footfall. I don't see the sleek greyness of her long nose, crowned by the white star.

The smell of hay and horse sweat assaults my nostrils, but at least it's cleaner than the main hall. I don't speak but instead follow the sound of a horse worrying at something.

There are others inside the stable. I can hear two querulous voices coming from the far corner of the building, the renewed sound of rain drumming on the thatch, but it's not them that concerns me.

I spy Ælflæd. There are tears in the corner of her eyes and streaming down her face, and she cradles the head of a sleek brown horse, only a little taller than she is, and the animal eyes her sadly.

I think I step quietly, but she startles and glares at me, cuffing the tears from her pale cheeks. She looks cold, her cloak hanging over the stable door, her hands almost blue. Her long blonde hair is in disarray, and there's a piece of hay behind her left ear.

'What are you doing here?' her voice is harsher than last time we spoke, no doubt upset at being caught crying.

'Sorry, My Lady,' and I bow quickly, thinking to move away.

'Why are you here?' she presses, the confidence back in her voice, even as she strokes her horse's neck.

'I heard crying. I was concerned.'

'Oh, and what did you think to do? Offer comfort?'

'I meant to find out if I could help,' I find it easier to speak to her here than when we first met. That relieves me.

'Well, you can't. You won't know anything about horses or how to treat my poor Sewenna. See, she has a cut on her lip, and the stableman has assured me he'll tend to it, but he's too concerned with another horse. It's been three days now, and I fear it will fester if not seen to soon. And I don't know what to do.' The final words seem to be filled with shame.

'Here, let me see,' I offer.

'Why? What can you do?'

As I move towards the stable door, she scurries backwards, taking her horse with her. That surprises me, but, of course, how would she know?

'I have some experience of healing. I was being taught, by the healer, at Tamworth, before King Ecgberht took it as his own.'

I see the surprise in the way her mouth hangs open.

'Then you better come and see,' Ælflæd quickly recovers. 'See, she's cut it, no doubt on the stable door or something. She doesn't like being cooped up in here, even though I tell her it's cold outside and she wouldn't like it there either.'

I eye the wound. It's not a long cut, but it's jagged, and I imagine that the horse has pulled it on a piece of a harness or perhaps the stray nail that holds the hay bale in place. It's pink and red, a little inflamed, but not worth crying over. Well, I don't think it is, but then, I would know how to treat it.

'Have you bathed it with warm, salted water?' I ask, my hands probing round the site, keen to see if there's any wound rot, but there isn't.

'No, should I have done that?' she asks uncertainly.

'Yes, any wound, animal or human, needs to be bathed and cleaned. We could add a poultice to it and apply some honey to promote healing. It wouldn't take long. But I suggest you get the stableman to remove that nail or drive it in more deeply.' I point to the offending nail. A sliver of blood can be seen glinting on it.

'Oh. Is that how Sewenna did it?' A thin edge of fury enters her voice. 'I will tell my brother,' she offers heatedly. 'Only, well, he won't care because the stableman is too busy with my father's horse, and he cares of nothing else at the moment. They say,' and here she speaks in a whisper, 'that the horse will not survive. It's not relieved itself for two days now.'

'Is that what they're doing over there?' I ask, pointing to the sound of the argument that's becoming more heated.

'Yes, but here, hold her, and I'll go and get some water, and some honey, did you say?'

'Yes, but I can get it if you want to stay here.'

But she's already flinging her cloak on and scurrying away.

'No,' she calls over her shoulder, 'the monks won't give you honey, but they can't say no to me.' And she's gone. I can hear her running across the muddy expanse towards the workshop of Lord Coenwulf's cooks.

I turn to the horse. Sewenna eyes me intelligently, and I run my hand over the rest of her body. I don't know a great deal about horses, but I think to check, she has no other wounds. I would do the same with Wine, and I've watched my uncle do it on many occasions.

Ælflæd returns quickly, a deep bowl in one hand, rags in another. 'Here, take these and I'll return with the honey.'

'I need your help,' I find myself announcing without realising I was going to say as such. 'You need to hold her head as still as you can. She's not going to like it.'

'Oh, of course.'

We change places, and quickly, I rip a rag, dip it in the water.

'It's scorching,' but Ælflæd's caution is too late. I wince at the bite of the heat and the salt into my fingers.

'It's fine.' I can feel the burn along my hand. It's unpleasant and yet lovely, all at the same time. It feels good to be so warm, even if it's only on one part of my body. 'I'll just wait a moment, though, before I clean the wound.'

When I deem enough time has passed, I quickly move to the thin cut on the left side of the horse's mouth. Ælflæd talks to Sewenna as though to distract her, but when I press the heat to the wound, the horse doesn't even stir. An interesting observation, I note. Wynflæd has assured me that horses feel pain differently from a man or woman. Perhaps she's right to say so.

Quickly, I clean the dirty wound, moving aside stray pieces of hay and oats stuck in there so that all I'm left with is a pink wound, gleaming from the heat of the injury and smelling much cleaner.

'I could attempt to stitch it shut,' I offer, eyeing it carefully. 'But I don't think it's truly long enough to need it.' I've not noticed that Ælflæd has moved round her horse's head and now watches me intently. 'What do you think?'

'I think you should do what you believe is right,' she replies slowly, her eyes focused only on the wound. 'It looks better already,' she admits with surprise.

'It's not as bad as it appeared,' I confirm. 'Not at all. The honey will keep the wound rot away, but I can't apply a bandage here, so we'll have to keep applying it until it heals enough that it's not needed any more.'

'Shall I get the honey now?' she asks, all traces of the upset young woman gone from her face. I can't even tell that she's been crying.

'Yes, please. A small pot and something to apply it with, a spoon or something, or we'll end up sticking to the hay and everything else as well.'

Ælflæd scoops to pick up the bowl and leaves me once more.

I stroke the horse's neck, but she doesn't need any reassurance. Instead, she stands still, as though aware I'm here to help her. From the far corner, I can now hear low rumblings and think I recognise the voice of Lord Coenwulf. I'm surprised he's in the stables, but then I recall Ælflæd's words. Quickly, I leave the stable and make my way to the group.

There are four men, Lord Coenwulf amongst them, and a tall horse, black from head to the tail with a sprinkling of grey around the eyes and the nose. I can hear the animal's heavy breathing and appreciate that it is in great distress.

Closer up, I realise that Lord Coenwulf isn't inside the stable and that another stands beside him, while two men inside the stable are sweating and breathing just as heavily as the horse.

I can see the animal's chest puffing, and I listen carefully to what's being said.

'You must save him. He was my father's horse. A king's horse.' An uneasy silence falls.

'It can't be done, My Lord. The animal is in too much pain. Two days, nearly three, since he last emptied himself. And he's not eating either.'

Again, I don't know a great deal about horses, but I agree with the man who speaks to Lord Coenwulf, his head entirely bald, his eyebrows black, heavy things hanging over eyes that are deeply recessed in a lined face.

'I've tended to him all these years, and I've never seen this before. Did you approach the monks? They might have some knowledge I don't possess.' There's no hope in the request.

'Brother Fassel told me that the great scholars didn't concern themselves with keeping a horse alive and just to end the animal's suffering.'

'Then there's nothing to be done. I've tried everything I know to assist the beast.'

'Have you tried a garlic purge?' I interject, noting the discharge around the animal's nose. It seems to me the animal has been ill for some time.

'What?' It's the stableman who asks; his black eyes fixed on me.

'A garlic purge. It should ease the suffering...' I suddenly quail under the furious gaze of four sets of eyes.

I don't know the man's name who stands beside Lord Coenwulf, but I know he sits beside him at mealtimes. Perhaps his clerk, or some such. An estate such as this would need a man who could keep excellent records.

'Well, have you, Hatel?' Lord Coenwulf demands to know. There's desperation in his voice.

'No, I've never heard of that or tried it?' Hatel announces slowly, seeming to consider my suggestion carefully.

'It works with people,' the clerk interjects, as though that will convince the others, and I feel I owe him my thanks.

'How would you know this?' Lord Coenwulf demands.

Unknown to me, Ælflæd has returned, a small, sealed pot in her hand.

'He knows about herbs and healing,' she interjects. 'He's helping me with Sewenna. The wound already looks better.' Her words ring with conviction that I'm not sure I deserve. Not yet.

Hatel looks uncomfortable at the reminder of the task left undone, but Lord Coenwulf doesn't notice it.

'Try it, and aid my man,' he informs me, licking his lips as he does so. 'But if it doesn't work, I'll hold you entirely responsible.'

I nod, holding my stance in the face of his evident fury at having to take advice from me. Perhaps I shouldn't have spoken my thoughts aloud?

'It should ease the animal's discomfort,' I confirm, determined not to be held responsible for everything. 'But the rest of the symptoms, his heavy breathing and ragged coat, they're not a new occurrence,' I announce, as though I'm an expert on such things.

A sudden silence falls, and I think Lord Coenwulf might well punch me, his hand clenching and unclenching, but instead he turns aside.

'Do as he suggests, and have him assist you. I'll make my own decisions on whether it works or not.'

With that, Lord Coenwulf flings his cloak tightly round him, pulling the hood over his head, and the clerk hurries to catch him.

'Ælflæd,' Lord Coenwulf pauses at the doorway, 'I expect to see you in the women's hall in good time and not here, tending to an animal who should be cared for by the stableboys.' And then he's gone, and we all listen to his wet footsteps before any of us speak again.

Ælflæd breaks the silence. 'I've got the honey,' she crows triumphantly.

Hatel speaks next. 'What else, other than garlic? And where will I get garlic from?'

'The monks have some,' I inform him quickly. 'In their herb garden. I've seen it growing there, or I can find some if Oswald lets me leave the compound.'

Hatel's lips settle into an uneasy line. 'I don't like either of those suggestions,' he admits, even as he makes to leave the stable, leaving the poor horse alone.

The horse quickly makes his way to the ground, chest heaving, and I wince to see him in such a state.

'How long has he been like this?' I think to ask the other stablehand, a younger man than Hatel.

'All winter. He's old. Near enough thirty winters to his name. But Lord Coenwulf has lost his father and doesn't mean to lose his horse as well.' The man's voice is filled with remorse.

I nod, unsure what else to say. I can't see the purge will entirely cure the animal, but it's not for me to say.

'I'll ask the monks for the garlic,' Ælflæd offers. 'They won't mind helping me. And you,' and she turns to me, 'can finish treating Sewenna.'

I take the jar, noting its weight and considering just how much the pot would be worth if it were to be sold. It seems that Ælflæd values her young horse just as much as her much older brother values their father's horse.

When she returns with the garlic, I've left Sewenna trying to lick her cut and with a caution that it should be left well alone. I can't see that the animal will do as I've requested, no matter how firmly I cautioned her.

I find Hatel, and his fellow stableman, discussing the contents of the purge for Ansfith. At least, I assume Ansfith is the horse. I don't know the other man's name. He looks similar to Hatel, although with a little more hair. Yet, I don't think they're brothers or even uncle and nephew. Perhaps they're cousins or not related at all.

'What do you suggest?' I expect resentment in Hatel's words, but there's none. It seems he's desperate for some assistance.

'Do you normally use purges?' I'm not entirely sure. For a man or woman with the same problem, Wynflæd would boil wormwood with sour ale and then add the garlic before making them drink it. I've seen the effects. They can be quite immediate.

'Yes, to remove worms. But I've not added garlic before.'

'Then I would suggest the same remedy, with the garlic added to it. Not too much to begin. Should it start to work, or not work at all, then we can reassess the quantity of garlic.'

'I'll fetch what we have,' the younger man offers.

Left alone with Hatel, he eyes me warily.

'You were brave to speak before Lord Coenwulf. If this doesn't work, I would be wary. Your uncle might not be best pleased that you've placed your continued stay here on the health of such an old animal.'

I swallow heavily then. I'd not honestly considered that.

Hatel chuckles darkly. 'Aye, boy. Sometimes, it's better to think before opening your mouth. A valuable lesson, and one I hope you don't learn in the next few days. It's perishingly cold out there at this time of year. And, as I understand it, you don't have anywhere else to go. At least these walls protect us from King Ecgberht of Wessex.' He turns aside and spits into the hay. 'He can send as many men to speak to Lord Coenwulf as he wants, asking for his submission, but provided Coenwulf does nothing to upset him; we're safe enough.'

I nod, words beyond me. I find it strange that Ælflæd doesn't attempt to defend her brother from the criticism, and that Hatel speaks so openly before her. She stands with a handful of garlic leaves, still dripping from where they've been cut from the plant. Am I the only person not to appreciate the seriousness of what I've done?

'I need somewhere to chop the garlic into small pieces.' I shake myself, seeking my confidence once more. I can just imagine Edwin's face should we be put out because I can't make the lord's horse shit. I daren't consider Cenfrith's response.

'Through there,' and Hatel points into what I think is just another stable but, I discover, is filled with the stableman's tools. There are wooden buckets for fetching water, more of them than I'd think necessary even for a hundred horses, stacked precariously against the far wall. There are also odd bits of equipment, pieces of leather, and metal tools that must be used for treating problems with teeth and hooves. I've heard Edwin complain often enough to know that horses suffer from all sorts of ailments.

There's also a random collection of brooms, shovels and saddles, but a small table sits in the middle of the room, its legs odd, canting to the left side, but it's clean. I can smell the stink of herbs used to clean it from where I stand.

I remove my knife and begin to chop the leaves and roots. Ælflæd has gathered a massive bunch of the stuff. I can't see that I'll need it all. She hovers at my side, watching me. I would tell her to move aside, but she's not doing anything wrong.

'I didn't know how much you needed,' she offers, watching me cut only a tiny portion of it.

'Me neither. He's a big horse.'

'Ansfith was my father's pride and joy. That horse took him everywhere.' There's a sadness in her words, and I'd ask her for more information, but I can't think how to word all of my questions. I'm amazed I've been able to hold as much of a conversation as I have considering my inability when we first met.

'Pega,' Ælflæd acknowledges the other man when he appears with a jar that smells disgusting. I immediately know what it is.

Holding my nose, I peer into the jar, surprised by the quantity of the purge. 'All of that?' I ask.

'Aye, the beasts need a great deal to aid them with their worms.'

I swallow around my disgust and begin to add in the small pieces of cut garlic.

'Stir it for me.'

And Pega does, using a long wooden spoon. I turn back to the pile of leaves and begin to cut more.

'Perhaps you didn't bring too much, after all,' I admit.

Ælflæd nods as though expecting the words, but there's a light in her eyes, and I think she's pleased with the compliment.

When I'm satisfied, I leave it to Pega and Hatel to administer the purge, hoping it will work. Ælflæd and I return to Sewenna. She meets us eagerly, and I grin. Some of the honey still smears her wound, and already it looks much, much better.

'You just need to leave her to heal,' I advise, once more relying on something I've heard Edwin say. Horses, he maintains, will heal themselves from most things given enough rest.

'You have my thanks for helping me,' Ælflæd offers formally, and I take that as dismissal.

As I leave the stables, I hear the sound of the two men struggling with Ansfith, and I spare a thought for them, finding it easier to shoulder their burdens than mine.

16

Throughout the next two days, I continue to tend to Sewenna, satisfied when her cut heals quickly, leaving nothing but a rough piece
of skin to show there was ever a wound. Ælflæd is pleased with me
too, while Hatel and Pega are more circumspect.

I eye the old horse, hanging my head over the stable door.
Ansfith still lies on his side, but his sides don't heave as much as
they did. Not content with just the one purge, Hatel has given the
horse two of them, yet nothing seems to work.

I stare at him regretfully. I don't know enough about horses and
their problems. In all honesty, I would expect Hatel and Pega to
know far more than I do. Perhaps, as Hatel advised me, Ansfith is
merely old. Maybe he even misses his master.

No one has spoken of the deposed King Coelwulf and his recent
death, and yet his presence hovers everywhere. There's the
reminder of who he was in the shields in the great hall. There's his
byrnie in the weapons store, and in the stables, his horse lingers on,
old and tired.

Abruptly, the great black horse surges to his feet. I turn, startled,
wishing I wasn't alone in the stables. Hatel has taken another of the

good mounts out riding round the complex, while Pega is busy lugging buckets of water to and from the nearby river. I've offered to help him, but he's bid me watch the horse instead.

And then, black tail raised, the most lurid green stream of horse shit I've ever witnessed in my life cascades from the animal's backside. The smell is so intense, I gag, forced to turn aside as the stench wafts and steams on the floor of the stable.

At the end of it, Ansfith watches me, and I almost think there's a look of relief in the drawing back of his lips to show me his teeth when I once more look at him.

Immediately, Pega is beside me, wafting his hand from side to side as though to dispel the smell with such a feeble movement.

'Good God,' he explodes, looking from me to Ansfith, a grin on his tight lips. 'It bloody worked,' he exclaims, moving aside and then returning with a shovel in one hand. 'I best clean this up,' Pega continues. And I swear, I've never seen a man so pleased to shovel shit.

'I'll help you,' I offer, but he shakes his head.

'No, lad, no. You've done more than enough. The old rogue won't take kindly to you in his stall. I'll do it. You can go and see to Sewenna.'

I bite back the retort that Sewenna is fine and find myself at a loss of how to keep myself occupied. Doing something that helped the horses gave me a reason to leave the smoky hall each day.

Outside, the sky is dull and overcast, and yet I can hear the cries of the warriors practising. Feeling strangely lethargic rather than pleased that my suggestion aided the black horse, I kick my way through the puddles and stand beneath the eaves of the women's hall, watching the men at work.

There are no more than sixteen of them. I would expect a lord such as Coenwulf to have more, but it seems not. Edwin stands amongst them all, while Cenfrith is to one side. He speaks with someone who shelters beneath a large black cloak, brown fur rimmed round the cuffs and hood. Whoever it is, they're wealthy and unknown to me.

Edwin catches my eye as he wrestles with a shield that's almost bigger than him. All the same, he holds his own well enough, and I find a tight smile on my lips. Edwin has finally found people who will train him to be the warrior he dreams of being. While I've lost my teacher, he's found his.

I feel a twinge of jealousy and stamp away, seeking shelter in the main hall, eyeing the shields that hang all around me. I will never be a warrior. I will never own such a trophy. I can't say that it worries me.

'Where is he?' I hear the roared words as I stagger towards the stables. In place of having nothing to do, I've found small jobs to distract me from our current predicament. Today, it's lugging water from the riverbank to the workshop inside which the cook beavers away. I have no idea why she needs so much water, but I'm just happy to have something to do.

I recognise the outraged tone of Lord Coenwulf and know a moment of fear. He's ill-tempered much of the time, but I can't be the object of his outrage. Ansfith has been well these past three weeks or so, coat brightening every day. I didn't expect Lord Coenwulf to thank me for aiding his father's ailing horse, and yet I didn't expect to be entirely ignored either.

A scurrying of steps and Ælflæd is before me, breathing heavily.

'Icel, you must hide away from my brother.'

'Why?' I ask, suddenly cold. It seems Lord Coenwulf does mean me after all.

'Ansfith, he died during the night. It wasn't your fault, not at all, but my brother won't hear reason. I fear what will happen if he finds you.'

I feel my mouth drop open in shock, even as I know a moment of sorrow for old Ansfith. He might have felt better these last few weeks, but Hatel warned me of continuing lethargy. It seemed the stableman was aware that the horse's time was limited. Not so, Lord Coenwulf.

But for all Ælflæd's warnings, I turn and deliver the water before making my way towards the stables. I'm not alone in seeking out the cause of the problems. Even as Ælflæd tugs at my arm, urging me away, I head to meet my fate.

I see Edwin in the crowd, eyes wide as he speaks to the youth beside him. He shakes his head on seeing me, and I think I should probably take the advice of him and Ælflæd. Still I don't. Surely, Lord Coenwulf will listen to reason.

'Ah, there you are, you bastard. You killed my father's horse.' His words ricochet round the enclosed space, echoing in the dampness of another drab day. The sky seems to touch the ground, leaving in its wake more and more water.

'My Lord, I assure you, I did no such thing.'

Lord Coenwulf's face is purple, and spittle follows the words he directs at me. I can't believe I speak to contradict him, and yet, I can't allow this. I helped his horse. I did what little I could. 'Then why, you little shit, is he lying cold and on his side?'

Behind Lord Coenwulf, I can see Hatel's sorrowful face, hands wringing, one inside the other, but he shakes his head as well, cautioning me. But no, Lord Coenwulf threatened me and my uncle, should Ansfith die. I can't have it.

'The horse was old. He'd been in ill health for a long time,' I try to reason with him.

'He wasn't old. And he was my father's horse.' The words are a shriek of outrage. 'If he were a man, you'd pay wergild for him, but he was a horse, and they have no such price attached to them, even as noble as he was. You, and your uncle and your friend, will leave here. You're no longer welcome and never were.'

With that, Lord Coenwulf strides towards me, and before I can dodge out of the way, his hand slaps my icy cheeks, and pain shoots up my nose. I stagger backwards, landing in a deep puddle, the coldness of the water seeping into my trews. My head rings, and before me, there seems to be more than one of Lord Coenwulf.

'You'll be gone with the sunrise. I'll not change my mind.'

Only my uncle steps from the crowd of those who've gathered to watch my humiliation.

'My Lord,' Cenfrith speaks respectfully, but I see the grimace on Coenwulf's face.

'What? You think to barter for yourself? After everything your family has done to mine?' It's almost a shriek.

'No, My Lord, I do not. I would merely ask you to keep the other boy, Edwin. He's no nephew of mine. He can stay here, train with your warriors, become one of your oath-sworn men.'

I can't believe what my uncle is asking. I can't even look to Edwin.

I think Lord Coenwulf will refuse the offer. I think Edwin will demand to stay by me side, but both are remarkably silent.

Finally, Lord Coenwulf speaks. 'Yes, the boy can stay. He's becoming a fine warrior. He'll be warm and sheltered inside these walls, and if King Ecgberht should think to look this way, he can fight for my family.' There's a harshness to the words, and dread fills me.

Yet my uncle bows his head, acknowledging the acceptance of his request, and still Edwin doesn't speak.

Lord Coenwulf rushes away, and I'm not the only one to watch him as he heads towards the church.

A firm hand reaches down to me, and I grip it, surging to my feet, bending to vomit as my stomach churns from the movement.

'You did your best,' Cenfrith offers me, but his words are edged with resignation. It seems that I've once again ensured we have no roof over our heads.

I spit aside the taste of vomit and blood, wishing I could dispute his words.

I seek out Ælflæd in the crowd, and she grins sadly before veering aside. Edwin won't even meet my eyes. His betrayal leaves a bitter taste in my mouth, as he too turns away, walking beside the young men with whom he trains.

Hatel claps me on the back, and I stagger while my uncle holds me upright.

'You gave that horse a better last few weeks than could be expected. At least he went quickly, in the end. One day, Lord Coenwulf will realise that. He's not truly a cruel man. Just one who's grieving.'

I nod and then regret it as a wave of nausea hits me. I appreciate Hatel's words even as I realise that whatever Lord Coenwulf's grief might be, I'm being punished for my uncle's part in taking the royal crown of Mercia from his father. And, as part of that punishment, I've lost my only friend. If he even is still my friend.

17

It's the noise that wakes me. Or rather, the lack of it. Where before there'd been the chattering of small animals and the calls of the birds, there's suddenly nothing. It's very different to when we lived at Kingsholm for those few short weeks. Now, I sleep beneath the sky, and with the beasts and the birds. Just like last summer.

Startled, I stagger upright, peering into the grey gloom I'm surrounded in, some of it shadowed by the trees and bushes that hide our current campsite. Something isn't right. I'm sure of it.

Quietly, I slither my way to where my uncle sleeps close to the hearth of stones I built; hand outstretched to touch his arm. His huge hand clasps mine, the strength in it enough to assure me that he hears and knows that something's very, very wrong.

Cenfrith doesn't speak to me, but I can feel him reaching for his seax on his weapons belt. When he releases my hand, he quests for where the shield lies abandoned on the summer-baked hard ground.

Our small shelter, cut into the spongy hill of the woodland floor, provides a roof, and some respite from the wind when it blows, but little else. I hope that we'll stay hidden even as I realise that won't happen.

I hear the sound of voices, men thinking they talk quietly and yet whose voices ring through the early summer's day. I don't understand their words, and I turn to meet my uncle's resigned brown eyes.

There are Raiders here, in our special place, and their intentions can't be good.

Laughter ripples through the air, and there's something in it that makes me believe it's given by one man ridiculing another. I recognise it from when Mercia's warriors used to mock one another in Tamworth.

Cenfrith is standing, eyes peering into the treeline in front of us, his head half turned as he listens. There are only the two of us now. Edwin left behind at Kingsholm. Cenfrith argued it was less likely we'd be found if there were just the two of us, when I demanded to know why he made such a request of Lord Coenwulf. 'If we're being hunted by the Wessex warriors, they'll be seeking a man and two youths, not one man and one youth.'

Equally, Edwin argued much less than he should have done. I've not forgiven him for that. I might not.

Foreboding holds me steady, as I think to join my uncle. It sounds as though there are any number of Raiders out there, and there are only three of us, if you count Wine, but two if you exclude me. I've never fought with blade and shield. I've never wanted to do so. I don't even have a shield.

I feel as though I'm being watched and imagine the Raiders can see me, although it's my uncle, urging me on with his hand to get to his side. I take a step towards him, wanting to feel safe behind his broad back, only the thick branches no more than three horse lengths in front of us rustle, and from their midst, an unmistakable booted foot appears, the leather well-worn.

Above the foot comes more of a leg, then half of a man, and then all of a man. I imagine they've smelt our fire, for all it's little but ash now.

The Raider grins; he can't be anything else with his dark hair tightly braided as it is, pulled back from his broad forehead, inkings pouring down his exposed arm, a silver arm ring settled on his upper left arm. Even if I'd not heard him speak, I'd have known him for what he is.

I can't believe that we've managed to evade the Wessex warriors of King Ecgberht but have been found by these deadly strangers.

The Raider keeps his eyes on me, even as he languidly calls over his shoulder. I don't need to understand the words to decipher the intent. There's more than just the one man.

The Raider has black hair, a black beard and an even blacker byrnie held tightly over his tunic and trews. I note the shimmering weapons, the seax and war axe, on his weapons belt, even as I realise he has no shield.

'Icel,' my uncle bellows, all pretence of silence forgotten. The words sound strong, but I detect the undulation in his voice. My uncle is terrified. He's not alone in that.

With more rustling branches, three more Raiders appear, all of them tall men, with muscles showing on their upper arms and a collection of cords hung round their necks, although I can't see what ornaments hang there. No doubt they'll be part of their religion, perhaps their god, Thor's hammer, or something similar. I've never actually seen them, but the scops tell such stories. Wynflæd says they do it to scare us all to our prayers. She says they're little more than trinkets, such as the holy men wear their wooden crosses round their necks.

The three men grin, calling one to another, and I swallow down the vomit that pools in my mouth. I'm going to die here. I just know it. These are men who mean to kill us and steal what small treasures we have. And we have treasures for men who have no shields or horses, even if they must share the spoils.

And then a further man appears. This one is squat, bright red hair spilling down his shoulders in running curls. I startle to see him because he looks like no Raider I've ever heard about in the past. The scops always say the Raiders are blonde-haired, powerful, lethal. Not all the men I've seen here fit that image. In his hand, the red-haired warrior carries a large war axe, the handle shining in the growing light, the axe head heavy-looking and menacing. And bloody sharp.

'Icel,' the snapped command and I'm next to my uncle. I know to obey him, and it's too inbuilt not to do it now.

Gasping for air, I sidle closer to Wine, as my uncle pushes me away from him, giving him room to prepare for what's about to happen. I wish I didn't feel so useless. But I trust my uncle. He's always protected me, and now I hope he'll do the same, even if he's vastly outnumbered.

The red-haired man looks to my uncle, lips curled, eyes narrowed, as he quickly assesses his chances against a warrior of Mercia.

The Raider opens his mouth to speak, a string of words that make no sense to me, but my uncle tenses. He must know what they say. Yet, my uncle must lack the words to reply, for he merely shakes his head, denying whatever the request was.

Even as the other four look on, the red-haired man rushes my uncle. His squat legs cover the distance between them far too quickly.

'Uncle.' The single word echoes with terror. I hate myself for showing such weakness. I reach for my belt, aware a seax rests there, beside my sharp knife, given to me by my uncle when we left

Kingsholm even if I don't know how to use it. But my hand is slick, and I lose control of it so that it thuds into the ground, only just missing my right foot.

I move to retrieve it, but my eyes are riveted on my uncle, and I'm frozen in place.

I know he's a great warrior, but I've never seen Cenfrith in combat. The men from the Welsh kingdom who found us on the hillside were all killed while I was hidden inside the shelter. I wish I could hide away again.

The red-haired man thinks my uncle an easy target, but when Cenfrith stands to face him, he becomes otherworldly. I gasp in both surprise and horror.

Cenfrith's leather byrnie moves with his body, not as bulky as some I've seen, and certainly made just for him. Not for Cenfrith the use of a dead man's byrnie. He holds his seax menacingly in one hand, his shield, showing the image of Mercia's eagle on a blood-red background, in the other. By the time the red-haired Raider is close enough to attempt a strike with his lethal-looking war axe, the shield is there to force aside the edge. The crash as the iron hits the wood thrums through me, jolting me. I stuff my hand into my mouth, trying to hold back my shriek of terror.

The Raider closes on my uncle once more. He gloats, his eyes alight, perhaps imagining what it'll be like to ride Wine, with her white-starred nose, to wear Cenfrith's byrnie, to own his weapons. The damn fool. He's too short to be able to mount Wine. He's too short to wear Cenfrith's byrnie. It'll drag on the floor should he attempt it.

The crash of Cenfrith's shield against the war axe startles me, the noise so loud in such a small space. I notice how Cenfrith holds his shield, using it as much to jab and punch as any fists. Not using it just to protect himself.

I turn towards the remaining Raiders, finally reclaiming my seax and standing upright. The space between them and me seems vast, the ground covered with the remnants of our camping equipment, the fire smouldering a hint of smoke into the air. We've been here for five days. It was almost comfortable.

I swallow heavily, knees weak, panting, for all I don't fight. My uncle skips into his opponent, using his speed as well as his weapons against the smaller man.

The other men jeer from the safety of the trees they've come through to find us. Their boots are well worn. These men have walked here. They hold their weapons aloft or hit them against one another. I notice they have no shields either.

Not that the red-haired Raider seems to need a shield. He has two weapons now, his war axe in one hand, his seax in the other. He thunders against my uncle's guard, trying one way and then another to place a blow on him.

Wine moves to block my view, and I swallow once more. I close my eyes. Perhaps I won't have to see what happens. But I must help my uncle. If he dies, the Raiders will come for me, and that thought turns my legs sluggish. I gasp, hot tears running down my face.

Holding my seax before me, I dart from behind the horse's rear, mindful of the pile of green horse shit on the floor. My legs feel leaden, but I place one in front of the other, aiming for some speed, trying to move my feet in time to the beating sound of the Raiders' weapons. I must aid my uncle, even though the thought terrifies me.

I note how the Raider fights with all of his strength, one blow and then another, war axe and then seax, sweat beading his helmless face. One of the other Raiders has rushed to join the battle. It's the man who first stepped through the bushes. Cenfrith fights against two, one short and one just as tall as him. Not that the two

Raiders seems to be unduly troubling my uncle. If I wasn't so terrified, I could enjoy watching him fight for the first time, but every
clash and clang of metal and wood sends more tears running down
my face.

A thin stream of blood arcs into the air, held immobile for a
moment, a cry of pain coming from the red-haired man. I can't see
the cut, but I know he bleeds. The sound reassures me that Cenfrith
will prevail, even against two of the five Raiders.

The three remaining Raiders leer at me. Terrified once more, I
decide my uncle can fight the remaining Raider alone. All I can
think of is returning to Wine. Perhaps she will gallop from this
place, taking me and my uncle with her. But in my fear, and with
my eyes fixed on Wine, I forget the smouldering fire and the stones
I placed around it. I stumble, the ground coming up to meet me
with a jarring thud, my breath stolen from me.

I spit leaves and ash from my mouth, vision blurry, scrambling
to find my feet. With my arms extended, my knees beneath me, I
feel a boot on my arse as I'm once more floundering on the ground.

I roll this time, arms over my body, looking into the fiery eyes of
a blond-haired Raider. He has a narrow face, a drooping beard and
a smirk on his face that promises nothing but my death; his seax
held ready for the killing cut. His smile only increases as he smells
the piss I can't contain. Embarrassment wars with my fear, and I
scream. To begin with, I don't even realise the sound comes
from me.

The Raider, wincing at the noise, backs away a little, arms up as
though to ward off blows. I scrabble on the ground, trying to get my
feet beneath me. But it's impossible. They skid away on the slick-
ness of my fear, and still, I scream. I think it's my uncle's name, but I
can't actually tell what I shriek.

I've lost my seax in the fall, and I have nothing with which to protect myself. Nothing but my knife used for cutting herbs. It's sharp and deadly, but only to nettles, radishes and carrots.

A gabbled conversation between two of the men, and the Raider menaces closer, his blade touching my throat even as I try to hold myself away from it. If only the ground would give, but no, it holds firm. I can feel the coldness of the blade. I can see where his hand holds firm, the hair on his knuckles as light as sunlight. I can smell my fear and my blood. I close my eyes.

There's a loud thud but no killing strike. Slowly, I open one eye and then another.

The Raider is gone, where I can't tell, not from here. I turn over, dig my hands into the ground and push upwards, looking only for the safety of Wine. As soon as I'm behind her, crouching low in the hope that the Raiders won't see me, I seek out my uncle. But he's not where he was. Wine nickers to me softly, as though to comfort, but it doesn't help me.

I swallow my fear.

My uncle clashes with the blond-haired man, with the narrow face who tried to kill me, his actions tight and constrained, each movement seemingly decided upon some time before he makes it, even though each and every move counters one the Raider makes.

I watch him in awe. I'll never fight like that. Never. I feel the dampness of my piss on my trews, and misery takes me. I'm no warrior, not that I ever wanted to be one. But I had half-hoped that if I ever needed to fight, I'd find the strength to do so. Once more, it's been proven that will never happen.

Only then do I realise why my uncle could come to my aid because the red-haired man is lying in a pool of his blood, the dark-haired man trying to stand upright, although blood leaks from his chest. I slither forward, keeping hold of Wine's long neck. I've seen dead bodies before, but never like this.

The men and women that Wynflæd treated at the end of their days looked peaceful in death. The red-haired man has his eyes wide open and staring, a perplexed expression on his face, as the halo of his hair is joined by more and more blood.

I grimace at the severed flesh of his throat. A thin trickle of blood pushes its way outwards, but really, it's all grey and white and exposed. I taste bile.

Cenfrith is busy beating back the remaining three Raiders, including the two who've decided it's time to join the battle rather than merely encourage their allies. One of them, a dark-haired man lacking a beard and a moustache, a rare sight, instead has his face inked. In the flickering sunlight, it appears as though a snake twists its way into and then out of his mouth. I almost gag at the scene.

Cenfrith thrusts his shield forward, his seax stabbing outwards, and none of the men can get close enough to him to land a blow. Seeing Cenfrith's strength and skill, I feel weak again.

The inked Raider is down on one knee, trying to stand, but he wavers. I imagine he's taken a blow to the head from Cenfrith's shield. The two remaining men seem less keen to meet my uncle's attack, even as Cenfrith menaces them with quick steps.

The kneeling snake-inked man, now some distance from the continuing battle between my uncle and the two remaining Raiders, watches me. He bleeds heavily from a wound in his left side, blood pooling down his leg. Yet, he smirks all the same. I taste my fear.

Cenfrith continues to battle, the blond-haired narrow-faced Raider falling to the ground so that he fights man against man, a swift glance meeting mine. He grimaces, and I fear he's injured as well. And then I can't look any more because the Raider my uncle left bleeding to death beside the red-haired man has reared up and comes towards me. He towers over me, war axe in his hand, bloodied and lethal-looking. My only weapon is my cutting knife and my padded byrnie, worn more for warmth than anything else.

I know what I have to do.

I stand my ground and push Wine away quickly. The Raider rushes me, war axe sweeping through the air even though the action pains him, face pale beneath the patchy sunlight, blood pouring from his torn chest. I thrust my knife upwards, hoping to at least counter the blow from the war axe because I don't have time to move away, but my grip is weak, and the Raider angry and far more skilled than I am.

My knife leaves my hand with a shriek of pain, my fingers aching from the contact, vibrating with the clash of both weapons colliding. An elbow reaches up to crash into my nose. I manage to avoid the heavy blow, but only by dropping low to the ground. My knees almost hit my nose instead, and I swallow blood from where I've bitten my tongue. The war axe is ready to take another sweeping blow against me.

I shuffle backwards, my hand encountering the hard stones that surrounded the firepit that tripped me in the first place, left me vulnerable to the blond-haired Raider who now battles my uncle.

Pleased to have another weapon, I fumble for one of the larger stones. Quickly, I aim for the Raider's head, hoping to unbalance him. He's almost dead anyway. Only, the stone thuds to the ground, not even covering half of the distance because I've thrown too quickly.

Now I grip a handful of warm embers, not burning ones, and this dust I fling at the Raider. It coats him so that he looks as though he's emerged from the grave, but for all his grey face and spitting aside of the foul-tasting ash, his steps don't stop.

I grasp another stone, this time testing the weight before I fling it. I surge upwards, taking the rock with me, back on my feet.

The Raider's eyebrows are blackened now, his lips grey, but his war axe is unaffected.

I catch sight of my uncle, a heavy blow from the shield connecting with his remaining foe's face. I glimpse the nose of the Raider for a moment, but he stumbles, and my uncle moves quickly. What happens next, I can't see, but I can hear hurried footsteps over the ground.

Hoping Cenfrith is coming to help me; I let lose the stone. This time it hits. The Raider collapses to the earth as though he has no bones or muscles. I hope he's bloody dead this time.

But now the snake-inked Raider approaches me, war axe sweeping from side to side, as though I'm little more than a head of corn to be scythed away from the ground. He's unsteady from the head wound he's taken, and from the blood that gushes from the wound in his side.

Fear takes me. I've no ability with a blade. I've shown that only too well. What skills do I have? I have only stones and ash to help me.

Once more, I see a blade aimed at me and know I can't avoid it. Time slows, the shimmering edge of the war axe aimed at my upper arm and throat. I'll take an impact for one of them, no matter what I do.

But, once more, even though I'm prepared, the final blow doesn't come.

I open my eyes, unaware they'd been shut. The Raider shudders before me, something heavy hitting him from the rear. I meet my uncle's eyes over the shoulder of the shaking man.

'Move, Icel. Move,' my uncle huffs, spittle following the words.

I scamper to do as he says, hand reaching to touch the slice through my byrnie from where the axe missed my arm but encountered my body instead. My fingers come away reddened, and I judder. That was too close.

The Raider grimaces, teeth reddened from my uncle's attack. His war axe has fallen, the weight suddenly too much for his arm. I believe my uncle has won this attack. In his wake, he'll leave five dead men. I'll have done nothing but fall and take a wound, oh, and throw a stone. As though to prove the truth of those words, I turn and immediately slip in the bloody mess left by the Raider.

I cry, more tears joining the ones that already stream from my eyes. Only Wine is there, her nose urging me to stand. With her help, I make it to my feet and then onto her back, ready to flee if my uncle should order. But he battles against the Raider, the inked man turning to meet this new attack.

Despite his wound, the foe-man lifts his war axe, revenge writ into the lines of his body.

I eye my uncle. He's not unscathed. A wound leaks slowly down his forearm, a dark mark on his lower left leg, speaking of another cut, but he's calm, steady, sucking in a much-needed breath. He lifts his chin to notice me. I try to smile, to thank him, but it's impossible. Water leak from my eyes.

I hope this is it, and there are no others.

The Raider's war axe moves toward Cenfrith to be intercepted once more by the shield. Only, the shield shatters at the force of the blow, pieces of wood sheering from the surface, the eagle falling to earth, to be torn to pieces by the hungry wolves who will gather to feast. My uncle has no choice but to close his eyes or risk being blinded by the thin slivers. The Raider doesn't have the same problem, and he forces himself closer and closer.

I scream in terror, the war axe far too close, and Cenfrith moves his broken shield and seax to counter whatever attack might be coming, although his brown eyes remain firmly closed.

It almost works, only the Raider adjusts his stance, and the war axe skips over the seax, the blow, when it lands, seeming to hit me more than my uncle. Cenfrith's byrnie darkens quickly, the blood flowing too fast. Hastily, I jump from Wine's back, hands scurrying for the saddlebags and my healing supplies contained within them.

When the sound of a body hitting the ground, just like a dropped sack of flour, echoes in the silence, I know it's not my uncle who's dead, but, with a wound such as that, it might not be long.

18

Shaking hands scurry through the saddlebags until I find what I
need. Rushing towards the smouldering hearth, I throw a handful
of leaves onto it, and a flash of flame greets my actions.

I need the heat. I need everything that Wynflæd has ever
taught me.

I wipe away the snot from my streaming nose, banging to the
ground where my uncle has slowly collapsed onto his knees.

He glances from the still Raider to me, a look of triumph on his
face.

'Careful,' I urge him. Should he fall forwards, I'll struggle to
turn him.

'It's all right, Icel,' his words surprisingly soft. 'They're dead,' he
states, as though that's my concern. And it was, but no more. Now I
need to save Cenfrith's life.

'Lie down,' I bark, the command in my voice surprising me just
as much as my uncle.

He nods, the movement slow and laboured.

'Help me,' he asks, and I do, taking the weight of his head as he
tumbles backwards. The blow I took to my nose has caused an ache

in my head that pulses with every breath. But I know what to do. I know how to save my uncle if I can.

I rip aside his byrnie as soon as he's lying, using my retrieved seax to cut through the thick material and expose the wound. It's bad, the cut deep, in the space between his throat and where his heart beats. I can see layers of grey beneath the pinkness of his skin, the blood loss already turning my uncle's face pale, his limbs lifeless.

Once more, I thrust a handful of leaves onto the fire, reaching for the waiting wood for today's fire and adding it as well.

I hold a torn piece of tunic against the wound, willing the blood to slow so that I can have the time to make the fire hot enough to seal the flesh against the injury.

It seems to take forever, my uncle's words becoming softer and softer, his words to me impossible to decipher, as I realise he's already delirious from loss of blood. He speaks faintly, urgently, his hand scrabbling for the cord he wears round his neck, but I'm too busy to listen to what he says.

Rushing back to Wine, I snatch the water bottle and, moving the sodden tunic, thrust the water against the paleness of Cenfrith's flesh, noting the matt of dark hair that covers his chest. I also see the other scars there, crisscrossed against his skin so that he looks like a patchwork.

I swallow my unease, seeing in those scars the promise that he's healed before and will again.

My seax is warming in the fire, the scent of blood burning from it, making me wrinkle my nose.

'Put the fire out,' my uncle commands, coming round enough to smell the smoke.

'Without the fire, you'll die,' I caution, batting aside his hands that reach for mine.

'There might be more,' he urges.

I nod. I've realised this. 'There might be, but without the heat, I can't seal your wound.'

Impatience wars with my knowledge that I need to wait longer. I offer my uncle water when he asks for it, but even such a movement makes blood flow freely again from the barely patched wound.

'Hold still,' I urge him, wrapping my hand in another tunic to grip the handle of my hot blade. All the same, I can feel the burn through my skin, the scent of smouldering linen adding to the myriad scents in the air of death, blood, piss and pain.

Quickly, I press the blade against the wound, my uncle's lips held firmly together, his breath too fast, chest rising and falling far too quickly. And I hold it for longer, gritting my teeth against the pain of the burn from the hilt. Only when he opens his mouth and roars in agony do I pull the blade aside.

The flesh is reddened and angry, the smell turning my stomach, burnt hair adding to the acrid tang.

My uncle's eyelids flutter, and he stills in sleep.

I take a breath, unaware I've even been holding it, and a sob escapes my mouth.

Wine comes closer, nosing her owner, perplexed when he doesn't respond as expected.

I hang my head low. I touch my uncle's forehead, feeling the sheen of his sweat but knowing he merely sleeps. And still, I watch him, assuring myself that his chest rises and falls, that he has no other wounds.

But, of course, he does. I lift his right arm, seeing where a thin snick has touched his arm just above his elbow, small but deep. I clean it quickly, returning the blade to the fire to seal this fresh hurt. I feel my way down his legs, finding the bleeding cut on his right leg, just below the knee. It's more blood than flesh, but I clean it, all the same, finding some semblance of normality in such a task.

When his arm wound has been seared, once more I thrust my

seax back into the fire to cleanse it and only then examine my burnt hand. There's an imprint of the seax hilt on my right hand. It's faint, but it aches, and I know it'll only get worse. Quickly, I swill cold water over it and then wrap it in another piece of torn linen. I know it won't heal; the burn is too deep. I recall one of Wynflæd's recipes for treating a burn, but I don't have woodruff or lily, or brooklime, to hand. I'll have to contend with cleaning it and ensuring it stays clean. Already, it's burned a vivid red and my hand aches even with just air passing over it.

Only then do I stand, my legs weary, my heart heavy.

I bend to check all of the Raiders are indeed dead. The red-haired one is lying face up, blood flooding a slight depression in the ground so that it looks as though rain has fallen stained with pink. His chest doesn't move, and when I lift his right hand and drop it, it thuds to the ground without feeling. But I knew he was dead anyway.

The next Raider lies curled round his stomach wound, hands bloodied as he tries to hold his innards inside, but he's as dead as the other man, head dented from where I hit him with the stone, although it's his belly wound that killed him. I kick him for good measure, but no man could survive such a wound. It's beyond even the healing skill of Wynflæd. No man would want to survive such a wound for he'd end his days stinking of his own filth.

The blond-haired man who thought to kill me has a wide gap where his throat used to be. I grimace at the sight. He's fallen heavily but has stayed upright, his knees beneath him, hand on his war axe, as though it props him upright, axe head on the ground, handle upright.

I nudge him, and he finally falls to the right in a clatter of weapons, his head bouncing loosely, as though it might sever itself from the rest of his body.

The other two men my uncle killed lie one face down, and one face up. I can see the ruin of the man's face who had his nose smashed. He's been stabbed across his belly as well and blood pools in the leaf litter. The fifth man is face down, and when I kick his arm, a wet sound tells me he's bled to death from a jab beneath his armpit.

I raise my head, look to the sky far above, where light clouds scud across, where there's the hope of a warm day and an even warmer night, and tears fall without ceasing.

I've lost my home, and I might just lose my uncle as well. I can't protect us both if more Raiders come. I was lucky to hit the man with the stone, but my uncle killed him first.

We're deep in the heart of Mercia's hinterlands, almost, my uncle warned me, tempting fate by stepping inside the Welsh kingdom of Powys. If my uncle is to survive, I need to get him to a healer, to Wynflæd. She's the only person I know who can cure him. I don't have the skills, of that I'm sure. But how am I to get him there when she's in Tamworth, the place I fled from, from where King Ecgberht of Wessex rules Mercia, as well as Wessex, and where the Wessex warriors are as much of a menace as the bloody Raiders.

If only it was possible. But it's not.

19

I want to do nothing but sob, but there's no one here to comfort me
other than Wine. And there's only so much she can do. Eventually, I
rub my wrists into my eyes, standing to assess the surroundings.

Our camp hadn't been elaborate. With the weather so fine,
there'd been little need for more than the trees above our heads
and the welcome trickle of the stream running to the far left-hand
side of the slight hollow in the steep wall at our back, forged from
the spongy ground where tree roots criss-cross, some exposed,
others deeply hidden. The stones for the hearth fire had been taken
from the depths of the nearby stream.

I need to drag the dead away from my uncle. While he lies,
insensible, I can't risk a hungry wolf coming to chew on him,
thinking him dead even though he yet lives.

I make my way to the furthest of the dead men, the last who
died from a wound into his armpit. I'm content that Wine will stay
close to my uncle. She can do little but make a noise if there's
danger, but it's better than nothing.

Before we made camp, we crested a steep rise, over one side of
which there was a long drop, where craggy rocks had fallen down

the steep slope. It's not ideal, but it will get the bodies far away from me without having to dig holes or find rocks and stones to cover them. I bend, grip the legs of the first warrior, considering and dismissing helping myself to his trinkets. Only then I drop the legs so that they thud, one, two, into the ground.

The man wears arm rings, silver, at the top of both arms. He also carries a pouch round his waist, the noise of something inside it clanging metallically. I bend, not wanting to touch any more of the dead man, and carefully remove the loop of the packet. It's heavy, but I don't stop to pick through the contents. Instead, I move my hands to the right arm, biting my tongue to hold back my squeamishness. I've touched the dead before. This should be no different.

Deftly, and with more care than others might show, I move the first arm band and slip it down the arm until it comes free over the less bulky muscles close to the hand. I'm surprised by the weight of the item, and then I'm surprised all over again when the second one, although just as wide, weighs half as much. It seems the Raiders aren't above a little misdirection.

Only then do I consider the weapons belt itself and the byrnie. A layer of blood coats everything, and yet, Cenfrith's custom-made byrnie is ruined, both thanks to the Raider who cut him and my need to remove it from him quickly. But, to take it from this man, I must turn him over, force him into a sitting position and then struggle to remove the byrnie over an unresponsive upper body and head, not to mention the arms.

I sigh, sweat already beading my face, standing to check on Cenfrith. He hasn't moved, and neither has Wine. I take that to mean all is as well as it can be. And so, the byrnie.

Resolved, I make my way round the man, using my feet to roll him over so that his eyes glare upwards now. Only then do I approach the rear of the body, bending to hook each hand under a shoulder, and then I thrust upwards. The dead man resists me for a long moment. I'm already thinking of giving up when I stagger forwards, the man's forehead resting on his legs, his body bent double, with a sharp crack and a more disquieting oozing noise, followed by a long fart.

'Bloody bollocks,' I whisper to myself, swallowing down nausea.

Working my hands beneath the byrnie, I begin to move it over the man's stomach, jarring away from the coldness of so much flesh touching my fingers. It really is too much effort, but eventually, I manage to free his left arm from the confines of the byrnie so that it's far easier to roll it free down his right arm.

I examine his nakedness with the detachment of someone used to healing, not maiming. His body isn't lacking scars, but few of them are deep, and most might even have been caused many years ago because they're small and puckered.

Either this man was an excellent warrior, or, and I think this is the truth, he was not one for engaging in an attack unless he believed himself the victor from the start. It speaks to his reticence to join even this small battle. At least that means the byrnie will have been little used.

Now, I grab his legs once more and pull him behind me. The ground isn't too rough, but even so, by the time I reach the sharp drop, I'm thinking that I'm not going to be able to do this with all of the men. And certainly not before darkness falls. The sun is already well past its zenith, and even the long summer's day won't be my ally forever.

I force the body forwards, dangling my opponent's feet over the precipice, before moving back so that I sit and use my feet to launch the body free. I don't wait to listen to the sound of it dropping. It'll be nothing compared to a bag of iron pieces dropped on a stone floor.

I quickly gather my treasures and return to my uncle's side. He's not moved while I've been gone, and I reach out to touch his forehead. His hand snatches mine, the grip fierce.

'Icel.'

'Aye, it's me,' I offer, trying not to show how much his movement shocks me.

'What are you doing?'

'Moving the dead.'

His eyes open slowly, squinting as though the diffuse light through the leaves high above us is too much. 'The Raiders?' Cenfrith's eyes are fierce as he gazes at me. 'Hand me the water. I'm bloody thirsty.'

I move without thought, retrieving the water from our pile of belongings.

'Who were they?' I ask.

'Raiders, lost in Mercia, no doubt. Or they were just trying their luck. It happens. They've probably become separated from a larger group and were lost.' My uncle speaks when he finishes drinking, handing me the half-empty bag. His words terrify me. 'There'll be no others. If there had been, we'd both be dead and not having this conversation,' Cenfrith states flatly, even though I've not yet asked the question.

All the same, as I return to my task, my eyes are fixed on the trees round me, seeking out more of the enemy, fearful of what they'll do to me, and seeing booted feet in the dense undergrowth.

I hurry my endeavours, labouring to remove the fine rings and chains from round the neck of the man curled round his wounds. Already, his innards stink, the hot sun encouraging even the smallest of creatures to his side. It's almost impossible to unfold him from the position.

I abandon any attempt to take his byrnie, contenting myself with his portable wealth and the weapons that remain on his weapons belt. All the same, I have to touch the hardening flesh.

Once more, I'm reminded that these dead bodies are different to ones I've helped Wynflæd with in the past.

These men are not Mercians, although they've died in Mercia.

My stomach growls as I check on Cenfrith once more. He's sleeping, his hand curled round his seax, Wine drowsy. I kick the fire with my foot, noting that I need to collect more wood as well as water.

But I don't pause to eat, not yet. I drag another of the bodies away, and then another. Sweat pools down my back, and my pile of treasure grows higher.

Cenfrith is awake when I return for the last body, hooking the feet beneath my armpits of the smaller man. He hardly feels less heavy than the others.

I make my way back slowly once I've disposed of his body and bend to refill water bottles in the brook. Wine has made her way to the stream whenever she's needed it. I've noticed her hurried steps as she returns to my uncle. Yet, I drag my feet, noting the marks gouged through the earth from where I've been busy at the grue-some task of moving the heavy dead.

This morning, I woke without thought, only fear.

I collapse to the ground beside my sleeping uncle. Soft snores come from his open mouth as I slowly place more pieces of wood on the fire. It's not cold, but I shiver all the same. I pour water into my mouth, thinking it might revive me, but it doesn't. As hungry as I am, I curve round the warmth of the fire, wrinkling my nose at my stench, but I'm asleep before I can think to change.

* * *

'Icel,' my uncle's words are harsh in the night.

I peel open my eyes with an effort, noting how dark it is. I reach over to touch my uncle, but he's not there.

'What?' I squint into the darkness, but still, I can't see him. 'Where are you?' I demand, but the only sound that returns to me is that of feet moving over the ground.

Hastily, I grab more twigs and branches, add them to the fire. The shadows leap high as soon as the flames are steady. Turning my head, I catch sight of my uncle pawing the ground.

'What are you doing?' I ask, exhaustion making my words harsh.

Only he doesn't look at me.

'What are you doing?' I repeat more softly, standing beside him, reaching out as though I'll touch his arm, but I don't.

He's down on his knees, I hardly know how, but I can feel the heat from him.

'Damn, you have a fever,' I coax, hoping he'll pliantly stand and return to the fire, but he doesn't seem to hear me. His hands continue to run over the surface as though seeking something frenetically.

'Icel,' the word is soft, laced with sorrow.

'I'm here, Cenfrith,' I speak slowly, loudly enough for him to hear, and his entire body shudders. Only then does he look up at me. I can see where tears streak his sweat-stained face. 'I'm here, now come on, back to sleep.' Now I touch him because he's aware of me, no longer walking between wakefulness and sleep.

'You're here,' he smiles, his breath foul in my face.

'You need to piss and drink,' I caution him.

He nods, turning to fiddle with his trews and then releasing stinking water into the ground he just examined. His breath is ragged as we retrace the few steps back to the fire. His head hangs low, and words rush from his mouth, too soft for me to hear. I've watched Wynflæd with such patients before. It's best not even to ask him to repeat what he says. It'll be the vague ramblings from someone in too much pain to understand what they say. He speaks of my mother, of King Beornwulf, of King Coelwulf, little more than words coming from his mouth. I fear to listen, lest his secrets spill from him.

With effort, I get him to sit and hand him the water bottle. He takes no more than a mouthful and tries to hand it back to me.

'Drink it all,' I urge him.

I think he'll argue with me, but he doesn't. Only then do I let him lie down. He shivers, unsurprisingly, and I cover him with my cloak.

For all my uncle quickly sleeps, I'm awake now, and I lie on my back, staring up at the sky overhead, rich with the lights of stars and the moon. My heart is heavy. I miss the sound of Edwin's loud snores now that he's safe at Kingsholm. With just my uncle and Wine beside me, the vastness feels too great.

A tear streams its way down my face once more, and I cuff it aside.

I need to sleep.

20

An urgent hand on my leg has me instantly alert in the morning. My uncle's bleached face peers at me in the grey light of dawn. 'We need to move.'

I understand the words more by watching his mouth than by hearing them. I nod but also strain to hear. What is it that's disturbed him from his sleep once more?

I can't hear anything, but my uncle is no longer slick with sweat. He's returned to the here and now. I trust his instincts even though he's had no time for his body to heal.

Hastily, I gather together our supplies, encouraging Wine closer with a gentle murmur. She comes and obligingly allows me to load her with the saddle and saddlebags. My uncle has quenched the fire with three handfuls of dirt, grunting with the effort of bending and standing. I stamp on it, keen to extinguish all the flames.

But then we both stare at one another. Cenfrith can't walk a long distance; that much is evident in his stooped frame. How then will he mount the horse?

'Bugger,' he staggers towards Wine, but even such a move pains him, and he hisses through his teeth.

Now I do hear the sound of something moving nearby. Whether it be beast or Raiders, I don't know. But it adds to the urgency of our predicament.

'Help me,' my uncle winces as he speaks. His face is pale, his chest bare because I cut his byrnie and tunic from him. If he can't mount a horse easily, he certainly can't put on a new tunic.

I move to his side, offering him my cupped hands as a means of mounting up. I don't believe he'll be able to do it. Neither do I think I will, not when his total weight is in my hand. I strain, desperate to keep my fingers laced together, my arms shaking with the effort.

Somehow, and I'm not sure how, Cenfrith manages to mount Wine. And it's only just quick enough. As she moves under my uncle's direction, turning to follow a concealed pathway running between the trees and the mass of growing green flowers and plants, I hear the predator come even closer.

I don't risk looking; instead, my hand on the seax my uncle gifted me, the one I used to seal his wound closed with fire, and which has developed a fiery ache, I struggle under the weight of all our excess bags. Sweat slicks my face, and it's far from daylight yet. The pain from my hand is only just bearable. It's going to be a long day.

At the last possible moment, I risk looking behind me and shudder at the piercing yellow eyes of the wolf who sniffs the air in our direction but turns back eagerly enough, the scent of day-old blood driving the animal to seek the source. I'm grateful the wolf is content with the easier meal of day-old flesh than attacking me and my uncle.

We travel in silence, other than the passage of my feet and the hoof falls of the horse. Cenfrith's breathing is laboured, but he doesn't complain, and he's managed to pull the cloak round him.

My misery grows. My feet hurt, my neck itches, my hand throbs and I stink. I should have immersed myself in the stream yesterday, but I was too tired. I regret that now. I'm hungry as well. I don't know when I last ate.

I don't ask my uncle where we travel. Since being ejected from Kingsholm, we've trekked through the hidden landscape beneath trees and thick woodlands with no real end in sight. I don't ask Cenfrith his plans. I think he still has one. And while I don't know that for sure, it allows me to feel some hope.

Overhead, the day is far from bright, grey clouds hanging low, although it's warm, and when we do emerge from the sheltering treeline, my eyes wince at the sharp brightness.

My steps grow slower and slower. I'm used to walking all day long, but today every step is an agony. I've not slept as well, or for as long as I might have wanted. Eventually, Cenfrith calls a halt to our meandering.

'Here, help me,' he calls to me, his voice ancient and filled with agony. We've not spoken during our journey. There's seemed little point.

Eagerly, I drop all of the bags I carry, almost fearing I'll float away without them to weigh me down.

'Catch me,' but his words are almost too late as he slithers down the side of a sweating Wine, and it takes all of my feeble strength to keep him on his feet.

He cries out with pain as his feet hit the ground too fast, and he shudders to the ground, unable to support his weight.

'I'm sorry,' I mutter miserably.

He surprises me by trying to smile. 'It's not your fault your uncle is such a heavy bastard.'

The words buoy me, and quickly I move to see to Wine, removing the saddle and bags and leading her to a trickling stream not far away. The water is clear, and we both drink eagerly. I leave her to drink and remove all of my clothes, allowing the cold water in a deeper pool, just lower down, to wipe away the grime, sweat and piss of the last day.

I'm disgusted by the filth that comes away from me, the rustiness of day-old blood flowing away, as I clean my trews in the cold water before slipping them back on when I emerge, dripping wet but smelling far better. The water torments my burned hand, and I'm careful not to rub at it, making it bleed all over again. My neck wound pulses as well but is far more manageable. It's not a deep cut.

I shiver at the coldness against my skin, but sooner that than the other.

Wine watches me with detachment before following me back to my uncle. I could wish Wine and I were more friendly towards one another, but she's my uncle's horse, and I think she knows I can't ride well. Cenfrith hasn't moved, is still slumped in the same place, eyes closed, sleeping propped up against the saddlebags that fell behind him.

'I'll collect some wood and stones,' I speak to Wine as I lead her to some long grasses and offer some oats as well with my hand. She eats them eagerly enough. She needs a good brush, but first, I need a fire. I need something warm to eat, and so does my uncle.

By the time Cenfrith revives from his sleep, a small fire burns before him, a pot of oats slowly cooking, flavoured with herbs I've found on my quest for wood and also taken from the small supply in my bags that's all I've got left of our winter in hiding. It's not much, but it doesn't need to be. As long as it's warm and filling, it'll ease my stomach and give my uncle the nourishment he needs to heal.

'I need to check your wounds,' I inform him, touching the small cut at my neck in sympathy, not wanting to show him the burn on my hand.

'Once I've eaten, you can,' he offers, lines on his forehead attesting to the pain he's feeling. His skin remains too pallid, and he still doesn't wear a tunic. His cloak covers him, but again, I see the glimmer of the emblem he wears round his neck.

I open my mouth to ask the question, but then don't. Cenfrith is ill, weak, wounded. I can't extract the truth from him now. It wouldn't be at all fair.

'We'll find somewhere to shelter for a few days.' The thought cheers me as we eat, and I tend to his wounds. The one on his chest looks red and angry, although the ones on his leg and arm are already knitting together. I know a flicker of worry, thinking of Wynflæd and what she would suggest. She certainly wouldn't have allowed Cenfrith to ride all day as he has. Neither would she have thought him healed, not yet. And by the morning, my uncle is once more delirious, and I can't get him to stand and mount the horse, no matter how much I try.

Furiously, I consider how Wynflæd might try to treat him, but I don't have the herbs I need: pennyroot, betony, yarrow and corn-cockle; and even if I did have them, I don't have cow's milk, let alone butter.

I assess our refuge, walking away from my uncle, to determine where we are. The seax in my burned hand, I wince as I grip the hilt, although I know I'm more likely to stab myself than anyone else,. But it's impossible. I don't know this path, and there's no clear view to be had, not with the mass of trees overhead. We've been avoiding the better trodden roads and paths. I wish we hadn't, but, of course, if we'd kept closer to them, it's more likely that we'd have been discovered, aroused the curiosity of those keen to win the approval of Mercia's new king.

Not that I'd have known where we were on the old road, either.

Next, I return to the stream, leading Wine with me, and while she drinks, I refill all three water bottles. We might not be going anywhere soon, but I'd rather be prepared.

I cook more oats, flavouring them with a small amount of honey, wary of using all of my carefully hoarded supply, in case I need it for my uncle's wound. I think longingly of the copious honey I used to heal Sewenna. Cenfrith wakes routinely, sometimes crying in his sleep and rousing himself, and occasionally just to drink. His eyes are far from bright, and I wish I could take him to Wynflæd at Tamworth, but it's impossible. I think of all those herbs I've prepared for her in the past, and of her knowledge, and could weep for the futility of it all.

Now that King Ecgberht holds Tamworth, Wynflæd's out of reach to me, even if she yet lives. I worry that she doesn't. The winter was hard, even in our shelter far up the hill, the snow deep, the days cold, the nights even colder. I mustn't forget that she's the oldest person I've ever met.

The day drags on, my feet itching to be on the move, my hand pulsing, my neck uncomfortably tight, but I can't get my uncle on Wine's back without his aid. And he'd need to be awake for long enough to do that.

I resolve myself to a day of doing little, collecting more wood, ensuring Wine is fed. I miss Edwin's camaraderie. We've kept each other company through so much of our exile from Tamworth, but now he's not here, and I resent him for being safe and well at Kingsholm while my uncle sweats and moans in his sleep.

Edwin would have made the day less tedious by telling me how he once helped King Beornwulf remove a stone from his horse's hoof and was rewarded with a silver penny. He would have told me of how one day he'd fight the men of Wessex and reduce that kingdom to the thin sliver of land it used to be.

I smile at the thought. Edwin has so many dreams and hopes. All I've ever wanted to do is learn to heal the wounded, but it seems I know much less than I thought. My uncle languishes, and I'm less than useless.

My uncle finally rouses only when the brightness of the day has dimmed. He blinks, coughs, winces and glares at me.

'Why did you wake me? I've only just fallen asleep.'

'I didn't wake you. And you fell asleep yesterday. You've slept the day away, just about.'

Cenfrith shakes his head, denying the words, and then winces again.

'I need to piss,' he complains instead, bunching his legs beneath his body to stand before stopping.

I rush to his side, offer him my shoulder so that he can stand with one arm draped over me. We manage it between us, but it's painful for him and me. We stagger only five steps away before he fumbles with his trews, and once more, the air fills with the stench of bad piss.

'You need to drink more.' I wrinkle my nose at the smell of him. He needs to bathe in the stream too, but it seems an unimaginably long distance away.

'We need to keep moving,' he retorts, something of his old vigour in his voice.

'Then one of us needs to stay awake for long enough to do so.'

He grunts, and I lead him back to his place beside the fire.

'We'll eat and move on, now. There's a bright moon. Better to head out now that I'm awake.'

Better for him, I think, considering I've spent the day awake already. But the urge to continue guides my steps when we set out. Exhaustion makes my strides drag throughout the long night. I don't have the chance to drowse, as my uncle does in the saddle, and my ears are alert to all the night-time sounds round me.

This is far from the first time I've walked through the darkness of the night, the sounds of the forest animals loud: the call of owls, the unmistakable sound of bats flapping through the trees. This, however, is the first time I've done so believing myself being watched. The sensation makes me itch, and more than once, I startle, glancing all round, only to see nothing but a hedgehog or a badger busy about their own business. I keep my seax close at hand but know the comfort it brings me is a lie. I have no skill with the weapon, and it pains me to hold it.

My uncle doesn't speak to me and, again, my thoughts turn to the current situation within Mercia.

I sigh. Since King Beornwulf's death, nothing has gone right, not within Mercia and not for me. Rage kindles inside me – rage at being ripped away from Tamworth and the only home I've ever known, rage at Wiglaf for being so weak Ecgberht overthrew him, and, most of all, rage at the bastard Raiders who are making the whole mess even more complex.

Mercia is no longer the kingdom it once was, that much I know, and it's a bitter disappointment to me. Just like my uncle's frailties, Mercia is weaker than I believed her to be. It's ruled by men who make stupid decisions and act rashly. If I were her king, I wouldn't rule as they do. And then I laugh at my words. Why would I ever think myself worthy of being Mercia's king? I can't even face one of the Raiders without pissing myself in fear.

* * *

We do the same the next day, only this time I sleep during the heat of the day, exhaustion dragging me under when I've only just managed to remove Wine's saddle and bags. My uncle drops to the ground, a hiss of pain through his tight lips, but I believe he's healing. He's no longer as hot as he has been and he's managed to force a tunic over his head.

But after a further three nights of travelling, we're no closer to finding a more permanent place to shelter. The forest trails we follow are deserted. I've seen no one since the Raider attack five days before. I believe my uncle is lost.

'We'll find somewhere soon,' he assures me, perhaps sensing my unease.

I grunt, nothing more.

He's recovering, his wound almost knit back together, but his mind isn't. Not as far as I can tell.

'You don't believe me, do you?' His words are hot, betrayal rippling through them.

'I do,' I retort but without conviction.

I'm tending the fire, once more feeding branches into the flames so that our dwindling supply of oats can cook. I wish I had the skills of a hunter and could trap the small animals that make this place their home, but after the deaths I've seen, I don't even wish to attempt it. Perhaps, I consider, I'll live only on vegetables for the rest of my life.

'I know you don't,' Cenfrith's voice is too high and quarrelsome.

I glance at him. His face is flushed, and his hands worry at the tunic that covers his wound. I wish there was more than honey to offer him to ease the pain. We don't even have ale or wine. Why would a warrior and a youth on a journey have required ale to drink?

'I do, Uncle. But we've been travelling for a long time now.' I don't mention that I'm sure we've passed some places more than once. I'm too weary to argue.

'I assure you,' and he sounds belligerent now, 'that tomorrow, we'll find the road, and then we'll find somewhere new to shelter away from the trees and those who hunt the woodlands.'

And he's right, but also wrong.

It's the sound of horses moving over a hard surface that forces me to
poke my head free from the treeline. I've been hearing the noise for
some time now. To begin with, I thought it only my heart thudding
in my chest, my bones weary beyond imagining, but then my uncle
heard it as well.

A grin of triumph touched his drawn face, only for Cenfrith to
wrinkle his forehead in thought.

'That's not right,' he mutters.

Now, I watch mouth open in shock at the mass of mounted
warriors moving along the remains of the ancient road over which
we've travelled both ways since leaving Tamworth. It's etched into
the landscape, as though a river forging a path between two
hillsides.

I recognise the white wyvern on the black shields slung over the
horses' backsides quickly enough and swallow against my fear.

I scan the expanse of horseflesh, noting the men travel ready
for war. They wear byrnies, even beneath the heat of the summer
sun. They have weapons close to hand, and they're alert as well.
Well, not alert enough to notice me, but they peer all round

them, their distrust of the landscape they travel through easy to see.

I seek out King Ecgberht. I've never seen him before. I've heard enough about him to know that I hate him, but I've never seen the man who's claimed Mercia as his own.

It takes so long to find King Ecgberht, I think he's not amongst his warriors, but then my eye catches on a helm festooned with white horsehair, and I know it's him.

I'm surprised he rides with his helm on. It must be sweltering inside the cloth cap he'll wear beneath the metal helm. I wouldn't like to be responsible for cleaning it. I can't see the horse he actually rides, surrounded by so many of his warriors. I watch through slit eyes, almost daring him to notice my scrutiny, but he doesn't.

'It's King Ecgberht,' I whisper to Cenfrith, returning to hide within the trees besides Wine and the rest of our supplies.

'It can't be,' my uncle gasps, and for a moment, I see the fear on his fatigued face. He's struggled into one of the pilfered byrnies. It was an effort, but at least he's protected now, even if it's nowhere near as good as the one I ripped from his body when I needed to stem the bleeding.

'Show me,' he demands, but I shake my head.

'No, there's near enough two hundred of them, if I'm any good at counting. They all have the wyvern on their shields. So why would it not be him?'

'Two hundred?' my uncle gulps, his face turning even sallower. 'It just can't be?' he whispers to himself.

I don't understand why he denies my words. I've never lied to him before, not about the path ahead.

'Where are they headed?'

'To the west.' I'm finding his questions frustrating and time-consuming. 'We need to leave here,' I urge. We can't risk using the road, not now, and it's taken all of my skill of persuasion to get

Cenfrith to agree to return to the same place we spent last winter. I'm hoping that the dead men have been discovered and buried, that no one thinks to go there now. Maybe they fear to travel to such a spot, thinking nothing but death from an unknown hand awaits them.

I could weep with the injustice of it all. Just as I've managed to get Cenfrith to agree with my decision, it's as ashes in the wind.

'He wouldn't?' still my uncle muses to himself.

I shake my head, reaching for the water bottle and swigging from it, before using my hand to hold a small amount of water so that Wine can drink as well, her tongue rough over my burn. There's a stream running along the far side of the road, but it's out of reach for now. It seems I'm always going to carry the imprint of the seax handle on my hand. In the correct light, I can just depict the beak of Mercia's eagle there. On the seax hilt, Mercia's emblem is etched in thin copper thread. On my hand, it ripples whenever I move it, depicted in pink and red against the lines of my hand.

'I need to see,' my uncle continues to complain, his words too loud.

'We need to be silent, or we'll be hunted down, and what explanation will we be able to give?' At the moment, Cenfrith could ride away, but I'd be left behind. I don't want to feel the edge of a blade at my throat again. Not anytime soon. It's only just knit together, the rough edges of the scab disappearing overnight while I slept.

'Then stop bloody talking,' Cenfrith argues with me, and I roll my eyes at him. I've always adored my uncle, admired him, but wounded and alone in these never-ending forestlands, I'm growing frustrated with his testiness. And he's growing ever more bad-tempered.

He urges Wine onwards, and I open my mouth to argue against the necessity of exposing both him and the horse, but it's still difficult for him to walk unaided. I snap my jaw shut and drink instead.

I watch him disappear between the green branches of two trees, the swish of the horse's grey tail showing her unease at the commands she must follow.

I drink, finally erasing the dryness of my throat. I might regret drinking my fill but not immediately.

Cenfrith is gone for too long. Shaking my head, I collect the sacks I've discarded and follow in his wake. It's not difficult to see where Wine has forged a path through the tightly packed leaves. There are broken branches and churned mud underfoot.

'Where have you been?' Again, anger laces his words as I approach him.

I bite my lip. There's no point in responding. Whatever I say will be wrong.

'King Ecgberht is with these warriors, riding at the centre of them.'

'And?' I demand when he offers nothing else. I told him that. It's evident he didn't believe me.

I can see the carts that accompany the horses and warriors, laden down with supplies and with a large man sitting beneath a huge hat, dozing in the heat of the sun. I take him to be the man who cooks the king's meals. My stomach growls at the thought, even as I'm envious of his hat that would keep the sun from my eyes and burning my skin.

'Where is he going?' There's a combination of interest and something I take to be fear, running through Cenfrith's voice.

'He's following the road,' I point out, jerking my head in that direction. 'Where does the road lead?'

'To the dyke and then into the Welsh kingdoms of Powys and Gwynedd,' my uncle states, his face furrowed in concentration.

'What's he doing?'

But I have an idea, and my uncle does as well. After all, it's what the rulers of Mercia have done for many years.

'We need to follow him. See if we're right in our assumptions.'

I'm already shaking my head. 'What does it matter? We wait for them to pass us and resume our journey.' I'm thinking of his wound, but more, of my poor feet.

'No, we follow them, and I'm not explaining or arguing with you as to why.'

I shrug my shoulders, stifling down my urge to yell at him. 'Then we'll have to leave some of these belongings behind. I can't carry everything.'

I'm surprised when Cenfrith eagerly nods in agreement.

'You're right. You need to move more quickly, or we'll lose sight of the horses. We'll find somewhere to bury what can't be carried.'

It's hardly what I was hoping to achieve, but I can tell it's useless to argue further with Cenfrith.

'Where would you have me bury these things?'

'Somewhere easy to find.' His words are riddled with mockery, as though he directs one of the sheep and not his nephew.

'Fine,' and I stalk through trees, far from hopeful that there'll be anything that fits such a precise requirement. And there isn't, not until I trip and tumble to the ground, arms wide apart, head thrown back, jarring my wounded neck and making my burned hand smart as I reach out to steady my fall on the uneven ground.

'Bollocks,' I exclaim, feeling the tell-tale traces of tears forming in my eyes.

'Hurry up,' Cenfrith helpfully hisses from his place inside the treeline. He still watches King Ecgberht and his trail of men.

I've put my foot down some abandoned hole made by a small animal. The soil has tumbled inside it, exposing the droppings and leftovers. It's as good as I'm going to find. Hastily, I scoop out the topsoil and I empty the equipment I took from the dead Raiders.

With that done, I cover the hole in the mud I disturbed and then collect five lichen-covered stones, random sizes and shapes. I don't place them over the spot; that would be folly. But, instead, I pile them close to the nearest tree, a small collection of pale stones, chalky on my hands. As a final sign, I gouge another tree trunk with my knife, leaving two sharp lines, one crossing the other, before pulling some fallen branches into place over the disturbed ground. I hope it's enough; it'll have to do.

Lighter now, it's almost too easy to throw my sack of provisions over my shoulder and return to Cenfrith.

He hasn't changed position and continues to watch the very end of King Ecgberht's line of warriors and supply carts. His expression is pensive, his hands twitching on the reins of the horse.

I open my mouth to speak, but he encourages Wine onwards, coming out onto the road, the dust cloud from King Ecgberht's passing hanging in the air.

'Isn't this too obvious?' I demand. We've not exposed ourselves for a long time, not since leaving Kingsholm. I can't help but think that Cenfrith wants the Wessex warriors to find him. All the same, Cenfrith shakes his head.

'Sometimes, and it's not often, but hiding in plain sight is to be preferred to scurrying round in the woods.'

I grit my teeth, stepping back to another tree and gouging the trunk once more. I set into my mind where a small stream trickles beside the remains of the old road, how a solitary thornapple tree, the leaves lush and green, stands there, and the clump of dandelions and long grasses that share the same piece of ground. It's not much to go on. I doubt I'll ever find this place again, and certainly not if I come in winter. But that doesn't concern Cenfrith.

He knees Wine to a canter, and I huff. It seems that having walked for days, I'm now expected to run.

Perhaps I should train to be a warrior after all. At least then, my lord would gift me with a bloody horse to ride, just as Edwin once complained to me.

* * *

With every step, I examine the ground before me. This ancient roadway has long since fallen to ruin. It consists more of grasses and weeds than gravel, with clogged drains running along the side of it. It's certainly not as well maintained as the road which runs from Tamworth to Wall, but then, these roads are less well travelled, and there are fewer people living on land that's so often disputed between the Mercians and the people of Powys.

The road is a trip hazard from beginning to end. I don't know how the horses stayed upright, and how the cook slept in the cart. He must have jarred his teeth.

After my first encounter with the hard surface, I take my time planting my feet. Ahead of me, my uncle travels more quickly than any time since we escaped from Tamworth. He sits upright in the saddle with no hint of injury at all. He looks every bit the feared warrior I know him to be. There's no trace of the wounded man who cried when I tended to his wounds, who spoke feverishly in his sleep.

I wish I could transform myself in such a way. But I'm still just Icel, the boy who wanted to be a healer, not a warrior. See where that's got me.

The sun is hot overhead, beating down on me, and in no time at all, I'm forced to stop. Panting, I reach for my water bottle. I call to my uncle to wait, but he mustn't heed my words and continues on his way.

'Nice,' I complain to myself. I'm under the distinct impression that Cenfrith has decided to forego all that talk of staying away from whoever rules in Mercia.

Having drunk enough to remove the dust and heat from my mouth, I resume my shamble, not wanting to be left behind, no matter my unhappy thoughts. If I don't have my uncle, then I'm truly alone. I can never return to Tamworth while King Ecgberht rules and no one has heard of King Wiglaf since he ran like a coward from the Wessex advance. Not that I'd ever seek him out either.

I keep turning to stare behind me, convinced that there must be more warriors rushing to join King Ecgberht of Wessex, but the road remains empty, apart from the odd scurrying creature, taking a chance now that the thunder of the hooves has faded away. A hare eyes me at one point, before returning to nibble at the dandelion stalks it's found. I laugh bitterly that it deems me to be no threat.

Ahead, I lose sight of Cenfrith and Wine quickly. But I continue to follow on. There are yet more trees, and the landscape is starting to climb higher. Finally, in the far distance, I can see the hills of the Welsh kingdom of Powys.

Even as dusk begins to fall, much, much later, Cenfrith still hasn't reined in Wine. She's not used to such long journeys and at such speed. Every now and then, I catch sight of her bowed head and limp tail. I'm more staggering than running now. Repeatedly, I consider just collapsing on the side of the road. But I don't. I need Cenfrith, and that requirement forces me onwards.

Before it's fully dark, I hear a hiss from the side of the track.

'Icel.'

'At last,' I huff, hands on my knees as I try to regain more breath with which to speak.

'Come here,' Cenfrith urges.

Feeling as though my legs no longer belong to me, I do as he asks, falling to the ground where he sits. I'm impressed he's managed to dismount without me. He's evidently feeling much better. Perhaps the thought of hunting down King Ecgberht, as crazy as it sounds, has reminded Cenfrith that he's a Mercian warrior.

'They're going into the Welsh kingdoms,' Cenfrith informs me, eyes bright with delight. 'He's taken the submission of the Northumbrians, as Lord Coenwulf told me, and now he means to subdue the Welsh as well.'

This doesn't surprise me as much as it might. Mercia's kings have long tried to overwhelm those who dwell on the borderlands.

'And?' I huff the one word. I can't believe I've run for so much of the day just so my uncle could determine something that seemed so clear to me from when I first saw the Wessex warriors. 'Where else would they have gone to?' I ask when my uncle doesn't reply. He's busy with the saddlebags, hunting for something, while Wine crops the grass on the ground beside me. I reach up and run my hand along her nose, an apology for such a long day. I inhale her warm breath and take it that she's just as apologetic as I am that I've been forced to run while she's had no choice but to canter.

'Somewhere,' my uncle's word comes back to me softly.

I shrug. He's started talking in riddles, and it's not because he's delirious. Not any more.

'This could be our chance,' he insists, turning back to me, eyes bright with fervour beneath the shimmering light of a clear sky overhead, half a moon shining almost as yellow as the sun.

'To go where?' I demand.

'Not to go anywhere. To save Mercia from King Ecgberht.' His words are sharp, concise.

'What?'

'King Ecgberht is going into the Welsh kingdoms. He means to fight them. Look at the supplies he's taking with him. It's a bloody risk and one that needs exploiting. If we let King Wiglaf know what's happening.'

I'm already denying his words.

'I have no intention of helping King Wiglaf. He has no more right to rule Mercia than bloody Ecgberht.'

'But Wiglaf is Mercia's king, Mercia's anointed king.' I'm

surprised by Cenfrith's argument. After so long in the wilderness, escaping from Wiglaf's abandonment of Mercia, I wouldn't expect my uncle to want anything to do with him.

'It should be the line of King Coelwulf who rules in Mercia.' I've become convinced of this. All of Mercia's problems began with King Beornwulf.

'What, so King Beornwulf and Ludica shouldn't have claimed Mercia either.' There's fury in Cenfrith's voice, and also something else that I don't understand. A hard edge, not quite mockery. But not far from it.

'No, they shouldn't,' I announce flatly. I've thought about this a great deal in the last year. Finally, I've been forced to put aside my childish belief that because I liked King Beornwulf, he did the right thing in usurping the kingdom from King Coelwulf.

'Then you want King Ecgberht of Wessex to rule your kingdom?'

I don't appreciate the emphasis on 'your' and I glare at Cenfrith, furious with him. I don't understand why we're having this argument. Not now. And not here.

'No, the Wessex king needs to bugger off back to Wessex, but neither should Wiglaf rule here.'

'Then who would you have rule Mercia? Coelwulf's son. I would have thought meeting Lord Coenwulf would have proved to you that he's not fit to rule.'

'There's a daughter as well.' I still can't believe how much I floundered when I first tried to speak with Lady Ælflæd. I remember her watching me as her brother ordered us from Kingsholm.

'And a woman would be better than a man when Mercia is surrounded by enemies?'

'A woman could have a husband.' I flail, unsure why Cenfrith is so passionate about this.

'No, we need to let King Wiglaf know where Ecgberht of Wessex is going.'

'Even if we wanted to, which I don't want to, how would we find him? Wiglaf hasn't been seen since he ran from the battle against Ecgberht, or so you've told me. If anyone knew where he was, then King Ecgberht of Wessex would have hunted him down by now, ordered his assassination, as well as that of his son.'

But my uncle is shaking his head. 'I know where King Wiglaf will be.'

My mouth drops open in shock at Cenfrith's assertion. 'And you would risk my life to tell Wiglaf what you know.'

'Sometimes...' And there's sorrow in my uncle's voice, but it doesn't stop my fury at his words. 'Sometimes, Icel, it's not all about you.'

22

We don't speak for the rest of the evening. Cenfrith lights a small
fire and, over its heat, the last of our oats boil and bubble. I eye
Wine. She seems to know that it'll only be grass from now on until
we can trade for more. Having coins isn't the problem, not since my
uncle killed the Raiders. No, we just need to find people, and with
the Wessex king on the march, that doesn't seem likely. Not in an
area so used to problems with the men of Powys and Gwynedd
anyway.

After eating, I roll myself in my cloak, not even asking my uncle
how his wounds fare. It's apparent that he won't heed my words, no
matter what they're about, so why should I bother.

I sleep, eventually, but when I wake, I'm as angry as the night
before. That only increases at my uncle's voice, floating back to me
through the trees.

'Hurry up.'

'What?' I glance round. The fire has been extinguished, Wine
no longer there, or Cenfrith. In fact, his voice comes from the road.
He hasn't even woken me.

Angrily, I stand, wrap my cloak into a bundle and thrust it into the sack I carry over my back. Only then I stop. I'll take my time, and Cenfrith will just have to wait for me, wherever he is.

I take myself to the trickle of water I've heard throughout my dreams, removing my tunic and cleaning myself thoroughly, my tunic as well. I smell bad, of too much sweat and too little water. Eagerly, I refill my water bottle in the burbling stream, listening to the birdsong overhead, and then drink it all back in one go before filling it again. My belly rumbles, but I don't have the means to cook more oats, even if I did have more oats to cook.

Instead, I bend and examine the mushrooms lying in the lee of a tumbled-down tree. They're brown ones that Wynflæd advised me could be eaten without fear of illness. I savour their texture and hastily remove all of them, stuffing them in the sack with my cloak. I might need them later.

When I emerge back onto the remains of the road, I'm unsurprised and yet angry all the same to find Cenfrith hasn't waited for me. Neither can I see him, not from where I stand.

'Bloody wonderful,' and I adopt the shambling run of the day before. Immediately, my calves start to ache, my breath ragged, all the water I've drunk churning in my belly. 'Bastard,' I direct at the world at large, startling a sparrow from where it pecks amongst the long grasses. It flies into the air, and I envy such ease. I wish I could fly. How much sooner would I catch up with my uncle.

But throughout the long, terrible day, the relentless sun overhead, I don't even hear Wine's hoofbeats, let alone see my uncle. My fury drives me onwards, long into the dusk, until unease begins to build. Cenfrith might be angry with me, but where is he? He must have realised long ago that I'd not rushed to catch up with him. Has he truly decided to abandon me entirely to fend for myself, even now?

In the distance, the road seems to buck before rearing up once more, and I see a deep ditch and a rampart, a strange green-brown stain running through the landscape. This then must be the dyke constructed under the command of the Mercian King Offa.

It's not at all what I imagined it would be like, but I continue to move towards it. I drink more water, testing the water bottle, realising I need to refill it and soon. But my uncle hasn't stopped, although I think he must before we actually reach the dyke. We can't risk going into the kingdom of Powys. I'm sure we have enough enemies as it is.

My ungainly run eventually trips me, and I stumble to the floor, remembering to roll into a ball so as not to injure my hands or head further. But it's not enough. I'm winded.

Lying flat out on the track, ignoring the rocks and weeds that press against my back, I gaze up into the night sky. The moon is sharper tonight, the stars seeming to ripple, sometimes almost close enough to touch, other times out of reach.

I laugh at my folly as my hand reaches upwards, thinking to steal one of the shimmering stars for myself.

And then a horse appears in my vision, a long pointed nose too familiar to me, and I startle upright, expecting to see Cenfrith on his mount, mouth tight with my folly. But the saddle is empty.

'Where is he?' I demand, jumping to my feet, exhaustion forgotten about apart from the dull throb of overworked feet.

Wine, of course, doesn't answer, preferring to pick at the grasses I've crushed beneath my back, releasing the pungent scent of a hot summer day. We could do with some rain.

I run my hand along Wine's grey coat, feeling that she's sweated, but not for some time. Her coat is warm but no longer sodden.

'Where is he?' I peer all round me, worry waring with rage. Is this some sort of test from him? Is he hiding in the trees far back from the road, or has something happened to him? I hardly know what to do.

The saddle is intact, the saddlebags as well.

'Where is he?' I demand from Wine again, but instead of answering, she moves forward, her nose still on the ground.

I look away, peering into the gloom, first behind me, and then in front. Only then I look where Wine is going, and I catch my breath.

Bending quickly, I place my hand on the dark mark visible against the whiteness of the old stone. My hand comes away stained and sticky. Blood. But is it my uncle's?

My eyes seek out more blood splotches and, too quickly, I find another, and then another. Then, finally, there's a circle on the road, almost a complete circle, as though someone laid a shield on the road and then ran a bleeding hand all round it.

I swallow heavily. My uncle came this way. His horse is alone. It can only be his blood.

But two distinct trails run from the circle, one further along the road, the other into the undergrowth. I know which one will be easier to follow with the light of the bright moon and stars, but that's not the one I should follow.

I scour the grasses and bushes, and just when I think there's nothing to see, I find another splash of maroon fluid. This one large and still slowly dripping to the ground beneath it. I notice that the branches are broken here as well, and more, Wine is following me.

'Cenfrith,' I call harshly, hoping my uncle might respond to me. But I don't know how badly wounded he is. Is it a fresh wound, or has he merely reopened his old wound? Neither option is reassuring.

I'm tense, my entire body quivering with unease, and Wine is being far from silent.

The ground begins to dip, a vast expanse opening up before me – a verdant valley. Somewhere close, a river rushes by, and I follow the sound. A wounded man needs water above all else.

The blood is more difficult to track here, but there's something else, the horse's hooves have left imprints in the ground that must have recently been covered with water, although there's been no rainstorm for days. Perhaps a flood that's slow to clear, or just boggy ground. I don't mind, not when I track the hooves to the river's edge and there find Cenfrith.

He's spread out on a flat rock that projects over the water. His hand uselessly hangs in the water, parting the flow, head turned to one side, eyes closed.

'Uncle,' I call to him, already on my knees, reaching into my sack for what I need, knocking aside the extra mushrooms from that morning in my haste. They tumble onto the rock, and Wine is there, snaffling them even though she won't like the taste. 'Cenfrith,' I urge, but there's no response. None at all.

Hesitantly, I reach out with my hand, place it on his back, desperate to be assured that there's movement. There is, but it's weak and laboured.

'Bollocks,' I exclaim, splashing into the water to get a look at his face. I lift his eyelids, noting how they're rolled back in his head. He's not so much asleep as unconscious.

I can't see where he's bleeding from, but the water has a pink tinge to it where it flows downstream. With tender hands, I feel for his barely healed chest wound, but there's nothing there. Even touching the bandages, my hands come away clear of blood. So he must have taken some fresh injury.

I need to move him away from the stream's edge, but I can't risk it, not until I know from where he bleeds. I could rip aside more skin. I could reopen wounds that have already begun to knit together.

I run my hands over his ill-fitting byrnie, feeling for gaps in it, hoping for some tell to guide me to the new openings in his skin, but there's nothing. So I stand frustrated and only then appreciate that it's not only his hand that's in the water, his left foot is as well, the boot almost entirely submerged.

'That must be it,' I talk to Wine, for all she's busy cropping the river weeds. I should check there's nothing poisonous there, but there's not enough light to differentiate between the small heads on the plants. I leave her to it, hopeful she knows enough not to eat something she shouldn't.

I move my uncle's foot with gentle hands, and he groans but doesn't wake.

I've found his wound, but now I need to uncover it. I hate taking boots off dead men and those too ill to do it themselves. There's just something about feet that makes it all but impossible. They flop into awkward positions, not wishing to relinquish their boots or shoes. Hands are little better.

I start to tug on the leather, one hand on the heel, the other on the top of his boot. Cenfrith groans again, words streaming from his mouth, spoken too quietly for me to decipher them.

I move slowly, carefully, but the boot won't budge.

'Damn,' and I resolve to force it from his foot without any care at all. His body buckles at the movement, but he still doesn't wake, and now, thanks to a sudden brightening of the moon as clouds move aside, I can see what the problem is.

My uncle's foot has been all but severed. A seax or, more likely, a spear, has pierced him, just below the ankle. It's exposed the innards of the foot. I gag at the sight of so much severed flesh and white bone. Wynflæd always teased me that I could stomach the sight of more blood than most, but the first sign of white bone and I would be nauseous. That's why she always encouraged me to help with broken bones, well Cuthred's broken bones. That boy must have broken his legs and arms more than once. I'm thankful to her now, although I resented it at the time.

I pour water over the wound, cleaning it as best I can, but not wanting to encourage it to bleed for longer, I reach for an old tunic in my sack and rip it to form a thin strip of bandage. I can't tell if the foot is broken, I imagine it is, but for now, I just need to keep it dry and in one place. And that place isn't beside the burbling stream.

I sigh. I'm aching all over, my feet throbbing, my hand pulsing, but my day's labour is far from done.

I stand, scouting the area, and decide on a favourable location to place him. It's far enough from the stream that the water won't rise to cover it, higher up than the line of hoofprints I've followed here and on a reasonably flat piece of land. There are trees and plants, but I can kick some of them aside and find room to place a wounded man.

I shake my head. Only now does my rage at my uncle resurface. Why did he rush out alone? What was he thinking? I've never known him to be so reckless before. What drove him to do something so out of character? I think back to our conversation the day before. My uncle hates the men of Wessex. Perhaps he hoped to kill them all.

Once more, I collect twigs and branches, a handful of stones from the river, and kindle a fire, placing a bowl of water in the smouldering flames so that it will boil. I need clean water.

Only then do I move my uncle. He's heavy, too heavy for me, really, but there's no one around to help, and although I consider enlisting the help of Wine, she doesn't have enough harness for me to make something that will work. It takes me a long time. When my uncle is finally where I want him, my muscles are shaking, and it's all I can do to check his foot no longer bleeds before I close my eyes and sleep.

The mumblings of my uncle awaken me. It's not that the words are overly loud, but they don't stop, other than for odd pauses, as though holding a conversation with someone.

'Why can't you, not now?' Cenfrith asks, but it's not to me that he speaks. 'Nothing has changed. It's your responsibility.' I shake my head. My uncle speaks in his dreams. It's not the first time.

'What?' I ask, just to be sure, but receive no reply from him. Wine nickers softly, reminding me that I've not removed her saddle. I stagger upright, feet pulsing, legs complaining, aware that daylight is beginning to flood the place. At the stream, I see a deer drinking and hold still, appreciating the beauty of the animal, its lithe body and springy legs. Others might think to kill her, devour the flesh, but I'd rather appreciate her grace.

Removing Wine's saddle, I brush her down with dry grasses and examine her. I have no oats left to feed her with, yet I won't be able to move my uncle without her. I might have resented her eating my mushrooms the previous night, but it was probably for the best.

Once Wine's free from the saddle and can lie down more comfortably, I return to Cenfrith. He sleeps, face sheeted in sweat, hands fluttering on the ground, fingers tapping a strange beat.

'What a mess,' I exhale, deftly unwrapping the binding on his foot. I don't know enough about such wounds to be able to say if it will heal. Certainly, I doubt he'll ever walk again, and not without a limp.

The flesh is hot to my touch, and I peer into the gaping wound. I need to seal it, somehow. I need Wynflæd's skills more than ever, but she's far from here. I don't even know where I might find her if she's run from Tamworth. Even though my uncle said she wouldn't be harmed, I'm not convinced. King Ecgberht of Wessex has moved against the Northumbrians, and now he seeks out the Welsh. I think an old woman and her healing craft might have also fallen beneath his blade, even though it pains me to think as such.

The water I left in the fire has boiled away. Frustrated, I up-end the rest of a water bottle into it, listening to the sizzle of cold water touching the heat. I also place my knife in the flames, having added more wood to the small fire. I know the heat will seal any wound, but the angle is so awkward, I don't know if it'll work on my uncle's ankle.

Perplexed, I consider the resources to hand. I have heat, fire, water, metal and some herbs. But I don't have a means of suspending his leg in the air, and I don't have enough food for the horse or myself. And, somewhere, probably not far from here, King Ecgberht and his Wessex warriors ride into the kingdom of Powys or Gwynedd, war on their minds. If they find us, what will they do to us? It seems evident my uncle has already fought at least one of the Wessex warriors and come off the worse for it. Where is the man he fought? Will they be looking for Cenfrith, or will they just assume he's dead?

I work quickly, deciding how best to seal the wound with my blade, and then I gaze down at my scarred palm. This time, I will use my knife, not my seax. The handle is less elaborate, any burn will leave less of an imprint. Only then do I expose my uncle's ankle and ready myself to lay the glowing blade against his skin. I eye him, seeing that he still sleeps, and then grip the handle tightly, using a tunic to keep some of the heat away from me.

I place the knife along the lower part of his foot, as tight to the ankle bone as I can get. The stench of searing flesh fills my nostrils, and Wine whinnies. My uncle stirs at the action, and I bite my lip with my upper teeth, and then move the knife a little higher. The skin sizzles and I press for as long as I can, sweat pooling down my cheeks.

When I move it aside, my uncle stirs, and I return the knife to the flames. I might need to repeat the action.

'Icel,' my uncle's eyelids flutter as he speaks. I'm amazed he only now wakes.

'Cenfrith,' I keep my voice neutral, even though I'm pleased to hear him speak.

'You must leave me here, find King Wiglaf, tell him what we've seen.'

I gasp, horrified by my uncle's words.

'You can't be moved,' I mutter, hoping such a statement will make him stop speaking. Instead, his eyes remain closed, only his lips moving, and his agitated fingers over the ground.

'I know. You must go without me. Take Wine.'

I laugh then, the sound as far from merry as it's possible to be. 'Where would I go and, more to the point, what have I actually seen?'

My uncle's eyes snap open at the words. They're clear, sparkling with fury. 'You saw King Ecgberht of Wessex, heading into the kingdom of Powys. He means to fight them, to take on the might of Cyngen ap Cadell as King Coelwulf did seven years ago when he overran Powys. And while he's gone, Mercia is ripe to be reclaimed for her rightful king.'

I tut in anger, both at the state of his ankle and his words. 'Wiglaf isn't Mercia's rightful king.'

'He's the only king Mercia has, for now.'

'Anyway,' and I lift my hands high as I speak, not wanting to replay the argument, 'where would I find him? Wiglaf has been missing ever since he ran from King Ecgberht's might, abandoning his warriors, his wife and his son.'

'I told you. I know where he'll be.' Cenfrith's words are urgent.

I eye him, aghast. 'Where will he be?'

'I can only tell you when I have your word that you'll do as I command.'

'Uncle, if I leave here, you'll die.' I speak plainly. I know he will.

He shakes his head, wincing, eyes open, his fire gone, resignation in them. 'I am but one man. I can do nothing alone, as you can see. This is what a single Wessex warrior did to me when I happened upon him. He must have heard Wine for all I thought I left enough of a gap. He didn't know who I was, only that I'm a Mercian. King Ecgberht's warriors are lethal, all of them.'

He stops speaking, and I think he's done, but he swallows his pain and looks at me again.

'Mercia is more important than just me.'

'Not to me,' I roar, unable to contain my growing sense of fear. Cenfrith is my only family.

'You must,' is his simple reply, and I feel tears on my cheeks. This is utter madness. I won't do it. I can't do it.

'Tomorrow, you'll leave me here. Gather all you can for me – water, wood, food, if there is any – and then travel to Bardney. That's where you'll find Wiglaf. Tell him of King Ecgberht's plans. He'll know what to do.'

I shake my head, unable to believe I'm having this conversation with Cenfrith. 'I don't know my way to Bardney. I don't know my way back to Tamworth, let alone Bardney.' The words tumble from my mouth with fury and panic.

'You'll have to find it. The future of Mercia depends on you doing this.'

I eye him hotly. I want to tell him he's a fool, he's mad, that he's ridiculous, but there's a ring of truth to his words that makes me hold back all of the arguments as to why I can't do what he demands from me.

For Mercia to thrive, King Ecgberht must be pushed back into his southern kingdom of Wessex. And the only person who can do so is King Wiglaf. There's no other. Not any more. No matter how much I might wish there was, because if there was another, they'd be protecting Mercia now, they'd have risen up against King Ecgberht, but no one has. Not even Lord Coenwulf, son of King Coelwulf, who shelters behind the walls at Kingsholm and does nothing to offend the Wessex king.

23

I gather together all I can for my uncle. I fill the water bottles with fresh water from the nearby brook where I found him. I hunt for and find mushrooms and other berries and even manage to catch a fish with my hands that's basking below a rock to evade the reach of the sun. It's a hot day, even the fish lethargic. I also gather wood and branches, enough stones to keep the fire contained, and long grasses upon which he can lie.

I know it won't be enough, but every time I produce my finds, Cenfrith pulls a smile from his tight lips, thanking me for doing all I can. I try not to see the pain he's feeling or to hear the moans he emits when he believes me far enough away that I'll not heed them.

I also bend and tend to his wounded ankle once more, as well as the one on his upper chest, which is almost healed, the skin tight and puckered, angry but under control. It seems impossible that his ankle will ever heal, but my uncle hasn't lived his life without injury, as the scars that cover his body attest, and in the past, he's recovered. Admittedly, with the aid of Wynflæd and good food.

In the grey half-light of dawn, I survey the scene before me, fixing it in my mind, fearful that whether Cenfrith lives or dies in my absence, I'll not find him again.

I've had some sleep, my uncle far less, and my head pounds with exhaustion and worry.

'Ride well,' Cenfrith offers me, reaching out to grip my arm. As he does so, I see the sliver of the cord round his neck once more. I know what dangles at the end of it, but I have no idea of its meaning. I open my mouth to ask. I don't want to leave here and never know, but I stop myself. To ask would be to admit that I might never see him again, and I won't be able to go to Bardney if that thought is foremost in my mind.

'And you look after yourself,' my words are jagged, spoken round a grief that threatens to undo my intentions to follow his commands.

'I always do,' Cenfrith assures me, smiling despite his pain. I've ministered to enough people to know the signs, the tight, dry lips and the flinching as though everything means to wound. 'Wine will see you right,' he assures me, his horse dipping her white-starred nose for a stroke.

'Does she know the way to Bardney?' I ask, only half-joking. I spent almost my entire life in Tamworth, with only the last year away from the place. The names of Mercia's settlements are just that, names.

I take a final look at my uncle, fixing him and where he is, in my mind, and then lead the horse away from him. We have a long distance to cover, and not much time to do it in.

But, first, I need to ensure the way for me to go is clear. Hovering on the edge of the treeline that borders the road down which I ran yesterday, and the day before, I gaze into the distance, both into Powys and into the heartland of Mercia, but there's no one around, not at this time of the morning.

Leading Wine to the road, I pause and mount up, my leg

twinging with the unexpected movement. I'm not a natural horseman. I use my cloak to cover as much of myself as possible. One final time, I peer into the woodlands I've just left, thinking of Cenfrith. But I have to do this. There was never really another choice.

* * *

The road remains clear that first day. I know it's the right one to take because Cenfrith told me as much. It feels strange to be out in the open, and not bending low to avoid overhanging branches.

I see no one until the sun is past its zenith, and then, it's only a cart being pulled by a slow ox. The man who walks beside the animal keeps his head down, not wanting to make eye contact, and I keep my mouth shut, refusing to call to him even though he'd be the first person I've spoken to for a long time who isn't Cenfrith.

Wine has adopted a constant canter beneath me, and I don't rush her onwards. If she injures herself or exhausts herself, it'll take me even longer to reach Wiglaf, and then my uncle's life will be in peril for a lengthier period of time.

It feels strange to ride so openly, even with my cloak over my head. For so long, I've kept myself hidden away, moving through the vast woodlands and forests, other than when we sheltered in the steading on the hill. I've hidden away from the problems in Mercia, determined to stay as far from the deposed and disgraced king Wiglaf as possible. But all that has changed now.

King Ecgberht of Wessex might have taken the submission of those north of the Humber, as we heard at Kingsholm, but the men and women of Powys and Gwynedd aren't going to bow to him anywhere near as easily. And in that overreaching of his resources, Mercia can reclaim herself.

As the long summer's day begins to come to an end, Wine and I move ever closer to the heart of Mercia, and we pass more and more dwellings, fields rich with crops, and herd beasts who pause in their chewing to eye us both with mild interest. Even seeing this is almost overwhelming. I've become too used to the trees and streams as the only witnesses to my actions.

'Here, boy,' a man calls to me from the doorway of his home as Wine stumbles on an overgrown root snaking across the road. 'You need to rest that animal, or she'll be no good to you come tomorrow.'

'Thank you,' I call, allowing Wine the time she needs to right her footing.

'Come, you'll be welcome inside. There's a stable for the horse and good oats.' As he speaks, the waft of something delicious cooking inside assaults my nostrils. Something I've not had to cook? The promise is too good to ignore, and I slowly dismount, eyeing him gratefully.

The man must be about Cenfrith's age, or so he appears in the growing shadows of dusk. His home is close to Watling Street, the road my uncle assured me would connect to the smaller one that I've travelled along for much of the day. There's a collection of buildings all hinting at a wealthy farmer. He walks towards me.

'My name's Osbert. What's yours?'

'Icel,' I offer warily.

'Then, young Icel, bring your horse to the stables. She could do with a long drink and a good rest.'

Wine is pliant on the end of her reins as I loop them over her ears. They twitch, disturbing a fly that's settled there. Round the back of the long building, roof hanging so low it almost touches the ground in places, I can hear the sound of more animals.

Osbert, his gait rolling as he moves to open a large wooden door on the first building, indicates the land to the building's rear.

'I have two horses and an ox, as well, for the heavy stuff. And twenty cattle, and fifty sheep. Not bad for a small steading.'

Now I'm closer to him, his face is more lined than I at first thought, and on glancing at his hands on the door, I see that one of them is reddened, as though burned, and the tip of his left ear is missing. His hand makes me think of my scar. It's finally stopped itching, and while I've been riding, it's been impossible to ignore the temptation of running my one hand over the other. It feels strange, I can't deny it.

'Lost the ear in an accident with a scythe,' he offers. 'The hands when my first steading burned down, fifteen years ago now. It's taken time to rebuild all that you see here.'

Wine eagerly enters the stall he indicates, and I remove her saddle and harness, using some of the straw to wipe her clean. Osbert brings a bucket of water, and she eagerly drinks.

'Where's a young lad like you off to in such a hurry?'

There, the question I've been eager to put off answering.

'I'm a messenger for the king, returning to Tamworth.'

'Aye, which king would that be?' His words have less warmth now. Suddenly I'm anxious. I thought the man generous to extend his hospitality, but now I fear I've erred.

'The king of Mercia,' I try to counter, only for his dark eyes to narrow.

'And which king would that be?'

'Wiglaf,' I state, head held high, chin out. My hands have bunched into fists at my side, ready in case he wants to start a fight with me.

'Then you'll not find him at Tamworth. The runt is in hiding, but I imagine you know that.'

'I do,' I confess, meeting his eyes once more, now that it seems we're not about to come to blows. 'I hope to find him elsewhere, with news of the Wessex usurper's attack on the kingdom of Powys.'

'Is that where all those warriors were heading earlier in the week? That makes sense to me,' Osbert muses as we make our way into his home.

Inside, there's light from a small hearth, over which a cauldron hangs, the source of the smell. I pick out three sets of eyes by the light: a woman sitting with spindle and whorl while two children are busy playing a complicated game with small counters and something that should be a die but isn't, instead flecked with different colours.

'My wife, Acha, and my two sons, Sigbert and Sigegar.'

They watch me with interest as I sit on the offered stool but don't speak.

'He's off to find our missing king. The Wessex one has decided to attack Powys. That's not going to end well,' Osbert quickly informs his wife, his tone flecked with both humour and confidence.

She nods, although I can see her lips moving.

'Counting,' Osbert announces as an explanation, moving to spoon pottage into a well-worn wooden bowl.

It's too hot to eat straight away, but I attempt it, all the same. I'm famished, my belly so worn out with rumbling that it's actually quiet.

'Take your time, lad. There'll be more yet,' Osbert cautions me, although his words are gently spoken. The mixture is rich with peas and beans and onions, and something else.

'Chicken?' I ask, and he nods, smiling as he does so. He doesn't offer any to his wife or children, and I take it to mean they've eaten, and this is something for the morning. And then he hands me a flat piece of bread, stale round the edges but good for dipping.

I can't keep the smile from my lips as I raise my hand high to acknowledge the addition to my meal.

'A lad like you needs feeding, or he'll always be scrawny, no matter how tall he grows. What have you been doing, living on berries and mushrooms?'

It's not far from the truth, and that startles me. But Osbert waves his hand aside.

'You won't be the first to have hidden away under our usurper king. God rot his bones. They tried to take my good oxen with them, but I refused, asked them how a man was to pay his taxes without the means to till his fields. The cur relented soon enough, but he had half an eye to my lads. And they're to farm, after me, not run off to some battlefield to feed the soil before their time.'

As Osbert speaks, he watches his sons, fierce resolve on his face.

'Tell me, what news is there?' Now that Osbert has worked out where I've been, I see no harm in asking after local matters.

'It's a mess,' Osbert warms to his subject quickly. 'King Ecgberht of Wessex thinks Mercia is good for little but filling his coffers. The men he's set over Mercia in place of the ealdormen, most of whom are in hiding, even that Sigered, which I admit, surprises me, ensure there's no justice, little peace and add their weight to any who transgress, provided they do so in the name of King Ecgberht. But,' and Osbert pauses now, leaning back to drink deeply of his ale. 'I hear rumours of Raiders on the borders, some even inside Mercia, and the Carolingians, those who back this here King Ecgberht in taking Mercia, have stopped sending him the aid he needs. There'll be no money from them, or warriors.

'Why else has he gone off to claim sovereignty over the men and women of Powys? Mark my words, the time is rife for King Wiglaf to make his reappearance. People might not have liked him, after everything that happened to poor old King Coelwulf, God rest his soul, but they'd sooner have anyone over them than bloody Ecgberht of Wessex.'

Osbert's words so mirror my uncle's that I startle. Sometimes, as my uncle suggested, it really isn't all about me.

* * *

'Thank you for your hospitality,' I offer Osbert early the following day, stifling a yawn.

He nods and holds Wine's reins as I mount up, a pensive look in his eyes. 'You tell King Wiglaf, when you see him, that he'll be forgiven if he gets his arse back to Mercia right now. If not, well, even with the Carolingians leaving bloody King Ecgberht without their support, I doubt Mercia will recover itself.'

'I will.' I promise, even as I doubt that I'll be able to say as much to King Wiglaf.

Osbert grins. 'You tell him that when he demands an oath from you. You give him yours in exchange for him doing what he swore to do two years ago. He needs to be the king, not some king in hiding.'

And with that, I place a silver coin in Osbert's hand that I took from one of the dead Raiders, which he snatches gratefully, and I'm on my way once more.

24

Wine's head hangs low as we follow the Foss Way northwards. Our journey has been too long, every step taking me away from my uncle. Just thinking about him makes me want to dismount and run onwards. I'll get there more quickly that way. But I don't. Wine and I have been on this voyage together. I won't abandon her. Not now. Not when we've endured so much together.

I've not ridden well, and she's been careful with me, somehow appreciating the aches and sores a body gets when it's not used to riding.

I've found the roads I've travelled since that first day remarkably busy, and yet every man who looked like a warrior I've encountered, head down, face covered by my cloak, has worn the white wyvern of Wessex on their shield, byrnie or helm. How many of the bastards are there within Mercia?

Surely King Wiglaf can't have enough to overpower so many of the Wessex warriors? Not now, when he's perceived as so weak. But I must do as Cenfrith commanded me. It might be the last thing he ever asks from me.

The last time I asked for directions from a woman picking berries from the hedgerow, a keen look in her eye at being hailed by a lad on a fine horse, she assured me I would reach Bardney that day. Yet, I'm still to see any sign of a settlement ahead, any settlement as I meander through the flat landscape. It shocks me after the hills of the borderlands with Powys and Gwynedd.

I'm weary and hungry and so too is Wine. But the end is close. I can feel it. I'll allow myself to rest, perhaps beg the use of another horse, and be on my way back to Cenfrith as soon as possible. He promised me he'd stay alive in my absence. I have to trust him to do so.

And then, between one tired glance and the next, something finally appears amongst the tedium of fields planted with low-lying crops, basking beneath the too-hot sun. There's not even the hint of a breeze to drive the sweat from my face. Beneath me, Wine finds some fresh speed and then I'm dismounting before the selection of buildings that rise from the flat ground, a thin strip of smoke leaking away into the cloudless blue sky.

'Hail,' the voice is gruff, not at all the sound I expect to hear from the man who's dressed as a monk as I bang on the door, announcing my presence.

'Hail,' my voice reeks of exhaustion, and before I know it, the monk is by my side, holding me as I all but slide to the ground.

'You're weary?' he announces, his words filled with understanding, as he supports me. I don't miss that behind us, the small doorway in a larger wooden gate, has slammed shut.

'I've travelled a long way. At the bequest of my uncle, Cenfrith.'

'Icel?' the word rings with shock, and I nod, even though I don't recognise the man.

'Where is Cenfrith?' The man looks behind me, and then notices Wine. 'Is he well?'

'No, not at all. But he sent me here, to find King Wiglaf. I have important information.' I still don't recognise the man, but he does push his hood backwards so I can see into piercing blue eyes, and I startle with recognition.

'Come inside.'

The gateway opens, and a small girl runs out to hook the reins from the horse's back and lead her inside, words cajoling. I don't recognise her from Tamworth. I wobble on behind, knowing that without the support of the monk, I'd fall to my knees.

The small door bangs shut behind me. I peer all round me, expecting to see no one, but behind the gateway and enclosure, there's a hubbub of activity, warriors training, iron clanging together, and from amongst it all strides King Wiglaf, a hand shading his eyes, peering at me. I wonder how I've not heard the noise from out on the road. Perhaps I didn't want to hear it.

I eye King Wiglaf uneasily. I don't like the man. I'd go so far as to say I hate him. I hate him all the more because my uncle bid me leave him with his life in danger in order to come here.

'My Lord King.' The monk casts aside his cloak, and I can see that he wears the trews and byrnie of a fighting man. A clever place to hide away. Even better because the inside of the monastery has enough space for the men and horses who take refuge there, clearly rebuilding their strength after King Ecgberht's attack. 'This is Cenfrith's nephew.'

'And why is he here, Ælfstan?' Anger fletches Wiglaf's words. Distaste flickers on his face, his brown beard with one or two flecks of white, downcast, just like his mouth. I don't know if it's because he recognises me, or because of my association with Cenfrith.

'Cenfrith sent him. On his horse, Wine.' Those words mean more to the pair of them than they do to me. A flicker of understanding softens Wiglaf's face. I can see where he carries a scar that wasn't there last time I met him. It runs from the corner of his eye to the tilt of his lips. A nasty wound. No doubt delivered by one of the Wessex warriors when they overpowered him. My uncle said Wiglaf ran without a fight, but that might not be the case after all. But why would my uncle have lied to me?

'My Lord King,' I can barely force the words through my dry lips, as I feel my eyes flickering closed with exhaustion.

'What is it, boy? Spit it out.' Wiglaf's words aren't sympathetic.

'King Ecgberht. He travels to Powys. Six days ago, no more. He was heading into the heart of Powys.'

Understanding kindles quickly on both the warrior-monk's face, who I now know to be Ealdorman Ælfstan, and also on Wiglaf's.

'You're sure of this?' The intensity in Wiglaf's voice jolts me to full wakefulness.

'I saw them with my own eyes. The white Wessex wyvern on black, on shields and saddles, on everything. The king with a helm crowned with white horsehair. I saw King Ecgberht himself.'

A slow smile spreads across Wiglaf's face. I can see his thoughts clearly. And he turns aside speaking as he does so.

'Feed him, let him rest. And then return to my side.'

I peer at Ælfstan, he's nodding slowly, resolve showing in the tight line of his jaw.

'Come on, we'll do as the king commands.' I sag against him, half of my journey is completed. But the most important part is still to be done.

'Is Wynflæd here?' I ask as the king moves away, his steps purposeful as he calls other men to him.

Ælfstan doesn't hear me, as he escorts me into a large hall and leaves me on a wooden bench. He goes to speak to a collection of women, and I note the figures at the top of the hall. Lady Cynethryth and her son, Wigmund. I feel bitter watching him sit in the king's hall rather than training with the king's men. He's no warrior, and he never was.

Quickly, a bowl of pottage is before me, piled high with chunks of white fish, fresh baked bread as well, and I eat as though I've not eaten for two weeks, trying to calm myself, take my time, but unable to, all at the same time. I'm also eager to avoid the scrutiny of the king's wife and his son. How I despise Wigmund.

No sooner have I finished eating and drinking the water offered to me than I feel my eyes close once more.

'This way,' one of the women smiles at me, her brown eyes filled with sympathy. Again, I don't recognise her from Tamworth. 'A good sleep and all will be well with the world.'

But it won't be. Not until I return to Cenfrith's side.

* * *

'Wake up, the king wants you.' The hand that shakes me is far from gentle. Groggily, I rouse, and peer at the same man who helped me when I first arrived, Ealdorman Ælfstan. 'Bollocks, you sleep like the dead, boy. Now hurry, the king requires you.'

I try to move quickly, summoned by the King of Mercia, but I'm too slow, and in the end, Ælfstan bends and assists me with my boots while I force my tunic over my chest.

'What does he want from me?' I think to ask, moving through the hall and outside once more. Here, there's a grey edge to the dawn, and I shiver at the dampness in the air.

The man doesn't answer, leading me to King Wiglaf in silence.

The king is surrounded by men and horses, all of them clearly ready to ride out to war even though it's barely light enough to see.

'Ah, here you are. You'll ride with me. I want you at my side.'

'But, My Lord King, I must return to my uncle. He's wounded, perhaps mortally. I need Wynflæd to help me heal him.' I'm staggered that I argue with the king, but I've only just woken. My thoughts are muddled. I expect the king to berate me.

This isn't what King Wiglaf wants to hear. That much is clear. His eyes harden and I feel the warrior behind me step closer, no doubt to prevent me fleeing.

'You fled from my domain when it was threatened, and now you bring me news of King Ecgberht being absent from Mercia. How am I to trust your word?' Only, King Wiglaf leaves me no time to answer. 'I can't trust you, even though you name your uncle as the man who sent you this way. But, with you at my side, I can punish you, should treachery be your intention.' The words thrum, seemingly louder than thunder. I shudder at the implication in them, even as I damn my uncle for forcing me into the wolf's lair. I shouldn't have trusted Cenfrith, not when he was delirious with pain.

'I must take Wynflæd to my uncle.' I speak with calm assurance, even though my legs tremble beneath me.

'You'll only have Wynflæd when I know your word is true. And not before. After all, you knew where to find me, even though no one else has yet found me. But you knew where I was, and you might have told King Ecgberht of my hiding place as well. This might all be a ruse. As soon as my men and I ride forth through these gates that have sheltered us for many months, the Wessex king might be there to kill me.'

'My Lord King.' I shriek, outrage in my words, fear as well. He's told me that Wynflæd lives, but I don't have time to absorb that information.

'Oh, so you do acknowledge me as your king then, the rightful king of Mercia.'

My pulse thuds in my neck, my mouth struggling to form words.

'I do, My Lord King, yes.' I rein my emotions in.

'Then you'll kneel before me and give me your oath as my sworn warrior.'

There's no time for this, none at all. But King Wiglaf is insistent. I can tell from the way his right hand clenches round his seax hilt that he's not far from cutting me with the blade.

I swallow. I feel a fool for thinking the king would be pleased to see me, to learn of what I knew. I think of my uncle, risking his life to tell the king what we'd discovered. I can do this for him. Not for King Wiglaf.

But first, I must speak again.

'I'm no warrior, My Lord King. Do you forget that Wynflæd was teaching me her knowledge, in Tamworth? I'm a healer, not a warrior.'

Distaste covers King Wiglaf's face, while Ælfstan, his cloak flung over both shoulders, startles. Does he think me moon-touched as well? I see his lips fall downwards.

'I'll still have your oath, as you carry a seax, and ride one of the finest horses a warrior could ever hope to own. You look like a warrior, with your height and your reach.'

'Very well, My Lord King.' I want to argue, refuse to do as he bids, but I must return to Cenfrith. If this is the means by which I do so, then I'll do it. I'll do anything to ensure Cenfrith lives. For a moment, I do consider Osbert's words from the first night of my journey, that I should demand from the king what he demands from me, but I don't want to delay any further.

I bend my knee, first the left one, and then the right, until, head bowed, I have both knees on the hard ground, a pile of horse shit just to the side of me, the scent almost too pungent. I'm aware that, round me, others have stilled in their tasks and watch this strange tableau.

Ealdorman Ælfstan steps forwards so that I can see only his feet and nothing else. In a melodious voice he intones the words I must say, for I don't know them. I've never witnessed men giving their oaths to the king. I certainly never thought to have to speak them myself.

'I pledge to be loyal and true to King Wiglaf of Mercia, and love all that he loves, and hate all that he hates, in accordance with my commitments.'

I mirror the words of Ælfstan, stumbling over some of them in my rush to have them spoken. He notices that much is clear, for the next words are spoken even more slowly, as though he means for me to follow his lead.

'And never, freely or deliberately, in word or deed, do anything that is intolerable to him; on condition that he keep me as is our covenant, when I subjected myself to him and took his service.'

When it's my turn to repeat the second part of the oath, I speak clearly, the words ringing from my throat, even if I don't mean them. I'll do this for my uncle.

'You'll ride by my side, to Tamworth. I'll claim back what's mine, and only then can you leave me, and only with an assurance that you'll return, once your uncle is healed. Both of you will be my sworn men, owing allegiance only to me.' Wiglaf's words are forceful.

Head bowed, examining his boots, I nod, and then clear my throat because Wiglaf won't have witnessed my movement.

'I'll do as you request, My Lord King. I swear it.'

Silence follows my pronouncement. I hold still, not wanting to shatter the sacred moment when I swore my life to a man I despise, and all for my uncle, and for my homeland.

'Good, then stand, and prepare yourself. We leave shortly. Take one of the horses from the stables. Your horse has been badly used and needs the rest.'

I return to my feet, refusing to look away from King Wiglaf. I trust him as much as he trusts me. More, the care he shows to my uncle's horse is so counter to his intentions towards me and my uncle that I want to do nothing more than spit in his face, turn my back on him. Never see him again. But I can't. I need Wynflæd.

Round me, the men preparing to ride to Tamworth, and the servants who assist them, scurry to return to their tasks. There's a maelstrom, and I'm entirely apart from it. I catch sight of Lady Cynethryth in the doorway of the church. Wigmund stands beside her. It's evident Wigmund isn't about to journey to war with his father. I wonder whose decision that is.

I turn back to King Wiglaf, and he grins, driving back the years that age him from a face grown harsh and severe ever since he ran from the Wessex king with the only thought for his life. If that is, indeed, what he did. I'm not so sure, not any more. If Wiglaf were such a coward, then why would so many of the Mercian warriors be here, ready to fight at his side? Equally, why would my uncle have lied to me?

'We'll retake the capital, Tamworth, and drive that bastard Ecgberht from my kingdom. And you'll prove yourself a man in the meantime. It's not all bad.' And he strides away, recalled to some duty he must perform.

I stand my ground, unsure what to do, or where to do it.

'You're lucky,' Ælfstan grunts. 'He's so desperate to believe you, he's prepared to forgive your treason easily. Should you play him false, he'll kill you.' The words are filled with menace, crowding my pounding head as I hold my stance.

I'm no warrior. I'm no killer, and yet, my uncle has sent me to the king of Mercia, and now I must fight in his war band. It's not going to end well. Far from it.

* * *

The horse assigned to me by a surly-looking stableman is a piebald stallion who dances uneasily beneath me. An animal as good as this one should surely belong to a king, or one of his ealdormen. But the animal is unruly, more inclined to do what it wants than follow my commands. I can see why I've been gifted such a beast.

I'm far from forgiven for coming here, or for disappearing from Tamworth, or for anything. Now they mean to test me with an animal that requires skills beyond my control.

If it weren't for Cenfrith, lying broken in the forest close to Powys, I wouldn't even attempt to master such a creature.

I pause next to Wine, where her head hangs tiredly over the stable door.

'Sorry, girl,' I offer, and she whiffles the scent of warm hay into my nostrils. 'I'll get him,' I promise her. 'I'll bring him back for you.'

Wine holds my eyes, as though she understands the words, and then she licks my hand. Her tongue is rough, and it rubs over the scar from the heated seax.

I nod. It seems we need say no more to one another.

No sooner have I joined the rear of the band of warriors riding under the king's command than the horse, named Brute by the stableman, although I don't know if it's the animal's name, or temperament, is rushing me towards the slowly opening gateway. The king is there, leading his men to reclaim his kingdom, but my horse has other ideas.

Crouching low in the saddle, when my heels and commands on the rein don't stop the animal, I decide there's nothing for it but to allow the horse to work through whatever complaints it has about its rider, and the conditions it's been kept in.

Passing the king, and trying to avoid his displeased and wide-eyed stare, I aim the animal down the roadway, aware someone else follows me closely. I risk a glance, and see Ealdorman Ælfstan, his forehead furrowed in confusion.

'The horse won't stop,' I call, words lost on the wind, as the road I travelled over so slowly only the day before rushes by far too quickly now. It takes all of my skill to hold on. I can feel my legs almost trailing behind, my arse aching from the unfamiliar bony back and saddle. No matter what I do, Brute won't stop.

I close my eyes, aware of a sharp bend coming soon, only then I hear more hooves, and startle as a hand closes over mine, pulling tightly on the reins. Even more tightly than I already was. Brute's speed begins to slow, and I turn to face the grinning face of Ælfstan who threatened me, should I be a traitor.

'Bloody arseholes,' he explodes. 'This horse shouldn't have been given to you. But now you have him, you need to learn to control him. He'll take direction, but only if it's sharply given. None of this pulling and then pulling more. A sharp tug will slow him. Heels in his flanks will only make him move more quickly. He's a contrary animal. I'm impressed you stayed seated.'

There's surprise and admiration in his voice. I'm just pleased to have slowed enough to be able to pick out the stones on the road, as opposed to them flashing by in a pale grey haze.

'My thanks,' I breathe as we come to a complete stop.

'The horse is worth too much to have let you run off,' now his words are gruff, and in the near distance, I can see the rest of the party beginning to catch us. 'Remember,' Ælfstan offers, 'firm and sharp movements, or you'll be upended before the day's out, and the king will curse you even more for being dead.'

I swallow down the argument I wish to voice. This man won't want to hear it, and worse, he already knows the truth about the horse.

'I know your uncle,' he clarifies. 'He's a good man. He should never have run when Wiglaf was defeated. If you handle this correctly, the king will welcome him back.'

'If he still lives,' I retort, face flushing.

'He'll live. Cenfrith is a stubborn git. Now, stay out of sight of the king. Then, he might forget all about you.'

I grimace. 'Easier said than done with this bloody horse, but I'll do what I can.'

'You'll do more than that. You'll succeed.'

With that, Ælfstan turns his horse, a black mare, tail swishing high in the air, a jaunty step to her.

He calls to the king. 'Damn fool's never ridden a decent horse before. That old nag of Cenfrith's is no comparison.'

I strain to hear the king's reply, even as I flush at those who stare at me as they ride past. I meet their gazes evenly. I won't be cowed by this trick. And, anyway, the king has already commented on Wine's pedigree. The king, no doubt, will be more than aware of what's happened to me.

* * *

We ride for the rest of the day without incident, following the track of the Foss Way. Some areas of the road are well-maintained, others clogged with grasses, and in one or two places, there's nothing to show there was ever a road there in the first place.

With some silent arguing, I manage to get Brute to follow my instructions and not vice versa. But it's a struggle. All day long, as soon as I lower my guard, even if only to swill water into my mouth, he skips sideways, or backwards or lurches forwards. By the time we stop for the night, I'm sweat-soaked and fuming all over again.

I shouldn't be here. I should be returning to Cenfrith. I can't even ride the damn horse the king ordered I was given. Perhaps it would be wise to tell him that I have even less skill with a seax, let alone a war axe.

Even though I travelled this road recently, I can't decide how far we've come. I've not been seeking out landmarks I saw on the way to Bardney. I've been trying to keep my horse from making an arse of me once more.

'Where are we?' I ask another of the warriors. He's a slight man, bow-legged, and with a mop of hair so blond, it's almost white.

'On the way to Tamworth,' his words are guttural, and only just intelligible.

'But where on the way to Tamworth?' I press, stepping clear of my horse as he tries to kick me in the shin.

'Somewhere,' is the only response I get.

I can smell smoke and something cooking, and my stomach growls. I have no idea where to go or what to do now that the troop has stopped for the night. I thought we would ride until the horses dropped, but it seems that King Wiglaf wishes to reach Tamworth, just not yet. Impatience gnaws at me.

I finish caring for my horse, leading him to drink from a brook and offering a sack full of oats, which he takes now I stand beside him as opposed to ride him, before carrying the saddle towards one of the first campfires I see.

'Not here,' a rough voice calls out, the man's back turned to me. 'We don't want your kind here.' I recognise him as the man who used to be Lady Cynethryth's guard in Tamworth, Oswy.

I would argue, but Ealdorman Ælfstan beckons to me, from another campfire, and I stamp out my fury on the way to him.

'Sit here, and keep your head down,' he urges me, indicating the cooking pot and implying I can help myself.

'Stay away from Oswy and his ilk. They're all troublemakers, but good for bashing heads together when needed. Especially Wessex heads, and Northumbrian heads.'

I scowl into the fire, settled on the trampled-down grass.

'It won't be long and you'll be away from the king,' Ealdorman Ælfstan offers eventually, after I've eaten my fill of pottage, flavoured with strips of pork. 'Provided you're not a treasonous git, that is,' he can't stop himself from adding.

It's far from reassuring. The only person here, other than the king, who seems to give a damn about me, and even he's far from sure.

'The king wants you.' It's Ealdorman Ælfstan who summons me from my place at the rear of the train of horses. As he suggested, I've kept out of everyone's way as much as possible. It's made the previous two days much easier on me, even if my hands ache from all the effort I've put into controlling Brute. My scar has added a blister to it. It's bloody painful.

I don't like the horse. He doesn't like me either. I'll be pleased to reclaim Wine, even if it's nice to ride instead of running on foot. I doubt I'd have enough coins to purchase a horse for myself, even if I collected all of the wealth buried in the rich earth close to the kingdom of Powys, and the remnants I keep in the money pouch taken from the Raiders.

I'd ask why the king wants me but appreciate that Ealdorman Ælfstan isn't going to tell me; that much is obvious from the way he doesn't meet my eyes but instead waits, impatiently, for me to join him to the side of the main body of men.

The dust on the road here is thick, covering my clothes and the coat of my horse. It's almost worth being summoned by King Wiglaf to move aside from the fug. It's too damn hot. Sweat clogs everything, and where sweat forms, dust is close behind. Overhead, the sun is fierce and unrelenting, no trace of clouds to be seen.

I sneeze, the sound jarring Brute to a quick canter and, hissing at the pain in my hand, I tug back on the rein, forcing him to obey me, which he does..

Ælfstan, having moved his horse aside at the movement, comes closer now.

'Well done. Have you mastered the beast so soon? I'm impressed.' And he sounds it. I search his face for some hint of mockery, noting the speckles of blond in his brown beard again, but there's none to find.

'You were right. Firmness. He doesn't like being given his head,' I reply, feeling that if he can offer me some praise, I can extend my thanks.

Ælfstan nods but offers nothing else.

I observe the horses and warriors as I make my way to the king. It seems everyone is just as hot and dust-streaked as I am. They don't ride in silence, but neither is this march categorised by the laughing and good humour I expect to hear. Instead, I detect something else, in sharp movements and heaving chests. Are these warriors of King Wiglaf's scared of what they'll find at Tamworth?

I can hardly believe that seasoned warriors would fear King Ecgberht this much. But then I reconsider. These men know only that two of Mercia's kings died on the blades of Athelstan of the East Angles' men, while Wiglaf has surrendered his kingdom to the might of Wessex rather than die for it. Many of these men might never have fought against such an enemy. If they're with Wiglaf now, most of them wouldn't have been involved in the battles against King Athelstan. If they had been, they'd be long dead.

Mercia is weak. The knowledge makes me uneasy when it's laid so bare before me.

'Ah, Icel.' But King Wiglaf smiles on seeing me. He's dust-covered as well, but not as much as I am. I scrub at my face, hopeful of removing some of the grime, but all I accomplish is to make it even worse.

'My Lord King,' I bow from the saddle of my horse.

'You're brave to do that, on the back of that horse.' Wiglaf rumbles, and I glance at him, eyes skirting between his and Ælfstan's. Now I think they both mock me, but there's no sign of ridicule on their faces again.

'He needs a firm hand.' I swallow round the words. 'I've heeded Ealdorman Ælfstan's advice.'

'Have you?' Now it's the king who looks from me to Ælfstan, his expression inscrutable. 'I want to hear about King Ecgberht again. You tell me he was heading into Powys?'

I nod, and then recall that I'm speaking to the king. 'Yes, using the remains of the old road, the one you can find to the west of Wall.'

'And why were you there?'

I hesitate, but the time for secrecy is long past.

'My uncle and I were hiding out in the woodlands close to the border. My uncle hoped to evade the reaches of King Ecgberht.' That's the truth.

'Well, that makes sense, at least. And you saw them on this road?'

'I did, yes.' And now I pause, remembering the Raiders. 'We encountered Raiders as well. That's why we were there.'

King Wiglaf meets my eyes, his gaze sharper than before. News of the Raiders will be unwelcome. I should have remembered that before now.

'How many of them?'

'Five. We killed them all – or rather, my uncle did. We saw no one else.' I should perhaps have taken some battle glory for myself, but I want to remind the king that I'm no warrior.

The king looks away, peering into the distance, at the fields lying beneath the blaze of the sun, at the road ahead.

'So, you've been in the borderlands for some time and only encountered these five Raiders.'

'Yes, My Lord King.'

'Then I must thank your uncle for killing them for me. Ealdorman Ælfstan, I task you with teaching Icel how to use that seax on his weapons belt. Ensure he can protect himself when he fights as my oath-sworn warrior.'

I consider shaking my head, denying his words. But he's the king. So I must do as he asks, no matter how much I know I'll fail.

'My Lord King,' Ælfstan's voice thrums with annoyance.

'Do as I command,' Wiglaf snaps, not quite with irritation. Whatever's happening here, I don't understand it.

I bow again, allowing the king to move on while I back Brute away from the train of horses and men.

'Wonderful,' Ælfstan complains, eyeing me without remorse for his harsh words.

'I'm not happy about it either,' I retort, colour flooding my face, making me even hotter than before.

'You'll try your hardest,' Ælfstan grunts, scrutinising me with the practised eye of a man used to sizing up his opponents. 'You'll do everything I say, and then, if you're lucky, you'll live through this and be able to return to your uncle if he lives.' But, of course, there's no hope of success in either of those statements, and my fists curl on the reins.

Ealdorman Ælfstan notices and laughs at me, his shoulders shaking with the motion.

'Well, there might be a bit of spark in you after all.'

* * *

That evening, Ealdorman Ælfstan seeks me out to begin my training as the king instructed. I'm sitting away from the rest of the warriors but still close enough that I can hear their conversation. As I suspected, it's doom-laden. These men don't believe they can win. That concerns me. It seems more than just the king think I lie about King Ecgberht being far to the west.

'Ignore them,' Ælfstan cautions me, as we find a clear space amongst the campfires and horses. 'These aren't the king's most skilled warriors. They're here for the numbers, more than anything. Wiglaf has his loyal household troop close to him. They fought to overpower King Ecgberht when he came for Tamworth. They would have succeeded if the Wessex king wasn't such a sly bugger. I'm sure you remember.'

I don't, but I nod all the same. I wasn't at Tamworth when King Ecgberht rode through Mercian land and came knocking on the door. My uncle had already arranged for me to flee. I'm still not sure I understand his motivations. I'm also surprised by the story. My uncle told me that King Wiglaf fled the battlefield when he was overrun, leaving good Mercians to die. He said he watched it happen. But it seems that's not the case. And that realisation has been worrying me ever since I arrived at Bardney. Did my uncle lie to me? Or did he simply not see what really happened?

'King Ecgberht held back no more than twenty of his men,' Ælfstan continues, even as he has me jabbing with my seax against his own weapon. He's covered the blades with pieces of linen wrapped tightly round just the sharpened edge. I still think it'll bloody hurt if he lands a blow on me, and my blister has popped so that it both hurts more and less now. 'And when King Wiglaf believed he'd won, his warriors as well and they began to relax, that bastard Ecgberht sent these twenty men in under cover of darkness, cresting the ditch and the rampart, and they almost killed the king during the night.'

'So, only twenty Wessex men caused Wiglaf to flee from Tamworth?' I'm startled. This isn't what I've been told. I didn't even know that Wiglaf made it back to Tamworth. I understood he'd bolted from the battlefield.

'In the end, yes. See here,' and Ælfstan lifts his tunic and shows me a long scar running along his back. It's ragged and pink in places where the stitches have been pulled too tight. I don't sense Wynflæd's hand in the work. 'One of the scum did this to me. True warriors would never fight from behind, using stealth and deception. A real man faces his enemy and stares him in the eyes. Remember that.' He jabs forward once his tunic is lowered, and I finally counter one of his strokes with my seax, but it's more chance than skill. 'Not bad,' he compliments me, coming at me again and again, pulling short when my blade is too slow. 'It'll come,' Ælfstan assures me when I slump to the ground, exhausted only a short time later. 'You have natural talent, like your uncle. He's a mean one in a fight, and the tighter the fight, the better he becomes.' I think Ælfstan speaks to reassure me, but he doesn't.

'I don't have his skill,' I admit softly, puffing through dry lips. 'When he fights, it's as though time slows, and his opponent's movements can never counter his.'

'Well, that's a fancy way of saying it, but remember, he had to learn his craft first. No man can just pick up a seax or spear and become competent in its use. Although, admittedly, some will find it easier than others.'

'Why are you helping me?' I pluck up the courage to ask.

His forehead crinkles in thought, and then he smirks, offering me his hand as he hauls me upwards, his intention to continue with our work evident. 'Everyone needs someone to show them the way and, of course, the king did order me to teach you to fight.' And he says nothing further, talking with his seax, not his mouth.

* * *

The following day, I startle on realising we're close to Tamworth. I expected King Wiglaf to form his warriors up before now and have them deployed so that they could rush the settlement and retake control, but it seems not. Instead, they continue to ride onwards, the only change I can detect, the six warriors who now guard the rear. I can only assume the same at the front.

I think to ask one of the other men, but none of them speaks to me, other than Ealdorman Ælfstan. Worry gnaws at me. I saw more of the Wessex king's men when I travelled to Bardney. Where are they all now? Do they suspect an ambush by Wiglaf? If Wiglaf fails here, my life might be in peril, and then how will I return to my uncle?

Brute is frisky beneath me. I appreciate he must sense my unease. I do my best to control my pounding heart, aware that the closer we get to Tamworth, the quieter the remaining warriors have become. If I were King Wiglaf, I'd be chivvying my men on, assuring them of victory. Certainly, that's what King Beornwulf would have done. But then, they're different people, very different people.

Before me, the sight of Tamworth resolves itself into the landscape, and I feel a pang of longing for the home I knew for all of my life until Ecgberht claimed Mercia. I know every nook and cranny inside Tamworth. I know the best places to hunt for all the herbs and mushrooms that Wynflæd needs for her healing potions, the gentle streams where garlic could be found, the dense woodlands where the most potent mushrooms would be hidden. I might have been able to find what I've needed in the woods, but it would have been much easier here.

I expect King Wiglaf to call a halt to the forward march, to have us wait until darkness falls to begin his attack. But, instead, I'm astounded when he simply rides through the open gateway to meet the curious eyes of those I've not seen since I left here.

'Where are the Wessex warriors?' Wiglaf demands loudly of Siric and the blacksmith, men who watch Wiglaf with disbelief in their eyes. I see Edwin's mother as well, although she doesn't notice me. I've brought Brute forward, the line disintegrating as the fearful Mercians realise there'll be no battle that day, and joy makes them careless of horses and people.

'They've gone, My Lord King,' the blacksmith bows low before King Wiglaf. He must have been forced to serve whichever king claimed Tamworth no matter his opinion on the subject. His skills would have ensured he lived. Cenfrith implied that all the men and boys would be put to death by the Wessex king. But that's evidently not the case either. Has my uncle purposefully lied to me again or is it more that he didn't wait long enough to find out what would happen?

'When?' There's a vein of frustration in King Wiglaf's voice. He came here to defeat his foe; to drive any Wessex warriors from Tamworth and reclaim it as his capital, fly his eagle banner above the sealed gates and from the rampart.

'Yesterday morning. A messenger came, and they took the west road. They didn't even leave warriors to guard the gates. It seems they knew of your impending arrival.' It's more of a question than a statement.

'Ealdorman Ælfstan,' the king calls for the warrior, and he quickly works his way to Wiglaf's side. The two converse, heads bowed, and then Ælfstan moves aside, collecting a handful of men as he goes. I try to avoid his gaze. I don't want to be involved in whatever's about to happen.

The men dismount, even as others shriek in delight at being reunited with people they've not seen since Ecgberht took

Tamworth. I don't see Wynflæd, though. Neither do I see Cuthred or Beornwyn.

And then my eyes are drawn to Ealdorman Ælfstan, as he leads the six men into the king's hall. I can hear them calling to one another before they emerge and move onto the next collection of buildings, the stables, Wynflæd's workshop, that of the blacksmith, the grain store, the animal shed, and on and on until they've been in and out of every building, often accompanied by shrieks of outrage from those who've not realised King Wiglaf has returned to Tamworth.

'Nothing, My Lord King,' Ealdorman Ælfstan eventually announces, his words loud enough for all to hear. There's no attempt to mask the fact that the blacksmith might have been lying to Wiglaf, and I can see Edwin's mother consoling him.

By now, all of the men, women and children left in Tamworth have flooded into the open space between the buildings. The ground is baked hard, and not even the horses manage to leave an imprint on the surface.

'Then they've really gone?' Even King Wiglaf doesn't seem quite to believe his luck. But, quickly, he recovers himself. 'I need warriors on the gate and warriors down by the river and more guarding the roadway to east and west.' These commands are quickly disseminated, although no one includes me in them. I dismount and lead Brute to the stables.

Edwin's mother seeks me out then. I meet her eyes evenly, noticing that I tower over her now.

'Where is Edwin?' she asks me, fear in her voice.

'We left him, at Kingsholm, before the winter ended. He should be safe and well.' I keep my anger from my voice. Wisely, she asks nothing further.

'And your uncle, where is he?' Her once black hair is now

streaked with grey, lines round the corners of her eyes. She's aged since I left Tamworth.

'Injured in the borderlands with the Welsh kingdoms. I must return to him.' My voice is fierce.

'Then you wanted the aid of Wynflæd?' I don't need to answer the question. She nods. 'She left, with Cuthred. King Ecgberht wasn't cruel to her, but I think she was terrified of him all the same. It hasn't been the same without her. So many succumbed to winter illnesses without her aid.'

'But do you know where she is?' I demand from her, knowing how desperate I sound. It seems the king has played me for a fool, promised me something I can't have. I want to rage at the injustice of it all, but now fear wars inside me. I needed Wynflæd but she's not here to assist me.

'No, I don't, and neither does anyone else. You'll have to cure your uncle with your own skills.'

The thought isn't comforting, even if she means to fill me with confidence. I watch her walk away, noticing how she stands taller, knowing her son lives. Just seeing her reminds me of how much I miss Edwin. Hopefully, he'll return to Tamworth once King Ecgberht has been forced back to Wessex. If not at the hands of the Mercians, then at the hands of the men of Powys or Gwynedd.

As soon as Edwin's mother has left, Ealdorman Ælfstan appears.

'The king has summoned you,' he announces as I attend to Brute's needs. The horse and I have come to some sort of agreement now our journey is done. He lets me curry him, and I allow him to do as he wants, provided he stays within the stable assigned to him. The stables have been left in good condition, although there were few enough horses before Wiglaf's men brought theirs within. It's remarkably cool inside. Even I appreciate the lack of the sun beating on my head.

'I'm coming,' I call to the other man, unsure why the king wishes to speak to me once more. I hope that he'll allow me to leave, but I'm not convinced. I've not yet forgiven him for lying to me about Wynflæd.

Once more, Ælfstan accompanies me in silence. I wish I knew more about him to decipher his thoughts.

I'm led to the king, where he stalks round the hall. Above his head, shields are displaying the white Wessex wyvern on a black background, and not the eagle on a red background. I'm reminded of Kingsholm, and of how, even now, Mercian shields decorate the home of the dead King Coelwulf. My lips curl at the sight. Wiglaf notices my expression.

'I quite agree. We'll have them brought down and destroyed. A good fire will see the end of them. I know you hope I'll release you now, but not yet. Tomorrow, you'll lead me to your uncle and to where you encountered the Wessex warriors, and the Raiders. This was too easy, far too easy, and King Ecgberht isn't the sort of man to give up on something so quickly. There's trickery here.'

I nod, meeting the king's eyes. I can't tell whether he means to accuse me or not, but I'm not tricking him, and my heart leaps to realise I'll not be hunting for my uncle alone. No, I'll have all of Wiglaf's warriors as well. I can't see how I'll fail to find him, not now.

'And Wynflæd?' I ask the question even though I already know the answer to it.

'I don't know where she is.' King Wiglaf admits quickly, 'I assumed she'd be here, but she's escaped, and no one knows where.' I want to shout and rage, but Wiglaf's honesty startles me.

'Unless she's with King Ecgberht,' Ælfstan offers.

'Perhaps, but why risk an old woman on such a perilous journey?' Wiglaf asks. And none of us knows the answer to that, and I fervently hope that she isn't with the hated Wessex king.

I bow low and, once released, rush to Wynflæd's hut. It's cold and damp inside, even though it's warm outside. I search for anything I might need, noting as I do, that some jars are missing, the desiccated rat as well. That reassures me that she still lives, and has indeed escaped. Who else would have wanted the horrible object?

Hastily, I grab what I can, even finding a jar of honey hidden behind a collection of dusty jars.

With a final glance to make sure I've not left anything behind that might be useful, I leave the workshop. It's not the comfort it should be to see the place where I once spent so much of my time, and it's not just because I'm so tall now, the cobwebs festoon my hair, one of the spiders thinking to leave with me. I pull him from my shoulder, place him on the abandoned table. I don't know where Wynflæd is, and I don't have time to search for her, as Edwin's mother said.

26

The trackway before me is familiar, and I spur Brute onwards. The smell of heat surrounds me. The road is too hot. The vegetation pungent. In weather such as this, man or beast could quickly become delirious from lack of water. I drink often but sparingly, seeking out those streams so that Brute can drink as well. The heat has driven the feistiness from Brute. My head is covered by my cloak, wrapped tightly round it; anything to try to stop the sweat from running down my face and the sun from shading my skin.

Behind me, King Wiglaf rides with Ealdorman Ælfstan and three others of his most loyal warriors close to him. The remainder of his force stretches behind. Most of the men from Bardney are here, but Wiglaf didn't follow Ecgberht's example of leaving no one to protect Tamworth. He also sent more warriors to Repton and Lichfield to evict any of Ecgberht's warriors who remained there. Well, to kill them, not evict them. Men who yet live can return to Wessex and alert Ecgberht's ealdormen of Mercia's resurrection.

It's taken two long days of riding to get this far, in complete contrast to the meandering journey my uncle and I took to reach it.

Already, I've taken Wiglaf to see the broken bodies of the Raiders, pleased that the king didn't press me but took my word for it.

The dead bodies were jumbled and rank, the impact of their fall from such a great height easy to see. I didn't get close enough to smell them. Even staying twenty paces away was enough.

'My Lord King,' Ealdorman Ælfstan, of course, had gone closer, his face impassive. 'They have the inkings and hair of the Raiders.'

Wiglaf had glanced round as though seeking more of the Raiders, the hands of his warriors on seaxes in case there were more.

'Well, you didn't lie about that,' Ealdorman Ælfstan had commented to me as we made our way back to the horses.

'Does the king still believe I lied?'

'The king has no reason to trust you, and you have no reason to trust him.' He'd shrugged his massive shoulders and moved on, but my concern remains.

And now I itch to move more quickly, but King Wiglaf keeps calling me back. Round us, the space feels empty, devoid of all others. I can't see that King Ecgberht is close. I'd expect to scent smoke or food cooking if he were, but perhaps he's still deep inside Powys. I hope the Welsh are triumphing over him.

Neither do I feel the gaze of others on me, well, none apart from Wiglaf and the remainder of his warriors. The only man I feel no suspicion from is Ealdorman Ælfstan. He's continued to help me with some training, with a shield and spear, but not a sword. I almost think he enjoys it, but it worries me. The king must still expect me to fight for him. I'm not a warrior, even if I now know which end of the war axe is which.

Once more, I note the hills in the distance, imagining I see the green shoots browning in the unrelenting heat, but my eyes are seeking out the small details I noticed when I left here; the piles of stone, the shape of a far distant tree, the curve of a stream, the unmistakable line of Offa's dyke. But, as of yet, I've not found that which I seek. I wish I could call to Cenfrith, but what good would that do? And King Wiglaf wouldn't allow it. He's had the men muffle their weapons. I think he'd order the horses' hooves covered as well, but that would take time, and he's suddenly impatient.

Not far now, and we won't even be inside Mercia any more, and there's still no sign of the Wessex warriors.

King Wiglaf hopes to find Ecgberht unprepared, perhaps beaten from a defeat against the men of Powys. With the knowledge that Tamworth is safe and once more under his control, Wiglaf wishes to chase Ecgberht from Mercia with such force that he'll never consider returning. Ever.

Behind us trail upwards of four hundred warriors, about fifty mounted, the rest sweating in the heat of the day. The ealdormen of Mercia, who've hidden away from King Ecgberht, have added their household troops to those of King Wiglaf. I'm almost impressed by the number of warriors there are.

Brute is pliant beneath my hands; the heat of the day, the lack of a cooling breeze, driving the spite from him. It's just easier to follow my instructions. It almost makes the terrible warmth enjoyable. At least my hands don't strain from holding him tight, and although I remain alert, my eyes can focus on the landscape we pass and not on directing Brute where I want him. Even my blister is healing.

King Wiglaf has sent no one on ahead. That concerns me. I'm here to prove my worth even while being used as a scout. Should the Wessex warriors, or even some Raiders, be close, it'll be me at which they first aim. And then Ealdorman Ælfstan joins me at the front of the train of men and horses, bringing his mount beside Brute.

'You look lonely up here,' he offers by way of an explanation. He grunts at the end of the sentence, and I consider offering him a smile but don't. All of a sudden, my skin is prickling.

'Do you sense that?' I ask him softly.

'Yes,' he sighs, hand moving to his seax. He holds his hand upright, signalling for the king to stop, even as our horses continue onwards. Here, there's a patch of trees stretching back on either side of the trackway. Anyone could be hiding amongst them. I lick my dry lips, consider removing my cloak from my head, but don't. The moment I do, I'll be temporarily blinded by the bright sun.

'Icel?'

I startle. The one thing I didn't anticipate hearing was my name, not here. And I turn with relief, taking Brute to Cenfrith's side. He's standing, just about, leaning against the trunk of one of the trees, green and brown branches far above his head. He's ashen and thin, and the smell of him is foetid. He has a hand on his seax, but what concerns me is the trickle of blood running down his neck.

'They're here,' he urges me. 'King Ecgberht's retreating men. Hurry.'

I can't believe it. My uncle yet lives, and yet as unwell as he is, he still fights for Mercia.

'My Lord King,' Ealdorman Ælfstan roars for the king, no longer concerned with being quiet, and a clatter of hooves rushing onwards fills the air.

'Well done, Icel,' my uncle says, slowly falling to his arse. 'Well done,' and his eyes close.

I'm on the floor, rushing to him before Ealdorman Ælfstan can summon me back to the king.

'Cenfrith,' I urge, hoping his eyes will open.

His brown eyes flicker, the sheen of sweat making him seem scaly, his skin in terrible condition. 'The Wessex warriors, this way. They've failed, been sent running from Powys. They've been abandoned by their king,' and he points, even while I shake my head.

I want to examine his ankle, ensure it's well, but I can smell it. His wound has soured. He shouldn't even be able to stand. I turn to rush back to Brute, thinking of the items I need from my saddlebag that I took from Wynflæd's workshop, but King Wiglaf is between the horse and me. He glowers at me, and I quake to see his rage.

'Mount up,' he orders me, voice ringing.

'My uncle—' I try, pointing, only to be interrupted.

'Knows what it means to defend Mercia. Now mount up. The Wessex men are near. We must fight them.'

I'm shaking my head, fists bunched, prepared to do what I must for Cenfrith. But the king is gone, to be replaced by another, his expression implacable.

'Get on your bloody horse,' he menaces.

If it were Ealdorman Ælfstan, I might stand a chance, but it's one of the king's three especial warriors, who never seem to leave his side.

I swallow heavily, furious at my predicament. I've done what my uncle asked me to do. I've done what the king asked me to do, and still, I can't do what I need to do. I know this man's name, Wulfheard, but it won't do me any favours.

'Hurry up, you little shit,' he taunts me, and quickly, I do as I'm bid, mounting Brute, thinking of my uncle, searching for his strength of will, which has deserted me.

Still, I manage to direct Brute close to my uncle and, with fumbling fingers, slide one of my bags to him, complete with a water bottle. Cenfrith's eyes flutter open at the action, and he looks up and up, meeting my eyes, and he grins, yellow teeth showing between his ragged moustache and beard.

'It suits you,' he calls to me.

'Drink the water, and find the bandages,' I urge him, fearful that his skin is already so translucent, I can see where his blood surges round his body.

'Aye, lad, I will. Now, fight for Mercia. Do it for me. Do it for Beornwulf,' he mutters as Wulfheard bellows for me.

'Hurry up,' the words echo back to me and, startled, I realise I'm the last of the mounted warriors to take the path Cenfrith directed us to follow. The men without horses have already run through as well. I hasten Brute. I don't want to be at the rear if the Wessex men attack. No, I want to be in the middle of it, hopefully avoiding every blade that comes close.

The passage of the horses has churned up the ground, but there are also scuff marks from previous fights, and beneath a tree, I see a body and surmise it must be the man that Cenfrith killed. The heavy buzzing on this hot day presages a bloody body, eyes mercifully closed. Where dark blood has seeped from the slit neck, flies are busy about their task.

I twist my head away, taste bile and spit it aside. I want to turn back, return to my uncle, have him sit bestride Brute so that we can escape from this place. Only, such an option is beyond me. I would never be able to move fast enough to outrun the king's horses with my uncle mounted beside me. Not even Brute could gallop with so much weight on his back.

I must fight for my uncle's life and Mercia's freedom, in that order.

27

THE BORDERLANDS BETWEEN THE KINGDOM OF MERCIA AND THE
KINGDOM OF POWYS

The scent of heat is pungent in the air, the air stifling between the expanse of hanging trees. There's no wind to cool me here, and sweat seeps down my back, down my face and even along my arms. I don't see how I'll even be able to hold a seax, let alone try and kill another man with it. I wish I could remove my byrnie.

Wulfheard rides in front of me, the black tail of his horse visible as he changes direction amongst the low-growing bushes and trees. The thought of slipping away takes hold of me as the cries of an altercation ahead ring too loudly in my ears. But there's no choice. I consider whether there was ever one anywhere other than in my thoughts.

'Quickly,' the word is a howl of outrage, and Brute hurries, even without my command. His head is rigid before me, his steps assured. I can feel the trembling of his legs, and yet he doesn't try to run away. Maybe he wouldn't even run in the opposite direction if I tried to make him. Have I finally found where Brute is most content? Riding to battle?

Catching up to Wulfheard and his mount, I'm about to speak to him when the space before us suddenly opens up, and there are warring men and milling, riderless horses as far as the eye can see. My mouth drops open in shock. How did we not find this place before?

It's a vast area, the trees seeming to hold back from filling the spread, and instead, a layer of green grass covers the ground, lush and verdant, the chime of a distant stream or brook explaining why the grass hasn't turned brown with the heat.

I try to make sense of the scene before me. I can see King Wiglaf and his warriors dismounted, formed into a tightly knit shield wall surging forwards. They rush a haphazard collection of warriors I take to be from Wessex. I catch sight of the white wyvern on black shields. But it's what happens behind them all that astounds me, visible because I'm still mounted.

This isn't a battle the Wessex warriors want. No, this seems to be a camp, perhaps set up for the wounded. No fully hale warriors guard them. There's not a single horse between them. There's no horse and cart to carry those too wounded to walk back to Wessex. Some of the men don't even rise from where they lie on the ground, dirty bandages covering legs, arms, chests and bodies. There's no canvas to be seen to protect them from the sun or the rain.

This is impromptu; maybe this is as far as the wounded managed to make it. They're retreating from a victorious Powys, just as Cenfrith said. It appears that King Ecgberht had finally met someone he couldn't overpower. The thought thrills me.

'Dismount and join the shield wall,' Wulfheard's voice is implacable. I find myself obeying even as I shudder. I've never fought in a shield wall. My uncle told me of it on odd occasions, but never in any great detail. I'm more than aware that the tall tales told by the scops are that. Men don't thrill to be cheek by jowl with their enemy. No, here men piss and shit themselves with fright.

I gag as my feet hit the ground, hand fumbling for a borrowed shield I never thought I'd need to use. My hand hits the metal rim, fingers crushed, and I wince, even as I thrust the reins round the saddle so that Brute won't tangle his feet should the horses be frightened away.

Emerging from behind Brute, the shrieks of men and the clash of iron loud in my ears, I tremble. All over. From head to foot.

'Put this on,' with rough hands, Wulfheard rams a battered helm over my head. The leather cap inside it stinks of another man's sweat, and it's too tight. All the same, I feel better wearing it. 'Stay by my side,' he cautions me, his feet moving quickly over the churned ground.

For a moment, I can't move, my feet frozen in place, my chest heaving, unable to catch enough breath. I fear tears will form on my cheeks, mercifully hidden by the helm.

A roar of outrage fills the space, my eyes darting all around, but now I've dismounted, my view has been compromised.

I anticipate Wulfheard ordering me to rush to the shield wall, and I fear I'll be unable to, my stomach a leaden mass of terror. But I catch sight of Ealdorman Ælfstan, his broad back easy to see even amongst the rabble of men, and resolve fills me.

I'll do this. I can do this for my uncle and Mercia.

I finger my seax, feeling the sharpness of its edge, knowing just how easily it will cut through flesh if I just get close enough.

And then I'm amongst the Mercians, to the rear of Ealdorman Ælfstan, where he fights with men he knows, the perfume of sweat and blood and piss almost making it impossible to inhale without tears forming in my eyes because of the bitter reek of it all.

Wulfheard pushes his shield over his head, his shoulder into the man before him, and I follow his actions. Immediately, the shield I hold becomes too heavy, my arm straining. The shield shudders, and I find myself ducking, even though the shield protects most of my head as well. Something runs across the shield, a stone or some such, and when it falls free, landing amongst the fury of the shield wall, a shriek of outrage assures me that the enemy has done nothing but wound one of their own.

It's stifling, with the breath of so many men filling the space. For all the open sky overhead, the scorching stink can't escape because it's being pressed down by the heat from the sun. I blink, wish I could wipe the sweat away, only for the man before me to stumble. All of his weight disappears from in front of me, and if not for Wulf-heard's hand on my shoulder, I'd follow him to the ground. I think to pull the man back to his feet, but when I look down, all I see is a rapidly spreading pool of blood from beneath his body. He's dead.

'Fill the gap,' Wulfheard shrieks at me. He didn't need to see the warrior to know he was dead.

My uncle told me a shield wall is only ever as good as the men who form it, and I'm hardly a man, but without me, the Mercians will be exposed.

I swallow heavily, offer a thought for my uncle, and carefully step over the dead man's bloody pool to fill the gap. The shield remains, held up by the other shields to either side even without a hand through the strap. I loop my hand through the leather handle, grimacing at the wetness of another man's sweat. Behind me, the shield I abandoned is above my head, or one like it. I place my weight behind the shield, positioning my feet wide apart, trying not to stamp on the dead man.

I'm grateful when I feel him being pulled away. Behind me, someone has thought to clear the obstacle of the dead Mercian.

Something hits the round shield, and my hand quivers, all the way to my elbow. Instinctively, I increase my grip, ensuring the shield remains firmly in place. A seax sneaks between my shield, and the one next to it, questing for flesh. I note it, trying to deter-mine if it's truly a threat. The shield wall shudders and the shields bang together, men taken unawares. A roar of torment informs me that the enemy has been caught off guard. The seax drops to the ground, a white hand all that remains. I slash it, taking three fingers before the shield wall shifts again and the enemy can retrieve what's left of his hand.

Blood shudders in the air, boiling and smelling of rust.

I find a tight grin on my face. Perhaps I can do this after all.

Only then something cold touches my left leg. I want to jump back, but Wulfheard is tightly behind me, and I can't move forwards for the enemy are there.

The men I fight beside huff and shove, one of them, far taller than I am, constantly muttering under his breath, the words unintelligible but important to him. I wish I knew his name. Blood oozes from a deep cut on his chin that's split his fair beard, but nothing stops him.

I stamp down on the spear beneath my foot, aiming for the wood, not the iron. But I miss, and the spear keeps on coming, closer and closer. I open my legs wider, and the spear darts forward. I feel movement behind me and know that Wulfheard has contained the threat.

As the men to either side of me do, I thrust my seax through one of the gaps between the shields, aiming high, not low, preferring the open space where the shields don't overlap to the promise of a broken hand and missing fingers from lower down.

But no sooner have I propelled the seax upwards than I feel a weight on my wrist, pulling me down. My shield has dropped, almost level with my knees. I manage to snatch my hand back. By then, I've seen the face of my enemy.

He leers at me, breath foul, speaking of too little water and too much ale, his nose bloodied and bleeding into a black moustache. The corner of his lips are encased in filth. I won't let this wreck of a man kill me. I vow it there and then.

Heaving my shield back into place, I stand my ground, panting heavily and trying to think what to do. I'm just pleased not to have pissed myself as I once more face one of Mercia's enemy.

To either side of me, the Mercian warriors are on the offensive. Both of them have war axes to hand, using the axe's head against their enemies' shield. They're trying to do to the Wessex warriors what the man tried to do to me – force the shield low and take a life in the process.

With my shield firmly in place, I watch them, even as the shield wall jostles forwards and backwards, the ground beneath my feet crisp with pine needles, the spongey surface absorbing all the blood and piss so that it doesn't foul my footsteps.

The man to my left quickly knocks the enemy shield aside but is left without the means to attack him, war axe wedged in place, and no matter how much he tries to release the weapon, it's remains firm. The strain on his foe's face is easy to see as he forces his shield higher and higher, my comrade struggling to retain his grip on the war axe.

Quickly, I thrust my seax through my weapons belt and reach over to add my height to the attempt. The war axe finally comes away from the Wessex shield, but only as the shield drops, and I'm weaponless and facing his enemy.

The man cackles, his eyes wild behind a helm that has no nose guard. A blade slices into that face and, behind me, Wulfheard snorts with the effort.

The shield wall of the enemy buckles, the death of the Wessex warrior with Wulfheard's blade through his right eye making it weak.

'Rush the gap,' Wulfheard hollers.

I go to do as he asks, but there's a hand on my arm, holding me in place.

'Not you, you damn fool,' the man to my right huffs, his grip painfully tight. 'Leave the ones who know what they're doing to it.'

Instead, I brace myself. If the shield wall is breached, I'll be the first to come under attack, provided I keep on my feet.

I reclaim my seax from my weapons belt, even as Wulfheard and the man in front of him force themselves against the fraying shield wall of the wounded Wessex men. For a moment, I see through the shield wall, note that there are fewer of the enemy than I thought, that the defence isn't even two men deep here. If the foeman falls, there'll be no one to take his place.

But Wulfheard and the other man are too slow. Somehow, the shield wall of the Wessex warriors closes round the gap, two shimmering shield rims slamming together, and we're back to the task of shoving and probing for weaknesses.

My arm begins to tire, my clenched hand round the shield strap begging to be released, but I can do nothing about that. The Wessex warriors might have countered the loss of one of their men, but I've seen their weaknesses. If only I knew how to take advantage of that.

Along the line of the shield wall, I once more feel a rupture somewhere. I'm pleased to have such firm footing. Glancing down, I notice a depression in the ground, and I carefully step over it.

'Ware,' I call, but the man to my left is already losing his balance.

I hear Wulfheard's shriek of annoyance, inarticulate, as our shield wall staggers now, the enemy opposite him using his war axe against the Mercian shield. Blood flies through the air, and the Mercian warrior falls even lower, gargling with the wet sound of a slit throat, his shield obscuring him as though a grave cover. The Wessex warrior raises his dark eyebrows at me, his intentions clear, as his bloodstained war axe once more begins to arc through the air.

'Bastard,' Wulfheard huffs. I can feel him moving to fill the gap, but it won't be quick enough. Even now, the shield wall's integrity is crumbling. More and more of the Wessex warriors can scent victory as those to my left stagger, their balance upset by losing one of their own.

I don't know what to do, but I need to do something. The man to my right has seen what's happened, a streak of blood on his helm assuring me that I'm not the only one to wear the blood of another.

Fear takes me one more time, only then I'm reminded of my uncle, when he fought to save me from the Raiders, of how he battled five men to keep me alive. Now, I have to do that. I have to live or my uncle will surely die.

I throw my seax at the Wessex warrior. My aim is compromised by my shield, by my angle, by fear which threatens to turn my bowels to water, but I risk it, all the same.

The seax, top-heavy, spirals end over end, and then, by chance and luck, and certainly not skill, it slides into the Wessex warrior's open maw, cracking his blackened teeth as it goes. A well of blood gurgles from his mouth, and he drops, dead, landing atop the dead Mercian, and Wulfheard is there to fill the gap.

A low whistle emits from either Wulfheard or the man to my right.

I reach for my weapon's belt, hunting for something else to fight with, only for Ealdorman Ælfstan to offer me a blade from beside me. His face is streaked with sweat and his helm is askew, but there's no blood on him. Not yet.

'Here, take this.'

I don't have time to examine the seax given to me, but its weight is good, remarkably similar to the one I've lost which Cenfrith gifted to me; the one which permanently marked me when I heated it to seal his wounds.

The enemy shield wall is undermined now, more and more of the Wessex warriors struggling to hold their ground. I rush the man before me, fed up with having to smell his stink. I all but run up my shield, landing on his showing the Wessex wyvern with all of my body weight. He tumbles backwards, head banging painfully on the ground, jarring his teeth so that he bleeds from his mouth as well. But he's far from dead. Not then.

I bend low, taking note of the bashed nose, the dull-looking eyes, as I run my seax across his exposed neck, only then stabbing down into his chest in the hope of making the death final.

His body goes limp, and now I turn, ready for the next of my attackers. I'm not alone. The Mercians are all doing the same, taking advantage of the splintering Wessex shield wall, where the wyvern has lost its ability to fly. Some of the enemies have even begun to run away, those that aren't too wounded to do so.

The cries of the wounded fill the air; those already too frail to defend themselves reach for whatever weapons they have to hand. I don't even think as I move amongst those still fighting. My seax is busy, cutting, slicing, when that's not enough, using my elbows or my knees to bring a man down, once or twice, my forehead as well. My face is covered in the blood of others, slipping down my nose as though my sweat. When the Wessex warriors are all dead, I can return to my uncle. It's the only thought that drives me. Damn King Wiglaf. I'll do what he demands, and then I'll insist he honours his words to me.

One of the warriors is still eager to fight. He's a squat man, his legs firmly planted beneath him. He eyes me with a semblance of respect, and I note that he has to crane his neck to meet my eyes. Immediately, he attacks. He has a spear in his hand, long and deadly-looking. He jabs for my feet and then, as I skip aside, aims for my belly instead, a much larger target at which to aim. He's too far away for me to get close enough for a killing blow with the seax. Instead, he makes me dance, first one way and then another. I'm sweating profusely now, the hollow sickness in my stomach of not having drunk enough threatening to make me dizzy and unable to defend myself.

And then the man stumbles, the point of another spear erupting through his stomach. I stagger, looking round to see who's saved me and catch sight of Ealdorman Ælfstan. But he doesn't acknowledge me because, by now, the shield walls have fallen apart. The fighting is frantic, in small sections where so many Wessex men counter the Mercians. I take the time to suck in a breath, unsure what to do now. The shield wall was bad enough, but this threatens to be much, much worse.

Wulfheard and two others fight against four of the Wessex men, and I think to aid them, but my eye has caught something else.

To my left, there's a heavy knot of fighting, three Wessex men against a solitary Mercian and I recognise the stance and the clothes. King Wiglaf is alone and surrounded.

If King Wiglaf dies, then who will save Mercia?

28

For all of a heartbeat, I consider what I should do, but there was
never really any choice. I don't even pause, rushing to King Wiglaf's
side, jumping over the dead and dying to get to him. I'm amazed he
fights alone. Only when I get close enough do I realise one of his
favoured warriors is down on the ground. Whether he lives or not,
his byrnie is blackening as blood seeps into it from some, as yet,
unseen wound. It seems Wiglaf didn't intend on fighting alone, but
now he does.

King Wiglaf is down on one knee while the Wessex warrior
presses against him, war axe against the king's sword, while the
other two wait for their turn. They mean to kill the King of Mercia,
and that can't happen. Not here. Not while I can prevent it. Without
Wiglaf, Mercia will never stand against the pretensions of Wessex
again.

'Ælfstan,' I call his name over my shoulder, hoping he'll see the
problem, but there's no resultant rush of footsteps, and I realise that
there's me and no one else to aid the king.

I pause. Perhaps, after all, there's another who can be Mercia's king, maybe even Lord Coenwulf, but I know the truth of that. For all Lord Coenwulf of Kingsholm's anger, he doesn't want to wear Mercia's warrior helm and rule as king. If he did, he wouldn't have hidden away from King Ecgberht of Wessex when King Wiglaf was overwhelmed.

No, Mercia needs King Wiglaf, and Wiglaf is alone, unprotected, and I'm alone as well, and the only one who can help him.

Seax ready, I rush into the knot of three Wessex warriors, reversing my grip so that I can stab upwards with my seax into the man's armpit who thinks to kill Wiglaf while he's down on his knees. I believe the attack won't work, even as I use my left fist to smash into the face of the second man, the action far from as strong as I'd like it to be. But my aim is good, the man shorter than I am, and I feel the crunch of bones as his nose breaks, and he chokes on the flood of hot blood into his mouth, his blond beard flashing pinkly.

It gives me the time I need to finish killing the first man, thrusting my seax even higher into his armpit before the pink-bearded warrior recovers. His war axe waves wildly in the air, aiming for Wiglaf and me. Wiglaf hasn't yet recovered his feet, and the third warrior is too far away for me to reach, as he advances on the king.

My seax is slick with blood, my face covered with the stuff, for a moment blinding me so that I have to blink it aside. In that brief moment, the pink-bearded warrior lashes out with his war axe, and I feel the cut into my left arm and yet don't respond to it. I could drip my last into this ground, and still, I would stand. For Mercia.

He also carries a blackened shield with a white wyvern on it which he thrusts upwards, knocking aside my seax, leaving me stumbling round, unable to see, and with the king still threatened by the third Wessex warrior.

'Ælfstan,' I call once more, fearing my failure, fearing the king will die, fearing I can't do enough to reverse what's happening. It's Wulfheard who responds.

'Duck,' he bellows, and I do so, unsure if he means Wiglaf or me. My head impacts something heavy, a loud ringing in my ears making it impossible to hear, even as I can't see.

And then there's a hand on my back, and my seax rushes to meet it.

'Hold,' Ealdorman Ælfstan's single word brings me up short, somehow making itself heard despite my ringing head.

I open my eyes slowly, blinking away the blood and sweat.

'Get off your king,' Wulfheard suggests immediately.

I meet the king's eyes, noting the lines etched into his skin, the cut on his chin, the scar obtained while King Ecgberht has claimed Mercia as his to rule. I apologise even as I stagger upright, but his eyes are hard. I wince away from his wrath, fearful that I've roused King Wiglaf's anger, grateful for the helping hand from Ealdorman Ælfstan.

The three Wessex men are dead; of that there's no denying. I didn't kill all of them; of that I'm sure as I observe their bodies. One bleeds from beneath his armpit, the pool growing, another has a war axe held firm in his chest and above which a pink beard wavers, yet another stands, motionless, a spear protruding from his bleeding belly that holds him upright.

No one speaks. Not a word. Round me, I can see the fighting is almost over. The Wessex warriors are either dead or attempting to flee. They won't get far. There are two who still desperately battle, protecting something behind them. I don't know what it is.

I reach up to remove my helm, noting disinterestedly that my hands are claret, almost as far as my elbows. It'll take more than a brush to remove the grime wedged beneath my clipped nails. I shake my head, and the world lurches up to meet me. This time Ælfstan grabs me, holds me upright, even as my stomach threatens to unman me.

'Take your time,' Wulfheard suggests conversationally, his words surprising me because he speaks without malice or conceit. 'A blow like that can leave a man without senses. I don't know how you're still standing.'

If I'd known that not standing was an option, I'd have stayed on the ground. I note that Wulfheard calls me a man. I'm not sure how I feel about that.

Wulfheard has assisted the king to his feet. Wiglaf limps a little, his right foot held just off the ground, while a bruise is already forming on his cheek, where his helm has been pressed too tight against it, no doubt. Perhaps my fault, I don't really remember all the details. His hair is in disarray; his byrnie ripped below his left arm. I notice the tremble in his right hand but quickly look away. He doesn't need to know that I've witnessed that. And, anyway, my entire body is shaking.

The king opens his mouth, and I think he'll speak, but then he shuts it once more, a perplexed expression on his face. He turns slowly, surveying what's happened here, and when he turns back, there's a sly smirk on his face.

'A great victory over the Wessex bastards,' he roars, the words startling me, and Ælfstan isn't unaffected either.

A peal of laughter fills the air.

'Now, bring me whatever those two were fighting so hard to keep from us.' The king strides away, no words exchanged between us. I'm pleased to be left alone as Wulfheard trails behind him.

'Bloody fool,' I think I hear Ælfstan mutter, but I've heard a man cry out in pain, another shouting for water. The wounded. And that recalls me to my uncle's predicament.

'Cenfrith,' the word burbles from my mind, and I shrug off Ælfstan's help, dashing back the way we've just come, trying to stay upright as the world lurches painfully from side to side. At the last moment, as my steps take me first one way and then another, I remember Brute and aim for him, where he stands to the edge of the mass of the Mercian horses. He watches my approach, and I think he'll hinder me, but he eagerly takes my commands from the saddle, and I'm ducking low to avoid the branches as I direct him through the overhanging trees.

The sounds of warriors mourning their allies, or riffling through the belongings of the dead, fades with his steady steps, and gradually, my heart begins to beat slower and slower. Lethargy has me nodding in the saddle, but Brute seems to know my mind.

* * *

As he draws to a stop, I jolt awake, looking for Cenfrith, dismay making me cry with sorrow.

My uncle is still where I left him, but a Wessex warrior lies bleeding on his side close to him, slick hands trying to hold in his slimy guts, and my uncle isn't moving.

'Cenfrith,' I call his name, jolting my feet and legs as I land badly on the ground, staggering to stay upright with the help of Brute, my ears still ringing from the blow to my helm.

I growl at the Wessex warrior, bending to plunge my seax into his panting chest.

'Cenfrith.' His eyelids flutter at my anguished cry and then startle open, a slow grin spreading over his face as he takes me in. What must he see? A boy covered in another's blood. It's not what I would want to find. It's not what I would want him to see when he looks at me.

'You fought for King Wiglaf?' His words are audible despite the breathlessness of them. He's bleeding, a seax protruding from his stomach where the Wessex warrior has given as good as he's got.

'Here, here, let me help you,' I cry, all thoughts of his injured foot banished from my mind. If he bleeds to death, it won't matter if his foot is infected with the wound rot or not.

'Leave it.' Cenfrith's words ring with the same authority as the king's.

My mouth drops open, my eyes seeking out his.

'It's too much,' he simply states, wincing as he does so. It seems that even breathing too deeply is agony for him.

'Here, here, water.' and I fumble to the bag I left him, finding the water and pouring it into his parched mouth. The sack I thrust at him hasn't even been opened. It seems he didn't have time to tend to himself.

Cenfrith swallows thirstily but soon shuts his mouth to the steady stream, and instead, I take some of the water. It's not the freshest or the coldest. It's hardly refreshing at all.

'I can help you,' I urge, frantic, hoping the words mean that I can, even though I know the truth of it. I've seen wounds like this before. I know why he holds the seax against his skin still, even though it must hurt. His skin is even paler now, beaded with sweat, even more translucent than when I first found him.

'It's too much,' Cenfrith says once more, and now he fumbles for something else, something round his neck. But with only one free hand, he can't get at what he wants.

'Here, let me help you,' my words are thick with emotion, but for now, there are no tears.

As much as I hate to admit it, my uncle is right. It is too much. His foot has soured, his belly is pierced, and he'll die. Even Wynflæd wouldn't be able to help him, and she's the most skilled healer I've ever known. If she weren't, the kings of Mercia wouldn't tolerate her and her desiccated rat in their royal enclosure.

Cenfrith's fingers scramble on the cord tied round his neck – the one I've seen before but never asked what it meant to him. The one I saw before I rode to Bardney but refused to question him about. My uncle, as much as I've always loved him, has kept his secrets from me.

Quickly, once more noting the blood on my hands, I fiddle with the knot, and when it still won't give, raise my freshly bloodied seax and cut through the cord, placing it, and the heavy item on it, in his waiting hand.

A lightness in his eyes assures me he won't last much longer.

The tightness in my throat increases. I'll be left entirely alone. Damn the bastard Wessex warriors. Damn the bastard Raiders.

'Take this, for me.' He presses the cut cord and the object into my hand.

I don't even look at it. I can't risk missing these final moments together.

'Take this to Lady Cynehild, at Winchcombe nunnery.'

I gasp. My uncle could have asked me to do almost anything, and I would never have guessed this final demand from him.

'Lady Cynehild?' I repeat, forehead furrowed.

'Yes. She'll understand.' He exhales, the words becoming fainter which I notice now that my hearing has returned to normal, following the blow to my head. 'Give me your oath.' There's harshness in his voice. I've already sworn an oath I don't plan to keep to King Wiglaf. This one is much easier to mouth, and to keep.

'I give my oath.' I promise, my throat tight as I try to force the words through dry lips.

He nods, just a little, in recognition of those words. I note his brown eyes, his face, so familiar to me, drinking in the sight of him so that I'll remember him for the rest of my days.

'You fought for King Wiglaf? You killed for King Wiglaf? For Mercia? You became a warrior of Mercia?'

I nod. It pains me to admit it, but it can't be denied.

'You did well?' he asks suddenly, worry on his drained face, even as he gasps with pain.

'I saved King Wiglaf's life, not that he's going to acknowledge it, but Ealdorman Ælfstan and Wulfheard witnessed it.'

And now Cenfrith's lips turn upwards, a smile there, although it looks more like a grimace on his colourless lips. 'A king will never thank you. You shouldn't expect it. I know you always wished to heal people, but that was never your path to take.'

Now the tears come. There's too much truth in his words, and it wounds me. Deep inside me, it hurts to think that if I'd come to this realisation sooner, my uncle might well still live.

His rough hand reaches out, rubs across my bloodied cheek, his nails filthy. 'You were always destined for this. It's not your fault that your path can't be avoided. Do well. Serve Mercia. Live a long and happy life, and remember, your mother loved you, your father loved you, and so do I.' So spoken, Cenfrith's hand falls to his wound, knocking against the seax, forcing it aside so that blood pours forth, staining the ground, but it doesn't matter. My uncle is beyond caring.

I lean back, my knees pressed to the pungent ground. Tears pour, without ceasing or effort, down my cheeks. I don't sob. They simply come.

I can't take my eyes from Cenfrith. I note all of the bruises and cuts and privations he's endured in recent weeks. I feel a slow fury begin to burn inside me, but worse than that, an acceptance that he's right. I'm a warrior. I didn't even know how to fight in the shield wall, yet I did it anyway. I didn't know how to do anything but defend myself with a seax, and poorly at that, yet I killed with one as well. I thought myself a coward, but I ran towards the king when he was in danger.

No longer will I behead dandelions for Wynflæd. I have new targets now.

Without looking, I place the item he gave me into my saddle-bags, ensuring it's well protected, and then don't know what to do. The stickiness of blood that coats me calls for me to walk to the brook or find a stream, but if I walk away, when I come back, it'll be to my uncle's dead body. I don't want to go. Not yet.

A questing nose from Brute has me push the animal aside, angry with him for interfering, but he's insistent, and I realise why, as I become aware we're no longer alone.

I jump to my feet, a hundred hurts making themselves known, as I menace with my seax.

'Who's there?' I call, mindful that I should probably stay quiet, wincing at the doleful crack in my voice.

'Ealdorman Ælfstan.'

I relax at the name and meet his sorrowful eyes.

'You were too late?' He looks behind me, to my uncle's breathless body.

'He was attacked by another of the Wessex scum,' I counter instead, jutting my chin towards the dead body of the Wessex warrior.

'He killed him?'

'Yes, they killed one another.'

Ælfstan holds his lips tightly together. 'You did well today.'

'My uncle is dead. I didn't accomplish anything.' The words are laced with bitterness.

'You would put your uncle's life before that of your king's?' His words are tight, edged as a blade.

I hold my tongue. I know enough not to answer that question.

'The king is pleased with you.'

I bark with laughter at that. 'He made that clear by ignoring me.'

Ealdorman Ælfstan won't meet my eyes at that statement. Instead, he looks to my uncle. 'Will you bury him here? It would be idyllic.'

'No, I'll take him to his home, bury him in the same church as my mother, his sister. I'll need someone to take me there. I've never been there. I don't know where it is.'

'Ah.' There's hesitation now. And I steel myself to hear something I don't want to hear. 'Then you should take him. I'll help you. The king will understand. He'll be busy chasing any more of the Wessex warriors back to their kingdom.'

'What do you mean?' Those words have me standing straight, even though I had bent to tend to my uncle.

'You're the king's man now. You owe him your oath and your life.'

I'm incredulous to be reminded of that while I mourn my uncle. If only King Wiglaf had moved more quickly, had trusted me sooner, all of this could have been avoided.

Ealdorman Ælfstan nods, his lips compressed but understanding in his eyes. 'You've got a great deal to learn, young Icel. A great deal. You've found your wings though, and now you must fly beside the king of Mercia, as I do, and Wulfheard. We're all men of Mercia, as your uncle was before you.'

I grunt, far from convinced. But I don't offer my true thoughts that time will tell what befalls me. I'm not yet reconciled to King Wiglaf. I fought on instinct, to aid my uncle, to drive bloody King Ecgberht from Mercia, although it seems the Welsh and Ecgberht's own overconfidence have done a great deal of the job.

Now my uncle is dead, and I already know that King Ecgberht of Wessex wasn't among the dead. The Wessex warriors we found, who first found my dying uncle, had been left behind by the

Wessex force. They must have been moving quickly, and that can only mean they were retreating from the wrath of the men of Powys, and using Mercian land in an attempt to keep them safe.

So, no, this battle with Wessex and King Ecgberht is far from done, but I have my uncle to think of now. Mercia will have to come later.

29

WINCHCOMBE NUNNERY

Winter AD830

I watch her emerge from the doorway, blinking with the brightness of the day, hand held above her eyes. I recognise her immediately. How could I not? For so much of my life, she was the one I was always most wary about?

In my hand, the object my uncle gave me seems to burn my flesh, even though I hold it lightly against my seax scar. As I thought, I will always carry the reminder of my actions on that terrible day. Even now, they come unbidden when I catch sight of the eagle's beak emblazoned on my palm when I eat, drink, wake in the night or train with my sword, seax and war axe.

I sigh heavily. I don't want to be here. Yet, Cenfrith begged me with his last breaths, and I gave my oath, and I can't go back on that oath, even if I wish I could.

I have buried my uncle. With the aid of Ealdorman Ælfstan, I found my way to my uncle and my mother's childhood home. I'd never been there, or at least, had no memory of it. Brute carried my uncle's body for me, bound tightly in one of Mercia's battle banners. The horse was remarkably pliant with such a cargo on his back. But I shake aside the memories of that journey, of my sorrowing steps, of the tears I shed without cease.

Before me, Winchcombe nunnery is a fine building, smoke pluming into the sky from a fire behind the stout wooden walls. It's suffused with something sickly-sweet.

'Cenfrith?' The gasp of Lady Cynehild's single word startles me as I quickly dismount from Wine, patting her neck as she nickers a greeting to Cynehild. I bow my head. I've assumed she knew of Cenfrith's death during the summer, but apparently not. Only then she scrunches her eyes against the glare of the sun. 'Icel.' The word is flatter now, and I notice how she tenses as though for a blow. She knows, after all. For that, I'm grateful to whoever told her. Until this very moment, I'd not even considered that she wouldn't know. After all, Winchcombe is a royal nunnery. Now that King Wiglaf once more controls all of Mercia, I would have hoped the nunnery would have been appraised of the change in rulership and how it was brought about.

'My Lady,' I bow quickly, still holding onto the reins of Wine, my uncle's horse, now mine. Having buried my uncle at Budworth, I returned first to Tamworth, and then to Bardney, taking Brute with me, to exchange him for Wine, but the stablehand bid me keep Brute as well as Wine. For now, Brute is at Tamworth. I needed a more gentle ride to Winchcombe nunnery. It felt wrong not to have Wine with me, although Brute is a fine mount. Even now, I think Wine knew I would return without my uncle. Her greeting to me was gentle, accepting, and she easily allowed me to saddle her, to bring her forth from the stables. I admit, when she nipped Brute's ears as he shifted and bucked beside her, I knew she would be my true mount. But she means to make Brute comply to my wishes.

'I didn't recognise you,' Lady Cynehild tries to laugh, but the sound is too hard, too brittle.

Once more, I consider what my uncle shared with this woman, who always hated me so much from her place on the dais behind her kingly husband, Beornwulf, the usurper king who did so much ill in the name of ruling Mercia.

'You've grown. You look, well, you carry the resemblance of your uncle,' she states quickly, gesturing with her hand so that a young boy rushes to lead Wine away.

I try to smile, but I know the movement slips from my face too quickly. She's not the first person to tell me how much I resemble Cenfrith. Edwin's mother has said the same. Edwin has yet to return to Tamworth. I'm not entirely sure he will, and his mother doesn't seem to mind, so I can't use that as an excuse to order his return. Perhaps Lord Coenwulf is an easier lord than King Wiglaf. Edwin deserves to have the future he dreamed about for so many years while we were little more than boys. It would be cruel for him to see me as one of the king's warriors when he is not.

I'm only pleased I can't see myself. If I could, it would be a constant reminder of my failure to save my uncle's life – the only task I set myself.

'Wynflæd assures me I still have some growing to do,' I speak with some trepidation. Already I tower over most men, and I count the king amongst that number. Wynflæd has been found at Repton, hiding away from King Ecgberht, along with young Cuthred. She's returned to Tamworth, and her workshop, sadness in her eyes for my loss, furious that King Wiglaf has taken my oath and I'm lost to her, but pleased to see me. Of that she assured me.

'I believe she's correct. She usually is.' Cynehild indicates a grass-covered path, and together we walk side by side amongst the gardens that surround the nunnery. I don't know where it takes us. I don't think it matters.

'Are you well? Here?'

'What, in the nunnery?' Now a soft tinkle of laughter burbles from her mouth. I don't think I've ever heard her laugh before. The sound is surprisingly light-hearted. 'It's not the life I imagined I'd have, but it's pleasant enough. I'm respected as the widow of King Beornwulf, even if people speak of his kingship with unease these days. Better that than at Tamworth and in the clutches of the odious Lady Cynethryth, King Wiglaf's wife. She and I were never friendly towards one another even when we were children.'

'Would you not sooner...' and I pause. I'm not sure how to phrase it or how to ask the question that burns on my lips.

Lady Cynehild knows where my thoughts take me, all the same. 'I would sooner not remarry, no. And anyway, no man would want me, not with the failure of my first marriage to produce children.'

I look away, uncomfortable at the frank words she shares with me. I want to state that it's not her fault, that her husband might have been at fault, but Wynflæd, when she knew of my journey, cautioned me to silence. There was something about the look in her eyes when she spoke to me that almost made me obey the directive. Now I wish I had.

'Anyway. I'm helpful here. I'm even learning the art of healing the sick. Wynflæd, for all she looks like an old crone, bent double and shaking, has a wealth of knowledge that I only now truly understand.'

I'm staggered by the amazement in Lady Cynehild's words. How could she have been unaware of the power that Wynflæd holds at her fingertips? I knew and from a young age. But then, Lady Cynehild was the king's wife, and I was merely a curious child with no mother to care for me. Now I look back on my childhood; it seems almost inevitable that Wynflæd would have aroused my curiosity. She knew things that no one else did, and she allowed me to share them with her.

'Now, I hear, you're a member of the king's oath-sworn men and lord over Cenfrith's lands, Lord of Budworth.' Her words hitch on Cenfrith's name, but only slightly. I wish I knew more about her. About why Cenfrith sent me here. It seems a strange task.

'Yes, somehow I've won the respect of the king.' I keep my voice neutral. My intervention to save King Wiglaf is something I still don't entirely understand.

'Somehow?' her eyebrows rise, and I notice the trace of fine lines at the corner of her eyes. I've never thought of her as particularly old, but then, I'm a man grown now, and she's always been King Beornwulf's wife. She must be older than I recall. 'I hear you single-handedly ensured that King Wiglaf could reclaim his kingdom. I hear that you stopped his death when his other warriors fell to theirs.'

'I was merely the messenger,' I offer, uncomfortable with any sort of praise and with being reminded of the battle that deprived me of precious time with Cenfrith.

'So, that's what you are now? A warrior in the same mould as your uncle?'

'I'm a warrior, but I'll never have my uncle's skill. I'm only beloved of the king because of what I did, not because of who I am. He tolerates me, nothing more.'

She turns aside, eyes on the path before us. I note the colour of her shoes where they peek below the hem of her long dress and fur-lined cloak. A pretty red colour. I wouldn't expect a nun to wear something like that, but then, she hasn't taken her vows, not as I understand it. This is merely the safest place for the widowed wife of a previous king of Mercia to be. I would expect Lady Eadburga to reside here as well, but I've been told that she's taken a new husband. A woman such as her, with proof that she can carry a child to full term and have it live, is powerful, even if that first child was a daughter.

In the future, some man will want to marry the girl, thinking she brings with her the promise of a kingdom.

'I doubt King Wiglaf tolerates you, Icel. I imagine he's scared of you and all that you've accomplished.'

'I hardly think the king of Mercia would be scared of a bastard child with no family to support him as he tries to survive at court.' She bites her bottom lip at my words, sorrow on her face, her eyes flashing, but not with tears. 'You must never think yourself alone. I am here. I will always do what I can do for you.'

For some reason, my throat tightens at those words. I look away, unsure what to say.

'And you have Edwin, and his mother, and her husband, the blacksmith.' The fact she knows so much about me, startles me. I would have thought myself beneath such notice.

Silence falls between us as we continue to walk. All round, I can see the ravages of the changing season in the drooping heads of dying flowers, in the balding trees, in the browns, instead of the greens. It's been a long year. And there's much here that needs harvesting to aid men and women with their wounds and sicknesses during the dark months. But that's not my task, not any more.

'I...' I start again, 'Cenfrith asked me to bring you something. I don't understand it, but he was adamant that I gift this to you.' I hold out my hand then, revealing the shimmering object that my uncle pressed into my hand with his dying breath. It's a beautiful object, an eagle, caught in half-flight. The silver catches the dying light from the sun, sparkling with the ice of the coming winter, only the red rubies of the eyes offering hope of the longed-for summer to come after the long winter.

Lady Cynehild gasps, snatching her hand out to quickly cover it. I feel the weight shift as she takes it into her slight hands.

She doesn't examine it further, as though it's an old friend. She quickly places it in the cloth sack that hangs at her waist, where it clinks against something else, perhaps coins.

Lady Cynehild nods when the object is once more hidden. I screw my eyes shut, feeling relief at the task accomplished, although I'm still confused by what it means.

'Thank you, Icel, for bringing me this. Your uncle never promised it to me, but as you can see, it means a great deal to me. But you must never tell anyone of this. It will be our secret.'

I nod, eager to agree. I have no intention of sharing this moment with anyone. I don't want others to know that my uncle loved his king's wife. That would not help me. It would surround me with more suspicions. King Wiglaf would still name me a traitor, had I not saved his life. 'You have my oath,' I confirm, eager to be away from here, the words slipping easily from my tongue. Being with Lady Cynehild reminds me of the people I've lost in recent years. I'm keen to be gone, even if that means returning to the king's hearth at Tamworth, to await his next command, which I know to be concerned with Lundenwic. King Ecgberht, while he might be gone from most of Mercia, clings to the wealthy trading settlement of Lundenwic, and he's not to have it.

'Send me word of how you fare,' Cynehild murmurs, her voice firm now, her shoulders straight, her back rigid. Some change has come over her. I don't understand it.

And then a thought strikes me, one that's been plaguing me since my uncle died. I didn't think to ask Lady Cynehild, but I know of no one else who will be able to help me.

'Tell me, Lady Cynehild. My uncle spoke of my father as he lay dying.' Lady Cynehild's eyes are fierce as I speak. 'I didn't believe he knew who it was. Do you?'

For a moment, silence falls between us. Lady Cynehild holds my eyes, her breathing calm, even as I feel my heart pound in my chest. I should like to know, I truly would.

And then she shakes her head. 'I'm sorry, Icel, no one ever knew who your father was. No one. Your mother assured your uncle that they were married, and that it would be revealed in good time, but alas, she died, and no one ever stepped forward to claim you.' The words are spoken evenly, no trace of judgment in them. 'Be grateful your uncle took you and kept you safe.' Her smile is brittle as she speaks.

I swallow down my disappointment, as I'm recalled to her words that I must send news of how I fare to her.

I nod my head, glance away, realising that I will never know who my father was. I thought I'd understood that for a long time, but there was always hope. There isn't any more.

'I will, My Lady. I will send word of how I fare.' And I turn, breathing deeply for the first time all day. I have no intention of revisiting this place. My oath is fulfilled to my uncle, and now, I must fight for the future of Mercia. The past is entirely that, the past, and I'll never see the silver shaped eagle emblem again. I find that oddly comforting.

NOTES FROM THE AUTHOR

Events in Mercia throughout the 820s seem to have slowly disintegrated, at least that's how the Anglo-Saxon Chronicle (ASC) portrays them (the main primary source for this time period). In a surviving charter issued at *Clofesho* in AD825, it states that after the death of King Coenwulf, who ruled from AD796–821 'much discord and innumerable disagreement arose between various kings, nobles, bishops and minister of the Church of God on very many matters of secular business' (D.P. Kirby, pg.188 *'The Earliest English Kings'*. Charter Sawyer 1435: https://esawyer.lib.cam.ac.uk/charter/1435.html#). In such an environment, it seems that the only solution some could find was to usurp King Coelwulf, who was Coenwulf's immediate successor (and brother, as Coenwulf's son had predeceased his father). The king who usurped the kingship was King Beornwulf. It isn't recorded when King Coelwulf died, but I have decided it was in AD828/9 because it fits with the story. (Historians trace the family connections of these rival royal families by looking for alliteration in the names – hence Coenwulf and Coelwulf are part of the 'C' dynasty. Wiglaf part of the 'W' dynasty.)

It's impossible to determine the true details of what was actually happening. We have a list of names, some references to those kings who died, but it's all muddled up with the career of King Ecgberht, who was the grandfather of King Alfred. And it was under King Alfred that the Anglo-Saxon Chronicle was written. No doubt, Alfred greatly admired and wished to portray his grandfather as a powerful man, doing all he could to expand and enhance Wessex.

Mercia doesn't have its own chronicle to tell the 'other' side of the story. (Northumbria has the words of Bede in his *Ecclesiastical History of the English People* to tell of its supremacy, and Wessex has the ASC – poor old Mercia has nothing, perhaps anything written was destroyed by the Raider attacks on the monasteries and nunneries where such records would have been kept).

The Mercian Registrar mentioned at the start of the book is fictional, although it is believed there was such a chronicle, and that it was used in the compilation of one of the surviving versions of the ASC. (While there was a 'Wessex' version of the ASC, there were also others kept in the monasteries, all of them shown to have some bias to the area they were written within.)

It's important to understand that Mercia was not confined to the Midlands of England at the peak of its power, under King Offa in the second half of the eighth century (AD750 onwards). Rather, Mercia had control of Kent, Essex, Sussex and East Anglia as well and was often to be found overpowering the Welsh kingdoms who were her neighbours, and oftentimes enemies.

When Wessex began to grow in strength, it was Kent that fell first, sometime between AD825–827, the dates hazy, but undoubtedly because of the battle of *Ellendun* (precise location unknown, but believed to be in Wessex) in AD825 between the Mercians and the Wessex warriors, which Wessex won, although Mercia wasn't overwhelmed, rather seeming to concede Kent, although that might not have happened until some years later.

Why King Ecgberht of Wessex was able to take on the might of

Mercia is a subject for conjecture, but it's believed that he had the support of the Carolingians, who ruled in Western Europe at the time, and with whom he'd been in exile when he'd been forced to flee Wessex because of the power of the Mercian kings earlier in the ninth century.

Equally, the kingdoms of what is now known as Wales ebbed and flowed during this period. In c.823, King Coelwulf, the first of his name, had a great victory against the Welsh of Gwynedd when they destroyed the fortress of Degannwy.

It is possible to find the names of the ealdormen of Mercia at this period, by consulting the charter evidence that survives, although there is not a great deal of it – three charters issued by King Coelwulf and three by King Wiglaf, and so I can find those who survived the intervening reigns of Beornwulf, Ludica and the imposition of King Ecgberht of Wessex. I haven't been able to determine where these ealdormen governed Mercia for this king. (Being an ealdorman was not the same as being a later earl. It was not a hereditary position and nor were ealdormen always governing the same area for the king.)

Charters were legal documents, 'witnessed' by the kings, their family, the ealdormen and the bishops of the period, and drawn up by royal scribes. (I say witnessed because they don't often sign them, but their names are listed on them, and some historians, such as Simon Keynes, would argue that the placing of the ealdormen's name on the charter shows their position at court). There's a resource available called the Electronic Sawyer (https://esawyer.lib.cam.ac.uk/about/index.html) for those who wish to fall down research holes. Charters are fascinating, although you may need to consult translations available in good non-fiction books, and there is, as so often the case, a whole world of expertise to wade into, which will be confusing at the beginning.

It must be remembered that propaganda is no new thing, and

equally, the charters that have survived have done so for a very good reason; they benefited someone, at some point, in the intervening years, often when future kings of England were trying to promote a claim to land that the monasteries owned. All the same, I enjoy finding the names of Mercia's long-ago ealdormen. It's good to use what knowledge is available.

In order to offer an accounting of the period, I have, for the first time, created, or rather used, a character who is entirely fictional, but well loved by readers of *The Last King**. Icel, with all his bluff and condescending statements after every battle fought by King Coelwulf, the second of his name, was begging to have his earlier years written about. But, as readers of *The Last King* will know, Icel is an extraordinary man. We'll now discover just how extraordinary he truly is as he takes us on a journey through the 830s.

I have never studied the medicine of Saxon England before, and I'm indebted to the book *Anglo-Saxon Medicine* by Cameron for much of my knowledge, and to an online translation of Bald's Leechbook, available at leechbookiii.github.io, for many of the recipes I have mentioned as being used by Wynflæd. It has been truly fascinating, and it's important to realise that there was knowledge of the Greek works on the subject and that while some of these were translated, no doubt in monasteries, there was also a body of work written in Old English and with local recipes, for as Cameron emphasises in *Anglo-Saxon Medicine*, many of the original ingredients would have been unknown in the Saxon kingdoms at the time.

My own plant knowledge is woefully inadequate, but wondering along country lanes during the summer months has shown me that weeds, nettles and wild flowers grow in abundance wherever good conditions allow.

As a point of note, there is a recipe contained in this body of

Saxon medicine that has been shown to be effective against the superbug MRSA. It seems they knew their stuff.

For the scene about horse health, I am indebted to a paper I attended at the 2021 VIMC given by Dr Christina C McKenzie, a vet who strongly advises that no Saxon remedies should be tried on the horses of today. Please ask a vet. And I would echo that in saying that Saxon remedies shouldn't be tried on humans either. Not without seeking medical advice.

The church at Tamworth is known as St Editha's, but this is a later naming, for a woman who lived in the 900s. I have chosen St Chad's instead as he was one of the men sent to convert the pagan Mercians in the 600s, and because there is a St Chad's in Lichfield, which would have been at the heart of Mercia's religious life.

Icel will be back. Thank you for reading.

MJP

*   https://www.goodreads.com/en/book/show/57825584-the-last-king

ACKNOWLEDGMENTS

As usual, huge thanks to my group of beta readers and cheerleaders – Ed, Stacy, Amy, Carole, James, Kelly and Michael. And to my daughters, A and M, for putting up with the constant horse-related/English language-related questions. I really couldn't do this without you.

Thank you to Flintlock Covers for producing an excellent map, even with all my dithering.

My sincere thanks to Caroline Ridding at Boldwood Books. Never has a single-sentence email had quite such a huge impact on me!

And to the rest of the Boldwood Books team and authors. Thank you for such a warm welcome. I'm hoping this is going to be quite a ride.

Finally, thank you to all my readers for allowing me to indulge in my passion for Saxon England, and for enjoying it just as much as I do.

MORE FROM MJ PORTER

We hope you enjoyed reading *Son of Mercia*. If you did, please leave a review.

If you'd like to gift a copy, this book is also available as an ebook, digital audio download and audiobook CD.

Sign up to MJ Porter's mailing list for news, competitions and updates on future books.

https://bit.ly/MJPorterNews

ABOUT THE AUTHOR

MJ Porter is the author of many historical novels set predominantly in Seventh to Eleventh-Century England, and in Viking Age Denmark. Raised in the shadow of a building that was believed to house the bones of long-dead Kings of Mercia, meant that the author's writing destiny was set.

Visit MJ's website: www.mjporterauthor.com

Follow MJ on social media:

 twitter.com/coloursofunison

 instagram.com/m_j_porter

 bookbub.com/authors/mj-porter

ABOUT BOLDWOOD BOOKS

Boldwood Books is a fiction publishing company seeking out the best stories from around the world.

Find out more at www.boldwoodbooks.com

Sign up to the Book and Tonic newsletter for news, offers and competitions from Boldwood Books!

http://www.bit.ly/bookandtonic

We'd love to hear from you, follow us on social media:

facebook.com/BookandTonic

twitter.com/BoldwoodBooks

instagram.com/BookandTonic